SUMMONER OF THE SERPENT GOD

"If I die—"

"Then your soul will wind up on the Fugue Plain, even without a gate," the demon said, "where, instead of being claimed by Ubtao and taken to the Outlands, it will be consumed by Dendar." The marilith smiled, revealing yellowed teeth. "As I'm sure you noticed, the Night Serpent has developed a taste for the faithful."

Karrell blanched at that but managed to keep her voice steady. "All the more reason to keep me alive," she argued, "since your soul will also be consumed."

"All the more reason to keep you close," the marilith countered.

Karrell gestured at the dretches. They had peeled back the skin of the dead one's neck and fought over the right to suck the spinal cord.

Destroy the House of Serpents

House of Serpents

Book I
Venom's Taste

Book II
Viper's Kiss

Book III
Vanity's Brood

Also by Lisa Smedman

The Lady Penitent

Book I
Sacrifice of the Widow
February 2007

Book II
Game of the Ancients
September 2007

Book III
Ascendancy of the Last
June 2008

R.A. Salvatore's War of the Spider Queen, Book IV
Extinction

Sembia
Halls of Stormweather
Heirs of Prophecy

FORGOTTEN REALMS®

VANITY'S
BROOD

HOUSE OF SERPENTS

BOOK III

LISA SMEDMAN

Wizards
OF THE COAST™

VANITY'S BROOD
House of Serpents, Book III

©2006 Wizards of the Coast, Inc.

Cover art by Raymond Swanland
Map by Rob Lazzaretti
First Printing: March 2006
Library of Congress Catalog Card Number: 2005928119

9 8 7 6 5 4 3 2 1

US ISBN: 0-7869-3982-6
ISBN-13: 978-0-7869-3982-4
620-95464740-001-EN

U.S., CANADA,
ASIA, PACIFIC, & LATIN AMERICA
Wizards of the Coast, Inc.
P.O. Box 707
Renton, WA 98057-0707
+1-800-324-6496

EUROPEAN HEADQUARTERS
Hasbro UK Ltd
Caswell Way
Newport, Gwent NP9 0YH
GREAT BRITAIN
Save this address for your records.

Visit our web site at **www.wizards.com**

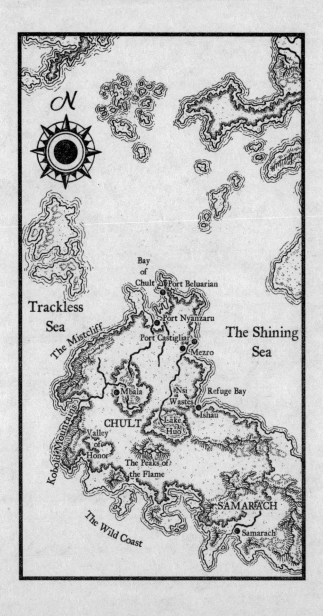

The air was hot, laden with the heavy scents of decay and mold. Black clouds of insects—tiny as gnats, but with a sting that made Karrell gasp—swarmed around her face, drawn by the sweat that trickled down her temples. She pulled a fold of her cloak across her mouth and nose to screen herself from the insects, but the fabric tore away in her hand. The acidic rains had rotted it, leaving it thin as pockmarked gauze. She cast the scrap of fabric aside, too weary from her trudge through the jungle to care if it was found by the demon that was searching for her.

She glanced up through foliage so thick it was almost impossible to see the mottled purple sky above. Vines wove through the branches overhead, giving the jungle canopy the appearance of a vast net. The stems of the vines coiled down the scabrous tree trunks like snakes, past clumps of gaggingly sweet-scented black orchids whose roots curled like shriveled white fingers.

Things moved through the jungle canopy above: dark, flitting shapes that startled her, then disappeared before her eye had a chance to fully register them. Their muted cries and sibilant hisses filled the air.

How long had she been fighting her way through the jungle? She had slept five times since escaping the cage the demon had kept her in since drawing her into the Abyss, but "nights" that strange plane were artificial ones. The sky was unchanging. It brooded, neither fully dark nor fully light, but somewhere in between, a perpetual almost-dusk.

Where *was* she? Whatever layer of the Abyss it was, she had been there several months, long enough for her pregnancy to make her slow and heavy, long enough for her to be dangerously close to the time when she would give birth. When those first labor pains struck, the demon would discover the truth—that it didn't need to keep her alive after all.

Karrell was no longer its prisoner, and she had to fend for herself. She was hungry all the time—the children were growing bigger inside her each day—but it was hard to find food she was certain was safe. The fruits that grew there were overripe, soft with bruises and rot, and the lizards she'd been able to catch had flesh that stung the tongue with its acidity. She worried, with each mouthful, whether she was doing harm to her unborn children. The only other option, however, was starvation. She had tried to summon a creature of her homeland—some small animal that she could kill and eat—but her prayer had failed. Wherever she was, it had no connection with her native plane.

She pushed her way through ferns that dusted her hands and arms with pale yellow spores, and vines whose curved, fang-sharp thorns left scratches in her flesh. With each step her feet crushed wide-leafed plants sticky with foul-smelling sap. The ground underfoot squelched as she walked. Spongy and soft, it was made up of layer after layer of dead and rotting vegetation, dotted with puddles of putrid water. In a normal jungle, she could pass without leaving any trace, but the Abyssal vegetation conspired against her, leaving behind a trail of footprints and broken branches that even the most unskilled tracker could follow.

She stopped at a pool ringed by foul-smelling yellow plants whose stalks were papery with peeling skin. Picking a wide leaf, she curled it into a cone and used it to scoop up a little of the scummy green water. A pass of her hand over the make-shift cup and a quick, whispered prayer turned the water clear. She drank thirstily, closing her eyes and wishing she could blot out the oppressive odor of decay that pervaded the place. Another scoop of water, another quick prayer, another drink—it still wasn't enough to quite slake her thirst, but she dare not cast the spell a third time—not there.

The jungle reacted to her prayers. A vine snaked toward her along the ground, brushing against her ankle with feather-soft tendrils. She jerked her foot away, tearing free of the vine, then rose to her feet and continued on her way.

She glanced around. Which way? Did it really matter? The jungle looked the same no matter which direction she went in. There were no landmarks, no trails, no bodies of water large enough to be called a lake. Months before—the first time she'd escaped—she had climbed as high as she could up a tree and bent back its branches so she could see out over the jungle. The view hadn't been encouraging. As far as she could see in any direction, there was nothing but unbroken jungle, green and matted from horizon to horizon—nothing that suggested a way out.

As she walked, something tripped her: a root that had humped up out of the spongy ground like a living snare. She stumbled forward, landing on hands and knees with her fingers in a brackish pool of water. The acid in it stung her skin; she wiped her hands furiously on what remained of her cloak. Then, hearing a slurping noise just ahead, she froze.

At the far side of the pool, no more than a half-dozen paces from her, through a screen of vegetation that hung like mottled green lace from the trees, a pale-skinned creature the size of a large dog lifted its head from the surface of the pool and sucked a purple tongue back into its small, sharp-fanged mouth. Squat and hairless save for a strip of matted black hair down its bulbous belly, the dretch had a round, bald head set on a thick, blubbery neck. It blinked tiny eyes, listening. Then, slowly, its head began to turn toward her.

With a whisper, she cast a spell. Her arms became branches, her legs roots, her cloak-shrouded body the trunk of a gnarled log. Her bulging stomach took the appearance of a burl on the trunk, and her long hair transformed into green-leafed vines. As the dretch loped toward her through the pool, its knuckles dragging through the water, she saw it out of peripheral vision only, unable to turn her head. It moved in close, pushing its head forward to snuffle in her scent through mucous-clogged nostrils. Then it sat back and cocked its head to one side. Extending a misshapen hand, it flexed a finger, revealing a dirty claw. With this, it scratched the bark of the "tree" it had just sniffed.

The scratch sent a spasm of pain through her; sap oozed like blood from the wound in her thigh. She remained motionless, trusting to her spell. The demon that was hunting her had sent dozens of small, stupid creatures out into the jungle to search for her, and she'd managed to avoid them all. Never before had any of them come close enough to touch her.

The dretch sat a moment longer, staring at her, sucking its claw. Its nostrils twitched. Lowering its nose to the trail she'd made, it loped away through the jungle, back the way she'd come.

When she could no longer hear it, she let the spell end, transforming back into human form once more. Blood trickled from the scratch in her thigh. She laid a hand on it, started whispering a healing spell, then thought better of it. Already the orchids above were reacting to the spell she'd just cast, sending a shower of tiny, waxy balls of pollen down on her. The pollen stuck to her hair, shoulders, and arms like a coating of pale soot, drawing first one buzzing insect away from the pool, then a dozen, then a swarm. Batting them away, she waded across the pond to mask her scent then fled into the jungle.

Some time later—long enough for her sweat to wash away the orchid pollen and leave behind a crusting of salt—she realized there was an opening in the trees ahead. Slowing to a walk, she approached it cautiously. The clear spot turned out to be a wide area of toppled trees and crushed undergrowth. It was almost as if a giant had stamped the jungle flat. Curious, she climbed over a fallen tree and moved cautiously forward. Something had happened there—something momentous.

At the center of the smashed jungle she saw a large structure, entirely covered in vines. It looked like a rounded wall of black stone, its sinuous curves reminiscent of a snake. She stood for several moments, staring at it, trying to decide whether it was safe to approach. The wall was the only structure she had seen in this wilderness of swamp and jungle—perhaps it enclosed something significant, a portal out, for example.

Cautiously, she walked toward the wall, trying to peer through the foliage that covered it. Vines had grown up through the toppled trees on either side of the wall, knitting together across its rounded top. Once again, she was reminded of a net—a living net—each strand as thick as her thigh and deeply rooted in the spongy soil. As she drew closer, she could see that the wall was made from a shiny black stone—obsidian, perhaps. Curved lines had been carved into it that resembled the scales of a serpent.

She followed the wall, ducking under fallen trunks and tearing her way through the ferns and spike-leafed plants that had grown up since the jungle here was felled. She came, at last, to the place where the wall ended in a blunt wedge, the head of the snake. There was a circular patch of smooth stone on the side of the wedge, nearly as wide across as Karrell was tall. A door? Heart beating with excitement, she tried to shift the vines that covered it. She succeeded in tearing off a few leaves, exposing the circle on the wall, but the vines themselves were as rigid as steel bars and did not yield, even when she planted a foot on the wall and yanked with all of her strength. Panting, exhausted by her efforts and the oppressive heat, she contented herself with tearing away the rest of the leaves. It was difficult work, especially with the last two fingers of her right hand missing—a legacy of her battle with the marilith—but she persevered. When a large space was clear, she pressed her palm against the stone, praying that it would open.

It did, revealing an enormous, slitted eye.

Startled, she jerked her hand back. "Ubtao protect me!" she gasped.

Even as the name left her lips, an angry hissing filled the air. Vines creaked as the mouth of the "wall" parted slightly, revealing the bases of curved fangs. A forked tongue strained to escape but could not, and the hissing intensified.

Realizing that she had just awakened an enormous serpent—its wedge-shaped head alone the size of a small building—Karrell staggered backward, stumbling over a fallen tree that sent her sprawling. The serpent blinked and strained against the vines that bound it, causing the ground to tremble, but it could not pull free. Its eye fixed her with a look of such utter malevolence that for several moments she was unable to breathe. Suffocated by a blanket of fear, she felt as if she were about to faint. Even bound, the serpent exuded power: raw, violent, untamed. It could consume her with less effort than a thought, could squeeze her between its coils until not even a smear of her remained. It hated her with a loathing deeper than death itself and equally cruel.

At the same time, Karrell sensed a terrible *need*, one that caused the serpent to plead, silently, with the one person who had responded to its call, even though that person served a god that was its sworn enemy.

Sobbing in a lungful of air at last, Karrell turned and ran, back into the jungle and the dangers it held. She didn't care if the dretches found her, and delivered her to their mistress.

Anything was better than facing Sseth.

CHAPTER 1

Arvin stared down into the bowl of water that served as his makeshift mirror, concentrating. Energy prickled through two of his body's five power points; he could feel it swirling in tight circles around his navel and flowing outward in ripples that concentrated again at the center of his chest. The air filled with the scents of ginger and saffron, the smells growing stronger with each long, slow exhalation.

A sheen of ectoplasm blossomed on his skin like glistening sweat as he manifested his power. Studying his reflection, he watched as snake scales erupted on his skin. With a thought he turned them from flesh-pink to black, banded with thin stripes of gray. His collar-length, dark brown hair also turned black and melded itself against his head, as did his ears, giving him a more serpentine appearance. Hornlike ridges of scale appeared above each eye—the distinctive trait of the adder he was impersonating. His mouth widened; opening his loosely hinged jaw, he watched as his eye teeth elongated into curved fangs. Bulges formed below each ear: poison glands. A gleaming drop of venom beaded at the tip of one fang. He flicked it away with a tongue that tingled fiercely; as he concentrated, his tongue lengthened, its tip splitting into a fork.

He turned his head, searching for any hint of the human he had been a moment ago. His sandals and clothes remained unchanged, though the loose cotton shirt and pants he wore caught slightly on his rough scales. Karrell's ring—a wide gold band, set with a large turquoise stone—was still on the little finger of his left hand. Seeing it there, he blinked away a sudden sting of tears. Then he concentrated on that finger, which had been severed, years ago, at the joint closest to its tip. Flesh tingled as the finger elongated and sprouted a new fingernail. It felt odd, having a little finger that was whole again. Odder still to see a layer of small black scales on his hands and forearms and on his face. The musky odor of snake rose from his skin.

He curled his lip at the smell.

His body had slimmed as it morphed, the belt around his waist loosening. He lifted his shirt and tightened it and felt his dagger sheath snug up against the small of his back. Then he raised a hand to his cheek and scratched the still-tingling skin. The scales were as itchy and rough as a new beard.

Satisfied that no one would recognize him, he bent and picked up his pack. His body felt loose, supple, and he swayed into the motion as if he had been born a yuan-ti. A satisfied hiss slid from his lips. It was the perfect disguise.

It wouldn't last long, and before it ended, he had a score to settle.

That very night, Sibyl would die.

He stepped out of the hut he'd ducked into to undergo his metamorphosis—one of the huts the city slaves stored their tools in—and walked up a narrow street hemmed in by high walls, a section of Hlondeth that was one of the oldest parts of the city. Several of its buildings were made of dull red stone, instead of the glowing green marble that had later become the city's trademark. Most were noble residences—coiling towers and domed mansions that mimicked the city's most famous landmark, the Cathedral of Emerald Scales. Behind the walls lay private gardens; Arvin could hear the fountains in them gurgling. He wet dry lips. It had been another sweltering summer day, one that left him feeling drained. Even though the sun was setting, the air was still sticky-hot. He'd love a drink of cool water but couldn't stop to slake his thirst.

The streets were narrow and shadowed, mere paths between the high, curved walls. They were used primarily by human slaves. Their masters—the yuan-ti—slithered along the viaducts that arched gracefully overhead.

As Arvin started to turn into a side street, he heard something behind him. A premonition of danger came to him. He whirled, fangs bared, ready to defend himself—only to see a small, scruffy-looking dog with golden fur. It stood about knee-high and had large, upright ears that gave it a foxlike appearance. It stared at Arvin, tongue lolling, probably hoping for a handout. Arvin hissed, and it scampered away.

The street dead-ended after a dozen paces at a simple, one-room shrine whose roof had long since fallen in. The walls on either side of the building pressed against it, squeezing it like the coils of a serpent. The door was gone, as if burst from its hinges under the strain.

The shrine had been built nearly thirteen centuries ago, shortly after the first great plague swept the city. It commemorated Saint Aganna, a cleric and healer who had lost her fingers to the rot caused by what came to be known as the clinging death. An icon of the saint was attached to the rear wall of the shrine, above the altar stone, its oils almost faded to the color of the wood it had been painted on. It showed the saint offering up her fingers on a platter to Ilmater. Despite the loss of her fingers, Saint Aganna had remained in the city, using her prayers to heal the sick. The clinging death had eventually taken her, but until it did she labored without pause, tending the sick until she was too weak to heal herself. Those whose lives she had saved kept her memory alive by building the shrine.

Hlondeth had been a human city in those days. In the centuries since, the yuan-ti had become dominant, and the yuan-ti worshiped the serpent god Sseth. Shrines like the one to Saint Aganna were all but forgotten, known only to the handful of humans who still worshiped the Crying God. Arvin, placed under the care of those priests in an orphanage, had been taken, years ago, to visit Saint Aganna's shrine as a "reward" for having knotted the most nets in a month. The sight of shriveled fingers on a platter, however, had terrified him, as had the faint rotten-egg smell that lingered within the shrine—an odor he had been certain was the lingering taint of plague. The priest, however, had explained to the near-panicked boy that the smell came from the shrine's cellar, which the yuan-ti had tunneled into and turned into a brood chamber. When Arvin had worried about the yuan-ti bursting out of the cellar to defend their eggs, the priest had chuckled. The cellar had been abandoned, he explained, many years ago. The yuan-ti no longer defiled it.

Arvin thanked Tymora, goddess of luck, for having woven that vital piece of information into his lifepath.

For the past six months, since returning from Sespech, Arvin had been gathering information about the ancient temple in which Sibyl had made her lair. He knew it had been built to honor the beast lord Varae, an aspect of Sseth, and that it lay somewhere beneath the city at the heart of an even older network of catacombs. Abandoned long before Hlondeth was even built, the temple had been rediscovered by the Extaminos family in the sixth century and used for several years as a place of worship by that House. It had been abandoned a second time after the Cathedral of Emerald Scales was completed. Over the intervening three and a half centuries, it had largely been forgotten. Nobody in Hlondeth—save for Sibyl's followers—knew exactly where it was or how to get to it.

There was a text, however—one of several obtained by Arvin at great expense through his guild connections—that described a way in. It had been written by a man named Villim Extaminos in the late sixth century DR. In it, Villim had made a veiled reference to a trap door that led directly to the temple catacombs—a door that could only be opened by "the lady without fingers."

Saint Aganna. The entrance to the shrine's "cellar" was probably behind the icon.

The altar, Arvin saw, had sunk into the floor in the eighteen years since his visit with the priest; any offerings placed on it today would slide off its steeply canted surface. He climbed onto it and stood, studying the icon. It was even more faded than he remembered. He could barely make out the white, wormlike fingers on the platter Saint Aganna held.

Arvin grasped one edge of the icon and gently tugged. As he'd expected, the painting was mounted on the wall with hinges—hinges that tore free, leaving Arvin with the heavy wooden panel in his arms. He staggered back and nearly fell from the altar. Once he'd recovered his balance, he lowered the icon to the floor and studied the portion of the wall it had concealed. A close inspection revealed five faint circular marks—slight depressions in the stone. Pushing them in the wrong order might spring a trap. A poisoned needle, perhaps, or a sprung blade that would sever a finger.

Arvin wrenched a splinter of wood from the top of the icon and used it to push each of the depressions in turn. He tried several sequences—left to right, right to left, every other depression—but nothing worked. Frustrated, he stared at them, thinking. They were arranged, he saw, in a slight arc. As if . . .

He lifted a hand, fingers splayed, then smiled. One depression lay under the tip of each finger and thumb. The solution, he realized, was to push all of them at once.

He did.

He felt movement under his forefinger and little finger—each sank into the stone up to the first joint. Then they abruptly stopped. Flakes of red drifted out of the holes when he pulled his fingers out.

The mechanism was rusted solid.

Arvin braced a shoulder against the wall and shoved, but nothing happened. He shoved again—then gasped as the altar teetered with a grinding of stone on stone. Realizing his weight was about to send it crashing into the chamber below, he leaped off.

"Nine lives," he whispered, touching the crystal that hung from a leather thong around his neck. Then he smiled. The secret door behind the icon wasn't the only way into the catacombs.

Placing his hands on the lower end of the altar,

he shoved. The slab of stone moved downward—then slipped and fell. As it tumbled into the chamber below, Arvin manifested a power, wrapping the block of stone in a muffle of psionic energy. Though the crash of the altar against the floor below sent a tremble through the shrine, the only sound was a soft rustle, no louder than a silk scarf landing gently on the floor.

Dust rose through the opening as Arvin peered down into it. Sunlight slanting through the hole dimly illuminated the chamber below. The floor was littered with what looked like deflated leather balls: the remains of yuan-ti eggs. All had hatched long ago; what remained was brown and withered. The walls bore some sort of plaster work, done in relief—knobby sculptural elements that Arvin couldn't make out from above.

He pulled a rope from his pack and laid it out on the floor, doubling the rope back on itself to form a **T**-shape. He tied a knot, then stretched the short bar of the **T** from one edge of the hole to the other, letting the longer piece dangle down inside.

"*Saxum*," he whispered. The rope turned to stone. He slid down what had become a pole, then whispered a second command word: "*Restis.*" The rope returned to its original form and slithered down into his hands.

He looked around as he untied the knot and stowed the rope away. The walls and ceiling of the chamber were decorated not with plaster reliefs but with human bones. On one wall, individual verte-brae and ribs had been arranged in floral patterns around a skull flanked by two shoulder blades that gave the appearance of wings. On another, leg and arm bones by the hundreds formed borders around still more skulls, arranged in circular rosettes. On the ceiling, thousands of finger bones were arranged in a starlike motif. A chandelier made from curved ribs and yet more vertebrae, wired together, creaked as it rocked slowly back and forth, disturbed by the fall of the altar.

On yet another wall was a gruesome parody of a sundial, arm bones dividing a circle of tiny skulls into the four quarters of morning, fullday, evening and darkmorning. Arvin's mouth twisted in disgust as he realized the skulls were from human infants. Stepping closer, he saw that the skulls were cracked, in some cases smashed in on one side; they must have been sacrificial victims. He touched one of the tiny skulls and it crumbled under the slight pressure of his fingertip, the fragments sifting down onto the floor like ash. The skulls were a poignant contrast with the hatched eggs that littered the floor—death and birth. The ones who had done the dying, of course, were human.

So were the ones who had done the killing. The Temple of Varae—and the catacombs—had been built long before the yuan-ti came to the Vilhon Reach.

There was one exit from the chamber, a doorway whose arch was framed in bones. It led to a flight of stairs that descended into darkness.

Arvin pulled a glass vial out of his pocket, pulled out its cork stopper, and drank the potion it contained. The liquid slid down his throat, leaving a honey-sweet aftertaste of night-blooming flowers and loam. The inky blackness that filled the staircase lightened as walls, stairs, and ceiling resolved into shades of gray and black.

He walked cautiously down the stairs, at several points having to duck to avoid decorative elements in the rounded ceiling where bones had been used to create mock arches. They gave the staircase an unnerving similarity to the gullet of a snake—something Villim had commented on in his text. Arvin shivered as a dangling finger bone brushed against the top of his head and clattered to the ground. He tensed, expecting one of Sibyl's followers to appear at any moment.

None did.

The air was cool and clammy, like cold sweat. He found himself missing the stifling heat he'd left behind.

The staircase should have ended in a hallway that led, according to Villim's text, to the temple. Instead, it ended in a jumble of fallen stone. In the eight centuries since Villim had penned his text, the ceiling must have collapsed.

Arvin swore softly and kicked at a loose stone. It rolled—farther than it should have. Bending down, he discovered a narrow gap, beyond which lay a wider passage. Clearing away the rubble that blocked it, Arvin realized it must be the tunnel the yuan-ti had used to reach the chamber in which they'd laid their eggs. It was too low to crawl through with a backpack on; he'd have to drag the pack behind him. He tied it by a short length of rope to one ankle then lay prone and wormed his way into the tunnel.

The narrow passage wound its way through the collapsed masonry, up and over sharp bits of stone that scraped Arvin's arms and legs and under jutting blocks that he would have banged his head against, had he not been able to see in the dark. Being in yuan-ti form helped. His increased flexibility enabled him to slither around corners a human would have been unable to negotiate.

At one point the tunnel constricted, forcing him to wriggle forward on his belly with arms extended in front of him. Claustrophobia gripped him a moment later when his pack got caught in the narrow section, jerking him to a halt like an anchor. He was trapped! He would lie there, entombed with Varae's victims, until he starved to death. He scraped at the rope around his ankle with his other foot, trying to free himself from it—then realized what he was doing. If he left the pack behind, he'd lose his chance to settle his score with Sibyl—the abomination who had killed both his best friend and the woman he loved.

"Control," he whispered.

He blinked away the sweat that trickled down into his eyes and licked his lips with a long, forked tongue. The sweat tasted slightly acidic, reminding him that he was in yuan-ti form. The serpent folk had wriggled through that narrow spot to reach their brood chamber, and Arvin should be able to do the same. It was just a matter of freeing his pack.

He worked it back and forth, prodding it with a foot, then jerked against the rope tied to it. Eventually the pack came free. Relieved, he crawled on.

The tunnel ended a short distance ahead, opening into a chamber illuminated with flickering red light that washed out Arvin's darkvision. A hissing noise filled the chamber: the soft, slow exhalations of serpents.

Dozens of them.

Arvin sent his mind deep into his *muladhara*, the source of psionic energy that lay at the base of his spine, then summoned energy up through the base of his scalp and into his forehead. He sent his awareness down the tunnel ahead of him, into the chamber beyond. The thoughts of the yuan-ti inside it, however, were not what he'd expected. He'd been prepared for guards, alert and suspicious. The thoughts of these yuan-ti were languid, jumbled, confused. As if . . . yes, that was it; they were dreaming. The mind of one was filled with images of a jungle, of a tree whose snake-headed branches had become tangled in a hopeless knot. Another dreamed that the viaducts that arched over Hlondeth were growing together, forming a stone lattice overhead.

A third dreamed she was basking on a stone that had suddenly grown unbearably hot, but someone held her tail, preventing her from slithering away. Others dreamed of gardens that had become choked with weeds, of hatchlings that struggled to tear open the leathery eggs that enclosed them, and of ropes that turned into snakes and slithered into a mating ball that could not be untangled. All of the dreams were different, yet all had one thing in common: a restlessness—a need to *do* something—and a frustrating inability to grasp what that something might be.

Arvin withdrew his awareness from the dreamers, wondering what to do next. He'd planned to pass himself off as one of Sibyl's worshipers, bearing tribute for the avatar. He'd spent months studying the practices of Sseth's faithful, learning the gestures of propitiation and the hisses of praise. Sunset was one of the chief times of worship, the time when the yuan-ti ended the day's heat-induced lethargy with feasting and praise.

He hadn't expected to find Sibyl's worshipers deep in slumber.

He couldn't wait for them to awaken, however. His metamorphosis would wear off soon. He crawled forward, determined to either find someone who was awake or to find Sibyl on his own.

As Arvin drew nearer to the chamber, a wisp of amber-colored smoke curled down the tunnel toward him, bearing an odor he recognized: a combination of mint, burning moss, and sap. *Osssra!* The flickering light, he saw, came from flames dancing across a bowl of the burning oil—the same oil whose fumes had nearly poisoned him when he'd forced his way into an audience with Dmetrio Extaminos, royal prince of Hlondeth. In morphed form, Arvin would be immune to the worst of its toxic effects—but that didn't mean he wouldn't wind up drowsy and dreaming, like the yuan-ti in the chamber, if he inhaled it. Worried, he crawled out of the tunnel and untied his pack from his ankle. If he moved quickly, he might make his way through the chamber before he breathed in too much of the smoke.

The yuan-ti were sprawled together in loose-limbed heaps on the floor around the burning bowls of *osssra*, heads lolling in slumber. Breathing as shallowly as he could, Arvin stepped quickly across them, making for the chamber's only door. This chamber, like the previous one, was decorated with human bones. Here, however, complete skeletons had been used. They were wired together and attached to the walls inside arches made of vertebrae. One of the skeletons, just to the right of the door, was that of a woman, the tiny skeleton of an unborn child arranged within her pelvic bones.

A wave of nausea swept over Arvin. Karrell had been pregnant when she died, pregnant with his children. Eyes stinging, he reached for the handle of the door, but before he could open it, something twined around his ankle. Startled, he gasped—then realized he'd inhaled a deep lungful of smoke.

Looking down, he saw the snake-headed arm of one of the sleepers, coiled around his leg. "Stay," it hissed while the rest of the yuan-ti's body slept. "Dream with us."

Made drowsy by the smoke, Arvin yawned, inadvertently drawing in another lungful of it. He shook his head, but it couldn't dislodge the cobwebs of dream that clung to the edges of his thoughts. In that dream, he ran through a jungle, trying to escape from a slit-pupilled eye the size of the sun. It stared down at him from above, then suddenly became a mouth, which opened, drooling blood. Out of it fluttered a brown, withered egg shell. It landed on the ground next to him, staring up at him with Karrell's face. Long black hair splayed around her severed head like the rays of an extinguished sun. Her eyes were flat and dead in the wrinkled brown face. The jade earring in her left ear wriggled free, and the small green frog opened its mouth and gave a squeaking croak—a baby's shrill cry of need.

Arvin shook his head, purging the nightmare from his mind by sheer force of will. Shaking the snake-arm off his leg, he wrenched open the door and stumbled into a brightly lit hallway. He slammed the door behind him and took in several deep lungsful of cool, clean air. How long had he been standing there, lost in the dream? However long it had been, it had cost him precious time. His body was already starting to tingle. His metamorphosis would end soon.

"Well?" a soft voice beside him asked.

A yuan-ti holding a parchment and quill sat a short distance away, her limbless lower body coiled on a bench against one wall. Long red hair framed an angular face, and for a moment Arvin was reminded of Zelia, the woman who had become his nemesis, but this yuan-ti had red scales, instead of green. She raised her quill, an expectant look on her face.

"Your dreams?" she hissed—softly, as if not wanting to break the tenuous thread that connected dreaming and wakefulness.

Arvin wet his lips—a gesture that sent his long forked tongue flicking out toward her, sending a drop of spittle onto the parchment she held. Her upper lip twitched, baring the tips of her fangs—a gesture that often preceded a bite.

Arvin started to flinch, then remembered that he was supposed to be a yuan-ti. No, he *was* yuan-ti, at least for the duration of his metamorphosis. Drawing himself up imperiously—yuan-ti never apologized, even to another yuan-ti—he bared the tips of his own fangs. He and the scribe locked eyes for a moment—and the scribe was the first to look away. As she did, Arvin manifested the power that would allow him to listen in on her thoughts. She swayed slightly, tipping her head as if listening to a distant sound, and her thoughts tumbled into Arvin's mind.

She was annoyed at him—how dare he threaten her! The mistress had given her a sacred task to fulfill, and she would not let a petty annoyance get in the way. Later, perhaps, she might exact her revenge, but for now, the important thing was to record whatever dreams the *osssra* had induced.

Arvin decided to get that part over with, then ask where Sibyl was.

"In my dream, I was in a jungle," he told the scribe.

She dipped her quill in the pot of ink that sat on the bench beside her and started scribbling. The script was narrow and flowing, a series of lines that looked like elaborately looped scratch marks, punctuated by blots of ink. Draconic.

Wary that his own nightmare might reveal some hidden human quality, Arvin repeated a dream Karrell had related to him just before she was killed: of being a mouse, struggling within the grip of a serpent. His voice cracked a little on the final words. He remembered how vulnerable Karrell had looked as she lay on the bench in Helm's chapel, her expression pinched and her fingers twitching as she fought, in her dream, to free herself. Seeing that, he'd been worried that Zelia had seeded her—that Zelia had used her psionics to plant, deep within Karrell's mind, a tiny seed of psionic energy that would eventually grow, choking out Karrell's own consciousness like a weed and replacing it with a copy of Zelia.

That hadn't been the case. The dream Karrell had been having was just a simple nightmare, rather than a dream-taste of Zelia's thoughts.

The real nightmare had come later, when Karrell was yanked into the Abyss by a marilith.

Arvin's awareness was still hooked deep inside the scribe's mind. She was disappointed by what he'd told her; it offered nothing new.

"That wasn't very helpful, was it?" Arvin asked.

"No," she agreed, blowing on the parchment to dry the ink. "It wasn't." Certainly not worth bothering Mistress Sibyl with, her thoughts silently added, especially in the middle of the welcoming ceremony.

Arvin's heart quickened. The scribe knew where Sibyl was. He needed to convince her that he must be conveyed to her mistress at once, but how?

He thought quickly. Slumber—and dream—were important parts of Sseth's worship. In midwinter, a select few of the serpent god's priests underwent the Sagacious Slumber, a month-long hibernation during which they communed with their god, gaining new spells, but that didn't seem to be what was going on here. It sounded as thought Sibyl was looking for something in the dreams of her worshipers.

Arvin had an idea what it might be: a clue to the whereabouts of the Circled Serpent, an artifact Dmetrio Extaminos had found during his restoration of the Scaled Tower one year ago. Sibyl's minions had managed to get their hands on half of the Circled Serpent, but the other half was still in Dmetrio's possession. He'd hidden it so well, even Karrell hadn't been able to find it.

If Arvin's guess was right, he would be conveyed directly to Sibyl, welcoming ceremony or not. If not
. . .

He decided he'd take the risk. He stared up at the ceiling as if lost in thought. "There was more," he told the scribe, "a second part to my dream."

"Yes?" she said, dipping her quill in the pot of ink that sat on the bench next to her. She gave a soft, hissing sigh. Her thoughts—which Arvin was still reading—held a note of bored indulgence. He was attracted to her—most males were—and he wanted to keep talking. He was probably making the second part up, she decided.

"There was a serpent," Arvin continued. "A silver serpent. Its body was coiled back upon itself in a circle." He sketched a circle in the air with his hands. "It was swallowing its own tail."

Arvin fought to contain his smile as he listened to the scribe's thoughts race. She scribbled furiously. It was *exactly* what she'd been waiting to hear. Mistress Sibyl had instructed her—personally instructed her!—to pay close attention to any mention of circled serpents.

"Go on," she prompted.

"A man was holding the silver serpent—a yuan-ti," Arvin continued, "a man with a high forehead, narrow nose, and dark, swept-back hair."

The scribe frowned as she wrote that down. Arvin had neglected to mention scale color and pattern, the first thing a yuan-ti typically mentioned, when describing another of his race.

"Oh yes," Arvin said, as if suddenly remembering. "There was something odd about him. He didn't have any scales. His skin was almost . . . *human.*"

He managed to inject a shudder of disgust into the word that satisfied the scribe. "Did you recognize him?" she asked.

"I think it was Dmetrio Extaminos," Arvin answered.

While she recognized the name, it didn't trigger the sudden rush of excitement Arvin had expected. The scribe, he decided, had been told only so much.

"Where was he?" she asked. "In your dream."

"He was in ..." Arvin said that much then deliberately halted.

He didn't know where the royal prince was. Nobody else in the city did either—at least, nobody the guild had been able to question. After being recalled from Sespech six months ago, Hlondeth's former ambassador had made a brief appearance at the palace then simply disappeared. Arvin had tried to contact Dmetrio with a sending, but it had met with the same lack of success as his attempts to contact Karrell. Dmetrio was either dead or shielded by powerful magic.

"Yes?" the scribe prompted.

Arvin drew himself up in a stiff pose and looked down his nose at her. "That, I think, is something for the ears of our mistress alone, hatchling." He used the diminutive term, despite the fact that he had assumed an appearance that wasn't much older than the scribe.

She hissed softly at the verbal bite. How dare he, she thought. She, a *ssethssar* of the temple, and he a mere lay worshiper! She started to bare her fangs then remembered the task she had been charged with. The mistress would be displeased, indeed, if this impertinent male died before his dream was recorded.

"Mistress Sibyl is too busy to meet with you," she began. "Tell *me* your dream. I will ensure—"

"Yes, yes, I know," Arvin said, waving a hand. It was tingling fiercely, the scales on it starting to shrink. Already the belt around his waist felt tighter. "The welcoming ceremony. I was supposed to be part of it but chose to dream instead. Take me to Sibyl—immediately."

That made her blink. He dared address the mistress by name alone? Perhaps she'd misjudged him. A few of the high serphidians had attended Dreamings in the past, but he wasn't one she recognized. She took careful note of his face—then blinked as she noticed it was changing. The black-and-gray scales were melting away into human flesh ...

A spy! her mind shrieked. I must—

The scribe raised her hands to cast a spell. As she began reciting her prayer, Arvin manifested a power. He was already inside her mind, which made it easier, but in order for his deception to work he needed to manifest two powers at once.

He peeled back her layers of memory, starting with the sound she was currently hearing: the tinkling noise that was his power's secondary manifestation. Working backward from there, he erased the moment of realization that he was a not yuan-ti, but human—a spy—and the memory of his scales disappearing and human features emerging. At the same time, he remanifested his metamorphosis, restoring his body to serpent form.

In the middle of his mental labors, the scribe's spell went off and a snakelike whip of glowing red energy lashed out from her hand. It slapped across his shoulder, burning through the fabric of his shirt and sending a hot wave of pain through the flesh below. Arvin gasped, fighting to maintain his concentration. For a moment, it almost slipped away—scales stopped blossoming on his body, and the scribe managed to lay down another layer of memory: an image of Arvin as he shuddered under her mystic lash.

Then he regained control. He stripped this memory away, together with several others, peeling her memories down to the point just before his metamorphosis had ended, leaving her with the memory of him ordering her to take him to Sibyl. At the same time, he completed his transformation, forcing his body back into yuan-ti form.

When it was over, he was no longer listening to

her thoughts, but he could guess what they were. She would wonder why he was suddenly panting and sweaty, why he was turning his shoulder away from her, as if hiding something.

"You're ... unwell?" she asked, her voice uncertain.

"Uneasy," he corrected. "The dream left me ... uneasy. It is sure to unsettle Si—Mistress Sibyl—as well. The sooner I describe it to her, the better." He waved a hand, as if dismissing her. "Take me to her now. I will follow."

"Yes, High Serphidian," she said.

Laying down her quill and parchment, she slid off the bench and slithered up the hallway. Arvin followed, shifting the strap of his backpack to cover the bright red stripe of burned flesh on his shoulder.

She led him for some distance through the catacombs along a route so convoluted Arvin became lost. He doubted he'd be able to find the dreaming chamber again, then laughed grimly as he realized that it probably wouldn't matter. He'd accepted the fact that killing Sibyl would probably be the last thing he ever did. With Karrell gone, his own life no longer mattered. What he needed to focus on was making sure the attack was successful.

After a while, the bone decorations were replaced by bare stone walls that had been carved in a pattern that resembled scales. Arvin's heart quickened as he realized they were approaching Sibyl's lair. Villim's text had described Varae's temple as having walls like these. Several times the scribe led Arvin through arches that had arcane symbols graven into their stonework. Arvin's skin tingled as he passed through their magical fields. Though his heart raced each time he felt the wash of magical energy, no alarm sounded. Karrell's ring protected him, shielding his thoughts and suppressing any auras that might have given him away as an enemy of Sibyl.

The ancient temple, a veritable stronghold, was crowded with yuan-ti. The scribe led Arvin past an egg-filled brood chamber that was warmed by crackling braziers and a great hall in which dozens of yuan-ti feasted on an enormous millipede whose head and tail had been staked to either end of a long dining table. The diners tore out chunks of the still-wriggling insect, and washed it down with blood-tinged wine.

Along the way, they passed several guards: grotesque, hulking blends of human and reptile that bore an unsettling resemblance to the hideous creature Arvin's best friend Naulg had become, after being forced to drink the Pox's transformative poison. Arvin gave a mental shudder as he passed them and had to work hard to keep his expression neutral.

Eventually they came to a chapel in which clerics coiled in reverent prayer before a statue, carved from gold-veined black marble, of a winged serpent with four arms and enormous rubies for eyes.

A statue of Sibyl.

One of the clerics turned to watch Arvin and the scribe as they passed—then hurried out of the chapel to clap a hand on Arvin's shoulder—his burned shoulder. With an effort, Arvin prevented himself from wincing. A sheen of acidic sweat broke out on his face.

"Where are you going?" the cleric hissed.

The cobra hood that surrounded his otherwise human looking face flared as he spoke. A forked red tongue flickered out of his mouth, tasting the air next to Arvin's cheek.

Arvin knew that his morphed body would smell as yuan-ti as the real thing, yet he was hard-pressed to damp down the unease he felt. The yuan-ti was a cleric, a serphidian of Sseth, and a powerful one, judging by the elaborate cape he wore. The scales sewn onto the garment had been fashioned of fingernail-thin slivers of precious gems, which glittered in the lanternlight that filled the corridor. The cleric would know dozens of spells, perhaps one powerful enough to strip Arvin of his disguise.

"We are going to the altar room," the scribe answered. "This one dreamed of the Circled Serpent. I am taking him to the mistress."

"The Se'sehen are arriving," the cleric said. "The mistress is busy welcoming them." He turned to Arvin. "Your dream can wait."

"That's true," Arvin said, shrugging his backpack off his shoulders, "but this can't."

As he spoke, he manifested a power that would allow him to falsify one of the cleric's senses—in this case, the sense of sight. The cleric was a difficult subject. Arvin had to force his way into the man's mind with a mental shove that he worried might give him away. The cleric shook his head, as if trying to clear his ears of an annoying ringing.

As Arvin opened his pack, allowing the cleric to inspect its contents, he shaped what the other man saw. The pack actually held a net Arvin had spent the past three months weaving from yellow musk creeper vines—a net ensorcelled with the ability to entangle its victim upon a spoken command—but what the cleric "saw" as he opened the pack was something entirely different:

A gleaming half-circle of silver.

Half of the Circled Serpent.

Arvin closed the pack and withdrew from the man's mind. When he looked up, the high serphidian had an eager look on his face.

Arvin could guess what the man was thinking—that he, rather than a lowly scribe, should be the one to deliver the Circled Serpent half to Sibyl. He was probably also weighing his chances of overpowering Arvin and taking the backpack from him. The cleric glanced at the distinctive ridges above Arvin's eyes then looked away, obviously deciding not to take on an opponent whose venom was more potent than his own.

"Who are you?" he demanded.

"Sithis," Arvin answered, giving a common yuan-ti name—one that was much more pronounceable with a forked tongue. "I'm one of Ssarmn's men," he added.

He waited, tense, wondering if his ploy would work. Ssarmn was the slaver from Skullport who had supplied Sibyl with the potion that would have turned the humans of Hlondeth into her slaves, had Arvin not thwarted her plan. That had been a year ago, but with luck—Arvin resisted the urge to touch the crystal at his neck—Ssarmn was still involved in Sibyl's operation.

"Ah," the high serphidian hissed. He waved the scribe away. "You may leave," he ordered. "Return to the dreaming chamber."

"But—"

The protest died on her lips at the look the high serphidian gave her. Cowed, she turned back the way she had come, but not without taking a good, long, quizzical look at Arvin's burned shoulder, revealed since he'd removed his pack. Arvin tried to manifest the power that would erase that glimpse from her memory, but before he could she had slithered out of range.

Motioning for Arvin to follow, the cleric led Arvin to a corridor that curved downward. The inside wall of the spiraling ramp was punctuated with vertical slits, and through these Arvin heard a sound like the hissing of waves on a beach. Glancing through one of the slits, he caught sight of a circular room, far below, bathed in lanternlight. Its floor was covered in thousands of snakes of every size and color imaginable. They slithered in a steady flow around a raised dais of glossy black obsidian.

Several times during their descent toward that room, Arvin heard a popping noise over the hissing of the snakes. He saw what was causing the sound when they reached the bottom of the ramplike corridor. One moment, the dais was bare; the next, a yuan-ti materialized on it. The dais must have been a portal, linked with some distant place.

The yuan-ti who had appeared on the portal was dressed in a white loincloth, high laced sandals, and a cape made from the pelt—complete with head—of a jungle cat whose golden fur was spotted with black. A necklace of heavy gold beads hung against his scaled chest, and on his head was perched an elaborate headdress decorated with circles of jade.

Arvin winced at the irony. The noble was from the Se'sehen tribe—Karrell's tribe—the people she'd come north in an effort to save.

Even though they were allies of Sibyl.

A cobra rose from the slithering mass and obediently presented its flared hood for use as a stepping stone. The noble stepped onto it. Other cobras did the same. Moving from one head to the next, the yuanti crossed the tangle of serpents that surrounded the dais, making his way toward a doorway whose frame was the gaping mouth of the beast lord's face. The cleric, meanwhile, led Arvin around the edge of the room—the snakes parted to clear a path for them—toward the same exit.

"Remain silent," he hissed. "I will announce you."

Arvin followed, tense with the knowledge that he was so close to his goal. Acidic-smelling sweat trickled down his temple, and he brushed it away. Ahead—down the curved corridor that connected the portal room to the one beyond—he could hear murmuring voices. Not one but dozens of Se'sehen must have come through the portal. In the chamber ahead, Arvin could see a large cluster of similarly garbed nobles. Moving among them were gem-caped high serphidians like the one Arvin followed, as well as a handful of yuan-ti in finery common to the Vilhon Reach: nobles from Hlondeth.

One of the high clerics, a woman, had hair that consisted of dozens of tiny, intertwined serpents. He knew her by reputation—everyone who lived in Hlondeth did—but had never expected to meet her face to face. She was Medusanna of House Mhairdaul, elder serpent of the Cathedral of Emerald Scales, high cleric of Hlondeth's most prominent temple, a yuan-ti abomination who was rumored to be able to petrify with a mere glance.

As the cleric led Arvin into the chamber, Medusanna turned to stare at them. She had been talking in the language of the Se'sehen with one of the nobles. Arvin's heart lurched as he heard a word he recognized—one that Karrell had taught him. *Kiichpan.* Beautiful. Swallowing his emotion, Arvin met Medusanna's eyes with a steady look and silently prayed that his disguise would hold—and that the rumors were wrong.

It did, and they were.

Instead of resuming her conversation, Medusanna continued to stare at Arvin as the cleric led him deeper into the gathering.

The chamber in which the Se'sehen and clerics had assembled had a ceiling whose stonework was set with a profusion of metal blades that hung, point down, giving the appearance of fangs. All were rusted and some had fallen out like rotten teeth, leaving holes behind. The walls to the right and left were carved with depictions of the beast lord in his various animal forms, each with a serpent draped around its shoulders and whispering in his ear. Between them were arched corridors that led off into darkness, five on either wall.

At the far end of the room stood a broad stone altar, carved to resemble a serpent coiled upon a clutch of eggs and flanked by two stone pillars—the twin tails of the serpent. Between these swirled a cloud of darkness that even Arvin's potion-enhanced vision didn't quite penetrate. Just in front of the altar, a rusted iron serpent statue held an enormous sphere of crystal in its jaws. Arvin swallowed, worried. If Sibyl appeared to her followers inside the crystal ball, instead of in person, all his efforts of the past six months would have been for nothing.

The darkness between the pillars began to swirl, as if an invisible fan stirred it. As it did, the yuan-ti assembled in the chamber fell silent. Then they began to chant. "Ssssi-byl. Ssssi-byl. Ssssi-byl." Arvin found himself swaying in time with the others. With an effort, he wrenched his mind away. Filling it with the memory of Karrell being yanked into the Abyss helped.

An enormous abomination burst out of the darkness. Ink black and nearly three times the height of a human, she hovered above the altar, lazily flapping her leathery wings. Two of her clawed hands held a spiked chain that glowed red as burning coal; the other two were empty. They rose into the air, drawing out the hissing adulation—then swept down.

A wave of shimmering energy swept from those hands, fanning out in front of her as it struck the floor. Arvin heard the nobles and clerics in front of him cry out in terror as it swept past them, saw them writhe and roll their eyes—and the magical fear crashed over him like an icy surf. Screaming, he sank to his knees, fighting for control and dimly noticing that others around him were doing the same. Even Medusanna had been driven to her knees, the snakes that made up her hair thrashing and spitting.

"Control," he whispered.

He threw up a psionic barrier, pressing with mental hands against the waves of magical fear emanating from the altar. The need to scream, to grovel, lessened a little, enough for him to glance in the direction of the altar where Sibyl sat coiled. Hatred helped him focus, but still a tiny part of his mind whimpered in fear.

Was Sibyl *really* the avatar of a god?

No, he told himself. Magical fear was something any yuan-ti could produce with a mere thought. Sibyl's was just more potent than the rest, potent enough to leave him gasping.

As the fear of those assembled in the chamber subsided to a subservient hiss, they slowly rose to their feet. Arvin rose with them. Sibyl stared with glowing red eyes down at her followers then smiled, revealing the tips of her fangs.

"Nobles of Se'sehen," she hissed in a voice that echoed throughout the chamber. "Welcome."

A lengthy speech followed: praise for the worthy and the faithful and a promise that they would soon reap their reward in Hlondeth as well as threats of swift and terrible vengeance against the unfaithful and unworthy. Arvin concentrated on calming his rapidly beating heart, on trying not to show his nervousness. The cleric who had led him there motioned for Arvin to give him the pack. Arvin nodded and started to slip it off his shoulders. The high serphidian obviously planned to present its contents to Sibyl himself—another of Tymora's blessings, since Sibyl was more likely to take it from the hands of someone she recognized. As long as Arvin was close enough when the pack was opened, he would be able to speak the net's command word and direct its attack. Doing so would instantly give him away, of course, but that was something he'd planned for. As soon as the net struck and began its deadly work, he would bite his own arm, injecting a deadly dose of yuan-ti venom, then end his metamorphosis. The instant he returned to human form, he would die and be forever beyond Sibyl's coils.

He touched the crystal at his throat. The last of his "nine lives" was about to end. In another moment, his soul would be joining Karrell's on the Plain of the Dead. He only hoped she would still be there to greet him—that her god hadn't already summoned her up to his domain.

Sibyl was still talking to the assembled yuan-ti, praising their efforts and making promises to the Se'sehen. Arvin didn't bother listening. In a few moments, it wouldn't matter anyway. He passed the pack to the cleric, wary of a sudden bite to the hand. He didn't want to die quite yet.

The cleric grasped the pack—equally cautiously. As he did, a loud rattling boomed out from the altar. The cleric and Arvin turned in that direction, both still holding the pack. The sound came from the pillars on either side of the altar. Their tails shook violently, filling the chamber with a noise that vibrated the floor beneath Arvin's feet.

When it stopped, a face appeared inside the crystal ball: one of the high serphidians. "Mistress," he hissed in alarm, "a spy has been detected within your sanctum."

Heart pounding, Arvin realized the scribe must have noticed the gap in her memories, realized that the burn on Arvin's shoulder was of her own making, and come to the correct conclusion, which meant that Arvin could no longer afford to wait for the cleric who had led him there to present the pack to Sibyl. Wrenching it out of his hands with a curt, "I'll present it to her myself," Arvin started to force his way to the front of the crowd.

Sibyl, meanwhile, hissed an angry rebuke at the crystal ball. The cleric inside it gave an urgent reply—"No, Mistress, within the temple itself!"

Sibyl's eyes blazed. She pointed at Medusanna. "Seal the temple. Find the spy."

Arvin elbowed the Se'sehen nobles aside as he desperately struggled to reach the altar, the cleric following in his wake.

"Mistress!" Arvin called out. "I found the—"

Before he could complete the sentence, Sibyl thrust herself backward with a mighty beat of her wings. The darkness closed like a curtain around her.

"No!" Arvin groaned, his voice lost in the murmur of confusion that swept through the chamber.

Rage and despair filled him in equal measure. He'd prepared for *six months*—had come up with the perfect weapon with which to kill Sibyl and been ready to sacrifice his own life, only to have the opportunity snatched away at the last instant.

His body tingled, and started to lose its shape. In another moment, his metamorphosis would end. He could restore it a heartbeat later—but not before the dozens of yuan-ti closest to him saw his human form. He couldn't alter that many memories.

If he was going to survive long enough to get a second chance to kill Sibyl, he needed to think of something else. And fast.

CHAPTER 2

Arvin withdrew his awareness deep into himself. Plunging it deep into his *muladhara*, he imagined the color leaching from his body, imagined his body fading, then disappearing altogether. At the same time he leaped to the side, vacating the spot he'd just occupied.

I was never there, he broadcast to the yuan-ti around him. You did not see me. You do not see me now.

He knew the manifestation was successful when one of the Se'sehen nearly walked into him. The power had clouded the senses of those in the altar room. Though Arvin could see and hear himself, he was invisible to them, impossible to detect even by sound or scent, and just in time. Looking down at his arms, he saw that the black scales were gone. His metamorphosis had ended. Putting his pack back on, he glanced around.

The altar room was in turmoil. The Se'sehen babbled at each other in their own language while the nobles from Hlondeth milled about in confusion. Clerics ran for the doors, shouting orders. The high serphidian who had led Arvin through the temple stood with hands on hips, searching the room—his gaze passed over Arvin without stopping—and began elbowing his way through the crowd toward Medusanna.

Arvin started toward the exit that led back to the portal room, then remembered the snakes that surrounded the portal. Several were venomous, and he no longer had the yuan-ti's natural resistance to poison he'd gained by assuming yuan-ti form. He could manifest another metamorphosis, but the concentration necessary to reshape his body would result in the loss of his invisibility.

Whispering an oath under his breath, Arvin looked for another way out. The altar room had ten other exits: the five arched corridors along each side wall, between the statues of Varae, but which to choose?

Even as he tried to decide, Medusanna cast a spell, her arms moving in sinuous gestures as she prayed. Malevolent glyphs sprang into view at the top of each exit and corridors beyond filled with a swirling mist. A whiff of it drifted out to where Arvin stood and stung his nose: acid.

His heart pounded. There was no escape. Then he laughed at himself; escape had never been part of his plan. Killing Sibyl had been, and Sibyl had disappeared into the dark cloud that still hung above the altar like a curtain—a curtain that Arvin's potion-enhanced vision allowed him to see through. Barely.

Through it, he saw the dim outline of the large corridor down which Sibyl must have flown. That it was also warded he had no doubt. The spells those wards contained would be fatal, he was certain, but he had to try and soon. Medusanna was casting another spell.

Swiftly, Arvin manifested one of his powers he'd only recently learned—a power that summoned ectoplasm from the Astral Plane. It was a risky choice. Psionic energy concentrated itself above and between his eyes then burst from his forehead in a spray of tiny silver sparkles that threatened to give his position away. The yuan-ti closest to him—all Se'sehen—were too busy to notice, talking together in slightly indignant voices. One of the them, a male with green scales and fingers that ended in snake heads, was close enough that Arvin's secondary display drifted down onto him like falling snow—fortunately, onto his back. The Se'sehen didn't notice them; he was intent upon some spell, holding the first two fingers out in a V and slowly turning.

Arvin's heart lurched as he realized the yuan-ti was casting a detection spell.

He sidestepped behind the snake-fingered yuan-ti as the fellow rotated, avoiding those splayed fingers. As he did, he completed his manifestation. He shaped the translucent, gooey ectoplasm he'd drawn into a vaguely human form and sent it running toward the portal room, roughly shouldering yuan-ti out of its way.

Medusanna took the bait, casting a spell at the construct. The spell had no visible effect, and Medusanna hissed in anger.

The snake-fingered yuan-ti, meanwhile, completed his spell and stared at the altar. He glanced over his shoulder—directly at Arvin—as he whispered something. For a terrible moment, Arvin thought he had been detected, but the Se'sehen's eyes were focused on something well behind Arvin in the rear corner of the chamber, something that, an instant later, made a loud, groaning noise.

Arvin turned just in time to see one of the statues of Varae tear itself away from the wall. With great, lumbering strides the beast-headed statue thumped forward, its heavy feet sending tremors through the stone floor. The vibrations rattled a sword loose from the ceiling, and the rusted blade clattered down amid the yuan-ti. One or two threw themselves to the floor, prostrating themselves before the statue. It strode right over them, crushing them to a bloody pulp.

Medusanna continued to direct her attacks at Arvin's construct. Whipping a hand forward, she sent a snakelike stream of energy toward it. The crackling line of force looped around the running figure like a constricting snake, but the construct passed right through it.

The statue lumbered forward, its body shedding chunks of stone as its joints ground against one another. Behind it, more stone fell from the ceiling above the spot it had just torn itself out of. Then one of the corridors next to where it had stood collapsed with a thunderous crash.

Arvin didn't wait to watch the rest. Making the most of the distraction, he hurried toward the altar. So did the snake-fingered yuan-ti. The Se'sehen was fast; he clambered up onto the altar a heartbeat or two ahead of Arvin, heading for the corridor at the rear of it. As Arvin followed, he realized that the Se'sehen might have been the one who had been detected; he was certainly acting like a spy. He'd animated the statue that was wreaking havoc at the back of the chamber, and praise Tymora, it looked as though he was going to clear a path to Sibyl.

Arvin touched the crystal at his throat and grinned.

Snake-fingers stepped into the darkness that shrouded the back of the altar. To Arvin, his vision still enhanced by the darkvision potion, it seemed as though the yuan-ti shifted from color to shades of black and gray. He watched as Snake-fingers took a deep breath and blew into the corridor. Inside it, on one wall, something glowed a faint blue. As soon as it did, the yuan-ti hurried into the corridor.

Arvin followed close on his heels. He tensed as he passed the blue glow—a symbol in Draconic that set his teeth on edge and made his eyes ache, even though he only saw it in his peripheral vision. Then he was beyond it.

The walls of the corridor were carved in a scale pattern, so he knew he was still within the ancient temple. It was enormous, with a rounded ceiling, easily large enough for Sibyl to have flown through it. After a short distance, the corridor forked. Snake-fingers hesitated and extended the first two fingers of each hand then pointed each down a different fork. A moment later, he continued up the left corridor. Arvin followed. As he did, he heard a thunderous crash from the altar room. Dust rushed up the corridor and the floor trembled. Glancing back, Arvin saw that the tunnel was blocked. The ceiling of the altar room had collapsed.

Snake-fingers glanced back and grunted in satisfaction then continued up the corridor, which grew steadily darker. Arvin followed, silent as a ghost, his psionics keeping him hidden. Soon he was relying entirely on his magical darkvision. The Se'sehen also seemed able to see in the dark, since he moved forward without hesitation.

Arvin wondered what the spy was up to. It would be the height of irony, indeed, if Snake-fingers had also come to kill Sibyl and had been given away by Arvin's blunder with the scribe. Curious to know if that was the case, Arvin tried to skim the spy's surface thoughts. He was surprised to receive nothing at all—not the faintest whisper of a thought. The Se'sehen didn't react at all; it was as if Arvin had never manifested the power. Snake-fingers must have had an amazingly strong will. Either that, or . . .

Arvin touched the ring on his left little finger—Karrell's ring. Was the Se'sehen protected by a similar device or by some spell?

The corridor forked a second time. Once again, the Se'sehen used magic to choose his course—and to reveal a nasty looking symbol positioned just inside the left fork. The Se'sehen disarmed it as he had the first, by pursing his lips and blowing. Arvin was close enough to hear the incantation he used. It didn't sound anything like Karrell's language, but perhaps that was because the yuan-ti's voice was lower, almost guttural—and strangely devoid of a hiss, which made Arvin wonder if all was as it seemed.

Once they were both beyond the symbol, Arvin risked another manifestation. Silver sparkles erupted from his forehead and his vision momentarily shimmered. When it cleared, he saw the person he'd been following for what he truly was.

He wasn't a yuan-ti at all.

He was a dwarf—but unlike any Arvin had seen before. His skin was so brown it was almost black, and his long, wiry black hair fell in what looked like matted braids across his shoulders. He was barefoot and wore only a loincloth made from a spotted animal pelt and two pieces of jewelry: a necklace of mismatched teeth and claws, and a band of gold set with a turquoise stone on his upper right arm. Faint white tattoos covered his body: the snarling faces of stylized animals. A small pouch hung from his belt. Next to it, tucked into the belt, was a hollow reed that might have been a wand. Aside from that, he seemed to be unarmed.

Arvin's secondary manifestation didn't go unnoticed. The dwarf whirled, blinked in surprise, then cast a spell of his own. Arvin felt no appreciable difference but could tell by the dwarf's widening eyes—and the way the shorter man glanced up to meet his eye—that he was no longer invisible. In that same instant, Arvin's manifestation ended. The dwarf's illusion returned, cloaking him in the image of a snake-fingered yuan-ti.

The dwarf raised his hands and snarled. A pulsing nimbus of red surrounded his body, washing out Arvin's darkvision.

"Wait!" Arvin said. "I'm a friend—an enemy of Sibyl."

Frantically, he tried to manifest a charm. Before he could, the illusion-cloaked dwarf launched his attack. Arvin twisted aside, but it was hard to tell where the dwarf's limbs really were. Arvin's attempt to parry passed through empty air. Something that felt like a hooked dagger—or a claw—caught at Arvin's belt and raked across his hip, opening a painful gash.

Dancing backward, Arvin reached for the dagger sheathed at the small of his back. He drew it but didn't use it. Instead he manifested another power, stamping his foot down on the floor.

More sparkles erupted from Arvin's forehead, and a low droning filled the air as the stomp sent the dwarf staggering sideways. He caught himself against the wall. His illusionary fingers looked like snakes but scritched against the stone. Claws?

Wincing against the pain of the wound in his hip—the slash was deep, soaking his pants with blood—Arvin at last was able to manifest his charm. He was thankful to see the dwarf frown as if listening to a distant, half-heard sound. The fellow could hear the power's secondary display.

"I'm an enemy of Sibyl," Arvin continued, backing away and still holding his dagger out to the side. "I came here to kill her."

The dwarf looked at him with a blank expression.

"Friend," Arvin repeated, tapping his chest. He was worried the dwarf didn't seem to speak his language. His charm wouldn't be any help if the dwarf couldn't understand him. Arvin spoke slowly, raising his dagger to make a violent cutting motion. "I want to kill Sibyl. Kill." With his free hand, he mimed a wing flapping, then a snake, as he repeated the cutting gestures, pretending to stab his own hand.

The dwarf shook his head like a dog throwing off water. His long, ropy hair whipped back and forth across his face. Then he charged.

Arvin dodged, still not using his dagger. He stared at the nimbus of red that continued to surround the dwarf, flickering like an angry flame. By concentrating, he could see where it was most prominent: around the smaller shape that was the dwarf's actual body. Arvin pretended to stumble, and as the dwarf leaped forward, caught him by the hair. Arvin touched the point of the dagger to the dwarf's throat, held it there for a heartbeat, then leaped away. Backstepping again, holding his left hand in a "wait" gesture, he returned the dagger to its sheath.

"Friend," he said again, in as loud a voice as he dared. He prayed that Sibyl wasn't just down the corridor, close enough to hear.

The dwarf halted, frowning. He said something in his own language and pointed at Arvin's extended hand.

Arvin spread his hands and shrugged. "I don't understand you."

The dwarf whispered something, raising his hands to his lips. Arvin tensed, but the spell produced no harmful effect. Instead the dwarf's words became intelligible. His illusion vanished—but the nimbus of red that had surrounded him didn't.

He grabbed Arvin's left hand and asked, "Where did you get this ring?"

"It belonged to a woman named Karrell."

The dwarf's grip on his hand tightened, and his claws pricked Arvin's flesh. "Where is she now?"

"She's—" the word stuck in Arvin's throat— "dead."

The dwarf's eyes blazed. In them, Arvin saw a mirror of his own grief.

"You *knew* her?" Arvin asked, incredulous. He thought quickly back over what Karrell had told him of her past—and her affiliations. "Are you one of the *K'aaxlaat?*"

The dwarf's eyes shifted at the question—answer enough. "Do you know what the ring does?"

Arvin nodded. "It shields thoughts."

The dwarf stared a challenge at him. "Take it off. Then tell me how you know Karrell—and how she died."

Arvin glanced warily around. "Here? Right now? What if Sibyl—"

"She is not that close. Speak quickly; there is still time."

Reluctantly, Arvin eased the ring off his finger. It felt like a part of Karrell—a part of him now. Speaking in a quick whisper, Arvin told the dwarf how he'd met Karrell, how they'd decided to join forces to fight Sibyl, and about how one of Sibyl's minions—the marilith—had yanked Karrell into the Abyss when it had been banished.

"It was my fault," he concluded. "I manifested the power that did it."

"Did what?" the dwarf asked.

Throughout Arvin's explanation, the red glow surrounding the dwarf faded. The hand that gripped Arvin's was normal again, without claws.

Arvin frowned. "I linked Karrell's fate with the demon's—but you should have been able to tell that from listening to my thoughts."

The dwarf shook his head. "My god has not granted me that ability."

"But—"

The dwarf nodded at Karrell's ring. "You were willing to remove it. I knew you were telling the truth."

"Then you believe me when I say that I came here with the same goal as you." Arvin shifted the backpack away from his injured hip. It was still bleeding. He took off his shirt, wadded it into a ball, and pressed it against the wound. He only needed to stay alive long enough to throw his net. "Lead the way."

The dwarf nodded at the blood that soaked Arvin's shirt. "First, there is something you need." He held out broad hands, as if in question.

Arvin nodded—then winced as the dwarf pinched the wound in his leg shut with his fingers. For several heartbeats, the pain was intense, but Arvin gritted his teeth against it. When the dwarf finished whispering, Arvin looked down at his hip and saw a threadlike vine, dotted with tiny leaves, holding the two edges of the cut together. The vine had a scent that reminded Arvin of a healing potion he'd once drunk. He flexed his leg. The muscle in his hip felt whole, and the pain was gone.

"Thank you, ah . . ."

The dwarf bowed, then supplied his name. "Pakal. Of the *K'aaxlaat*, as you guessed."

"I'm Arvin, of . . . no particular affiliation. My motive for wanting to kill Sibyl is strictly personal: to avenge Karrell."

"Thard Harr grant that your wish is fulfilled, some day."

"Today will be just fine," Arvin said. "Just lead me to Sibyl."

Pakal pointed back the way they had come. "Sibyl went in the opposite direction. She took the right passage when the tunnel first forked."

Arvin blinked. "You're not here to kill Sibyl? But I thought—" Then he guessed why the dwarf had disguised himself and come to the temple: for the same reason Karrell had come north to Hlondeth. "You're looking for the Circled Serpent."

Pakal nodded, and Arvin wondered if Pakal knew that Sibyl only had half of it.

"You can tell where it is?" Arvin asked.

"Yes." Pakal raised his hand and extended the first two fingers in a **V** shape. "With these." He pointed in the direction he'd been going. "The Circled Serpent lies in that direction."

"Is that so?" Arvin mused under his breath.

He remembered what Karrell had told him—that her search for the half of the Circled Serpent that Dmetrio had retained had been thwarted by something as simple as a lead-lined box. Surely Sibyl would have used a similar protection. Pakal had extremely powerful magic—he'd demonstrated that by getting past the wards Sibyl used to protect her lair—but even so . . .

"Doesn't this seem a little *too* easy?" Arvin asked. "We're deep in Sibyl's lair, yet there's been no sign of her minions."

"Any that might have pursued were squished like worms."

"That doesn't explain the lack of guards in these corridors," Arvin said. "It's almost as if Sibyl *wants* the Circled Serpent to be found. The easiest way to catch a mouse, they say, is to set out bait."

The dwarf grinned. "I am one mouse the serpent's coils cannot catch."

Arvin started to protest further then realized that if he was right—if Sibyl appeared in person to spring her trap—he'd get a second chance to snare her with his net, and Pakal seemed pretty confident of his own escape. The dwarf might have been deluding himself, but it was his decision. He'd been warned.

"You've got a way out, then," Arvin said. "Good."

Pakal stared up at him. "Don't you?"

Arvin shrugged. "That doesn't matter. Killing Sibyl does. Now that Karrell's . . ."

Arvin's eyes stung. He blinked.

"You loved her," Pakal said.

"Very much," Arvin agreed. Then he squared his shoulders. "I'm coming with you," he told the dwarf. "I've learned a few tricks from the guild. If there are traps guarding the Circled Serpent, I may be able to disarm them."

Pakal smiled. "Did you think I would come so ill prepared? I, too, can neutralize traps, but come. We have wasted enough time."

The dwarf led Arvin deeper into Sibyl's inner sanctum. The passage forked three more times, and each time, the dwarf paused to determine their direction and disarm another protective glyph. The corridors they followed continued to be empty, heightening Arvin's suspicions that it was a trap. At last the tunnel turned a corner and dead-ended in a massive stone, carved in the shape of a snarling, bestial face, that filled the corridor like a plug.

"It's here," Pakal said, "behind this door."

"How do we open it?" Arvin asked.

"With a spell, but first. . . ."

Whispering a prayer, Pakal moved his hands over the face, his palms not quite touching the stone. The mouth began to glow a dull red. For a terrible moment, Arvin thought the dwarf had activated a magical trap, but Pakal merely nodded.

"Trapped, as I suspected," he said. He stepped back and whispered a prayer, raking the air with curved fingers. Then his shoulders slumped. "The magic is too strong," he said as the glow faded. "I can not dispel it." He turned to Arvin. "I can still open the door, but without knowing what the trap does, it will be risky."

"I might be able to help," Arvin said.

Turning his palm in the direction of the massive stone face, he tapped the energy that swirled around his navel, drawing it up into his throat. A low droning filled the air and a thin sheen of ectoplasm glistened on the stone face as his power manifested. A psychic echo of the past flowed into his mind: a vision of a yuan-ti in old-fashioned clothing, carrying a lantern, who approached the face and cast a spell. The mouth yawned open, giving a brief glimpse of a chamber beyond, and the yuan-ti bent to slither through. As he entered, rubbery black tentacles erupted from the mouth, filling it like a nest of snakes. They lashed out at the intruder, wrapping around his arms, legs, and neck. Then they yanked, each in a different direction. The yuan-ti was literally torn to pieces; his limbs and head wrenched from his body with wet tearing noises. The tentacles released what remained of him and retreated. Then the mouth slammed shut.

Arvin shuddered as the vision ended.

"I know how the trap works," he told Pakal. "The doorway is the mouth. The trap is inside." He described what he'd just seen. "I have a rope that might be able to entangle those tentacles long enough for us to get through."

Pakal shook his head. "I have a better idea. Even tentacles cannot grasp the wind." He glanced up at Arvin. "With your permission, I will turn your body to air. When the mouth opens, float through it. I will make you solid again once we are safely inside."

Arvin hesitated. "What about my pack?" he asked. "And the things inside it?"

"They will become air also," Pakal assured him, "and will return to solid form after."

"All right," Arvin said. "Do it."

The dwarf uttered a prayer, moving his hands in a fluttering pattern. He started at Arvin's feet and moved up his body, standing on tiptoe to finish. Arvin felt a prickling numbness spread upward as Pakal cast the spell. Looking down, he saw his feet, legs, hips, and hands dissolve into individual motes of matter, then disappear. His body did not fall to the floor but remained standing upright. His heart lurched, however, as his arms and torso became fully gaseous. He felt a moment of panic as he realized he could no longer feel his heart beating. His breathing, too, had halted. Then his head became insubstantial as well. He floated, a detached awareness inside a swirl of air, somehow still able to see and hear but unable to feel. The only time he had ever come close to such a sensation was when he was deep in meditation—so deep, he feared he would lose his sense of self.

Beside him, Pakal cast another spell. He raised a fist and rapped once, smartly, on the stone face, then stepped quickly back. As the mouth groaned open, he rendered himself gaseous as well.

Follow me, a voice whispered.

Arvin felt the air next to him shift. It flowed toward the gaping mouth, leaving a swirling void where Pakal had been a moment ago. Arvin strained to follow it, but his legs wouldn't move—and he remembered he no longer had legs. Fighting down his fear, he concentrated on where he wanted to go—through the mouth—and felt himself drift in that direction.

Pakal hovered next to him, a swirl of coherency that Arvin could sense but not touch. They entered the mouth one after the other. As they did, the trap sprang to life. Tentacles uncoiled violently and lashed out at them, thrashing through the space that Arvin and Pakal occupied. Arvin instinctively recoiled as one of the tentacles whipped around his face, but the tentacle passed right through his gaseous form. His thoughts spun crazily as the gas that was his head swirled in its wake, then became coherent again. He concentrated on his objective—the chamber beyond—and drifted in that direction.

Once inside, his body solidified the same way that it had become gaseous: from the feet up. Blood rushed through his veins, sending a fierce tingle through his body from feet to head. He gasped and fought to keep his balance. As soon as the dizziness cleared, he reached over his shoulder to touch his pack. It was still there, the net inside it still weighing it down. Arvin heaved a sigh of relief.

The chamber was circular, its walls carved in the by-now familiar scale pattern. Against one wall lay the skeleton of an enormous snake, coiled in a neat loop where it had died.

"More bones," Arvin muttered.

He nudged the tail of the long-dead guardian with his foot, but the skeleton didn't react.

A simple wooden box sat on the floor; its hinged lid didn't appear to have a lock. Pakal materialized beside it—his feet, legs, torso, then head coalescing from air—then squatted to study the box. He pointed forked fingers at it, whispered something under his breath, and said, "The Circled Serpent is inside."

He reached for the lid.

"Careful," Arvin warned. "It's certain to be trapped."

"I sense no traps," Pakal said. He lifted the lid.

Arvin winced, but nothing happened.

The box was lined with black velvet. Inside was a silver tube twice the thickness of Arvin's thumb, bent in a half-circle. At one end of the half circle was a snake's head, its fanged mouth open wide and its eyes set with gems. The other end was tapered slightly; that would be where the other half of the Circled Serpent would join with it. Arvin held his breath, waiting for something to happen—for the mouth-door to close, for an alarm to sound, even for the snake skeleton to suddenly rear up and attack. Nothing did.

Pakal looked up at Arvin, a concerned expression on his face. "Only half? We thought that Sibyl had both pieces."

"Perhaps she does," Arvin said, thinking of Dmetrio's disappearance. "Perhaps that's why she decided that leaving this half in an easy-to-find location would be worth the risk; whoever found it would be tempted to waste time searching for the other half. Sibyl knows there's a spy in her lair; this is obviously part of a trap to catch that spy." He shrugged the backpack off his shoulders and began unfastening the straps that held it shut. He nodded at the door; the writhing tentacles that had filled the mouth were gone, but the mouth was still open. "Odd, don't you think, that the door hasn't shut yet."

Pakal tapped the half-circle of silver with a fingernail, making the metal ring faintly—probably making sure it was real and not an illusion—then closed the lid. He picked up the box and rose to his feet. "The other half of the Circled Serpent—"

"Will still be inside its lead-lined box, where your

magic can't locate it," Arvin said. He rose to his feet as well, holding his pack, ready to toss the net inside it at the door the moment Sibyl came through it. A musky floral smell rose from its fibres. "Go," he told Pakal, "while you still can. You've got half of the Circled Serpent; be content with that."

"You are not—?"

"No," Arvin said. "I'm staying. Sibyl's bound to arrive soon."

Pakal nodded and said, "May Thard Harr guide your—"

The dwarf grunted and staggered forward, crashing into Arvin. The box tumbled from his hands as he fell, spilling Sibyl's half of the Circled Serpent onto the floor. Arvin heard a rattling noise: the sound of bones moving swiftly across the floor.

He swore and leaped backward. The skeleton—animated after all—reared up with its mouth open, ready to strike again. It had already bitten Pakal, and the back of the dwarf's left arm leaked blood. Empty eye sockets stared at Arvin across the dwarf's rigid body. Then the serpent began to sway.

Arvin dropped his pack and flung his hands outward toward the skeleton. Silver sparkles danced in the air between them as long strands of glistening ectoplasm shot from Arvin's fingers, coiling themselves about the undead snake. They looped through the ribs, and with a twist of his fingers Arvin knotted them there. Another yank pulled the cords of ectoplasm tight, cinching together the coils of the skeleton's body. Its head and neck, however, continued to sway.

A fog crept into Arvin's mind. He stared at the snake across Pakal's body, unconcerned about whether the dwarf was alive or dead. He felt dazed, thick-headed, as if he'd drunk too much wine. He could feel his body moving in time with the serpent's swaying motion.

The skeleton opened its mouth wide to bring curved fangs into play. Head and neck still swaying, it hunched toward Arvin, awkwardly dragging its ectoplasm-bound body behind it.

Arvin meant to take a step back but took a step forward instead. His foot struck something that skidded across the floor with a metallic rasp. Glancing down, he saw it was the upper half of the Circled Serpent.

The interruption gave him a heartbeat's respite from the skeleton's mesmerizing motion. Arvin sank into one of the poses Tanju had taught him, raising his left arm as if to fend off a blow. He imagined himself in the Shield form, whirling to protect himself on all sides. As he did, energy exploded outward from the power point in his throat in a loud drone. It formed a protective barrier around him—one that helped him fend off the effects of the skeleton's swaying dance. His mind cleared.

Knowing that most of his psionic powers would be useless—the skeleton had no mind to attack—Arvin yanked the stone rope out of his backpack. Whipping it through the air, he shouted its command word. The rope stiffened into a pole of stone. It struck the skeleton just below the head, shattering the uppermost vertebrae. The head clattered to the floor, followed by the rest of the bones. Whirling a loop of the stone rope up and over his head, Arvin brought it crashing down into the serpent's skull. Bone exploded across the floor as the head shattered. The stone rope smashed as it struck the floor, and pieces skittered across the room.

Panting, Arvin looked down at what remained of the creature. Already the ectoplasm that bound it was evaporating. The skeleton, however, did not move.

It appeared to be dead. Arvin touched the crystal that hung at his throat.

"Nine lives," he croaked.

He crouched beside Pakal and pressed fingers against the dwarf's neck. Pakal's blood-pulse beat faintly beneath his leathery skin. His eyes were open and staring, his breathing shallow. The skeleton's bite had paralyzed him.

Arvin stared at his pack, wondering what to do next. Sibyl still hadn't come to investigate. What was keeping her?

Arvin heard a noise on the other side of the door; it sounded like the scuff of leather on stone or the slither of scales. Scooping up his backpack, he flattened himself against one wall. His heart pounded as he heard a woman's voice whispering an oath in the language of the yuan-ti. Certain it was Sibyl, he tried to yank the net from his pack. It wouldn't come free. He yanked harder, but it still wouldn't budge. He cursed silently as he realized what had happened: the yellow musk creeper vines he'd woven the net from had rooted in the soft leather.

Arvin yanked his dagger from its sheath, determined to cut the net free. As he drew it, he heard a furious thrashing sound from inside the mouth-door as the tentacles inside it were activated. Realizing it wasn't Sibyl but someone else coming through the door—or trying to—Arvin reversed his dagger, holding it by the blade, ready to throw. Whoever the intruder was, he was likely to be dangerous. Arvin reached deep into his *muladhara*, preparing to tap its energy.

Something stepped through the doorway—something that looked like the silhouette of a woman. In the blink of an eye, it expanded, becoming three-dimensional. The woman was a heavyset human with a double chin and brown hair with a streak of gray at one temple. Arvin's mouth dropped open as he recognized her. Naneth—the sorceress who had summoned the demon that had killed Karrell.

Or rather, he amended as he saw the sway in her body as she found her feet again and stared down at Pakal, a mind seed. The mind in that body was no longer Naneth's. It was Zelia's.

Arvin manifested the power that would cloud her mind, hiding him from her, and not a moment too soon. The wary Naneth-seed looked around the room then chuckled as her eyes fell upon the upper half of the Circled Serpent, lying next to Pakal's body. She bent to pick it up.

Knowing he was unlikely to surprise her with psionics—his secondary display would give her the instant's warning she needed to retaliate in kind—Arvin resorted to cruder methods. While she was distracted, he hurled his dagger. It struck home, burying itself between her shoulders. The blade would have killed someone with less fat padding her body, but the Naneth-seed merely grunted with pain.

She whirled around, her small eyes searching the room. Arvin gasped aloud as pain shot through his own back. It felt as though a dagger was embedded there. Something wet oozed down his back: not blood, but ectoplasm. The Naneth-seed must have manifested a power that transferred the pain of her wound to him.

The pain shattered Arvin's concentration, giving the Naneth-seed a brief glimpse of him. Her second psionic attack followed the first, swift as thought. Arvin tried to throw up a shield against it but wasn't quick enough.

Air exploded from his lungs in a rush as an invisible band of psionic energy looped around his chest then tightened. His own psionic power faltered as he fought for breath—and failed. He was visible.

"You again," the Naneth-seed said, the hissing of her secondary display overlapping her words.

Arvin struggled to draw a breath. He tried raising a mental fortress, but the Naneth-seed beat it down. He started to form a construct out of ectoplasm to attack her, but before it was fully shaped she usurped control of it and ran it headlong into a wall, splattering ectoplasm everywhere. He would have tried charming her, but there was no breath left in his lungs. He couldn't speak, couldn't even beg. He did manage the most tenuous of links with her mind and found a faint source of hope: she was debating ending the power that was preventing him from breathing and replacing it with one that would force him to take his own life. That would draw out his death, allowing her to savor it.

Then she changed her mind. No, she would end Arvin's life more quickly. Returning with the upper half of the Circled Serpent was more important, especially since Sibyl had been alerted.

When the Naneth-seed finally noticed Arvin listening in on her thoughts, she gave a brutal mental shove, propelling him from her mind. Then she squeezed harder.

Arvin sagged to his knees as darkness clouded the edges of his vision. He blinked furiously, trying to find the force of will to resist the Naneth-seed's manifestation. As he struggled, he thought he saw Pakal's arm move. A moment later, despite the dark spots that clouded his vision and the roaring in his ears, he was certain of it. The paralysis the skeleton had inflicted was wearing off.

Pakal's eyes fluttered, then opened to stare at the Naneth-seed. One hand crept toward his hollow reed while the other fumbled open the pouch at his belt.

The reed scraped against the floor. The Naneth-seed turned toward the sound.

With the last bit of his consciousness, Arvin manifested a power—one of the first he'd ever learned. A faint droning filled the air. Instead of completing her turn toward Pakal, the Naneth-seed glanced at the doorway, distracted.

The last thing Arvin saw before losing consciousness was the dwarf raising the hollow reed to his lips.

The next thing Arvin knew, Pakal was slapping him awake. Groggily, Arvin pushed him away and drew a shaking breath. He sat up—and had to wait for the room to stop spinning before he could speak. He felt as though he was going to be ill.

"What happened?" he asked.

Pakal pointed at the Naneth-seed, who lay face-down on the floor. She'd landed with one arm stretched out above her head, pudgy fingers splayed. One of her fingers, Arvin noticed, was encircled with a band of amber: the teleportation ring she'd used to spirit Glisena out of her father's palace. A tiny feathered dart protruded from the back of the Naneth-seed's neck, just above Arvin's dagger. He stared, not believing his eyes, at his defeated foe.

"Is she—"

"Dead." Pakal offered Arvin his hand.

Arvin sighed with relief. The fact that the dwarf had saved him was a sobering thought. Arvin should have, with his increased powers, been able to deal with the seed on his own. He took the dwarf's hand and climbed to his feet.

"Nice shot," he said.

He nudged the big woman's body with a toe. He half expected it to rise from death, as the skeletal serpent had.

Pakal picked up the Circled Serpent and placed it back inside the box, then pointed forked fingers at the room's only exit. His face paled as he lowered his hand.

"Sibyl comes this way," said the dwarf. "Are you certain you will not come? I can turn your body to air once more."

Arvin picked up his backpack and glanced inside. The net had indeed knotted itself into the pack, but a few quick strokes of his knife would cut it loose.

"I'm not leaving until I kill Sibyl," Arvin replied.

He yanked his dagger from the Naneth-seed's back and got to work.

The dwarf shook his head. "I will be gone before then. Even if you succeed, you may be trapped here."

"No, I won't," Arvin said. He tilted his head at the Naneth-seed's hand. "Her ring is magical. It can teleport me out of here. Assuming, that is, that I survive."

As he spoke, he continued working to free his net. It was tricky work; one slip and he'd sever a strand of the net itself, ruining it. He could hear the *whuff-whuff-whuff* of wings in the corridor beyond the chamber, as well as running footsteps and the slither of scaly bodies. Sibyl and her clerics drew closer.

Pakal laid a broad hand on Arvin's shoulder. "You are a braver man than I. Thard Harr grant you strength." He began the prayer that would turn his body to air.

It was cut short by an angry hiss from the corridor outside. "Naneth!" Sibyl shouted. "You will regret betraying me."

A heartbeat later, a wave of magical fear boiled into the room, even stronger than before. Panic filled Arvin's mind as he whirled, searching for a way out of the chamber. There was only one exit, and it led straight to Sibyl. He was trapped . . .

No. There was another way out. Shoving his way past Pakal, who cringed on the floor, Arvin grabbed the Naneth-seed's hand. He sobbed in relief as he located the band of amber on one of her pudgy fingers. Yanking it free, he threw it onto the floor.

"Ossalur!" he cried.

The ring expanded.

Waves of magical fear lashed Arvin toward the circle of amber, which had grown to nearly two paces wide. Safety lay just a step or two away. Outside the chamber, he could hear Sibyl's furious hissing, could feel the rush of air from her wings as she approached.

No! he thought, fighting the compulsion to flee.

Rallying, he turned and scooped up his pack. The moment he'd been waiting for, planning for six months, was at hand. Sweat erupting on his brow from the strain, he plunged a hand into the pack. He'd almost freed the net. One good yank and it would be in his hands, ready to throw.

Then another wave of fear struck. Pakal leaped to his feet, wide-eyed. He clutched the box tight against his chest in white-knuckled fingers, trembling like a mouse about to be consumed by a serpent.

Arvin, fighting against the icy blasts of fear that threatened to sweep him off his feet like a hurricane, turned toward the doorway and saw Sibyl, her wings folded against her back, slithering through the hole. He started to yank the net from his pack . . .

Then Sibyl looked at him. *Saw* him. As a third wave of magical fear struck, the courage Arvin had found a moment before melted to slush in his veins. Screaming, his pack dragging behind, he darted for the ring. He grabbed Pakal as he ran past, yanking the dwarf with him into the circle of amber.

The scaled halls of the Temple of Varae vanished. So did the magical fear.

Arvin cursed. Six months of planning and preparation, ruined. Despite the fact that his terror had been magically induced, he was disgusted with himself. He was a psion, a master of mind magic. His will should have been stronger than that. He ground his teeth together then reminded himself that all was not lost. At least he'd had the presence of mind to pull the dwarf to safety and to bring his pack with him. Maybe, gods willing, he'd get a second chance to throw his net at Sibyl.

Still trembling from the after effects of the magical fear, Arvin extricated himself from Pakal and looked around. The ring—shrunk back to its normal size—had teleported them to a rooftop garden under an open, starry sky. A fountain tinkled, spraying the nearby potted plants with a cool mist. Arvin took a closer look at the plants, each fashioned into a topiary of a coiled serpent. He'd seen them before. Even as the realization struck him, he heard a gate creak open. A woman swayed into view from the staircase leading to the railing-enclosed rooftop—a woman with long red hair, and a freckling of green scales.

Zelia.

"Arvin!" she hissed. She glanced down at Naneth's ring. "What have you done with my seed?"

CHAPTER 3

Arvin stared back at Zelia for a heartbeat—then threw up a mental tower around himself. A loud droning burst from his throat as he imagined himself in the form Tanju had taught him: one hand clenched above his head, a wall of iron around his will. With a thought, he expanded the walls of his mental tower outward to include Pakal, imagining his free hand extended to the dwarf behind him. Zelia was certain to attack their minds, but she wouldn't kill them before finding out what they were doing with Naneth's ring. Arvin's psionic tower would shield them from the worst of it.

The attack came immediately. Arvin heard the distant, tinkling-bell sound of Zelia's secondary display and felt her try to force her awareness into his body. Her will slithered around the defense he'd thrown up like a tide of snakes trying to find cracks in a tower wall. One forced its way through and entered his right hand. His fingers spasmed open, no longer under his control, and the backpack he held fell to the floor. The tendril of will wormed its way upward inside his arm, its scales rasping against bone; Arvin shoved it down and out with a mental push.

"Pakal!" he shouted. "Your darts!"

Instead of reaching for his blowpipe, the dwarf grunted a prayer and fluttered his hands. Pakal's body began disappearing as it turned to air. Arvin groaned, realizing Pakal was about to abandon him.

Zelia, meanwhile, had managed to find another chink in Arvin's defenses. Her mental snake slid inside his neck. It wrenched his head to the side, forcing him to look away from her. Two more tendrils of will forced their way into his legs. Zelia swayed forward, eyes triumphant.

"Kneel," she ordered. "Submit to me."

Arvin's knees buckled under him. Zelia smiled. Arvin tensed, terrified that she was about to seed him.

Her attention, however, was divided. She turned toward Pakal, a frown of concentration on her face. Pakal, however, continued his transformation. He stared at Arvin with eyes that held a hint of remorse and said something in his own language then vanished from sight. A breeze stirred the top of the nearest plant, then rippled away across the topiaries and over the wall.

Zelia cursed.

Her hold on Arvin lessened a little—enough for Arvin to manifest another power. Summoning energy into a power point at the base of his scalp, he created an illusionary image of himself prostrated at Zelia's feet. At the same time, his real self vanished from sight. Zelia frowned at the spot where the illusionary Arvin lay, probably wondering why he had capitulated so easily.

Arvin began drawing ectoplasm from the Astral Plane, shaping it into a vaguely human-shaped blob. Sparkles of silver light burst from his forehead as he worked, giving his position away. Zelia's head whipped up—but in that same moment the construct's fist slammed into her temple, snapping her head to the side. She collapsed in a boneless heap, crashing into the side of the fountain as she fell. Mist drifted down on her splayed body and closed eyelids.

Its chill didn't revive her.

Arvin ended his manifestation, and the construct disappeared. Shaking, he rose to his feet. He couldn't believe it. A year ago, he'd felled Zelia with a similar trick, using a simple psychokinetic power to levitate a knot of rope and knock her unconscious. Shaking his head in wonder, he touched the crystal at his throat.

"Nine—"

A hiss of laughter sounded behind him. Whirling, Arvin saw a second Zelia enter the garden.

"Surely you didn't think it would be that easy?" she said, closing the gate behind her.

She cocked a finger at him, as if inviting him to try something. Arvin heard a sound like the tinkling of tiny bells.

He stomped his foot. Zelia staggered but did not fall, nor, strangely, did she hurl an attack back at him. Arvin used the respite to yank ectoplasm from the Astral and braid it into the massive construct he hoped would overpower Zelia.

As he did, he felt a curious, hollow sensation at the base of his spine. The construct was taking far longer to manifest than it should have—and was drawing power at an incredible rate from his *muladhara*.

Arvin tried cutting the manifestation short in mid-flow but couldn't. Energy spiraled out of his *muladhara* at a faster and faster rate, spilling into the air around him like water from a torn wineskin. He tried fighting it, tried sending his awareness deep into his *muladhara*, only to have his consciousness nearly shredded by the violent whirlpool he found there. A moment later, the last of his psionic energies spilled out and were gone.

Zelia smiled. "I see you've learned a thing or two since we last met," she said, "so have I."

Terrified, Arvin whipped a hand around his back. Before he could draw his dagger, Zelia's eyes flashed silver as if reflecting the moonlight. Her hand shot out and slapped his cheek. Arvin stumbled backward, unbalanced. His forearm was stuck to the small of his back. When he tried to wrench it free, it felt as if the skin was ripping. His free hand brushed against his hip—and stuck there, the cloth of his pants melting away as flesh fused with flesh. He stumbled, one knee knocking against the other. They stuck fast as well.

Completely unbalanced, he crashed to the floor. Clothing melted away from his body like paper in the rain as his calves were forced up against his thighs, his arms stuck to his sides, and his chin to his chest, the flesh fusing together like clay being smoothed by an invisible hand. He crumpled down into a fetal ball. As he blinked, his eyelids tried to fuse shut. With an immense effort, he managed to tear one of them open again. Even as he did, his ears closed over, blocking out the sound of his own ragged breathing.

Terror gripped him. He prayed to Tymora, to Hoar, to Ilmater—to any god or goddess who would listen. He could feel the crystal his mother had given him pressing into his throat. The flesh had grown over it, sealing it inside.

He watched with his one open eye—not daring to

blink, lest the eyelid seal itself shut—as Zelia stepped out of view behind him. The dagger at the small of his back had likewise been buried inside folds of fused flesh—or rather, its sheath had. Arvin felt the blade slide out of the sheath as Zelia drew it. His heart beat with faint hope. Was she going to end his suffering? Would she truly show mercy?

She stepped in front of him again, holding the dagger. She jabbed its point into first one ear, then the other, cutting the flaps of skin that had grown over them. Then she sliced open his lips. Arvin gasped at the pain and began to choke on the blood he'd inhaled. When he was able to speak again, he told Zelia what she wanted to hear.

"You've beaten me," he said, blood dribbling from his lips onto the floor. He stared up at her with his one good eye. "What now?"

Instead of answering, she stepped over to the first Zelia—the one that lay either unconscious or dead. She laid a hand gently on that Zelia's neck, as though checking for a life pulse. Instead of continuing to rest gently on the neck, however, her fingers sank deep into it, as if into soft dough. Then the first Zelia began to shrink. Head and legs and arms shriveled into the torso, and the torso itself collapsed around the second Zelia's hand.

Zelia closed her hand around the last vestiges of the body it as it flowed into her palm and closed her eyes, taking a deep breath. She shivered and her head lolled back—and groaned in pleasure. Her fist fell open, empty. She opened her eyes and bent down to pick up Naneth's ring.

"How did you come to have this?" she asked.

Arvin stared defiantly up at her. Maybe she wasn't going to seed him after all. His lips were raw with pain, and he spat out the blood that had puddled in his mouth.

"Abyss take you," he swore.

Zelia swayed closer, tossing her long red hair. "You *will* tell me," she said, "one way or the other. When you've finished telling me, I'll end your suffering." She smirked. "Perhaps by compelling you to kill yourself."

Her eyes flashed and a soft tinkling filled the air as she manifested another power. Arvin felt it brush against his mind as softly as a cobweb—then tear apart, as if it were equally fragile.

Zelia frowned, then grabbed his hair and used it to roll his body back and forth like a ball as she examined him. Her eyes flashed a second time and a soft hissing filled the air as she concentrated on her manifestation. Her hand paused briefly over the braided leather bracelet on his right wrist, and hesitated a second time over the lump that had been Arvin's left hand. She probed with her fingers.

Arvin realized she had found Karrell's ring.

With quick, deft slices that sent fresh spasms of pain lancing through his hand and up his arm, Zelia cut Arvin's little finger apart from the rest, then yanked the ring from it. She held the ring in the fountain until the blood was gone from it, then gave it an appraising look.

A tear welled in Arvin's open eye. He said nothing, however. Zelia would have enjoyed listening to him plead for Karrell's ring. He stared at the backpack, lying no more than a pace away. He'd never be able to kill Sibyl. Zelia would no doubt claim the net inside it, as well ...

His breath caught as he realized there might be a way out. If he could trick Zelia into speaking the net's command word while still holding it, the magical net would kill her. Arvin would be free once the manifestation she'd used to fuse his flesh together ended.

Assuming it ever did end.

Zelia's eyes flashed silver a third time as she manifested the power that would allow her to listen in on Arvin's thoughts. Without Karrell's ring or his own psionics to counter it, he had only his own raw will to defend himself with—and Zelia tore through that like a knife through cloth. Arvin pretended to panic, filling his mind with thoughts of his backpack. He prayed—falsely—to Tymora that his luck would hold, that Zelia wouldn't take the net inside it, that she wouldn't speak its command word—*pullulios*—and toss it on him. That would inflict a terrible agony, one that would cause him to crumple and succumb to whatever she wanted.

Arvin felt Zelia push deeper into his mind. She chuckled. "Try that trick on someone who's going to fall for it." Then she continued to sift through his thoughts.

Arvin's mind reeled as his thoughts were peeled back, layer by layer. Memories flashed before his eyes, terrible memories of confronting the marilith and watching in horror as the fate link he'd manifested yanked Karrell into the Abyss with it when the demon was banished. And wonderful memories of making love to Karrell—just a flash of that, and a long sequence, replayed more slowly, of the conversation they'd had just before.

Zelia rifled through his memories of everything Karrell had told him about the Circled Serpent, then through more recent memories of sneaking into the temple and getting close—but not quite close enough—to exact his revenge on Sibyl. She saw him meet Pakal, get past the tentacled mouth and undead snake to claim half of the Circled Serpent, confront the Naneth-seed and defeat it, and she saw them found by Sibyl then teleporting to the rooftop...

"The Circled Serpent was *here?*" Zelia hissed,

releasing his mind at last. She glanced around, wary, then kicked Arvin. "Where did the dwarf go?"

Arvin slumped, exhausted in both mind and body. "I don't know," he answered at last. He stared, unseeing, at the fountain. He'd been violated. Used.

Zelia swore under her breath. She sputtered for several moments, her fangs bared, then got control of herself again. She turned back to Arvin.

"You are certain the Naneth-seed is dead?"

Arvin supposed she would kill him for that, especially since she'd learned all that his memories could tell her. He tried to nod, but his fused body just rocked back and forth on the floor.

"She's dead," he answered.

Zelia gave a false-sounding chuckle. "Just as well. I was growing tired of her. Mind seeds can be so ... infuriating ... at times. Naneth was constantly complaining about the body I chose for her. And she was getting ... defiant. They all do, given enough time—" she stared down at Arvin—"some of them even before their seed has blossomed."

Arvin met her unblinking stare with his one good eye. "What do you expect?" he said. "They're all just as self-centered and vain as you are." Blood pooled in his mouth again, and he spat. "Now shut up and kill me."

Zelia's eyes widened in mock surprise. "Kill you?" She tilted her head. "Oh, no. I never waste anything I can still use."

Swaying into a crouch, she brushed a hand against his cheek. A shiver rushed through Arvin's body and a thin sheen of ectoplasm blossomed on his skin, forcing its way into the folds of fused flesh. His arms and legs sprang apart and his eyelid fluttered open. He rose, shaking, to his feet. Blood still dripped from his lips, his ears, and his left hand. He stared down at the latter, and saw that the little finger and the one next to it were sliced open along their lengths. He picked up one of the scraps of cloth that remained from his shirt and wrapped the fingers together, debating whether or not he should attack Zelia. He glanced at his backpack. It was within reach, but the net had probably rooted itself back into the leather again.

Zelia saw his glance and bared her fangs: a warning not to try anything. She held up Karrell's ring. "You think she's dead, don't you?"

Arvin stared at the floor. "The demon drew her into the Abyss. Nobody can survive there."

"It drew her into Smaragd, you mean."

Arvin glanced up. "What are you talking about?"

"Smaragd is a layer of Abyss, the layer where Sseth dwells. That's where Karrell would have wound up."

"How do you know that?"

"Mariliths range throughout the Abyss, but this one was summoned by a servant of Sseth. It's the most likely place for the demon to have come from, and its banishment would have returned it there."

Arvin pressed his damaged lips together. The sting of cut flesh helped blot out the ache in his heart. "Even if she did get dragged into ... there, she's still—"

"Dead?" Zelia gave a hiss of derisive laughter. "You humans know so little. Smaragd is dangerous but not completely inhospitable to mortals, especially if the mortal is yuan-ti. Your precious Karrell may still be alive."

Arvin felt a surge of hope. Karrell—alive? Zelia knew more about the Abyss than he did. Maybe she was right about this Smaragd layer being survivable, except that Karrell's god, Ubtao, was an enemy of Sseth. The serpent god would have immediately killed any cleric of Ubtao's that showed up in his realm. Zelia was toying with him, tempting him with the one possibility that she *knew*—now that she'd raped his memories—would most torment him.

He walked over to the fountain and splashed water onto his face, washing away the blood. "Quit lying to me," he told her, "and let's get this over with. Tell me what you want." He turned to her, his face dripping. "Why am I so 'useful?' Because I have something that can kill Sibyl?"

Zelia laughed. "That too," she said, her eyes glinting, "but also because you have eyes in Smaragd."

"Eyes?" Arvin echoed. He'd expected Zelia to send him on his way, to either order him back into the temple to make another attempt on Sibyl or to chase after Pakal and retrieve the Circled Serpent—perhaps after seeding him first, though he was starting to suspect she might have used her last power stone when she seeded Naneth.

"Eyes," Zelia repeated. "Karrell's eyes."

"She's dead." Arvin touched the lapis lazuli embedded in his forehead under a layer of scar tissue. "I tried sending to her, every day for more than a month."

"You kept my stone? How touching," she mocked. Her voice grew serious again. "A sending doesn't always penetrate to another plane. Smaragd lies deep in the Abyss—more than seventy layers shield it from this plane. There is another power, however, which can be used to view a mortal on another plane, even one as remote as Smaragd. And by viewing that mortal, to get a glimpse of what is happening on that layer of the Abyss."

Arvin's head came up. His breath caught as hope blossomed a second time in his chest. "You really do think Karrell's alive, don't you?"

Zelia gave a slow serpent nod.

Arvin hesitated, wondering if she'd just tricked

him somehow. "What . . . is it, exactly, that you hope to see? Sseth?"

Zelia smiled. "Aren't you the smart little monkey?" She passed Arvin back his dagger then sank down, cross-legged, and patted the floor next to her. "Sit."

Arvin sheathed the dagger, hesitated, then did as she'd ordered. Aside from tatters of his clothing he was naked, and the stone floor felt cool against his skin. The only sound was that of water tinkling into the fountain. He glanced across the city's rooftops, glowing green against the night sky. He couldn't believe that he was sitting in that rooftop garden, talking to the woman he most feared. It was as if he'd stepped back in time to the night when Zelia taught him to master his psionic powers. But if there was a chance that Karrell was alive—even a small chance—he wanted to hear what Zelia had to say.

"For some time now—more than a decade—Sseth has been . . . strangely muted," she began. "His clerics are still granted spells, and the god still answers their prayers, but the voice of Sseth has changed in subtle ways. They say it has deepened, become somehow drier, more whispery . . ."

"Drier?" Arvin asked.

Zelia shrugged. "I am not a cleric." She toyed with the ring in her hands. "But I do serve House Extaminos, and that noble House controls the Cathedral of Emerald Scales. Anything that is of concern to its clerics disturbs Lady Dediana, and that, in turn, disturbs *me*."

"The clerics think something's happened to Sseth?" Arvin asked.

Zelia nodded. "A little over two years ago, I had a troubling dream, a dream of a larger serpent swallowing a smaller serpent, tail first. As the smaller serpent started to disappear into the larger one's jaws, it twisted and took the larger serpent's tail in its own mouth, and started consuming it in turn. Each serpent choked the other down, until both disappeared."

She paused to flick away the venom that had beaded on her fangs with a blue forked tongue. "I wasn't the only one to have this dream," she continued. "Dozens of other yuan-ti shared it—or one similar to it." She nodded at the ring. "Karrell was one of them. She told me of her dream when we spoke in Ormpetarr. She was one of the few to recognize the snakes in the dream for what they were: the two halves of the Circled Serpent."

Zelia obviously expected a startled reaction. Arvin didn't grant her one.

"Go on," he said.

"That same winter, a restlessness gripped the yuan-ti. Dmetrio Extaminos began his restoration of the ancient city, and Sibyl arrived in Hlondeth. Lady Dediana, deep in winter torpor, didn't recognize the danger Sibyl posed at first, not until Sibyl had killed her cousin Urshas and lured half of the cathedral's clergy away by claiming to be Sseth's avatar. By then it was almost too late."

"What's this got to do with ... Smaragd?" Arvin asked, stumbling over the unfamiliar word. "And with Karrell?"

"That's what I hope to find out," Zelia said. "Why has Sseth not struck down an imposter? Does he condone what Sibyl is doing? Or is he merely ... keeping silent?"

Arvin frowned. "You hope to find that out just by looking at Karrell? Why not look in on Sseth himself, or *ask* him?"

"Because I can't," Zelia hissed. "No one can—not even his clerics. Something is preventing it, but that same something may not prevent us from viewing a mortal in Sseth's realm. Your Karrell may be the crack in the wall that will allow us a glimpse into Smaragd."

"Why do you need me?" Arvin asked.

"If I tried to contact her, Karrell would resist, but she won't resist you. She trusts you."

"Why should I trust *you*? Given the way your mind seeds scheme behind your back, it looks as though you can't even trust yourself."

Zelia's lip twitched, revealing the tips of her fangs. Arvin's taunt had struck home. He knew, thanks to the dreams he'd had while seeded, that at least one of Zelia's seeds—a dwarf—had turned on her. He wondered how many others had betrayed her over the years.

With a visible effort, Zelia composed herself. "Don't you want to find out if Karrell is alive?"

Arvin stared back at her for a long moment. At last he nodded and said, "There's just one problem. I don't know the power that will let me view someone at a distance."

"That's easily remedied."

Silver flashed in Zelia's eyes. She sat silent, staring out over the wrought iron railing that enclosed the rooftop garden. After several moments, a finger-sized crystal rose into view and floated toward her. She caught it then passed it to Arvin.

He glanced at the crystal. It was deep blue and blade-shaped: thin, with a chisel-like point at one end. Azurite.

"A power stone," he said.

Zelia nodded.

Arvin closed his hand around it. "You trust me to tell you what I see?" he asked.

Zelia laughed. "No. That's why I'm going to look through your eyes."

Arvin shuddered. He'd had Zelia inside his head—or rather, a fragment of her—a year ago when she planted her mind seed. Having her coiled around his thoughts wasn't an experience he wanted to repeat, even briefly, but it was something he had to do. If Karrell *was* alive. . . .

"Let's do it," he said through gritted teeth.

Zelia stared into his eyes. Silver flashed across her pupils, then was gone. An instant later Arvin felt a soft fluttering under the scar on his forehead, the lapis lazuli silently alerting him to the fact that someone was watching him—from inside his own skull. As Zelia settled in behind his eyes, he saw her as she viewed herself: confident, poised, powerful—desirable. Then it was gone.

"How do I hail the crystal?" he asked.

"By its name," Zelia said. "Gergorissa."

Arvin whispered the name. He sent his awareness deep into the crystal and felt it awaken.

Yes? a female voice hissed as a mote of pale green light bloomed in the darkness. The voice was unsettlingly close to Zelia's own, and for a moment, Arvin thought Zelia had spoken to him. She must have created the power stone.

Arvin grasped the mote of light with his mind. He felt its energy rush into the base of his skull, filling the power point there. Suddenly he *knew* how to view Karrell anywhere on any plane of existence.

Assuming she was still alive.

Holding his breath, he manifested that power—and gasped as Karrell appeared in his mind's eye.

She sat slumped on the floor of a dripping jungle, arms clasped around her round, protruding belly. She was still pregnant, but otherwise she looked terrible. Her cheeks were hollow, her eyes dark, her hair tangled. The dress she wore was in rags and her arms and legs were covered in angry red scratches. The scar on her cheek from the sword wound the marilith had inflicted was barely visible under the dried mud that smudged her face. A tear trickled down her cheek, eroding a furrow through the grime. Despite her condition and the desperate, exhausted look in her eye, she was beautiful. Arvin's breath caught in his throat. He ached to reach out and touch her, to hold her.

To save her.

Karrell glanced up, startled.

"Karrell," Arvin whispered in a choked voice. "It's me."

Her eyes widened. "Arvin?" she gasped. "You're alive?"

Arvin almost laughed. Six months in the Abyss, and she was worried about *him*. "It's me, *kiichpan chu'al*. I'm alive."

Karrell's image blurred as tears formed in his eyes. Suddenly, they blinked rapidly: Zelia, trying to clear them. Arvin tried to push her from his mind.

Don't, she cautioned, shoving back hard enough to make his eyes bulge. *Talk to her, before the manifestation ends. Ask her what's happened to Sseth.*

Karrell continued to stare at Arvin. "Where are you?"

"In Hlondeth." He shook his head, still not quite willing to believe his eyes. "How did you survive?" he asked. "It's been so long."

Karrell gave him a weary smile. "By Ubtao's will," she said, "and through my own resourcefulness." She laid a hand gently on her stomach. "Because I had to."

Zelia gave him a mental jab that made his mind ache.

"Where are you?" Arvin continued. "In Smaragd? With Sseth?"

Karrell didn't seem to find his question odd. "Yes. The serpent god is stuck fast. His jungle has bound him. I escaped from the marilith, and now it's searching for me. It still thinks our fates are linked. It's been protecting me, but when I start to give birth, and it doesn't feel my pain . . ." she shuddered. "I can't let it find me."

Ask her more about Sseth, Zelia interrupted. *Is the god asleep? Awake?*

Arvin ignored her. He stared at Karrell's stomach. "The children. Are they still . . . ?"

Karrell smiled. "Alive? Yes. And kicking—at least one of them has feet, and not a tail." She bit her lip. A haunted look crept into her eyes. "It won't be long now. When my time comes, I won't be able to run any more. The marilith—"

"I'll get you out of there," Arvin promised. "I don't know how, but I will. I'll find a way."

"Find Ts'ikil," Karrell said. "She'll know what to do."

Sseth, Zelia insisted. *Tell her to go to where Sseth is.*

Karrell looked warily around. "Arvin! Did you hear a hissing noise?"

"It's nothing," Arvin lied, mentally shoving Zelia back as he spoke. "Who is Ts'ikil? Where is she?"

"She's—"

Their connection broke. Arvin found himself staring at Zelia across the rooftop garden. He leaped to his feet, furious. "What did you do that for?" he shouted.

Zelia gave him a long, unblinking stare. "You were supposed to make her go to where Sseth is."

Arvin almost laughed. "Karrell? I can't *make* her do anything." He sighed. "You got what you wanted—you heard Karrell. If she says Sseth is bound, he is."

Zelia thought about this for several moments, her eyes narrowed. Then she lounged back against the fountain, a lazy smile on her lips. She looked like a serpent that had just swallowed a juicy, squirming morsel.

"Karrell's pregnant?" she hissed. She gave him a

withering look. "By you—a *human?*"

"You can hardly talk, given what *you* like to sleep with," Arvin shot back at her, "and Karrell's pregnancy is none of your business."

"Oh but it is," Zelia said, rising smoothly to her feet. "It makes you so much more . . . motivated."

"To do what?" Arvin asked, his voice tense.

"To rescue her." She let the silence stretch out between them for several heartbeats, then added, "Wouldn't you like to know how? Or would you rather let your children be born in the Abyss? I don't think they'd last long. Karrell couldn't possibly protect them. They'd be no more than a soft, squishy mouthful for any passing—"

"Get on with it," Arvin snapped. "How do I rescue her?" His hands balled into tight fists.

"By using the Circled Serpent. It can open a door to Smaragd."

"You lie," Arvin said in a low voice. "It opens a door to the Fugue Plain, to the lair of Dendar, the Night Serpent. If that door opens and Dendar is released, thousands will die."

"That's true," Zelia said, "but the Circled Serpent opens more than one door. There is a second—the door that Sseth used nearly fourteen centuries ago, when he vanished from this plane and became a god, a door that leads directly to Smaragd . . . and to Karrell."

Arvin stood rigid, stunned. "You're . . . making this up," he said. "It's a trick." He thought back to the little he had learned of the serpent god's lore from the dreams he'd had after Zelia seeded him. "Sseth left the realm of mortals by flying into a volcano," he told her, "one of the Peaks of Flame in Chult. Your own memories of the Cathedral of Emerald Scales told me that much."

Zelia hissed with laughter. "You believed them?"

she taunted. Then the mocking smile fell away from her lips. "That's the official version," she said, "the one the clergy teach the laity. The clerics themselves know that Sseth left his plane of existence through a door, not an erupting volcano. The trouble is, nobody remembers where that door is, save that it is somewhere on the Chultan Peninsula. Over the centuries, the legends became intertwined. Some—Sibyl, for example—mistakenly conclude that Sseth entered Dendar's lair and somehow slipped from the Fugue Plain into Smaragd, though this is a ridiculous notion." She paused to shake her head, as if disappointed in Sibyl. Then her eyes glittered. "Using the Circled Serpent, you can open a door to Smaragd and rescue Karrell."

"There's just one problem," Arvin said. "I only know where half of the Circled Serpent is—with Pakal—and I don't know where he is."

"You'll find him," Zelia said.

"Maybe," Arvin countered, "but then what?"

"Dmetrio Extaminos still has the second half."

"I don't know where *he* is, either."

"I do," Zelia said. "His mind has been dulled lately by too much *osssra*, but he's still perfectly capable." She pointed at the scar on Arvin's forehead. "When you retrieve the first half from the dwarf, use my stone to contact me. I'll tell you where Dmetrio is—and where the door to Smaragd is. Together, you and Dmetrio can open it."

Arvin hesitated. He knew he couldn't trust Zelia, but what if the Circled Serpent *would* allow him to rescue Karrell? It was the only shard of hope he'd found. He clung to it, even though it cut deeply.

He met Zelia's eye. "You know I'll try to take Dmetrio's half of the Circled Serpent and open the door myself."

"Yes," Zelia answered, a gleam in her eye.

"Then why trust me?"

"I don't," she hissed, "but if you don't do exactly as I say, I'll tell the marilith that its fate is no longer linked with Karrell's. When the demon catches her—and it will—Karrell will die ... and so will your children."

Arvin felt the blood drain from his face. He should have expected as much. Zelia always made sure she had something to threaten him with—and Karrell herself had handed Zelia just the weapon she needed.

"I'll need Karrell's ring back," he said at last.

Zelia tossed it to him—an offhanded gesture, as if the ring meant nothing to her. Arvin caught it and squeezed it tight in his hand. He stared at Zelia.

"What's in it for you?"

"The eternal gratitude of Lady Dediana Extaminos," she answered, "when it is her son—not Sibyl—who enters Smaragd, frees Sseth, and reaps the rewards of service to a god."

Arvin let out a long, slow breath. Dmetrio also wanted to become Sseth's avatar? For a year, Arvin had struggled against one arrogant yuan-ti who wanted to become a god, and Zelia was proposing that he join forces with another—with a man who had callously used then abandoned a woman who had been pregnant with his child, a man who had the backing of Arvin's most feared enemy.

Arvin rubbed his temples. It was a dangerous game he was about to play. In order to rescue Karrell—and not release an evil god in the process—he would need to find a way to defeat Zelia.

"Well?" she asked.

He closed his eyes and shuddered. Zelia still controlled his destiny, as certainly as if she'd seeded him. She liked watching him squirm.

"I'll do it," he whispered, "for Karrell and our children."

CHAPTER 4

Arvin winced as the fleshmender turned his hand over, studying his lacerated fingers.

"Strange wound," she said.

Arvin merely nodded. "Can you heal it?"

The cleric was a young, blonde-haired woman who might have been pretty save for the deep lines in her forehead, the price to be paid for taking on the suffering of others. She returned his nod.

"The Crying God feels your pain, my son," she intoned.

Dressed in ash-gray tunic, trousers, and matching gray skullcap, she had Ilmater's symbol—a pair of bound hands—pinned over her heart.

Arvin remembered that symbol well from his childhood. The severed hands—he always thought of them that way—and the other symbols of martyrdom had decorated the orphanage. Ilmater's martyred clerics were painted in vivid glory, spotted with plague sores, being torn apart by wolves, or covered in open, weeping wounds. All had their faces turned toward Shurrock, a savage domain of broken hills, torrential rains, howling winds, and wild beasts. Ilmater's dwelling place—the domain where his faithful would reap their reward of eternal suffering.

Arvin could have gone to a guild healer, but that would have meant answering unwanted questions. The guild frowned upon members taking on "outside work." But in the Chapel of Healing that catered to the humans of Hlondeth, the only demand made was a coin or two—whatever the petitioner could afford—in the wooden donation box.

Darkmorning had almost ended, and outside the chapel, the streets were quiet. Only Arvin sought healing. Come sunrise, however, the chapel's stone benches would be filled with petitioners.

The cleric murmured a prayer—one that Arvin could recite from memory, even though healing prayers had been used infrequently at the orphanage; the clerics believed that suffering built character in children. The wounds on his fingers slowly closed. She touched his mouth and ears, and the sting of each wound faded. When she was finished, she held his left hand in hers and touched his abbreviated little finger.

"This," she said, lifting his hand slightly, "is too old a wound for me to heal. It requires a Painbearer's touch."

"That's all right," Arvin said. He had no desire to meet any of the senior clerics. The only reason he'd come to the chapel was that it was run by the order's most junior clerics—men and women who weren't old enough to dredge up unpleasant memories. "I'm used to it," he told her.

He didn't bother to explain what the guild would do to him if they found he'd removed their mark. One day, perhaps, when he was finally clear of Hlondeth, he might seek out a cleric who could regenerate his finger, but....

She released his hand. "You have the face of someone who has seen much suffering. Ilmater bless you and help you to bear your load."

Arvin stood. He was grateful for Ilmater's healing, but that was as far as it went. The last thing he needed was another god meddling in his life.

As he dropped coins in the donation box, a disheveled woman rushed through the door, an infant lying limp in her arms.

"She's been bitten!" the woman shrieked. "There was a snake! A snake in her swaddling basket! She started to cry—it woke me—and I saw she had its tail in her fist. It bit her. Please, oh please, can you save her?"

The cleric turned her attention to the baby, touching its tiny hand and intoning a spell. Arvin watched a moment—the mother was panting from her run, and it was probably already too late for the poison to be neutralized—then he slipped out the door. He really didn't want to see the outcome. As he walked away from the chapel, he heard the cleric murmur condolences and the mother break into loud sobs. At least, he thought grimly, the woman had known the joy of holding her child in her arms, if only for a short time.

He wondered if Karrell would live to do the same.

As he walked the narrow, curving street, awash in the faint green glow from the buildings on either side, he struggled with his conscience. Karrell would be wary of his forced alliance with

Zelia—she'd made the same mistake herself, six months before, with near-disastrous results. She would certainly condemn any plan that ran the risk of both halves of the Circled Serpent falling into the hands of one of Sseth's devotees. Arvin ached to speak to Karrell again, but the sending he'd attempted after leaving Zelia's rooftop garden had failed, just like the rest of them.

He still couldn't quite believe that Zelia had let him go. She'd tossed a blanket at him when he requested something to hide his nakedness—he'd since retrieved a change of clothes and tossed the blanket on a garbage heap—then escorted him out of her garden and down the ramp to the street. He'd followed her warily, expecting her to seed him, but she hadn't. Perhaps she thought recovering Pakal's half of the Circled Serpent would take more than seven days.

He paused beside one of the city's public fountains and scooped up a drink of water in his hands. A line of scar tissue ran down the finger the cleric had just healed, wavy as a snake. He wiped his fingers dry on his trousers. Zelia had drained his *muladhara*, but he still had his lapis lazuli. If he was going to steal the Circled Serpent from Pakal, he'd better get on with it.

He closed his eyes, concentrating on the dwarf's face. The scar tissue on his forehead tingled as the lapis lazuli activated, and Pakal's image solidified in his mind. The dwarf was awake, sweat trickling down his face as he walked through the darkness. Arvin couldn't see Pakal's surroundings—a sending only showed the person contacted—but it looked as though the dwarf was trudging up a steep incline.

Choosing his words carefully, Arvin spoke directly to Pakal's mind. He'd already decided to tell the truth—part of it, anyway. *Karrell's alive*, he said, *in trouble. She told me to find Ts'ikil. Where are you? I need your help. Use few words; this spell is brief.*

Pakal halted, his eyes wide. He stared straight ahead for a moment—he would be seeing, in his mind's eye, a faint image of Arvin's face. Delight, then caution played across the dwarf's face. At last his expression settled into a look of contrition, and he spoke. Though the words were into the dwarf's own language, Arvin understood them as they flowed into his mind. *I will take you to Ts'ikil. Meet me at the temple on Mount Ugruth. I will wait there.* He paused, then added, *I am sorry I fled, but duty—*

Pakal's image vanished as the sending ended. Arvin frowned, wondering why Pakal would be heading for another god's temple, especially one dedicated to Talos, god of destruction. Arvin wouldn't be able to ask him, however, until the next night. The lapis lazuli would only allow him to contact any given individual once per day. He stared over the city, toward Mount Ugruth. A smudge of black smoke wafted from the volcanic peak up into the gradually brightening sky.

Arvin realized he was exhausted. He'd been awake for a day and a night, but he was too keyed up to sleep. He had to get moving to rescue Karrell.

As he turned away from the fountain, something brushed against his foot. He glanced down and nearly jumped as he saw a slender orange snake with large, bulging eyes slither out of a crack at the base of the fountain. The snake met his gaze and hissed a warning. Slowly, Arvin backed away from the fountain. Whether it was a natural snake or a yuan-ti in serpent form, he didn't want to make any sudden moves, not with its fangs bared and ready to strike.

The snake turned away and slithered up the street. With dawn approaching and the shadows lifting from the street, Arvin saw dozens of snakes emerge from cracks between buildings and holes in the ground. They slithered uphill, toward the section of Hlondeth where the nobles lived. Several of the snakes had scale patterns he'd never seen before: checkered beige-and-black with a circle of white crowning the head; jet black with a creamy pink belly; and cream-and-black bands with large red dots on each cream band. He was reminded of the legend of how Lord Shevron had summoned snakes to defeat the kobolds that crept through Hlondeth's sewers in the Year of Tatters to attack the city, except that these snakes slithered up from the sewers, not down into them. They were headed for the palace, rather than emerging from it.

Something was up—and Arvin was certain Sibyl was behind it. A fragment of her welcoming speech to the Se'sehen in the altar room came back to him then, her promises that those loyal to her would soon reap their reward . . . in Hlondeth. The oddly patterned snakes must have been yuan-ti from the south—the Se'sehen, breaking their longstanding alliance with Hlondeth. With that realization, a rush of anger filled him. One of those serpents must have been responsible for the death of the infant in the chapel.

A door opened to Arvin's left, and he waved back the sleepy-looking girl who emerged with a water jug.

"Bar your door!" Arvin shouted at the her. "The city is under attack."

Startled, the girl fled back into her home.

Arvin activated his lapis lazuli a second time. He paused, wondering who to send his warning to. He had never spoken with Hlondeth's ruler face to face, but he had seen her from a distance. He could visualize Lady Dediana well enough to contact her, but she wouldn't know who he was and might not heed his warning. Instead, with great reluctance, he visualized Zelia.

She was sleeping, but her eyes sprang open at Arvin's mental shout: *Zelia—wake up! Sibyl and the Se'sehen are attacking the city. They're moving toward the palace in serpent form, even as I speak.*

Zelia didn't even bother to reply. She merely nodded then with a brusque mental push, broke off the sending. Arvin shrugged; it was exactly what he'd expected. He'd acted instinctively in sending the warning. Hlondeth had been his home for too many years for him to ignore a threat to it, especially one that came from Sibyl. But did it really matter, to the humans who lived there which faction of serpents ruled them?

A gong sounded from somewhere up the hill, followed by another, farther in the distance. A bright flash of yellow seared the air above the section where the nobles lived, followed a heartbeat later by a thunderous boom. There were cries close by—humans, no doubt startled to find so many serpents slithering along the streets. Hlondeth's yuan-ti traditionally kept to the viaducts that arched overhead.

Arvin could hear shouted questions as people asked what was going on in the nobles' section, where a pillar of vivid green flame had just whooshed down out of a clear sky. Some cried that Mount Ugruth was erupting, while others, feeling the rumbling tremors under their feet, shouted back that no, it was an earthquake.

Arvin's part in this battle over—he'd passed on his message, and it was up to Zelia to relay it. He ran for the nearest city gate. People spilled out of doorways on either side as he ran past, some frightened, some clutching children or valuables to their chests, all looking confused. A half-elf holding his unlaced trousers up with one hand glanced sharply at Arvin as if he'd recognized him, then flicked his free hand to get Arvin's attention and gave a quick gesture in the silent speech: *What's happening?*

War, Arvin signed back as he ran past.

The guild member broke into a grin and grabbed an empty leather sack that had been hanging just inside the door. Then he ran toward the sound of the fighting.

Arvin turned into a wider street with shops on either side. Though none were yet open for business, the shuttered windows on their upper stories had been flung wide. People leaned out of them and called to each other across the street. Several shouted down at him, asking what was happening. Arvin ignored them; he needed his breath for running. He felt a tickle under the scar on his forehead. Zelia, looking in on him psionically? He slowed to a trot, expecting her to manifest some communication with him, but nothing happened. The tickling sensation continued. Someone, he realized, was scrying him.

An unpleasant possibility occurred to him. If Sibyl's crystal ball had survived the collapse of the altar room, it might be the abomination observing him. She'd gotten a good look at both Arvin and Pakal just before they'd teleported away with her half of the Circled Serpent; she'd be able to home in on him.

Fortunately, Arvin still had the net he'd created to kill her inside the backpack that bounced up and down against his shoulders.

He started to run into a circular plaza with streets radiating from it in five directions. At its center was a wrought-iron streetlight in the form of a rearing cobra. Something about it caught his eye, and he skidded to a stop. The streetlight was smaller than usual and of brightly burnished metal, rather than a dull black. It didn't have a glowing white stone in its mouth—and it was *swaying*.

As the metal snake turned and fastened glowing red eyes on Arvin, the sensation in his forehead intensified. This creature—whatever it was—had been using divination magic to search for him.

One of Sibyl's creatures!

With a scrape of metal on stone, the iron cobra slithered toward Arvin.

Unable to manifest his psionics due to his depleted *muladhara* and certain his dagger would be useless, Arvin turned and ran. Behind him, the scraping sound quickened. The iron cobra hissed like hot steam escaping from a boiling kettle. Panting, Arvin turned down a narrow alley, only to find that it dead-ended against the city wall. He leaped, activating the magic of his bracelet as he hurtled through the air. He slammed into the wall, knocking the air from his lungs, but his fingers and toes found a grip. The iron cobra lunged, and Arvin heard a *clang* as it struck the wall just below his foot. Venom splattered onto his boot. He scrambled up the wall, praying that the metal serpent wasn't capable of following.

It wasn't. As Arvin climbed, it remained coiled at the base of the wall, hissing softly, bathed in a faint green light from the glowing stones. It flared its hood and watched with ember-red eyes as Arvin climbed to the top of the wall and hauled himself onto the battlements. Then it turned and slithered back up the alley.

Arvin stood, panting, hands on knees. "Nine lives," he whispered, touching the crystal at his neck.

From inside the city came distant screams and more explosions. A militia member ran toward him along the wall, sword in hand. The soldier's flared helmet and scale armor reminded Arvin of the serpent he'd narrowly escaped.

"Out of the way!" the soldier shouted as he shoved past Arvin.

He clattered down a staircase a short distance beyond. Then he cried out in alarm. Arvin heard the clash of metal on metal—a single *clang*—then a *thud* as something heavy hit the street below. He straightened, wary. A heartbeat later, a metal head rose from the staircase and looked around. The iron cobra.

Cursing, Arvin clambered over the far side of the wall. He climbed down as quickly as he could, but the smooth green stones had been designed to offer little to grip, even to someone with a magical bracelet. Above him, Arvin heard a rasping noise as the iron cobra slithered through a slit in the battlements. Realizing it was about to drop on him, Arvin shoved off the wall, twisting as he fell. He landed awkwardly, crashing down onto hands and knees in a tangle of gourd vines. As he scrambled to his feet, nearly tripping over one of the large, rock-hard gourds, he heard a *thump* behind him and a soft, metallic hiss.

Arvin looked around. The sun was rising—it was finally light enough to see clearly—but the iron cobra was screened by the vines. It was somewhere between Arvin and the wall. If he ran right or left it would merely change course and outflank him. Arvin wished he had a magical entangling rope—the net in his backpack would work only on living flesh—or even a sturdy club or a tree to climb, but the field he'd landed in offered none of those.

As he turned, the tingle in his forehead intensified. He smiled as he realized which direction the attack would come from. He started to sling his backpack around to the front, thinking he might be able to shove it at the serpent like a shield. Then he had a better idea. Yanking out his dagger, he slashed one of the vines and lifted the yellow gourd, holding it like a morningstar.

"Come on, you scaly bastard," he breathed, turning in the direction the magical tingling came from. "Come on ..."

A gleam—morning sunlight on burnished iron scales—gave him a moment's warning. The iron cobra lunged up from the vines in a lightning-fast strike. Arvin whipped the gourd forward, slamming it into the serpent's head, but it was like hitting a solid metal door. The iron cobra's aim was knocked off only slightly—just enough that its teeth snagged and tore the hem of Arvin's shirt—but the blow itself didn't harm the cobra in the least. It reared back, body coiled beneath it, glowing red eyes watching the gourd, then lashed out again.

Arvin started to swing the gourd—but checked its motion, pulling the vine through his hand until the gourd was against his fist. He punched it into the cobra's gaping mouth, forcing the gourd down its throat. Metal fangs scraped along the gourd, then hooked fast. The vine was yanked through Arvin's fingers as the cobra tore its head away.

The iron cobra hissed and shook its head back and forth, trying to fling the plug from its mouth. It tried to gulp down the gourd, but couldn't swallow it. The metal bands that made up its body wouldn't expand enough. It lashed its tail in fury, ripping the vines around it into a tangle.

Arvin didn't wait around to see how long it would take to get the gourd out. He plunged through the field, tripping over gourds and falling several times as vines snagged his ankles. Ahead lay the road from the city's northern gate. People streamed out of Hlondeth, fleeing the fighting that echoed within the walls.

Arvin ran toward a cart being pulled by a horse. As he closed the gap, an elegantly painted ceramic jug spilled out the back and smashed on the road in a spray of dark red wine. The driver continued whipping his horse, trying to force it through the crowd, heedless of the missing cargo. Arvin vaulted up onto the cart and tried to find a place to stand among the rolling jugs.

The driver started to glance in Arvin's direction, then stared at something beyond him and gasped. Arvin glanced over his shoulder and saw the cobra rearing, its head level with the cart, its mouth clear. It lashed out, its fangs missing Arvin's hand by a hair's breadth. Then the cart veered off the road and into a fallow field. The horse broke into a trot, leaving the cobra behind. It followed, but the cart was moving too quickly for it to catch.

The driver of the cart turned again, met Arvin's eye, then broke into laughter. Arvin, taking a better look at him, was equally bemused. The driver was the half-elf Arvin had warned earlier, the one with the unlaced trousers. His long black hair was tangled and dusty, and one of his eyes was starting to purple. Someone must have thrown a punch at him. His trousers were laced and belted, and a thin black wand was tucked into the belt. A leather bag sat between his feet, bulging with something that clinked as the cart jostled along. Passing the whip into the hand that held the reins, he extended his left hand. Arvin took it and clambered onto the seat beside him.

"Good haul, hey?" the half-elf grinned, tipping his head at the dozens of jugs the cart held.

Arvin nodded, still panting from his mad scramble across the field.

"Was that a yuan-ti chasing you?" the driver asked.

"It was a—" Arvin paused, not really sure what it was. Better not to say too much. "Yes," he lied. "I think so."

Once they were ahead of the refugees the half-elf tugged on the reins, steering the horse back onto the road. "I just hope whatever you got was worth it."

"My life," Arvin muttered, touching a finger to his crystal.

The driver grunted. "You can call me Darris," he said, holding out a hand.

Arvin clasped it. "Call me Vin, and thanks for the ride."

Darris made a circle with forefinger and thumb and flicked it open, then tapped his index fingers lightly together: *It's nothing, friend.*

"Where are you headed?" Arvin asked.

Darris glanced back at the city. A mansion in the noble section burned, throwing a plume of dirty gray smoke into the air. Figures struggled in combat on the viaducts. Arvin saw two tiny shapes fall, snake tails flailing, into the street below.

"Away from that," the half-elf said at last. "Somewhere I can stash this until things cool down." He glanced at Arvin's abbreviated little finger and added. "Somewhere the guild won't take their cut."

Arvin nodded at the road that switchbacked up into the hills, toward Mount Ugruth. "There's an old quarry about a day's journey up the aqueduct road," he said. "Lots of broken rock, lots of places to hide things. The Talos worshipers use it as a stopping place on their way up the mountain, and they've built some huts out of the rubble."

"Sounds like as good a place as any," Darris said, flicking the reins.

Arvin whispered a prayer to Tymora, thanking her for sending Darris his way. Riding in a cart, he stood an excellent chance of catching up to Pakal.

He glanced back at the city one last time. Sunlight glinted off an object that slithered along the road, causing the refugees to draw away from it in fear. It was the iron cobra, still following him, and still producing a tickling sensation in the scar on Arvin's forehead.

"What's wrong?" Darris asked.

"It's the ... yuan-ti," Arvin said. "He's following us."

Darris flicked the reins again. "Don't worry. He won't catch us, not unless he sprouts wings."

Arvin nodded, uneasy. The metal construct might not have wings, but Sibyl did. The battle of Hlondeth was keeping her busy for the moment, but when it was over, the iron cobra would lead her straight to him.

❖ ❖ ❖ ❖ ❖

The cart jolted to a stop. Shaken awake, Arvin rose from the space he'd cleared for himself between the jugs of wine and looked around. By the slant of the sun, it was late afternoon. They had reached the quarry. Arvin recognized the cliff that had been cut into the forested hillside, the large blocks of broken stone that littered the ground, and the crude shelters that had been built out of unmortared stone and tree branches. When he'd been there a year ago, the place had been crawling with Talos worshipers. It had since been deserted.

Arvin rubbed the scar on his forehead. The tickling sensation was gone. The iron cobra had either given up its search, or they'd left it far behind.

"Looks like we've got the place to ourselves," he observed.

"Not for long," Darris said as he climbed down from the cart. "We passed a gaggle of doomsayers on the way up here. They wanted me to stop and sell them wine, but I told them they'd have to wait until they reached the quarry." He looped the reins of the horse around a tree branch and lifted the leather sack down from the driver's seat. It must have been heavy; he staggered slightly as he stepped back from the cart. "I wanted a chance to dispose of this first."

The cart had pulled up under the aqueduct that ran alongside the road. Mist drifted down from above, a welcome respite from the heat. Arvin turned his face toward it and closed his eyes, savoring the spray.

"Go ahead," he told Darris. "I won't look."

"That's right," Darris said, his tone changing. "You won't."

Arvin opened his eyes and saw Darris point the wand at him.

"Darris! Don't—"

A thin line of black crackled out of the tip of the wand and struck Arvin in the face.

He was blind.

"Stay where you are," Darris said. "I'll be right back."

"Darris, wait!" Arvin shouted. "I won't . . ." His voice trailed off as he realized the futility of pleading. Guild members didn't trust each other at the best of times, and they certainly didn't trust those who had "robbed" from the guild—as Arvin's amputated finger announced for all the world to see—which was ironic, because Darris was doing exactly the same thing: betraying the guild by denying them their share of his loot.

Arvin sighed. He'd just have to wait it out and pray that the wand's effects weren't permanent.

He heard the horse whickering, the splatter of water dripping from the aqueduct above, and the distant grumble of thunder as storm clouds built over the Vilhon Reach. Somewhere in that direction, the rulership of Hlondeth was being contested. Serpent versus serpent—a battle that needn't concern him. He said a prayer for the few people he actually cared about in that city, though there weren't many. Tanju was away for the summer, off on another mission for House Extaminos, and so would be safe. Gonthril and his followers had gone to ground, and Arvin hadn't seen the rebel leader in a year. Nicco had wandered off about four months past, summoned by his perpetually angry god on another mission of vengeance, but Drin, the potion seller, was still in town. So was little Kollim, eight years old and chafing under his mother's heavy hand. Tymora grant both of them luck.

The nap in the back of the cart had been uncomfortable, but it had refreshed him somewhat. He felt strong enough to perform his meditations. Arvin felt his way down from the cart, placed his pack on the ground next to him, then stripped off his shirt and tossed it aside. He lay down on his belly on the road, then levered his upper torso into an arch by extending his arms. Stretched out in the *bhujang asana*, his neck craned back and sightless eyes staring up into the sky, he pulled his awareness deep inside himself. It was even easier without sight to distract him, or it would have been, had he been certain that his eyesight *would* return. His mind was crowded with worries. There was no guarantee that Pakal would wait for him at the temple. The dwarf had abandoned Arvin once already, and there was also the iron cobra to worry about.

Arvin took a deep breath and pushed these thoughts from his mind with the exhalation.

"Control," he breathed.

It was Zelia's expression, but it served. In order to get through what lay ahead, he'd need nerves as steady as hers. He breathed in through one nostril, out through his mouth, in through the other nostril, out through his mouth, slow and deep, savoring the smell of sap from the pine trees nearby, restoring his *muladhara* with each long, extended breath.

When it was full, he rose gracefully to his feet and began the five poses of defense and five poses of attack that Tanju had taught him, alternating one with the other. He raised his hands and tilted his face back, then swept his hands through the air in front of his face, as if scrubbing his mind clean. Then he brought both hands to his forehead and thrust them forward, feet braced like a man shoving against a boulder, picturing his thrust shattering the rock that was an opponent's mind. He spun in a circle with hands extended and one leg parallel to the ground, forming an imagined barrier with both palms and the sole of his foot, then whipped his arms forward, one after another, imagining himself lashing an enemy's confidence to shreds and so on, through each of the ten poses, one flowing gracefully into the next.

When he was done, sweat covered his body. By sound, he found his way to one of the trickles that fell from the aqueduct above and caught the water in cupped hands. As he drank, he listened for Darris. The thief should have been back by then. Arvin hoped nothing had happened to him—especially if that wand was required to restore his eyesight. Already he could feel the air cooling slightly as evening approached.

The sound of footsteps caught his attention.

"Darris?" Arvin called.

More footsteps. Voices. Men and women, weary. Then a cry: "Smoke! The Stormlord speaks!"

The cry was followed by a rush of excited shouts and the sound of people—several dozen of them, by the sound of it—thudding to their knees. Arvin knew, from his experiences the previous summer, what they would be doing: tearing at their clothes and faces. His guess was confirmed by the sound of ripping cloth.

Above the commotion, he heard someone speak. "Wine!" the voice cried. "The wine merchant stopped here, just as he promised."

Arvin heard the people moving toward him. His nose crinkled as he caught the smell of hot, unwashed bodies and fresh blood.

"How much for a jug?" a woman's voice asked.

Arvin heard the clink of a coin pouch. He turned his head, trying to figure out where she was, and heard a male voice whisper: "He's blind."

Then a second man added, in a smirking whisper, "Pay him in coppers; he won't know the difference."

Arvin nudged his pack with one foot, making sure it was still there.

"Silence," the woman's voice hissed. "I will buy the wine, and you will drink only as much of it as I serve you. We must reach the temple tonight."

"Yes, Stormmistress," the second man said, contrite.

A hand touched his cheek, turning his face—a woman's hand, by the soft feel of the skin and the sweet-smelling, almost overpowering perfume she wore.

"I'm over here," the Stormmistress said in a silky, sensuous voice, "and I'd like to buy some wine for my fellow pilgrims. How much?"

"Five pythons a jug," Arvin answered, naming the price of the most expensive bottle of wine he'd ever seen ordered at the Mortal Coil. Judging by the fine ceramic jugs, Darris had stolen the stuff from a noble household, and it was probably worth that much or even more.

"Done," the woman said, not even bothering to haggle. "I'll take three." She caught Arvin's hand and pressed coins into it. He rubbed one of them. There was a snake embossed on one side of it, and what felt like the House Extaminos crest on the other. Judging by its weight, it was gold, not copper.

The woman leaned past him to lift a jug of wine from the cart. As she did, Arvin caught a whiff of what the perfume was hiding: the musky odor of snake.

That startled him. The clergy of Talos were all human as far as he knew. Yuan-ti scorned the Raging God as one of the lesser Powers, inferior to their serpent deity. To the yuan-ti, Sseth was the only god worth worshiping.

That brought up an unpleasant possibility—that the woman who'd just purchased wine for her "followers" had some ulterior motive for being there.

A moment later, when he listened in on her thoughts—hiding his secondary display by kneeling on the ground and pretending to search for his shirt—he discovered that it was even worse than he'd thought.

She was indeed a worshiper of Sseth.

One of the clerics who served Sibyl.

CHAPTER 5

Arvin patted the ground, pretending to search
for his shirt, as he probed the mind of the
"Stormmistress." She was delighted to have
stumbled across the wine; that would make
her job all the easier. She planned to mix
something into it before serving it to the
Talos worshipers. A word drifted through
her mind: *hassaael*. Arvin wasn't sure if it
was the name of a potion, a poison, or the
yuan-ti word for blood. All three concepts
seemed to be braided into the word. She'd
been given it by a yuan-ti in Skullport
named Ssarm—the same man who had
provided the Pox with their deadly transformative potion.

   He probed deeper, worming his way into
her memories of Sibyl. He was relieved,

somewhat, to find that her most recent meeting with the abomination was more than a tenday in the past, and that she had no knowledge of the events unfolding in Hlondeth or Arvin's role in them. The cleric—Thessania, her name was—had been on the road with the latest batch of worshipers, who had come all the way from Ormath on the Shining Plains. Her instructions had been to herd them to the temple, where they would be killed. If they didn't die that night, Sibyl would be displeased.

An image of what Thessania intended flickered through her mind, swift as a snake's darting tongue: Men and women, piled in a heap, their faces bright red and eyeballs bulging.

Arvin shuddered. The followers of the Raging God might be crazy—they had to be, to view volcanic eruptions, hurricanes, and lightning-strike wildfires as something to celebrate—but that didn't mean they deserved to die.

Once again, Sibyl was taking advantage of human gullibility. The first time, it had been the Pox then it was the pilgrims. If Arvin could stop whatever was happening, he would.

He heard another grumble of thunder, out over the Reach. A natural storm? Or the voice of Hoar, god of vengeance?

Arvin cracked a wry smile.

"Vin!" a familiar voice cried out. "I told you not to sell any wine until I got back."

Arvin turned in that direction. Daris had said nothing about the wine. He was up to something, and Arvin decided to play along for the moment.

Suddenly, Arvin could see again. Darris strode toward him, the leather sack gone. He had one hand behind his back, inside his collar, as if scratching his neck. It was an old guild trick, a way of dropping something you'd palmed into your shirt. Probably the wand he'd just used to restore Arvin's eyesight.

Pretending to still be blind, Arvin held his hands out in front of him. *Play along,* he signed. Aloud, he added, "Darris? Is that you?"

Meanwhile, he studied Thessania. The surprise of his eyesight returning had broken the link with her mind, but he'd learned what he needed already. He committed her appearance to memory as he stared "blindly" past her. She was one of those yuan-ti who could pass for human. Her pupils were round and there was no sign of a tail under her robe. Ash-gray gloves covered her hands, which were human-shaped, and the only skin showing—her face, framed by a tight-fitting black cowl—was devoid of scales. Arvin noticed, however, that she kept her teeth clenched when she spoke, giving her words a tense, clipped sound. She probably had a forked tongue.

She was dressed as a cleric of Talos, in a long-sleeved black robe that reached to her ankles. Lightning bolts were embroidered on it in gold thread, and the sleeves ended in jagged hems, braided with more thread of gold. The front of the cowl bore the god's symbol: three lightning bolts in brown, red and blue, radiating out from a central point, representing the destructive powers of earthquake, fire, and flood. A black patch covered her left eye—another symbol of the one-eyed god she pretended to worship. Her face, Arvin noted, was unscratched, unlike those of the real worshipers.

She held the three jugs of wine she'd purchased in the crook of one arm, a traveling pack in the other. The worshipers clamored for the wine, insisting their throats were dry from the long march up into the hills. She rebuked them sharply, telling them to quench their thirst with water instead. The wine, she said, would be served with dinner.

"Start preparing our meal," she ordered.

The worshipers crossed their arms over their chests and bowed, then scurried away.

Darris, meanwhile, strode up to Arvin. "How much did you charge her for the wine?" he demanded.

"Five vipers a jug." Arvin held out the gold coins while staring slightly to one side of Darius.

"Five?" Darris asked, his voice rising. Pretending to scold Arvin, he waggled a forefinger at him, then brushed the front of his nose. *Pretend.* "I told you to charge six!" He slapped the forefinger into an open palm. *Fight.* Glowering, he shouted, "What did you do? Pocket the balance? Up to your old tricks again, are you?"

He grabbed Arvin by the shoulder and shook him. The gold spilled from Arvin's hand onto the ground. Arvin knew what Darris had in mind; the mock argument was an old guild trick. Arvin was supposed to shove Darris toward Thessania, who watched the two humans with a bemused look on her face. The rogue would stagger into her, grasp at her robe in an effort to keep from falling—and in the process, slip a quick hand into a pocket. A neat trick—if you were dealing with a human and not with someone who could kill with a single bite.

"You never said six," Arvin said in an even tone. "You told me five, and that's what I charged." *No*, he signed.

A bored look in her eyes, the yuan-ti turned away to follow the worshipers.

Darris raised his palm and jerked it forward—*Push!*—then slapped Arvin. Hard.

Arvin took the blow like a blind man, without ducking; the worshipers still watched the fight. He lifted his hand to his mouth, as if to wipe away the blood from his split lip. Two fingers curled like fangs, he turned the wipe into a flowing motion while nodding in the direction of the fake cleric. *She's yuan-ti.*

That stopped Darris cold. "Ah," he said. Then, loudly, "I remember now. You're right; this *is* the five-viper wine. Sorry for the misunderstanding, Vin." He clapped an arm around Arvin's shoulder, using the gesture to whisper in Arvin's ear. "A yuan-ti *Stormmistress?* Are you sure?"

Arvin nodded.

"What's in her bag?" Darris breathed.

"Poison," Arvin whispered back. "She plans to mix it into the wine."

"I see," Darris said. He gave the worshipers a long, appraising look. "They look skinny as slaves," he said, using an old guild expression for someone with nothing worth stealing. Then he shrugged. "No sense hanging around, if you ask me. If the doomsayer really is yuan-ti, she'll demand first pickings."

Arvin, disgusted, realized that Darris thought he was suggesting they stay behind to loot the bodies once the poison had done its work.

"That's not what I meant," he said. "We've got to stop her from poisoning them."

Darris removed his arm from Arvin's shoulder and stepped back. "What she does is none of my business," he said. He watched the yuan-ti as she walked with swaying steps to the spot where the worshipers piled branches for a cooking fire. "What makes it yours?"

"Those people will die," Arvin answered.

"So?" Darris asked. "Sooner or later, one of the floods or fires they keep praying for will kill them, anyway." He tapped his temple. *Crazy.*

Arvin scooped up his pack and glanced at the worshipers out of the corner of his eye. One was a boy not yet in his teens who was being ordered about by an older, gray-haired man—probably his grandfather, given the resemblance between the two. Like the rest of them, the boy had ripped his shirt and gouged scratches in his face. He kept touching his cheeks however and wincing, giving his grandfather rueful looks.

"That one's just a boy," Arvin whispered. "He deserves a chance to grow up, to make his own decisions about which god to worship."

Darris listened, eyebrows raised. Then he nodded, as if enlightenment had suddenly come to him. He lowered his voice once more.

"You won't find my stash."

Arvin sighed. "I don't plan on looking for it."

The rogue chuckled. "Strangely enough, I believe you." He picked up the five coins and shoved them in a pocket, then clambered up into the cart. "People will be leaving the city—and they'll be thirsty. I'll have the rest of this wine sold in no time. Give me a hand, and I'll split the profits." He lifted the reins. "Last chance. Coming?"

Arvin shook his head. Thessania had disappeared inside one of the huts; she was probably lacing the wine with poison even as they spoke. Arvin was tempted to tell Darris what he thought of him but knew his words wouldn't change anything. The half-elf was a typical rogue; all he cared about was himself.

Darris released the wagon's brake, then paused. "If the doomsayer really is yuan-ti, you'd better watch yourself."

"I've dealt with them before."

Darris grinned. "I'll bet you have, and . . . thanks for the warning." He touched a thumb to his temple, then closed his other fist around it. *I'll remember you.*

He flicked the reins. The cart rumbled off down the hill, back in the direction of Hlondeth.

Arvin could feel, once more, the faint tickle in his forehead that warned him that magic was being used to search for him. The iron serpent must have been drawing nearer. He'd wasted too much time already.

But before he left, there was something he needed to do.

He sent his awareness deep into his *muladhara*. You don't see me, he mentally told the Talos worshipers. I'm invisible.

They continued going about their evening tasks, pulling food from their packs, tending the cooking fire and gathering water from the aqueduct in worn-looking iron pots. One or two turned to watch the cart as it left. As they did Arvin slipped an image into each of their minds of himself, seated next to Darris. Meanwhile, he picked his way carefully over the uneven ground toward the hut the yuan-ti had disappeared into.

She had hung a cloth over the entrance of the hut, preventing him from simply looking inside. The hut itself proved to be of better construction than the rest. Arvin couldn't find any gaps between the stones to peer through. That didn't matter, however. Retreating to a spot where the trees screened him from sight—he didn't need to be close to manifest the power he had in mind—he allowed himself to become visible again and imagined the interior of the hut. Psionic energy spiraled into the power points in his throat and forehead and a low droning filled the air around him as silver sparkled out of his "third eye." He sent his awareness drifting with it in the direction of the hut.

Slowly, its interior came into focus.

Thessania was pouring one of the jugs of wine into a wooden bowl. The other two jugs lay empty on the ground beside her. She must have been certain none of the worshipers would disturb her; she'd pushed her cowl back, revealing a hairless scalp covered in vivid orange and yellow scales. She had no ears, just holes in the side of her head. She had also removed her gloves; the scales covered her hands and fingers as well.

She set the empty jug down and rummaged inside her travel bag, then pulled out a glass vial containing an ink-black liquid. Unstoppering it, she poured a drop onto her finger, then stroked it along her wrist like a woman applying perfume. After repeating the application on her other wrist, she poured a few drops of the liquid into the wine. That done, she raised first one wrist to her mouth then the other.

At first, Arvin thought she was sniffing her perfume. Then he saw a drop of blood fall into the wine and realized she'd bitten herself. Thessania squeezed each wrist, milking herself of blood. As it dribbled into the bowl, the wine turned a vivid green. Thessania bent low, sniffing it, and licked her wrists clean. Then she spat into whatever the wine had become.

She pushed the stopper back into the vial—very little of the black liquid had been used—then pulled on her gloves. As she adjusted her cowl, Arvin skimmed quickly through the thoughts of the worshipers, searching for those who already had doubts about the stormmistress. From these he gleaned their names and a handful of recent experiences he hoped might be useful. By the time Thessania emerged from the hut, holding the bowl of wine, Arvin was ready. He stepped out of the forest and thew a mental shield between himself and the yuan-ti—who immediately turned in his direction as soon as she heard the droning of his secondary display.

"Worshipers of Talos," Arvin shouted. "You have been deceived."

Thessania bared her teeth in what would have been a hiss, had she not checked herself in time. She sent a wave of magical fear rushing toward Arvin, but his psionic shield deflected it.

"Thessania is no stormmistress," Arvin continued.

Thessania's charm spell hit him next. "Poor man," she said. "The sun has addled your wits. You don't know me; we've never met before. You have mistaken my voice for that of someone else. Come and drink wine with us."

Arvin's mental shield held. He needed to speak quickly. Once Tessalia realized her charm had failed, she would start tossing clerical spells at him.

"I may be blind," Arvin said, "blind as Talos's left eye, but by the god's magic I can still see." Silver sparkles—bright as the stars reputed to whirl in the empty space behind the Storm Lord's eyepatch—erupted from Arvin's forehead as he sent a thread of his awareness inside the hut. He pointed at one of the men, a tall fellow with bright red hair. "You wonder, Menzin, what Thessania was doing in the hut."

Arvin wrapped the invisible thread around the vial and lifted it into the air. With a yank, he pulled it out of the hut.

"She was adding poison to your wine."

Thessania whirled and spotted the vial. Bright green wine slopped over the edge of the bowl, staining her glove. Arvin sent the vial crashing against the wall of the hut, shattering it. Poison dribbled down the stonework like black blood.

The worshipers stared at it. Menzin muttered something to the man next to him.

"Ridiculous!" Thessania said. "Smell it—that's my perfume."

They did, and turned, glowering, toward Arvin.

Thessania pointed a slender finger at him. "This man has been sent by the Prince of Lies to stir up mistrust and strife among us. Don't listen to him."

"Cyric didn't send me," Arvin said, naming the god he'd frequently been warned about by the priests at the orphanage. He wove the name of Ilmater's chief ally into the lie: "Tyr did. The god of justice has allied himself with Talos to expose Thessania's trickery."

"The Raging God stands alone," said Thessania. "He allies with no one."

"Save for Auril, Malar, and Umberlee," Arvin said, hurling back the deity names he'd plucked from one of the worshiper's thoughts. "Though Malar would turn on the other Gods of Fury if he could—would send one of his beast minions sneaking like a serpent into Talos's tower to slay the Storm Lord, if he dared."

"Deceit!" Thessania cried. "More lies!"

She spat, and the glob of poisonous spittle hurtled through the air toward Arvin.

He imposed a psionic hand in front of it just before it struck, and smiled as it splattered on the leaves behind him. Thessania had moved precisely the playing piece he'd hoped she would.

He addressed one of the female worshipers—a thin woman who stared at him with narrowed eyes. "You've been wondering, Yivril, why your storm-mistress didn't smite the blasphemer in Ormath with a lightning bolt."

The worshiper's eyes widened.

"Odd, isn't it, that she's not hurling one at me now," Arvin continued. "Instead she's spitting at me . . . like a snake."

With that, he used his manifestation to yank back Thessania's cowl.

Some of the worshipers gasped; others gaped in open-mouthed silence.

"It's an illusion," Thessania cried, yanking at her cowl. "Pay it no heed!"

Several of the worshipers began babbling at once.

"So that's why she refused to—"

"I thought it was strange that—"

"We've been tricked!" Menzin shouted, lunging at Thessania and knocking the bowl from her hands. "She's a yuan-ti!"

Spitting with fury, Thessania bit him.

Menzin collapsed, gasping, his lips already blue. The other worshipers, however, were not easily cowed. A handful were driven back by Thessania's magical fear, but the rest mobbed her. Arvin caught a glimpse of Thessania shifting to snake form in an attempt to get away, but then Yivril rushed forward, a chunk of broken stone in her hand. She smashed it down on Thessania's clothes. Even from where he stood, Arvin could hear the crunch of bones breaking.

Satisfied, he slipped away into the woods. As he did, he touched the crystal at his throat. "Nine lives," he breathed, thankful that none of the gods he'd falsely invoked had seen fit to take notice of the fact.

He circled through the woods, putting some distance between himself and the quarry before returning to the road. The tickling in his forehead grew stronger; the iron cobra was getting closer. Though Arvin was still tired—it hadn't been a very restful sleep, being jostled about in the cart—he needed to get moving again. Talos's temple was still a day's journey distant, and he doubted the cobra needed to rest or sleep.

Fortunately, his meditations had replenished his *muladhara*. If the iron cobra did catch up to him, he'd have mind magic to fight back with. He doubted the thing had a mind to affect, and it was probably immune to ordinary weapons, but there were one or two manifestations he might use to at least slow it down a little.

A branch rustled in the forest. Arvin whirled, then saw it was just a small bird that had flown from a tree. The tickling in his forehead was starting to get to him. He needed to get moving, to cover a lot more ground than his human legs were capable of. He decided to use his psionics to morph his body into something speedier, perhaps into a giant like the one he'd met the previous winter, or . . .

Watching the bird climb into the evening sky, he had an inspiration. He would morph into something with wings. A flying snake, perhaps—he'd seen enough of them in Hlondeth. He made sure his backpack was snug against his shoulders, then began drawing energy up from his navel and into his chest. He held his arms out, imagining they were wings.

Something sharp touched Arvin's throat—a curved sword blade—as a hand grabbed his hair from behind. A high-pitched male voice panted into his ear. "Where is it?"

"Where is what?" Arvin gasped, his heart pounding. "Listen, friend," he said, attempting a charm. "I don't know what—"

"None of that!"

The blade pressed against his throat, opening a hair-thin cut. Arvin didn't dare swallow. The charm obviously hadn't worked, so it was time for something less subtle. Raising his open hands in mock surrender, he imaged a third hand grasping his dagger. As the energy built he felt it begin to slide out of its sheath.

"Please, don't kill me," he pleaded, feigning fear.

At the same time he jostled the person behind him to cover the movement of the dagger. He guided it behind his attacker and turned it so the point was toward the man's back. Then he nudged it forward, manifesting a voice behind the man the instant he felt the dagger point poke flesh.

"Release him," it said, "or die."

The scimitar was gone from Arvin's throat as his attacker whirled to meet the illusionary threat. Arvin flung himself forward, wincing at the pain in his scalp as his hair was yanked out of the man's fist. As he tumbled away, he caught a brief glimpse of his attacker: a small, skinny humanoid with a doglike head, wearing a starched white kilt. The dog-man swung his scimitar through the space where an invisible dagger wielder would be. Still directing his dagger with his mind, Arvin slashed at the stranger's sword arm, opening a deep wound. The dog-man emitted a high-pitched yip and slashed once more through empty air, then backstepped to a spot where he could see both Arvin and the dagger.

It also gave Arvin a better look at him. The fellow stood only as tall as Arvin's shoulder and had a humanlike body but with thick golden fur on his neck, shoulders, and arms. Atop his lean body was a doglike head with a slender muzzle and large, upright ears. Those ears looked familiar—the fellow had the same face as the dog that had startled him near Saint Aganna's shrine. The dog-man must have been a lycanthrope of some sort, of a species that Arvin had never seen or even heard of before.

"Why are you following me?" Arvin asked. "What do you want?"

The dog-man merely stared at him. "You should learn," he said in a high, quick voice like that of a yapping dog, "to let sleeping serpents lie!" Then his eyes began to glow.

"I . . ." That was all Arvin managed before his gaze was locked by those large, golden eyes.

He dimly realized the dog-man was unleashing magic that didn't require words or gestures—just as a sorcerer or psion would. Arvin tried to mount a defense, but even as energy flowed into the power point at his throat his eyes closed. He felt himself falling . . .

When awareness returned, he found himself lying on the road in the spot where he'd been waylaid.

Sunlight slanted through the forest as the sun slowly moved toward the horizon. Not much time had passed then. He sat up, rubbing an arm that must have banged against a rock when he fell. He blinked, yawned, and shook his head, willing himself to come fully awake.

The dog-man was gone. Blood marked the spot where he'd stood.

Arvin yawned again and rubbed his eyes.

More blood was on Arvin's dagger, which lay next to his pack. The pack was open.

Arvin scrambled toward it. He turned it over, inspecting it. The musk-creeper net was still inside—it looked as though the dog-man had the presence of mind to leave it alone—but the contents of the side pouches had been pulled out. Arvin's magical ropes and twines were scattered about, as were the mundane bits of equipment he'd gathered together after leaving Zelia's rooftop garden. There were smears of blood on several of them. The dog-man hadn't stopped to bind his wound before rifling through the pack.

Stuffing the items back into their pouches, Arvin wondered what the dog-man had been looking for. Had he, like Pakal and the Naneth-seed, also been searching for the Circled Serpent? He didn't look—or act—like one of Sibyl's minions, which meant that some other faction must be involved, but who?

Arvin didn't know much about ordinary tracking, but it was clear from the drops of blood on the road which way the dog-man had gone. Uphill, toward the temple. Toward Pakal. A faint paw print in the dust marked the spot where he'd shifted back into a dog then started to run.

Arvin turned in the other direction and felt the tickle in his forehead intensify. The iron cobra was close—very close. He'd better get moving.

He slung his backpack onto his shoulder and drew deep from his *muladhara*. Ectoplasm sweated out of his pores and the scents of saffron and ginger filled the air around him as he began his metamorphosis. He pressed his legs together and spread his arms, and willed his body into a tiny, slender, snakelike form. It unnerved him, a little, feeling his legs join together to form a tail—it was a little too close to what Zelia had just put him through—but he clamped down on his trepidation and forced himself to concentrate.

Arms feathered into wings, his tongue split into a fork, and his pupils became slits. He felt his body shrinking, contracting, becoming sinuous and light-boned. He flapped his arms experimentally—and found himself hovering, his tail dangling just above the road. By concentrating, he was able to rise a little farther, but it was awkward; the form was so alien to his own. It was difficult to control, difficult to find his balance.

From behind him came the scrape of metal on stone. Glancing back, he saw the iron cobra slithering up the road toward him. Red eyes gleamed in the dusk as it spotted him and gave a malevolent hiss.

Silver burst from Arvin's forehead and coalesced as a sheen of ectoplasm on the cobra's body as Arvin manifested another of his powers. The ectoplasm solidified into transluscent ropes, and he gave them a mental yank, binding the cobra up in a tight ball. It thrashed, and two of the coils of rope burst apart, spraying ectoplasm, but the rest held.

Before the entangling net he'd created evaporated, Arvin drew still more ectoplasm from the Astral Plane and gave it human form. It was difficult work, manifesting yet another power while hovering in mid-air with unfamiliar wings, but by concentrating fiercely he managed it. He was still a beginner when it came to creating astral constructs—he couldn't yet imbue them with the ability to discharge electricity or do extra damage with a chilling or fiery touch—but the constructs he created could punch and stomp. The one he manifested then did just that, pummelling the cobra with massive fists and feet. The cobra's iron body rang with each blow, and several of the metal bands that made up its body were dented. The astral construct gave it a final kick, and the iron cobra's metal head snapped back, its neck bent at a sharp angle. It clattered to the ground.

The ropes of ectoplasm faded then disappeared. Still the iron cobra didn't move. Arvin hovered just in front of it, waiting. Even given that invitation, it didn't attack, and the tickling sensation in Arvin's forehead was gone. Satisfied, he let his astral construct fade.

He climbed into the air. He rose above the treetops and began winging his way above the road to the distant temple. It lay higher up Mount Ugruth, on a bare area with burned trees to either side. Higher still, the peak of the volcano smoldered, a dim red glow that rivaled the setting sun.

Arvin flew toward it, hoping that Pakal still waited for him.

It was middark by the time Arvin reached the temple. He spotted it by the red glow in its central courtyard. The building had been built in a square surrounding a deep fissure in the ground, one that plunged like a knife wound all the way down to Mount Ugruth's molten heart. The white marble tiles surrounding the fissure were splattered with glossy black stone: lava that had cooled and hardened. Heat hazed the air above the crack, carrying with it the smell of sulfur. The inside wall of the building surrounding the courtyard had a wide portico supported by massive pillars that glowed a dusky red, like tree trunks in a burning forest. The rest of the building lay in shadow.

Farther up the mountain, Arvin spotted movement. He flew in that direction and saw a large group of people—about a hundred or so—climbing a narrow path that led toward the peak. Arvin swooped down lower and saw that they were Talos worshipers following a cleric—one who walked with a swaying gait. Suspicious, Arvin dipped into the cleric's thoughts.

The cleric—another yuan-ti in disguise—was leading an even larger group of worshipers to their deaths.

Not too much farther up the mountain was a large fissure, one that vented ash and poisonous fumes. The worshipers would be told to walk to its lip and breathe deeply. By breathing the fumes, they would "embrace" Talos and prove themselves worthy of him. If any of them dared to question their cleric's orders or realized what was happening and tried to run away, the wand would take care of them, just as it had taken care of the lower-ranked clerics. One way or another, they would die.

Arvin skimmed the thoughts of the worshipers closest to the cleric, hoping to find some spark of resistance. There was none. What their god had instructed them to do, they would do, no matter how odd his command seemed. Their thoughts were sluggish, as if they had been drugged.

The cleric glanced up at Arvin. *Strange*, he thought. *I didn't know Thessania kept a pet.*

Arvin broke contact. He wheeled back in the direction of the temple, searching for Pakal along the way. There was no sign of the dwarf, just as there had been no sign of him on the road leading to the temple. Nor did Arvin see anyone else. The temple seemed to be abandoned.

No, not quite. As Arvin circled over its roof, he spotted a solitary figure standing between two columns of the portico. Behind him was an arch that must have been the temple's main entrance. He was a tall man, his hair and beard as black as his clerical robes. Arvin might not have noticed him save for the javelin the man held. Its point, jagged as a lightning bolt, gave off a faint shimmer of electrical energy that illuminated his face. He leaned on the weapon, using it like a staff, staring into the courtyard with an unfocused gaze.

Arvin circled overhead, once again manifesting the power that allowed him to read minds, wondering if he'd discovered another yuan-ti. He was surprised to find nothing serpentlike at all about the man's thoughts. They were very human—and very troubled. The man wondered if he'd done the right thing. Did Talos truly demand more sacrifices? Already the clergy were gone, and they were forced to use lay worshipers from distant cities. The signs were all there, it was true—the smoke that rose from Mount Ugruth's peak, the lava that had bubbled up into the courtyard, the fire that had broken out on the hillside after the lighting strike—but was *sacrifice* what was truly required? And of the entire flock? Talos only seemed to be getting angrier with each passing day, yet if the high stormherald himself had sent word that sacrifice was necessary, it must be so.

He couldn't help but wonder, however, if he shouldn't have communed with Talos himself, just to be sure. If only his furies hadn't insisted on being the first to die, he might have consulted with them. Perhaps he should go after Siskin, ask the newly arrived cleric to wait until ...

Arvin withdrew from the man's thoughts. The cleric—the stormlord of the temple, Arvin guessed—had been duped by the yuan-ti, but his mind was still his own. If Arvin could convince him to listen, perhaps the slaughter that was about to happen on the hillside above could be stopped. The worshipers would surely listen to their stormlord.

Arvin landed outside the temple's entrance and allowed his metamorphosis to end. His tail sprang apart and became two legs again, and his body grew as it took on human form. He flexed his muscles, getting reacquainted with the feeling of arms and legs, then used his psionics to alter his appearance slightly, creating the illusion of deep red scratches in each of his cheeks. The stormlord would be more willing to listen to a warning if it came from one of his own followers.

Arvin strode through the entrance into the courtyard, he formed a cross with his arms against his chest as he'd seen the Talos worshipers do.

"Stormlord," he said, bowing, "I bring urgent news. May I speak with you?"

The brooding man turned. Close up, Arvin could see more details of his appearance. The stormlord's nose was long and sharp, his forehead creased with deep lines. Heavy black eyebrows were drawn together in what looked like a perpetual scowl. The right side of his face was puckered with white scar tissue and his hairline on that side was slightly higher. It looked as though he'd suffered a burn some time in the past. A wide metal bracer embossed with silver lightning bolts encircled each forearm.

"Approach," he said, "and speak."

Arvin rose from his bow and stepped closer. He had no idea what the protocol was for a lay worshiper addressing a cleric of this faith. He was taking a big chance. If he angered the stormlord, the man might strike him down with a lighting bolt. But he couldn't just let those people die—not when there was someone who might be able to do something about it.

"Stormlord," Arvin said, "I've just come from Hlondeth. I learned something there—something terrible.

The cleric who just left the temple … Siskin. He isn't human. He's a yuan-ti."

"Nonsense," the stormlord said. "Siskin has been touched by Talos. I saw the burn mark myself."

Arvin was about to counter that the burn had probably been an illusion when he realized something. The stormlord's breath had a sweet odor to it. He'd been drinking wine.

Wine that smelled like Thessania's perfume.

Arvin had been certain, back at the quarry, that the black liquid was poison, but he started to wonder. Perhaps it was something else, something more insidious. Something that would bend a person's thoughts along paths they wouldn't ordinarily follow, until even the most horrific suggestions sounded perfectly reasonable.

"Siskin served you wine earlier tonight, didn't he?" Arvin asked. "And he insisted that all of your flock drink, as well."

The stormlord nodded. The furrow in his brow deepened. "What of it?"

"Did the wine taste unusual?"

"It was sweeter. Flavored. It came from the east," he said.

"After drinking the wine, you talked," Arvin said. "Siskin suggested that the lay worshipers be sacrificed. Tonight. It sounded reasonable at the time, but less reasonable now that you've had a chance to think about it."

The stormlord started to nod, but just then, the ground trembled. Deep in the fissure that split the courtyard, something rumbled. Arvin heard a wet *splat* as lava shot out of the crack. He could feel its heat through his shirt.

The stormlord stared at the cooling rock, which was already losing its glow. "It is … necessary," he said. "Talos demands a sacrifice. Without it, he will level

Mount Ugruth. Thousands will die. Hlondeth itself may be wiped out. We cannot allow that to happen. The sacrifice is ... necessary."

Arvin blinked. For a moment, the stormlord had sounded like Karrell. He'd sounded as though he cared about Hlondeth and its people. Arvin, like most folks in Hlondeth, had been taught that the clerics of Talos reveled in destruction and death, but the stormlord's comments gave him cause for thought.

"You *don't* want the mountain to erupt?" Arvin asked.

The stormlord glared at him. "You're not one of us," he rumbled.

"No," Arvin admitted. "I'm not. Nor is Siskin. I'll bet that when he arrived here, he was as much a stranger to you as I am." He spread his hands, entreating the cleric to listen. "Think about it—of the two strangers, who gives you more cause for concern? The one who is asking you to listen to your own doubts before it's too late—or a 'cleric' who got you drunk on a strange-tasting wine, then suggested you kill off all of your worshipers?"

The stormlord blinked and blinked again. A shudder ran through him. He shook his head like a man trying to throw off a dream. When he looked at Arvin again, his eyes were clear and hard. "Thank you—friend—for the warning. May Talos's fist never strike you."

Then he wheeled, javelin in hand, and ran through the temple, out into the night.

Arvin activated his lapis lazuli. It was time to find Pakal. He imagined the dwarf's face, but though he could picture it clearly—dark, tattooed skin framed by ropy hair—Pakal refused to come into focus. Arvin, worried, wondered if Pakal had decided not to wait for him. Even if the dwarf had moved on from the temple, a sending still should have been able to reach him.

Unless...

A terrible thought occurred to Arvin. Maybe the dog-man had caught up to Pakal, killed him, and taken the Circled Serpent.

Then again, Arvin realized, Pakal could just be in another form, as he had been in Sibyl's temple, cloaked in an illusion that fooled the sending—an illusion, for example, that would help him blend in at Talos's temple.

"Pakal!" Arvin shouted. "Are you here? Pakal!"

Arvin heard what he expected—silence. He could guess where Pakal was: on the footpath above the temple, somewhere among the hundred or so others who were walking to their deaths.

He bolted in the direction the stormlord had gone.

The path up the mountain was a steep one, made treacherous by loose volcanic rock that skittered away with each step. Arvin slipped repeatedly, scraping his hands and knees. The night was overcast, and Mount Ugruth lent an ugly red glow to the clouds above. Smoke and ash rose into the sky from its peak. Perhaps the mountain really was about to erupt. Arvin ran until his lungs ached, but instead of stopping to catch his breath, he pressed on.

The air was hotter than it had been below. Here and there beside the path, heat waves danced in the night air over a crack in the ground. Glancing down into one of them, Arvin saw glowing lava. It bubbled out onto the trunk of a dead tree. The bark smoldered, then burst into flame. A thin stream of molten rock oozed out of the hole and flowed downhill, cutting across the path.

From above, past a point where the path rounded a knoll that hid what lay above from view, came confused shouts then screams.

As Arvin reached the knoll, a bolt of lightning lanced out of the sky, then forked horizontally just before striking the ground, as if it had been deflected by something. One bolt hit a rocky outcropping just a few paces away from Arvin. He threw up his hand to shield his face as splinters of rock rained down on him. He scrambled up the path, manifesting the power that would allow him to see through illusions as he ran. Sparkles flashed into the night in front of his forehead then were gone.

As he rounded the knoll, he saw the stormlord locked in magical combat with the yuan-ti—and it didn't look good for the stormlord. The yuan-ti menaced the worshipers with bared fangs, using his magical fear to drive them toward a stream of flowing lava. The stormlord was several paces back, caught in a dead tree that had wrapped its branches around him like a magical entangling rope. One of the cleric's hands was free, and he swept it up and down as he shouted a prayer. A pillar of lava burst from the flow, arced toward the yuan-ti in a streak of red, then plunged down.

The yuan-ti raised a hand above his head, magically deflecting the molten rock. It shot back toward the stormlord then veered aside and splashed onto the ground in front of him, splattering the worshipers. At least a dozen were badly burned, and they fell to the ground screaming.

The yuan-ti retaliated with a flick of his hand that engulfed the stormlord in a cloud of magical darkness. Then he turned his attention back to the remaining worshipers with an angry hiss. They recoiled and stumbled backward, screaming and weeping. At least a dozen ran blindly into the lava and were killed, their hair and clothes bursting into flame and their flesh sizzling as it roasted from their bones. One or two managed to resist the fear and tried to run back down the hill past the yuan-ti, but the false cleric was faster. Whipping a wand out of his belt, he pointed it at them. A pea-sized mote of fire burst from the wand, growing as it streaked through the night. It struck the back of one of the worshipers and exploded into an enormous ball of white-hot flame. In the blink of an eye, all that remained of those who had fled were twisted, blackened corpses.

The yuan-ti turned back toward the remaining worshipers and began swaying toward them, driving them like cattle with its magical fear. Behind him, lightning bolts arced out of the darkness that surrounded the dead tree where the stormlord hung, entangled. None came close to the yuan-ti. One struck a worshiper, blowing the man into the air.

Arvin searched the crowd, looking for Pakal. It took him a moment, even with his psionically clarified vision, to spot the dwarf under the illusionary human body he'd created for himself. Pakal tried to lift his blowpipe to his lips but kept getting jostled by the worshipers who ran toward the lava, lashed on by the yuan-ti's magical fear. The dwarf also suffered the compulsion's effects. The blowpipe trembled in his hand as he fought against the desperate desire to flee. He took one step back, then another—then someone ran into him, knocking the blowpipe from his hands.

Arvin needed to do something. Fast. He tried tossing a psionic distraction at the yuan-ti—only to hear Pakal scream his name from somewhere behind him. Arvin whirled then realized his distraction had bounced back at him. Whatever shield the yuan-ti had thrown up against the stormlord's magic also worked against psionics.

That must have been why Pakal had been trying to shoot the yuan-ti with a poisoned dart instead of using his spells. The dart lay beside the blowgun, useless, while Pakal was driven back toward the bubbling lava by the other worshipers. The man just behind him stumbled, weeping, into the lava. Pakal looked wildly around. His eyes locked on Arvin's. They were desperate, pleading ...

Suddenly, Arvin realized he *could* use his psionics. He drew energy into the third eye in his forehead and sent it whipping forward in a thin, silver thread. He wrapped it around the dart then yanked. The dart flew from the ground and buried itself in the yuan-ti's neck.

The yuan-ti staggered backward then turned. Unblinking, wrath-filled eyes stared at Arvin and magical fear punched into his gut, making him want to vomit. Then it was gone. The yuan-ti crumpled slowly to the ground, dead.

The worshipers, freed from the effects of the yuan-ti's fear aura, let out a collective sob of relief. Several started to pray. Others turned to the tree, calling to their stormlord as the darkness seeped away from it into the ground. Arvin ran forward, toward Pakal.

The dwarf clasped his arms and said something in his own language. It sounded like a thank you, and possibly an apology. Hearing it, Arvin felt guilty at the wave of relief he'd felt upon seeing the cloth sack Pakal carried—a sack that had something square inside it.

"Do you still have the Circled Serpent?" Arvin asked.

Pakal frowned, said something in his own language, then intoned what sounded like a prayer. "What do you ask?" he repeated.

Arvin repeated his question.

"I have it." Pakal glanced at the stormlord. Talos's worshipers were breaking off tree branches, freeing him. Other worshipers tore the clerical robes off the yuan-ti and pummeled his lifeless body with feet and fists. "We should go," Pakal added, "before my illusion wears off. I would not want them to think that I, too, am an enemy."

They moved quickly through the crowd, Pakal leading the way. They headed uphill, following the path. Soon the Talassan were well below them.

"Where are we going?" Arvin asked.

Pakal gestured at the peak. "Up there. To a portal that leads home."

"Where's home?"

"A jungle, far to the south. It is where Ts'ikil dwells."

"On the Chultan Peninsula?"

Pakal nodded. He glanced back at Arvin as they climbed. "Is Karrell truly alive? When we met in Sibyl's lair, you told me she was dead."

"I know," Arvin admitted, "but since then, I've been able to contact her. This time, for whatever reason, my sending worked. That's how I got Ts'ikil's name. From Karrell."

"Gods be praised," Pakal whispered. There was a catch to his voice; he must have cared deeply about Karrell, as well.

"Indeed," Arvin agreed, touching the crystal at his neck in silent thanks, "but Karrell's in deep trouble. She's still in the Abyss. In Smaragd."

"Sseth's domain," Pakal said.

"Yes." Arvin shuddered, imagining Karrell alone there. Giving birth. Vulnerable. "This Ts'ikil person will know how to get her out, right?"

The dwarf shook his head. "There is no escape from Smaragd."

"That's not true," Arvin countered. "I've learned there's a door that leads directly to Smaragd from this plane, a door that can be opened with the Circled Serpent. We can use it to reach Karrell, to rescue her, and we won't have to worry about the serpent god getting free. He's apparently been bound by his own jungle."

Pakal stopped. He turned to face Arvin, a wary look in his eye. "Who told you this?"

Arvin decided to tell only part of the truth. Pakal didn't need to know the details of what Zelia had forced upon him. "The woman in the rooftop garden—the one who attacked us after we escaped from Sibyl's lair. Her name is Zelia; she's a yuan-ti. Her agent—the human woman you killed with the dart—had also snuck into Sibyl's lair to look for the Circled Serpent. Zelia hopes to use it to open the second door, the one that leads to Smaragd. Like Sibyl, she hopes to free the serpent god."

Pakal's eyes narrowed. "Why would she tell you all this?"

"She didn't *tell* me," Arvin said. "I used mind magic to pull the information directly from her thoughts, after I defeated her."

"Where is this 'second door?' "

Arvin shook his head. "She didn't know."

"This Zelia recognized you," Pakal continued. "Why is that?"

Arvin smiled. That one he could answer with the truth. "Our paths have crossed before. She's an old enemy. She tried to kill Karrell and me when we were in Ormpetarr."

Pakal considered that.

"When I contacted Karrell, she told me to find Ts'ikil," Arvin continued. "She said that Ts'ikil would know what to do. I assumed that meant that Ts'ikil would help us use the Circled Serpent to open the door to Smaragd and free her."

Pakal folded his arms across his chest. "The Circled Serpent must not be used. Dendar must not be set free."

"We won't be opening *that* door," Arvin protested.

"If there *is* a second door, the Circled Serpent may cause both it and the one that would free Dendar to open at once."

"What if that isn't the case? What if the Circled Serpent only opens one door at a time?"

Pakal gave a firm shake of his head. "Ts'ikil will not allow it to be used. We cannot run the risk of Sseth emerging as an avatar. That would be as perilous as allowing Dendar to escape. The Circled Serpent must be destroyed. That is why we have been searching for it. Why *Karrell* was searching for it. Karrell herself would insist that this be done."

Arvin didn't like the sound of the word "destroyed." Maybe getting Pakal to take him to Ts'ikil wasn't such a good idea. He threw up his hands, exasperated.

"I thought you cared about Karrell, that you'd want to help rescue her."

"I do care about her," Pakal said, an intense look in his dark eyes, "and I would like to rescue her, but the life of one woman—even one to whom you owe your own life—does not negate the risk opening that door poses." He sighed and spread his hands. "This is an empty argument. We only have half of the Circled Serpent, and half cannot be used to open any door." He gave Arvin a level stare, as if warning him not to try anything.

"I know who's got the other half," Arvin said. "Dmetrio Extaminos."

Pakal's eyebrows shot up. "The yuan-ti prince from Hlondeth?"

It was Arvin's turn to be surprised. "You know him?"

"He claims to be on our side—to want to destroy the Circled Serpent. Why would he not tell us that he has—"

"Dmetrio is in Chult?" Arvin guessed.

Pakal gave him a look that made Arvin wonder if he'd spoken a little too enthusiastically.

"It's just that he disappeared from Hlondeth nearly six months ago," Arvin continued. "No one's heard from him since. I'm truly surprised to hear he's still alive. Everyone in Hlondeth thought he was dead."

"He's not dead," Pakal answered. He paused. "When we reach Ts'ikil, you must tell her what you have just told me."

"I will," Arvin agreed, uncertain whether he'd be able to keep that promise.

If Pakal was right about Ts'ikil not wanting the Circled Serpent to be used, maybe Arvin should grab Pakal's half and try to get to Dmetrio before the dwarf and Ts'ikil did. He was suddenly very glad of Karrell's ring. If the dwarf did turn out to have the ability to read thoughts, he wouldn't like what was going through Arvin's mind.

Arvin glanced up the path. "The portal is somewhere up above us, right?"

Pakal nodded. "Only a short distance ahead, but there is no hurry. The Talos worshipers are not following us."

"They're not what I'm worried about," Arvin said. He rubbed the scar on his forehead. It tingled again. "When I left Hlondeth, one of Sibyl's constructs was following me: a cobra, made of iron. I killed it, but my mind magic is warning me that Sibyl may have more than one of these constructs. If we don't get to the portal right away, it may lead Sibyl straight to us."

Pakal just stared at him.

"What?" Arvin asked.

"There is a problem," Pakal answered. "The portal can only be used at sunrise."

"Ah." Arvin thought for a moment. "We'll stay awake in turns until then and keep an eye out for the cobra. Maybe you can turn us to gas once we reach the portal. It may not be able to find us then."

"That I cannot do."

"Why not?"

Pakal sighed and spread his hands. "Thard Harr grants me only so many blessings each day. I can gain no more until I have prayed."

"Can't you pray now?"

"If I did, Thard Harr would not hear me," Pakal said. "The prayers must be said in daylight. The traditional time is when dawn first breaks."

"That's unfortunate," Arvin said.

He knew how Pakal felt. Arvin too was close to the limit of his own powers, already. His *muladhara* felt flat, a hair's breadth away from being utterly depleted. He needed to meditate.

He turned and stared down the mountainside. The stormlord and his worshipers were walking back to their temple, carrying the injured. Beyond the temple, the road vanished into darkness. Somewhere below, he was certain, another iron cobra slithered toward them.

CHAPTER 6

Arvin bolted awake, his heart pounding.

"Karrell!!" he shouted. "No!"

It took him several moments to realize that it had been a dream. A nightmare. Not real.

He could remember every detail. Sibyl, sending out waves of magical fear that turned into lava and burned the flesh from his bones, leaving him a walking skeleton that reeked of seared meat. Zelia, cracking open enormous eggs and slurping out the screaming infants they contained, her neck bulging grotesquely as she swallowed them down. The marilith demon, hacking open Karrell's pregnant belly with its swords—inside was a nest of dead snakes tied in an intricate knot.

Sweat trickled down Arvin's temples, and he wiped it away with a shaking hand.

The nightmare had been so vivid, so *clear*. Usually, in dreams, some of the senses were blurred, but in this dream every detail of smell, sound, touch, and taste had been present. Even though Arvin was wide awake, the dream wasn't fading. It hung in his mind's eye like a gruesome painting.

He closed his eyes and concentrated on Karrell's face, trying to contact her, but nothing happened. As before, his sending was blocked. The nightmare had left him more worried than ever—had the marilith found Karrell? Killed her? He remembered the prophetic dreams that had woken his mother, screaming, in the middle of the night. Was this what they had been like?

A hand touched his shoulder—Pakal's. The dwarf had been standing watch while Arvin slept.

Pakal muttered something, then spoke. Halfway through, his spell took hold and his words became intelligible. "—you dream?" he asked.

Arvin shivered. It was still dark, though the sky to the east was growing lighter. Almost dawn. "A nightmare," he answered.

Pakal grunted. "I, too. Earlier, when I slept." His face was difficult to see in the gloom, but the shudder that ran through his body made his feelings clear. "I dreamed of the jungle reduced to ash, like this place." He waved a hand, indicating a blackened tree that stood like gaunt shadow a few paces away.

They were almost at the peak of Mount Ugruth. The mountainside was bare black rock, freshly spewed from the volcano. Gray ash and chunks of porous rock covered the ground where they sat. Hot, sulfurous gases vented from a deep crack in the ground a few paces away. The landscape was desolate, like something out of the Abyss.

Nearby, at the bottom of a crater in the loose volcanic rubble, was a stone dais, much like the one in

Sibyl's lair. It too was of glossy obsidian—red obsidian. Glyphs, carved in Draconic script, encircled its rim. When the sun rose, they would activate.

According to Pakal, the portal was ancient. It dated to the height of the Serpentes Empire. Despite its incredible antiquity and the recent eruptions that must have pelted it with hot ash and chunks of falling stone, the dais looked almost new. Its edges were sword-sharp. Not a single chip had been knocked from them in all the centuries since its creation.

Arvin turned to Pakal. "Do you ever dream the future?"

The dwarf tossed back his braids. "No."

"My mother did. She dreamed of her own death—she couldn't prevent it." Arvin took a deep, steadying breath. "I dreamed about Karrell, and about our children. It was . . . terrible."

"Something has happened," Pakal said. "Dendar is not doing her job."

For a moment, Arvin wondered if the spell was translating Pakal's words incorrectly. "Her job?" he echoed. "I thought the Night Serpent was a monster who fed on mortal souls."

"Should she ever be released, that is what she would feed upon," Pakal said. "For now, she sustains herself on our nightmares. The dream fragments we remember upon waking are the crumbs she has left behind. Last night, for some reason, she did not feed."

Arvin sat up a little straighter. "Does that mean Dendar is dead?" he asked. If she was, he wouldn't need to worry about the door to her lair opening.

Pakal held up a hand. "I know what you are thinking," he said. "The answer is still no. The Circled Serpent must be destroyed."

Arvin nodded, feigning acceptance. He noted Pakal's wary look and the way the dwarf shifted his sack to his far hand. Arvin had been about to charm him but decided against it. He needed Pakal to show him how to use the portal. If the charm failed, Pakal would have even less reason to trust Arvin. As soon as they had stepped through the portal into the jungle, however, a charm would do the trick. If it failed, Arvin would take the Circled Serpent by force and amend Pakal's memory to erase any knowledge of the event.

Arvin glanced at the eastern sky. There was still some time before the sun rose. "Do I have time to meditate?" he asked the dwarf. "I need to restore my magic."

At Pakal's nod, Arvin adopted the *bhujan asana* and began his meditations. It felt good to slow his mind; it helped push the terrible images of his nightmare away. When he was done, the sun was peeping out from behind Mount Aclor. Slowly, it climbed higher in the sky.

Pakal climbed down into the crater, sending small avalanches of loose rock and dust toward the dais. Arvin forced himself to wait a moment before rising—casually—to his feet and following. The dais was knee-high on the dwarf but came only midway up Arvin's calves. One quick step would put him on top of it.

Together, they watched as sunlight crept across the dais, illuminating it like a waxing moon. As it did, the ash that had settled on that half of the dais vanished.

"What do we do?" Arvin asked. "Step onto it once it's fully in sunlight?"

Pakal nodded.

"Will Ts'ikil be waiting for us on the other side?"

"She will come once I call her."

Good. That would give Arvin some time. As the sunlight crept toward the western edge of the dais, the symbols that were already illuminated began to glow with a ruddy light. It looked, Arvin thought, as though their grooves had suddenly filled with lava. He passed a hand above one of the symbols but felt no heat.

"Does the dais work like the amber ring?" he asked. "Do we need to be touching to go through together?"

The dwarf eased himself to the side, slightly increasing the distance between them. "No. Once activated, it will transport anyone who steps onto it, but only for a brief time. Be ready."

"I will."

Arvin was glad the portal was almost ready. The tingling in his forehead had grown strong. If it was an iron cobra, it was getting closer by the moment. He risked a glance up at the lip of the crater but saw no sign of a snake, iron or otherwise.

As he started to turn back to the portal, something in the sky caught his attention. A creature flew toward Mount Ugruth from the direction of Hlondeth. It was big, with a serpent's body and four arms. With a sinking heart, Arvin realized who it must be.

"Sibyl's coming!" he warned. "She's headed straight for us!"

Pakal glanced in the direction Arvin had pointed then back at the dais. "She is still far enough away," he said. "We will be in the jungle, with the portal closed behind us, before she can reach us. The portal will not reactivate until tomorrow's sunrise."

Arvin nodded, only partially reassured. Sibyl a day behind them was all well and good if the Circled Serpent was destroyed by then, but destroying it wasn't Arvin's goal. A day wouldn't give him much time to trick Zelia into telling him where Dmetrio was, steal the second half of the Circled Serpent, and rescue Karrell.

"There," Pakal continued. "You see? It is ready."

He was right. The entire inscription glowed. Pakal placed a foot onto the dais. Arvin did the same. The tingling in his forehead turned into a steady burn...

A loud hiss and clatter of loose rock startled Pakal. One foot on the dais, one foot on the ground, the dwarf stared up at the source of the noise and cursed. Arvin, realizing it must be the cobra, grabbed the dwarf by the arm and boosted him onto the dais, leaping up after him. As the world beyond the inscription began to shimmer, Arvin saw the iron cobra he thought he'd defeated come skittering down the slope. Its hood was bent flat against its head and several of the iron bands that made up its body were jammed together, but it was moving again. Fast. With a screech of metal it heaved itself up onto the dais with them and bared bent fangs.

"Watch out!" Arvin yelled, yanking Pakal back. "It's going to—"

The mountainside vanished. For a heartbeat there was nothing under Arvin's feet as he fell sideways through the dimensions, still holding tight to Pakal's arm. Then his feet landed on something solid. A roaring filled the air: water. It slammed into Arvin's calves, knocking him prone. He had just enough time to register the fact that the portal had transported them to the bottom of a narrow, cliff-walled canyon filled with a rushing river before the force of the water dragged him off the submerged portal they'd materialized on. Then the river swept them away.

Karrell heard something moving through the jungle off to her left. She froze. Rain pattered on the slab of bark she held over her head like a shield, making it difficult to hear. Already the bark felt spongy; the acidic downpour was eating through it.

Whatever was moving through the jungle, it was big, larger than the dretches the marilith had sent to search for her.

Karrell touched her belly, soothing the children inside her. They could sense her fear and were kicking. She began to whisper the prayer that would disguise her as a tree but realized the sounds of branches breaking and sodden vegetation squelching were moving away. She sighed in relief.

The sounds stopped. A voice she recognized grated out guttural words—the marilith, casting a spell.

Karrell croaked out a prayer. "Ubtao, hide me in my time of need. Protect me from my enemies; obscure me from their sight and do not let them find me."

The jungle reacted to her, just as it did each time she cast a spell. Thorny branches slashed at her bare arms and the ground underfoot became soggier, causing her to lose her footing. Gnats erupted from a nearby pool in a belch of foul-smelling air and swarmed her face. She squinted and waved them away.

Somewhere in the jungle to Karrell's left, the marilith continued to chant. Something that flashed silver rose into the sky. After a moment, she realized the flashes were coming from the marilith's swords, which circled above the treetops. Just as it had done in Baron Foesmasher's palace, the demon had summoned a barrier of blades.

Perhaps the demon was under attack, but if so, why had it flung the blades into the sky?

Karrell's heart beat faster. Perhaps, she thought, the blades had been driven there by some unseen adversary. Had Arvin done as he'd promised and found a way into Smaragd?

Tossing her makeshift rain shield aside—she could move more quickly without it, and the rain was slowing anyway—she pushed her way through the jungle toward the spot the swords circled above. She caught only glimpses of them through the thick vegetation—brief glimpses, for though the acidic rain had no effect on her skin, it stung her eyes.

As she got closer, she spotted the marilith. Its tail was coiled beneath it as it stared up at the circle of blades. All six arms were raised above its head, directing the whirling blades. Squatting next to it were two dozen dretches, drooling and idly scratching their bulging, hairless heads. The marilith guided the swords down through the trees, tilting the circle so that it was perpendicular to the ground.

In the middle of the circle, Karrell could see a flat gray plain with a walled city in the distance. The wall that surrounded the city had a greenish glow. Hlondeth? No, the landscape was wrong. The walled city wasn't a port; the gray plain continued behind it as far as the eye could see. Her heart beat faster as she realized the demon had opened a gate to another plane. Which one, Karrell had no idea, but it looked habitable. Somewhere on the prime material plane? Wherever it was, it had to be safer than Smaragd.

Moving as close as she dared, Karrell readied herself. Leaping through the gate with a bulging belly would be difficult, but it might be her only chance at escape.

The view through the gate shifted as the link between planes adjusted itself. With a rush that dizzied her to look at it, the view zoomed in toward the city. When it stopped, it was focused on a field of rubble. Huge blocks of masonry lay jumbled together with rusted bits of twisted metal and splintered wood. It looked as though a giant had trampled on whatever buildings had once stood there. A crowd of people milled around the rubble—humans in torn clothing. Several had scratches on their cheeks. All looked terrified, and all cried out. Karrell could not hear what they were saying, but she could guess—their actions made it clear that they were praying to their gods.

Behind them was a river of bubbling black water; beyond that, a stalagmite-encrusted cave.

The marilith pointed at the gate. The dretches grunted then leaped through it, all but one of them making it through the circle of whirling steel. That one was instantly sliced to pieces. Blood sprayed outward in a circle and chunks of flesh were hurled into the jungle. A hand landed next to Karrell.

The other dretches seemed to rapidly shrink, and Karrell had to strain her eyes to see where they'd gone. She spotted them next to the milling crowd. The dretches drove the crowd forward like cattle, toward the cave.

The marilith, meanwhile, concentrated on keeping the gate open. Karrell edged closer, making sure she kept behind the demon. The prayer she'd uttered earlier had only hidden her from scrying and other divination spells. If the marilith looked in her direction, it would see her. She would have to time her escape just right. Slowly, glancing between the gate above her and the demon, she crept forward.

In the place beyond the gate, the dretches used magical fear and clouds of nauseating smoke to drive the crowd toward the cave. The humans screamed and wept as they stumbled into the water then into the cave. Karrell's heart ached for them, for they were clearly in torment. She eased closer still . . .

Her foot slipped on a wet branch and splashed into a pool of stagnant water. She halted, ready to chant a prayer. The marilith, however, didn't seem to have heard. It was intent on the gate. It watched, chuckling, as the first few ranks of the crowd disappeared into the cave.

Screaming erupted from inside it—the anguished cries of those within. Karrell pressed her lips together in a grim line, wishing she could do something for them, but realized she could do nothing until she was through the gate. She moved cautiously forward, taking a careful step, then pausing, then easing forward through the branches, then pausing again, all the while with one eye on the demon. Just a few steps more . . .

The last of the humans had been driven into the cave, and the field of rubble was empty again, save for the dretches. They loped back toward the hole, knuckles scuffing on the ground. Karrell, realizing the marilith would close the gate once they'd returned, quickened her pace, no longer caring if the movement of a branch betrayed her.

Behind the dretches, a head emerged from the cave. The head of an enormous serpent with midnight-black scales, its neck was as thick as the cave it emerged from. The serpent stared past the departing dretches at the gate, its tongue flickering in and out of its mouth.

"More," it hissed.

Karrell felt an icy cold settle in her stomach as she recognized the serpent and realized where the gate led.

To the City of Judgement and the lair of Dendar—grown large enough that she barely fit inside her cave. To the Fugue Plain.

A plane that could only be entered by demons, and the souls of the dead.

Karrell, still living, would be unable to pass through the gate the marilith had opened, even if she wanted to.

The dretches had driven the souls of the freshly dead—those whose gods had not yet claimed them from the Fugue Plane—into Dendar's gullet. Why?

The shock of this realization was Karrell's undoing. One of the dretches pointed and gabbled out a cry of glee. The marilith spun, spotting her. The gate slammed shut, slicing three dretches to bloody pieces.

The marilith lunged at Karrell, seizing her.

Arvin fought for breath as the river tumbled him away from the portal. He was above water, submerged, broke the surface, then was under water again. Choking, sputtering, he tried to fight his way back to the surface, but it was impossible to swim while clutching Pakal's arm and with a pack that had filled with water weighing him down. The dwarf thrashed about, kicking Arvin in the stomach, either trying to swim or just trying to get away from him. Arvin's head broke through the foaming water just as he and Pakal were slammed against the side of the canyon. Arvin lost his grip on the dwarf's arm. Pakal lost hold of the sack. As it swirled away in the current, the dwarf shouted and flailed toward it. Arvin was quicker. He kicked off the wall and lunged forward.

His hands closed around the sack.

Pakal grabbed him by the shoulders an instant later. The dwarf shouted something at Arvin, but his words were lost in the thunder of water. They struggled, Pakal clambering over Arvin—and nearly drowning him in the process—and at last grabbing the sack. The river swept them into a whirlpool, which spun them crazily around then out again. Arvin caught a glimpse of a tree that had fallen from the cliff above. It lay in the river at an angle, partially submerged, just ahead. The river was going to carry them right into the tree—and Pakal's back was to it. Arvin shouted and gestured frantically with his free hand then submerged, still clutching the sack. Pakal fought back, kicking up toward the surface.

Then, suddenly, Arvin was the only one holding the sack.

He burst from the water just in time to see the dwarf caught on the tree, his limp body draped across its trunk. Then the river turned a bend in the canyon, sweeping Arvin away. Cursing, he tried to fight his way back upriver, but it was no use. Even if he'd had both hands free and wasn't wearing a backpack, he would never be able to make headway against the current. It took all of his efforts just to keep his head above water. Kicking furiously, he quickly felt the sack to make sure the box that held the Circled Serpent was still inside. It was.

He began searching for a way out. It was some time, however, before he found one. By the time he battled his way over to a ledge that he could climb onto without being smashed against the wall of the canyon, Pakal was far behind.

Dripping wet, exhausted, Arvin opened the sack and took out the box. He opened it and saw a crescent-shaped object wrapped in crumpled lead foil resting on a bed of soggy black velvet. Carefully, he peeled back one edge of the foil, revealing the object it had been wrapped around. Gems glinted in a silver serpent face. The upper half of the Circled Serpent was in his hands.

He smoothed over foil and closed the box then touched the crystal at his neck. "Nine lives," he whispered. Then he tucked the box securely inside his pack.

Using his magical bracelet made the climb out of the canyon an easy one, but above the cliff, the jungle was thick and deeply shadowed. Something orange flashed through the trees. Instinctively, Arvin ducked and reached for his dagger, but it was only a tiny flying snake, its wings no larger than Arvin's hands. Its coloration made it stand out vividly against the jungle foliage, most of which was a green so dark it bordered on black. He wondered whose pet it was, but a moment later, when a second flying snake flitted past, he realized the creatures must be wild.

The jungle was filled with life, despite the fact that a thick canopy of trees blocked most of the light, throwing what lay below into shadow. Birds with bright turquoise, yellow, and red feathers cawed at him from the branches above; a centipede the length of his arm scurried out of his path; and tiny monkeys with bright orange fur leaped from tree to tree, chattering to each other. He saw at least a dozen more of the tiny flying snakes. Each would be worth a hundred gold pieces or more in Hlondeth, a fortune on the wing.

Despite the river that frothed through the canyon below, the air was oppressively hot. His clothes quickly went from being soggy and wet to just damp with sweat. Arvin combed his hair back with a hand. It was as hot in the jungle as the inside of Hlondeth's Solarium, but with the added discomfort of oppressive humidity that left him feeling slightly lightheaded. He was used to a dry heat and air that smelled of hot stone and snake musk.

He stood, debating what to do. He had the upper half of the Circled Serpent, and so he needed to find out where Dmetrio was and trick him into giving up his half.

Easier said than done, however. Arvin had no idea where Dmetrio was—no idea where *he* was, either. Pakal had seemed confident that the portal would convey them to his homeland but had seemed surprised to be deposited in a river. Had the portal malfunctioned and sent them somewhere else?

Pakal would know the answer to that question—but Pakal was draped, unconscious, over a log in the middle of a raging river, maybe even dead by now, if the river had swept his body away.

There was an easy way to find out.

Arvin started to summon energy into his lapis lazuli then hesitated. If Pakal was alive, a sending would allow him to see Arvin as well, and Arvin didn't want to give too much away. He took off his backpack and hid it behind a nearby tree. Then he resumed the sending.

Closing his eyes, he pictured the dwarf's face in his mind. A moment later, it came into focus. Pakal was bedraggled, his wet braids plastered against a bloody scalp, but alive. Both hands were gripping tightly to something and one foot was braced while the other was searching for a foothold. He'd not only survived but was trying to climb out of the canyon.

Pakal! Arvin said. *You're alive! I tried to swim back to you, but . . .* He paused, realizing that was eleven words, wasted. *Where are we? Did we reach your homeland?*

Yes, but we did not arrive where I expected. The portal must be—

He stopped, looked closely at each of Arvin's empty hands, then leaned to the side as if trying to see Arvin's back. Arvin turned slightly—a casual looking gesture designed to let Pakal see that his pack was gone.

Pakal's expression turned grim. Arvin could guess what he was thinking: that the box had been swept away by the river. The lead foil around the Circled Serpent would make it impossible to find.

Return to the fallen tree, the dwarf replied. *I will tell Ts'ikil to meet us—*

Having reached its limit, the sending ended.

Arvin grinned. Tymora must have been smiling on him; everything had worked out perfectly. All he had left to do was trick Pakal—or Ts'ikil—into telling him where Dmetrio was. First, however, he needed to hide the Circled Serpent.

Where?

He needed to get a good look around. The best way to do that would be by morphing into a flying snake again, much as Arvin hated the idea. The musky smell that clung to him even after he'd morphed back again was as bad as a dunking in Hlondeth's sewers. Sighing, he picked up his pack and put it on.

A scream made him jump—a bad thing to do so close to a cliff. One of his feet slipped off the edge, sending a stone clattering down toward the river. Arvin recovered quickly and reached for his dagger. The scream had come from somewhere close—no more than a few paces away—and it had sounded like a woman.

She screamed again, but her cry choked off suddenly. Arvin hesitated. Did he really want to get involved? Then he thought of Karrell. She, too, was alone and in trouble.

He plunged into the jungle toward the spot where the scream had come from. The vegetation was thick, and he was forced to push his way through a tangle of vines and bushes that blocked his way. When he was certain he was at the spot the screams had come from, he stopped. He searched the ground for tracks but saw none. The air smelled of dark soil and growing things, of sweet-scented flowers—and an acidic smell, like yuan-ti sweat.

Belatedly, he realized the jungle around him was silent. The monkeys, birds, and flying snakes were gone. A sharp smell hung in the air, one that stung his nostrils. He glanced down and saw tendrils of yellowish fog whisping out from under a waxy-leafed bush to his right. Then, with a loud hissing, the fog billowed out full force, enveloping him.

It became difficult to breathe or to see. The acidic fog tore at his lungs and throat with each breath. He doubled over, coughing. He could see no more than a pace or two in any direction. He tried to run but tripped over a vine.

It wrapped itself around his ankle. Then it tugged, sending him sprawling, and began dragging him along the ground.

He slashed at the vine, but three more came snaking out of the jungle after it. Coughing so hard he began to retch, he tried to crawl away, but his limbs moved at only a fraction of their normal speed. It was as if the air around him had turned to thick mud. The vines had wound around both legs and pulled him steadily along. He threw his body in the direction they dragged him, causing them to go slack, and slashed through another of the vines. But more came snaking through the air toward him—a dozen at least. Four more wrapped around him.

The vines belonged to an enormous plant. Yellow mist spewed out of the base of its trunk, and waxy green leaves fluttered like feathers around four flower buds that were each the size of a horse. One of these buds gaped open, revealing a mouth lined with row upon row of thornlike teeth. Another was clenched firmly upon the body of a monkey; the animal's limp leg and tail dangled from it. Arvin cursed as he realized it must have been the monkey that had screamed. The open bud swayed in Arvin's direction as the vines pulled him toward it.

Arvin cast his awareness toward the thing, trying to connect with its mind, but its thoughts were slow and ponderous, as impossible to grasp as the eye-stinging yellow fog that surrounded him. The plant would not respond to a distraction or to an illusion. An astral construct might be able to tear apart one of the buds, but not before the other three—all gaping open and turning hungrily in Arvin's direction— gobbled him up.

Instinctively, Arvin tried to slash at one of the vines that quested toward him, but his arm, like the rest of his body, moved too slowly. The vine wrapped around his wrist, immobilizing his weapon hand. If only, he thought feverishly, his body would move as quickly as his mind. . . .

That gave him an idea. He summoned energy into his third eye and sent out a streak of silver that wrapped itself around the vine. Rotating it swiftly, he uncoiled the vine from his wrist. Another line of silver burst from Arvin's forehead as he repeated the manifestation. He used it to grab his dagger and slash at the vines that held his legs. He manifested the power a third time, and a fourth, and a fifth, yanking back the vines that were still snaking toward him. He grabbed the end of each, then moved his energy-hands back and forth, over and under, tying the vines into a knot. Meanwhile, the dagger slashed through the last of the vines holding his legs. Slowly, sweat pouring from his body, Arvin crawled backward, moving at the pace of a slug.

Vines kept snaking through the jungle toward him, but he caught each one with a psionic hand, knotting it around the branch of a nearby tree. Coughing, his throat and lungs raw, he at last found the edge of the cloud of fog. He crawled into clean, clear air—and moved at his normal pace again. His pent-up muscles were sent leaping forward, and his shoulder slammed into the trunk of a tree.

In the branches above, a monkey screeched angrily— again, a very human-sounding cry—then swung away through the jungle. A piece of half-eaten fruit landed at Arvin's feet.

He rose, still coughing, and stared at the chewed-up fruit, its pulpy red seeds spilling out of its torn skin. "Nine lives," he whispered, touching the crystal at his throat.

Standing there, staring, he felt a tingle awaken in his forehead.

The iron cobra. It must have passed through the portal as well. It was still looking for him.

Arvin needed to get out of there. He drew energy into his navel and chest and manifested the power that would alter his body. It was disturbingly easy to morph into a flying snake; after his long flight to the temple, the wings that sprouted out of his arms felt familiar. Even feeling his legs meld together into a tail didn't bother him. He had an anxious moment as his backpack flattened into a brown patch of scales on his back, but the Circled Serpent in its box, like everything else in his pack, as well as his clothing, melded with his body. Exhaling the scent of saffron and ginger, he rose into the air, his snake tail lashing with each stroke of his wings.

He rose above the treetops and hovered, getting his bearings. Assuming no time had passed during their passage through the portal, the direction where the sun hung just above the horizon was east. The river snaked through the jungle in a roughly north-south direction. Its headwaters sprang from the slopes of a volcanic peak that resembled a broken serpent's fang. The river emptied, far to the south, into an ocean that stretched to the horizon. Another large body of water, a lake, lay to the east. To the west, about an equal distance away across thick jungle, was a range of mountains. Another chain of mountains lay to the north beyond the volcano.

Between these features, the jungle extended, unbroken, in every direction save one. About halfway between the river and the mountains to the west, enormous pyramids rose above the treetops. Arvin expected to see a city surrounding them but the jungle seemed to grow right up to their bases. Staring at the pyramids, he could see that their tops were jagged and broken—a ruined city.

He decided to follow the river; that way, he wouldn't get lost. Pakal was somewhere upriver, so the opposite direction was the way to go. He flew downriver along the canyon, looking for a place to hide the Circled Serpent.

CHAPTER 7

Arvin descended toward the limestone bluff he'd spotted from the air. It was one of the few landmarks in the vast sea of dark green, rising above the jungle canopy at a spot where the river made a **U**-shaped bend. There were a number of small caves in the bluff, any of which would make an ideal hiding place, assuming the caves weren't inhabited.

Dozens of flying snakes swooped in and out of the caves like swallows; they probably nested inside. Arvin joined them. He paused above the bluff, listening, but heard only the rush of the river in the canyon below and birds calling to one another in the jungle. Somewhere in the distance, a larger creature roared, and Arvin could see the treetops shake as something big moved between them.

He was doubly glad just then that he'd chosen not to make his way through the jungle on foot.

He chose a cave that was apart from the others, about halfway up the bluff, and sent his awareness drifting into it. Ectoplasm shimmered in the cave mouth as he probed for thoughts. The only ones he detected were those of the flying snakes, including some that appeared to be coiled up, sleeping, deep within the cave. Otherwise, the cave was empty.

He fluttered inside. The off-white walls had a wrinkled appearance. Here and there, a mounded stalagmite rose from the floor like a sagging column of dough. They were, however—as Arvin discovered a moment later when he accidentally brushed a wingtip against one—as hard as any other stone.

He glanced around, looking for a place to hide the Circled Serpent. There were no obvious choices, no convenient cracks into which the box could be wedged. Then a flying snake flew past him, toward the rear of the cave, and disappeared behind a natural column of stone that stood close to the rear wall. It didn't return. Curious, Arvin flew in that direction. Behind the column, he discovered a passage that had been sealed with clay bricks. Two of the bricks had fallen, leaving a small hole. The passage beyond the wall led up at an angle from the cave, worming its way deeper into the bluff.

It looked like the perfect hiding place. He flew into the gloomy passage, deciding that he would go only as far as the sunlight penetrated. After a short distance, the tunnel opened up into a second cavern. He gasped, barely remembering to flap his wings. For several terrible moments he thought he was staring down at Sibyl.

The abomination nearly filled the cavern, its serpent body a tight coil on the smooth floor. Its wedge-shaped head rested, eyes closed, on arms that were folded beneath it like a pillow. Its scales were black and shiny as obsidian, like Sibyl's, but it had no wings. It was dead, and the body had shrunk like a drumhead around the skeleton; every rib stood out in sharp relief.

There was no odor of rot. The air was only slightly less hot and humid than the steaming jungle below. Surely a body would decompose quickly, yet—Arvin sniffed—the only smell was that of herbs or perhaps flowers, a sweet, pleasant scent.

The cavern it lay in wasn't natural. Its walls were perfectly circular and smooth, with an equally smooth ceiling and floor, a tomb.

As Arvin's eyes adjusted to the gloom, he made out more details. Several of the yuan-ti's scales had nut-sized gems embedded in them. Though Arvin couldn't make out their colors, he was certain, given their size, that they were extremely valuable. Any one of them would probably feed, clothe, and house him for a year.

The flying snake he'd followed into the tomb flitted around the chamber. After several circuits of the tomb it fluttered past Arvin, back the way it had come.

Arvin landed on the floor and morphed back into human form, braced and wary. He waited several moments. If the tomb had any magical protections, they so far hadn't activated. He shrugged off his pack and unfastened its flaps, then pulled out the box that held the upper half of the Circled Serpent. After a moment's thought, he realized that the best place to hide it would be inside the corpse. Wary of touching the dead abomination—especially after facing the skeletal serpent in Sibyl's lair—he used a psionic hand to pry open its mouth. It was a struggle—the shriveled sinews of the jaw were tough as old leather—but slowly the mouth creaked open.

A second sparkle of silver briefly illuminated the gloomy cavern as he used his psionics to lift the box into the air. He nudged it inside the mouth, cushioning it between the forks of the rotted tongue. Then he pushed the jaw shut. Fang clicked against fang like the closing of a lock.

He put on his pack and started to turn away. Then he turned back to the abomination again, unable to resist temptation. Drawing his dagger, he pried the largest gem from the body—one with a unique, star-shaped cut that would double its value—and caught it in his free hand when it fell. He stood, waiting. Nothing happened. Breathing a sigh of relief, he slipped the gem into his pocket and walked back to the tunnel that was the tomb's only exit. Steadying himself on the wall with one hand, he prepared to morph into a flying snake.

A soft hiss, just ahead of him, made him jerk his hand back.

A snake poked its head out of the wall near the spot where his hand had just been, out of solid stone. Then it was gone.

A second hiss, soft as the first, came from the ceiling just above his head. Arvin ducked as a swift-moving ripple of shadow flashed past his face. He caught a glimpse of curved fangs. Then that serpent, like the first, disappeared.

He glanced around, his heart beating rapidly, trying to see where the serpents had gone. There was a faint smudge on the wall where the first serpent had appeared—a wavy line that might have been a ripple in the limestone or a shadow cast by one of the columns at the far end of the tunnel. From somewhere deep inside the stone came an eerie hissing.

The tomb was protected, after all—by shadow asps.

Arvin had once had a close brush with one such creature of the Plane of Shadow many years past.

A wizard the guild had paired him up with had the bright idea of making a "robe of shadows" from the shed skin of one of the magical serpents. The experiment, however, had fatal results. When Arvin had arrived at the wizard's workshop, he'd been met not with a living wizard, but the shadow creature the man had become. The shadow asp had escaped its bindings and bitten the poor wretch.

Arvin decided that one gem, no matter how valuable, wasn't worth dying for.

As a shadowy head emerged once more from the wall, Arvin yanked the gem from his pocket and rolled it across the chamber, back to the abomination. It worked; the shadow asp slithered after it. As it did, Arvin morphed into a flying snake. Wings flapping as rapidly as his heart beat, he streaked down the tunnel. A shadow asp emerged from a wall to watch as he dived through the hole into the first cavern, but it did not attack.

Back in sunlight again, safe from the shadow asps, Arvin morphed once more into human form. He touched his abbreviated little finger, thankful for his time in the guild. If he hadn't seen what had happened to the wizard, he never would have recognized the shadow asps.

The upper half of the Circled Serpent was safely concealed, but one more thing was required to ensure that it stayed hidden. Arvin took off his backpack and pulled out a few items he thought might come in handy in the next little while, including his trollgut rope, then placed the pack behind a stalagmite near the cave mouth—an easy hiding place to find. Pulling out a few items more, he arranged them around the pack to make it look as though someone had rifled through its contents.

His shirt was torn. He stripped it off and changed into the spare shirt he'd been carrying in his pack.

He used his dagger to cut a length of fabric from the old shirt and wound it around his head like a loosely wrapped turban; it would keep the worst of the sun off. He cut the remainder of the fabric into long, thin strips.

Those he braided into a thin cord. At several points along its length, he worked intricate knots into the braid. When he was done, he dropped the cord next to the pack.

Then he manifested a psionic power—one he'd never used on himself before to the best of his knowledge. It was odd, hearing his own secondary display. The tinkling noise sounded just like the tiny silver bells, shaped like hollow snake teeth, that had decorated the hem of one of his mother's dresses. It was odder still, feeling the power take hold of his own mind and reshape it. Sharp as a dagger, it sliced away neat chunks of memory, excising everything from his finding of the tunnel to his narrow escape from the shadow asps. He left in the memory of himself hiding the pack behind the stalagmite but removed the part where he'd knotted the cord. He felt the remaining memories braid themselves together again and—

Arvin stood near the mouth of the cave, staring at the spot where he'd just hidden his pack. It wasn't possible to see the pack from the entrance, but still he wondered if he'd chosen the best hiding place. He glanced at the back of the cave, wondering if there might be a better spot there, but no, that cave was one of dozens in the bluff and was one of the less accessible. The chances of someone stumbling across Arvin's pack were slim.

He morphed back into a flying snake; the transformation was even easier than it had been before. He launched himself into the air and flew upriver again, toward the spot where he'd agreed to meet Pakal.

When he reached it, the dwarf wasn't there.

Perhaps Pakal was trying to find him. Arvin flew back downriver to the spot where he'd climbed the cliff. Worried that Pakal might have fallen victim to the carnivorous plant, Arvin circled above that spot. The plant had torn apart the knots he'd tied in its vines, but its bud-mouths were open. It didn't look as though it had swallowed anything lately, at least nothing dwarf-sized. Pakal, being native to the jungle, would surely know how to avoid the danger it posed.

He flew back along the other side of the river, back to the spot where he'd last seen Pakal, and continued on upriver, searching its banks, but saw no sign of the dwarf or of anyone who might be Ts'ikil.

Worried, Arvin hovered above the canyon. He wouldn't be able to sustain his metamorphosis much longer. He needed to find a safe place to land and somewhere he could spend the night, since he wouldn't be able to use a sending to contact Pakal again until the next day. The lapis lazuli only allowed him to contact a particular person once each day.

A short distance from the river was a place that looked suitable: a roughly circular clearing in the jungle. He flew toward it and saw that it was the plaza of what must have been a small city. A dozen low hills encircled the plaza: ruined buildings the jungle had long since grown over. Each structure was topped with an enormous serpent head carved from stone. It looked as if some ancient foe had decapitated a nest of serpents then set each of their heads upon a leafy green cushion. Their sightless stone eyes stared at the plaza like brooding serpents plotting their revenge.

Arvin landed on top of one of the heads, whose upper surface was as wide as a feast table. It afforded an excellent view of the plaza. The open area was paved with enormous red flagstones; bushes had thrust their way between them at several points, giving the stones the appearance of flotsam on a heaving sea. He morphed back into human form and stood. The sun beat down from above, and the weathered stone was uncomfortably hot, even through his boots. His feet were sweltering, but he didn't dare take the boots off. The jungle was full of strange insects, bristling with spines and pincers.

He wished, belatedly, that he'd filled his water skin from the river. It felt as though the heat had wrung every drop of moisture from his pores. Sunlight glinted off water that had collected in a murky green puddle in a hollow in one of the flagstones, and he decided to climb down and see if it was drinkable.

As he looked for the best way down, a movement at the edge of the jungle caught his eye. Something—or someone—was moving toward the plaza. At first, Arvin took it to be a human child or perhaps, given its short-limbed, heavy build and childlike face, a halfling. Its naked body, however, was covered in patches of what looked like green scales and it had a tail, not long and serpentine, like that of a yuanti, but thick and stubby, like a lizard's, and entirely covered in green scales. It moved with a bow-legged gait. When the half-man, half-lizard turned, Arvin could see that he held a crude spear.

Slowly, wary of any sudden movement that might catch the half-lizard's eye, Arvin settled into a crouch on the stone head then slid down beside it, out of sight. He watched, trying to decide whether to venture closer. The half-lizard was probably native to the jungle. He might know where Pakal was—might even know where Dmetrio was. If Arvin could get close enough, he could read the strange creature's thoughts.

The half-lizard walked more or less upright, but as he approached the water, he dropped to all fours and scuttled. He scooped up water with a cupped hand then drank, his eyes ranging warily across the plaza. Then, as if sensing Arvin's eyes upon him, the half-lizard looked up, startled. A bright orange flap of skin shot out just under his chin, expanding into a half circle like a fan, as his head bobbed up and down several times in rapid succession.

Something moved through the jungle toward the plaza, something big—something that sent birds screeching out of the trees in flocks as it shouldered the trees aside like a man moving through a field of corn. It had to be as large as a dragon.

The monster smashed its way into the plaza a heartbeat later, knocking over a tree that slammed down onto the flagstones. It was an enormous reptile, its head level with the treetops. It stood on its hind legs, tiny forelegs scrabbling at the air, as if still tearing jungle vines out of the way. Slowly, it tilted its head from side to side. One eye fixed on the half-lizard. The giant reptile threw back its head and roared. Its mouth was filled with rows of teeth that looked easily as long as Arvin's dagger.

The half-lizard grabbed his spear and fled into the jungle. The gigantic reptile charged after him, its clawed feet gouging flagstones out of the plaza with each step. It smashed into the jungle and disappeared from sight. Only after it was gone did Arvin realize that there had been what looked like a saddle on its back.

He watched the rippling wake it left in the jungle, thankful that he'd chosen somewhere elevated to land. His eyes ranged over the jungle. Dmetrio was out there somewhere—but where?

Something occurred to Arvin then, that perhaps he didn't need Pakal to tell him where Dmetrio was. Maybe a sending to Dmetrio would work, since Arvin was on the Chultan Peninsula himself. It was certainly worth a try.

He activated the lapis lazuli and pictured Dmetrio in his mind. The yuan-ti noble's features were easy enough to remember: high forehead, dark, swept-back hair, narrow nose, slit-pupil eyes, and flickering forked tongue. The connection wouldn't come, no matter how vehemently Arvin mentally whispered Dmetrio's name.

Dmetrio had either shielded himself—or he was dead.

Then Arvin realized there was a third possibility: that Dmetrio *was* dead in a manner of speaking, dead at Zelia's hands.

Zelia claimed to serve House Extaminos, but the mind seed she'd planted in Arvin had given him an intimate knowledge of where her loyalties truly lay. She thought of herself not as a subject of Lady Dediana but as working for herself, and she craved power. If the opportunity presented itself for her to become Sseth's avatar, she would have seized it.

The Naneth-seed had been Zelia's ticket into Sibyl's lair. With Naneth in place, there was a good possibility of both halves of the Circled Serpent falling into Zelia's hands if she could also control Dmetrio. Seeding the son of Hlondeth's ruler would have been a dangerous move for Zelia to make, but the fact that Dmetrio was headed south, where few knew him, made it slightly less risky. A seeded Dmetrio would explain why none of Arvin's sendings to the prince those past few months had been successful.

Still holding the image of Dmetrio's face in his mind, Arvin shifted his thoughts slightly. He imagined an identical body that housed a mind that went by a different name.

Zelia.

Immediately, his mental image of Dmetrio animated. The mind seed was lounging, his predominantly human body bent backward in an approximation of a coiled serpent. He was holding a languid conversation with someone Arvin couldn't see, but he broke that off immediately as the sending manifested. Slit-pupil eyes stared at Arvin for a long, appraising moment. Then the Dmetrio-seed's tongue flickered out of an anticipatory smile. Its mouth hissed a silent word: "Arvin."

Arvin took a deep breath. *Dmetrio,* he began, *Zelia sent me. I have the upper half of the serpent. Tell me where you are, and I'll bring it to you.*

The Dmetrio-seed smiled. A heartbeat later, Arvin felt a familiar tingling in his forehead. *Stay where you are,* the seed answered. *The jungle is dangerous. I'll come to you.*

"I'll bet you will," Arvin muttered as the sending ended. It had been just the response he'd hoped for. He had no doubt that the Dmetrio-seed had just scryed him. The stone head would be a familiar landmark, and the seed would be there soon.

He glanced again at the water the strange creature had drunk from then decided not to chance it. Quenching his thirst would wait. He needed to get ready.

❧ ❧ ❧ ❧ ❧

It was early evening, and still the Dmetrio-seed hadn't shown up. Arvin wondered if he'd guessed wrong. Maybe he wasn't in Chult, but some other, even more distant place. He'd finished his meditations long ago and sat, hidden in the foliage a few paces distant from the stone head, but still there was no sign of the seed.

Finally, low in the sky to the west, Arvin spotted something. At first he took it to be a soaring bird, but the movement and proportions were all wrong. It was, instead, a person seated on a carpet.

He was reminded of the magical carpets of Calim-shan. He'd once been hired to repair one—though it had turned out to have a more deadly purpose than flying. As the person on the carpet drew closer, Arvin rendered himself invisible and created an illusionary image of himself sitting cross-legged on the stone head. Ectoplasm shimmered on the stone then swiftly evaporated in the heat. He toyed with the ring on his finger—he was counting on it to hide his thoughts from any probe the seed might do of the general area around the stone head—and watched as the flying carpet approached. As soon as it was close enough for its passenger to manifest a power against him, Arvin threw up a psionic shield.

On the carpet sat a yuan-ti, not Dmetrio, but a female. She was dressed as the Se'sehen had been, in a cape—hers made of overlapping "scales" of turquoise feathers—and a clinging, gauzy tunic that ended just below her waist, where her snake tail began. Both her skin and her scales were a dark brown. A band of gold encircled her left wrist, and a round plug of jade as wide as Arvin's thumb pierced the skin between her lower lip and chin. Instead of hair, a ruff of scales framed her face.

Wary that she might be yet another of Zelia's seeds— or the Dmetrio-seed itself, cloaked in illusion—Arvin probed her mind as soon as she was within range. To his surprise, he encountered no resistance. If she saw the silver that sparkled out of thin air when he manifested the power, she gave no sign.

She studied the illusion, mentally comparing it to the description Hlondeth's prince had given her. She was surprised by how human Arvin looked. Dmetrio had led her to believe the person she'd been sent to fetch was a halfblood.

She spoke. Arvin, inside her mind, understood the words, even though they were spoken in Draconic.

She asked if he was the one she'd been sent to fetch. He made the illusion nod.

Meanwhile, he probed deeper. The yuan-ti's name was Hrishniss, and she was a noble of House Jennestaa. She was one of those who had greeted Dmetrio when the prince had come to her tribe nearly six months before on a highly secret mission from Hlondeth. House Extaminos was poised to turn against its former allies, and assisted by the Jennestaa and Eselemaa, it would conquer the Se'sehen in a surprise attack.

She obviously had no idea what was going on in Hlondeth.

Hrishniss had no psionic powers, no clerical spells, also no attack or defense forms, aside from those native to the yuan-ti race. She had come alone and knew nothing about Arvin save that she was to fetch him back to Ss'yin, the ruined city he'd spotted in the distance. Her thoughts gave Arvin the city's full name—Ss'yin'tia'saminass—a word Arvin knew he'd never have a hope of pronouncing without a serpent's forked tongue.

Arvin's attempt to lure the Dmetrio-seed to him had failed. It looked as though Arvin would have to go to the seed instead—to place his head inside the serpent's mouth, so to speak.

Still wary but seeing no reason why he should continue to hide, Arvin ended the illusion and allowed himself to become visible. Hrishniss blinked but otherwise didn't react. Yuan-ti didn't startle easily, and she was no exception. She hissed something at him—an invitation for him to climb onto the carpet with her.

Arvin took a closer look at it. The "carpet" was a section of shed snakeskin with dozens of wings from the tiny flying snakes sewn into its hem. The translucent skin looked fragile, as if it would tear if too much weight were placed upon it. He climbed onto it—the skin gave slightly but seemed strong enough—and seated himself facing the yuan-ti. She turned her back to him and stared to the west, and the carpet moved in that direction.

As they flew toward the ruined city, Arvin wondered what was going on. It wasn't like Zelia to delegate a task, especially one as important as retrieving someone who claimed to have half of the Circled Serpent. She didn't trust anyone but her seeds—if indeed she trusted them. Arvin worried that Hrishniss might be part of some elaborate scheme but couldn't for the life of him figure out what it might be.

With a growing sense of unease, he rode the carpet toward Ss'yin.

❧ ❧ ❧ ❧ ❧

The ruined city was even larger than Arvin expected—three times the size of Hlondeth at least. It stretched through the jungle for a vast distance. Tree-covered mounds that had once been buildings gave the jungle canopy a bumpy appearance. Here and there Arvin could see the jagged remains of a partially collapsed arch or viaduct rising above the treetops. Circular patches of lighter-colored vegetation marked the spots where plazas had once been. In the center of some of these were the lower coils of enormous serpent sculptures.

The setting sun filled the spaces between the ruins with ominous shadows. Dozens of yuan-ti slithered and strode those shadows.

As the carpet descended, a depression in the ground caught Arvin's eye—it looked like the remains of an enormous cistern. The rim of it was lined with hundreds of needle-like spikes that faced inward and down. It looked as though there were people inside it, and as the carpet passed over the cistern, Arvin got a better look. He was stunned to see a dozen halflings in ragged clothing, huddled in a group. One was smaller than the rest, probably a child. Two of them looked up listlessly as the carpet flew overhead. The rest stared at the floor.

Arvin once again manifested the power that would allow him to read Hrishniss's thoughts, then tapped the yuan-ti on the shoulder and pointed down. She spoke in her own language, but Arvin heard the words as they formed in her mind just before each was spoken.

"Monkey-men," she said. "Soon to join the other slaves, once we have altered them."

The word she'd used—"altered"—had several other meanings rolled into one. It was also the word for "improved" and "magically changed," and strangely enough, the word for "fed"—specifically, for feeding a liquid to someone.

With a growing horror, Arvin realized what Hrishniss meant. The halflings below were going to suffer a similar fate to his friend Naulg. They would be fed a potion that would transform them into lizard creatures, just like the half-lizard Arvin had spotted in the plaza.

Arvin swallowed down the bile rising in his throat. His best chance at doing anything for the wretches below lay in feigning indifference. He stared back at Hrishniss, his face impassive, and nodded his approval.

They landed, as the sun was setting, in the deep shadow of a pyramid. It was shaped like a coiled serpent but was missing its head—this lay in the jungle nearby, blank eyes peering out of an overgrowth of vines. The broken neck was hollow. The serpent's mouth must have been the pyramid's original entrance.

As Hrishniss and Arvin stepped off the carpet, one of the half-lizards scuttled out of the shadows to retrieve it—a female with dull brown hair that had fallen out on the left side of her head to be replaced by scales. She smelled as if she had not bathed in several tendays and her clothes hung in rags. There were twin punctures in her left arm—bite marks—each surrounded by a nasty looking patch of red. Her eyes had a tortured, half-mad look that reminded Arvin of the way Naulg had looked just before he died.

Hrishniss hissed an order. The half-lizard flinched.

Arvin balled his fists. He exhaled, long and slow, breathing out his anger. He couldn't offer the transformed halfling so much as a sympathetic glance. He turned away and followed Hrishniss up the pyramid.

They entered the neck of the snake and descended through the pyramid's spiraling interior. For several circuits, they moved through darkness. Arvin had to listen for the sound of Hrishniss' footsteps as her feet slid along the stone. He walked with one hand brushing the wall, sliding his own feet forward to feel out any debris or sudden gaps, but he didn't encounter any. Despite the great age of the pyramid, its interior was clean and smooth.

The spiraling corridor lightened, and a yellow light flickered up ahead. The air felt drier. Arvin could smell sweet-scented smoke. Rounding the last bend, they entered a circular room illuminated by a enormous metal brazier, filled with oil, that occupied the center of the room. Yellow flames rippled across its surface, occasionally crackling as one of the chunks of resin floating on the surface burst into flame. Shadows danced on the walls, which were pierced around the circumference of the room with eight circular tunnels, including the one Hrishniss and Arvin had just emerged from. Each had been carved to resemble the open mouth of a serpent, and was framed by elongated, stylized fangs that stretched from roof to floor like curved pillars.

Inside one of those tunnels—the one directly opposite where Arvin stood—the Dmetrio-seed lounged, naked. His back was against one wall, his feet propped up on the other. His tongue flickered in and out of his mouth as he stared up at Arvin through the brazier's dancing flames. One hand made a lazy gesture.

"Leave us," he hissed.

Hrishniss bowed then backed out of the chamber.

Something tickled Arvin's forehead: his lapis lazuli, warning him that someone was using detection magic. Someone was scrying him.

There was nothing he could do about that now. Ignoring the tingling, he mentally braced himself. He stared at the Dmetrio-seed, ready for the psionic attack he was certain was coming, one thread of his awareness deep in his *muladhara*, touching the energy it contained. Worried that the burning oil might contain *osssra*, he breathed as shallowly as he could. He felt clear-headed, however. Sharp. Ready. He had defeated one of Zelia's mind seeds already, and he would match another, blow for blow, and beat it down, too—but not until he absolutely had to. For the time being, he'd play the game, pretending he didn't know it was Zelia.

The Dmetrio-seed rose to his feet and moved toward Arvin. The body might be male, but the swaying walk was feminine, seductive. Arvin wondered if the seed realized he was doing it. Arvin kept his eyes firmly on the Dmetrio-seed's face, deliberately not looking down at the spot in the yuan-ti's groin where his genitals were hidden.

"Lord Extaminos," Arvin said, bowing.

"Arvin." The answer was in a higher, softer tone than Dmetrio had used. "Zelia told me to expect you. Did you bring it?"

"No," Arvin said. "It's hidden. When the time comes, I'll go get it."

He felt a finger-light tickle touch his mind and heard the tinkling of Zelia's secondary display. A surge of magical energy tingled up his arm from Karrell's ring, sweeping away the seed's attempt to read Arvin's thoughts. Arvin drew energy up through his navel, into his forehead, preparing to manifest a defense against whatever the seed hurled at him next.

The Dmetrio-seed merely smiled.

Sweat trickled down Arvin's temples. This was unlike Zelia. He had to know what was going on. Taking a big risk, he redirected the energy that swirled around his navel and third eye into the base of his scalp instead. The Dmetrio-seed frowned slightly and turned his head, as if a distant sound had caught his attention.

Then, amazingly, Arvin was in.

It was Zelia's mind, all right. She stared at Arvin with tightly controlled loathing. He was a human—a member of a lesser race. An insect. Like an annoying gnat, he kept coming back to pester her over and over again. She ached to manifest a catapsi and watch his psionic energies bleed from him, then kill him. Slowly. For the moment, he was a gnat she dared not swat, not after all of the work the original Zelia had done to set things up. Of course Arvin hadn't been foolish enough to bring the other half of the Circled Serpent with him; Juz'la had said to expect that. Juz'la would worm the secret of where it was hidden out of Arvin. Yes, the seed would leave that to her.

Arvin blinked. Who was Juz'la? Whoever she was, the Dmetrio-seed was deferring to her like a subordinate. Arvin was shocked to hear even a seed of Zelia admitting that someone else was more powerful and capable. It was inconceivable.

He dug deeper and was surprised at the ease with which he read the Dmetrio-seed's thoughts. It was as if he were walking a well-worn path. The seed offered no resistance. Was he playing some sort of game—one that involved luring Arvin deeper into his mind? Arvin pushed on warily.

In a matter of moments, he had learned where the Dmetrio-seed had hidden the lower half of the Circled Serpent: inside a ceramic statue of Sseth that had been part of the tribute he had presented to the Jennestaa upon his arrival at Ss'yin, a statue that now sat in a place of honor on one of their altars. Bound up with that information was a much more recent memory—from five nights before—of the Dmetrio-seed bragging to Juz'la, over a glass of wine, how clever the hiding place was. No yuan-ti would dare smash open a statue of the god.

Arvin frowned. Juz'la again.

He found a picture of her in the Dmetrio-seed's memories: a dark-skinned yuan-ti woman with a bald head covered in orange and yellow snake scales that dipped down onto her forehead in a widow's peak. The image was nested amid a memory of the Dmetrio-seed seducing Juz'la. Memories of that seduction drifted to the surface of the seed's thoughts: Juz'la straddling the seed, naked, her muscular body glistening with acidic sweat, an indifferent look on her face. Skirting those images—which were fuzzy and incomplete, like the memories of a drunken man— Arvin explored the connection between the two. Zelia and Juz'la were old friends. They had known each other, long ago, in the city of Skullport.

The Dmetrio-seed had been surprised to learn that Juz'la had left Skullport, but he'd accepted Juz'la's explanation of needing to leave the city quickly, something about having run afoul of a slaver there. As for how Juz'la had wound up in the Black Jungles, that was simple. She had taken passage on a ship that had sailed through one of Skullport's many portals—one that led to the Lapal Sea—then made her way west. The seed thought it odd that Juz'la had wound up here in Ss'yin shortly after he did, but life was like that—people's lives entwined in the strangest of ways.

Stranger still was the fact that Juz'la, once human, now appeared to be yuan-ti. That part, too, Juz'la had explained. She'd drunk a potion, one that had transformed her into a yuan-ti. It was something she'd always wanted. Venom is power, she'd said.

All of this had the ring of truth—or at least, the truth as the Dmetrio-seed believed it to be. Something still didn't sit right, however. Zelia never accepted stories at face value, and one of her seeds would *never* look up to a human—even one who had since been transformed into a yuan-ti—with the kind of admiration and respect, even awe, that Arvin heard echoing through the seed's thoughts.

The Dmetrio-seed stared idly at the flaming oil—again, a most uncharacteristic behavior for one of Zelia's seeds. "Beautiful, isn't it?" he hissed. "Just like a slitherglow."

Arvin looked around, pretending to study the chamber. "This city must be ancient," he said, stalling as he tried to think what to do next.

"It was built centuries ago," the seed answered, "at the height of the Serpentes Empire."

"It's very remote."

"Yes."

"Why did you come here?" Arvin asked. He already knew the answer, but he wanted to hear what the seed thought about Dmetrio's mission.

"To forge an alliance," the seed answered. "House Se'sehen has turned its back on House Extaminos. We need new allies in the south."

That much was the truth. Dmetrio—the real Dmetrio, before Zelia had seeded him—had been ordered south by Lady Dediana on a secret mission to build up the Jennestaa forces in preparation for an attack on the Se'sehen. That, it was hoped, would draw Sibyl south. If all went well, Sibyl would be killed in the resulting battle, thus removing the thorn that had festered in Hlondeth's side those past two years. With Sibyl dead, Dmetrio could claim her half of the Circled Serpent, use it to free his god, and become Sseth's avatar.

Zelia, of course, had no intention of letting this happen, nor did she intend to let her seed become an avatar—that much was clear in the seed's thoughts. The Dmetrio-seed had been given strict orders to get the second half of the Circled Serpent from Arvin, kill him, and hand both halves over to Zelia.

The seed, of course, had his own thoughts on that matter. The idea of becoming Sseth's avatar—of gaining powers far beyond those the original Zelia possessed—was a tempting one, but also one that gave the seed pause. Zelia was a more powerful psion and a dangerous woman to cross. Seeds who had attempted betrayal before had all met a swift death.

Arvin pressed deeper. Had the Dmetrio-seed learned where the door was? Arvin couldn't find it anywhere in the seed's thoughts. That was disappointing, but there was still more to be learned. Whether the seed had told Zelia that Arvin had contacted him, for example.

"Was that why the Se'sehen attacked Hlondeth?" Arvin continued. "Because of the new alliance?"

The Dmetrio-seed blinked. He'd had no idea Hlondeth was under attack.

"You didn't know?" Arvin continued, even though he'd already heard the answer in the Dmetrio-seed's thoughts. "Zelia didn't tell you?"

The seed, he learned, hadn't been in touch with Zelia since receiving the message that Arvin would get in touch with him soon. The seed had wanted to alert Zelia to the fact that Arvin had just contacted him with a sending—that Arvin had the other half of the Circled Serpent—but Juz'la had advised against it. Amazingly, the seed had acquiesced.

"When did this attack take place?" the Dmetrio-seed asked.

"Two days ago."

The seed hissed. An attack on Hlondeth, he was thinking, might mean an attack on Ss'yin was imminent. The Jennestaa had been working hard to create an army, but they were nowhere near ready yet. After a moment, however, his agitation eased. He'd ask Juz'la for advice; she'd know what to do.

"War makes odd bedfellows," Arvin prompted, hoping to hear more about Juz'la.

The Dmetrio-seed didn't take the bait. His lips quirked into a smile. "That it does. The Jennestaa are wild and uncivilized—they find beauty in the power of the jungle to break apart even the largest stone. They'd like to see every city laid waste and reclaimed by the jungle."

"Even Hlondeth?"

The Dmetrio-seed touched Arvin's arm, drew him closer. "Even Hlondeth," he breathed in Arvin's ear. "Fortunately, they'll never get that far."

Arvin started to draw away—then stopped, as he smelled a faint but unmistakable odor. A perfume-sweet scent, overlaid with wine.

Hassaael.

That was what was muddying the Dmetrio-seed's thoughts and making Zelia as passive as a slurring drunk. Like the Talassan on Mount Ugruth, she had fallen entirely under the sway of whoever had fed her *hassaael*.

Arvin could guess who that was.

Juz'la.

It all fit. Juz'la had run afoul of a yuan-ti slaver in Skullport, and she'd drunk a magic potion that transformed her—a potion that sounded hauntingly familiar to the one the Pox had used to transform Naulg. That potion had come from a slaver named Ssarm, a man who was also a supplier of *hassaael* to Sibyl's minions.

Juz'la was one of them, a minion powerful enough to have conquered Zelia—or rather, one of Zelia's mind seeds. Zelia, Arvin was certain, didn't know that yet. She'd noticed the "dulling" of her seed's mind but had put it down to his *osssra* use.

A slithering footstep drew Arvin's attention to one of the tunnels. He glanced up in time to see Juz'la step into the chamber. She held a wine glass made of delicate green crystal in her hand.

"Ah," she hissed. "Our guest has arrived." She held the glass out to Arvin. "You must be thirsty after your journey. Here, drink."

CHAPTER 8

Thank you," Arvin said, taking the wine glass.
He pretended not to notice the twin puncture
marks on the inside of Juz'la's wrist. "I am
indeed thirsty. This is the hottest place I've
ever been."

He swept the improvised turban off his
head and mopped his brow with it, then pretended to stuff it into his pocket. When he
removed his hand, the fabric was inside his
sleeve. He transferred the glass to this hand
and raised it to his lips. He was tempted
to manifest a distraction but was wary of
alerting Juz'la with a secondary display. If
she'd associated with Zelia in the past, she'd
certainly know all about psions. He'd already
noted the glance she'd given the crystal that
hung at his neck.

The Dmetrio-seed stood slightly behind Juz'la. Arvin glanced in his direction and gave his head the slightest of shakes—just enough so Juz'la would notice. As he'd hoped, she glanced behind her to see what the seed was up to. Arvin used the opportunity to turn slightly to the right, to screen what he was doing from the seed, and tip the wine down his sleeve. The fabric inside it soaked it up, and any that bled through to his shirt would blend in with the sweat that already dampened it. He allowed the dregs of the wine to wet his tightly closed lips. As Juz'la turned back toward him, frowning, he wiped his mouth with the back of his free hand. If she saw any wine stains on his sleeve, she'd likely attribute them to that; few people could remember which hand, exactly, had been used in such a casual gesture.

"Unusual taste," he commented.

Juz'la glanced at the burning oil—probably making sure he hadn't poured the wine into it—and smiled. Her eye teeth were slender and curved, like a snake's. Scales covered her hairless scalp, her neck, and her arms, which were quite muscular. She wore a tight-fitting dress of a gauzy material that did nothing to hide her breasts or the darker patch of scales at her groin. If she'd been fed the same potion that Naulg had, it had left her mind remarkably unscathed; her eyes shone with a keen intelligence.

A black bracelet encircled her left wrist. Only when it lifted its head did Arvin realize it was a tiny viper. Juz'la lifted it to her lips and kissed it, then whispered an endearment to it as the tiny serpent twined around her fingers.

"Who are you?" Arvin asked, putting just a hint of suspicion into his voice.

"An old friend of Dmetrio's."

Arvin gave a mental nod. Juz'la was keeping up the pretense that Dmetrio was still himself. The

Dmetrio-seed himself probably hadn't realized that Arvin knew his secret.

"What's your part in this?" Arvin continued.

"The same as yours. To help Dmetrio accomplish his goal."

"I see."

Arvin glanced at the seed, who followed their conversation with a passive look on his face. He wondered how much Sibyl's spy had been able to glean from the seed. "Dmetrio" would have all of Zelia's memories up to the time the seed was planted; if Juz'la had been rifling through those, she might know as much about Arvin as Zelia did. Presumably, she'd lifted more recent information from the seed, as well. Arvin had to assume Juz'la knew about the deal he'd struck with Zelia, and about Karrell. She would know that Karrell served Ubtao, a god that was Sseth's enemy, and that Karrell was in Smaragd.

Arvin was suddenly very glad that Sseth's worshipers were no longer in communication with their god.

"Where have you hidden the Circled Serpent?" Juz'la asked.

Arvin was surprised by the blunt demand. It had obviously been intended to startle. Juz'la whispered something to her viper again as she played with it, disguising the words and gestures of a spell. Arvin felt energy flow up his arm: Karrell's ring, blocking what must have been an attempt to listen in on his thoughts.

He manifested a power of his own. If she heard its secondary display, she might think it was because he was blocking her spell. His attempt to charm her, however, was met by a force that pushed his awareness back so hard it made his head ache. Either Juz'la had an amazingly strong mind, or magic shielded her.

"How about this," Arvin said, meeting her gaze with a challenging look. "You show me your half of the Circled Serpent, and I'll show you mine."

If Juz'la was disappointed by her spell's lack of success, she didn't show it. "You've made a mistake," she said. "It's not me you need to bargain with. I'm only Dmetrio's ... assistant."

The Dmetrio-seed stepped forward. "I realize you don't trust me, Arvin," he hissed. "You're no more likely to hand me your half than I am to give you mine. Juz'la is our compromise. When the time comes to open the door, she can put the two halves together and wield the key."

Arvin wondered how much the *hassaael* would have affected him had he drunk it. It was probably safe to express a few lingering doubts. He glanced at Juz'la.

"Why should I trust *her*? We've only just met."

The Dmetrio-seed smiled—a slight upturn of the lips that was all Zelia. "Talk to her," he suggested. "Get to know her. Then decide." The smile widened. "Take your time. From what Zelia told me, I'm sure Karrell can wait."

Hissing with laughter, the Dmetrio-seed transformed into a serpent and slithered from the chamber.

Juz'la turned to Arvin. "Hungry?"

Arvin quickly considered whether Juz'la might drug any food he was served then decided that she probably wouldn't bother after having plied him with *hassaael*. Besides, he needed to show that he was starting to trust her.

"Famished," he answered. "I haven't eaten since yesterday."

Juz'la smiled. She turned and hissed something; a moment later, one of the mutated halflings—a male—carried in a platter bearing a selection of bright orange and green fruits. The half-lizard had a stubby tail and a scattering of yellow scales across his face, back, and chest. Four horns that looked as if they had only recently budded rose from his forehead, and his elbows and knees were scabbed over with what looked like fresh scales. He walked erect, however, still more halfling than lizard.

Kneeling, the half-lizard placed the platter on the floor. He started to back out of the chamber on his knees, but Juz'la flicked a hand at him.

"No need for that, Porvar," she said.

The half-lizard hesitated.

Arvin hid his frown just in time. Juz'la's attempt to show him that she treated the slaves well was failing miserably.

"You may go," she hissed.

Porvar turned and scurried away.

Juz'la indicated the platter with a wave of her hand. "Please eat," she said.

Arvin did. The fruit was thirst-quenching and tasted sweeter than any he'd eaten before. He licked the juice from his fingers.

Juz'la watched him in silence. Then, abruptly, she spoke. "Dmetrio told me about the bargain you struck with him," she said. "You want to enter Smaragd to rescue your woman—Karrell."

"Yes," Arvin said.

Juz'la gave him a conspiratorial smile. "You don't need Dmetrio for that."

Arvin played along. "Yes, I do. He has half of the Circled Serpent, remember?"

Juz'la gave him an unblinking stare. "So what? I know where it is."

"Ah," Arvin said, stroking his chin thoughtfully. "I see how it is, now." He used the gesture to hide his breath, which should have smelled strongly of the drug. His back was against the dish of flaming oil. Pretending its heat made him uncomfortable, he stepped away from it, putting more distance between himself and Juz'la. "Why betray Dmetrio?" he asked her. "What's in it for you?"

"It's not Dmetrio I'm betraying. It's Zelia."

Despite his years of hiding his reactions from the guild, that one made Arvin blink. "I don't understand."

"Yes, you do. You know who Dmetrio really is—why do you think I left you alone with him so long? I know about your powers. You can listen in on other people's thoughts, sift through their memories." She held up a hand when he started to protest. "You tried to do that with me a few moments ago."

Arvin shook his head. "I merely—"

"Here's what you would have learned, had you been able to probe my mind, as well," Juz'la continued. "I discovered, shortly after my arrival in Ss'yin, that Dmetrio is one of Zelia's seeds, and I decided to take my revenge upon her by thwarting whatever the seed hoped to accomplish."

"Revenge for what?" Arvin asked.

"Years ago, Zelia and I both worked for the Hall of Mental Splendor in Skullport, an organization similar to a rogues' guild that offered spies for hire. We became ... friends.

"A few years ago, I was assigned the task of gathering information on one of Skullport's slavers, a man named Ssarm. Around the time of that assignment, Zelia announced that she was leaving Skullport. She told me she was setting out on her own—she'd just learned how to plant mind seeds, and meant to build up an organization similar to the Hall—but there was more to her departure than that.

"The day after Zelia left, Ssarm learned I'd been selling his secrets. To say that he was furious about this would be an understatement. He ... punished me."

For several moments, her eyes shone with a fierce hatred. Then she smiled. "I know what you're thinking—

even without my spells. Ssarm is Sibyl's man, but no, I'm not one of the abomination's followers."

For a heartbeat or two, Arvin actually believed her. Juz'la was that good. A strand of truth ran through everything she'd just said, but the end of the braid was frayed in two places.

Back at the portal, Pakal had said that the Dmetrio-seed had been in contact with Karrell's organization, the *K'aaxlaat*. Juz'la must have known this. If all she wanted to do was thwart Sibyl's plans, she could have handed the Dmetrio-seed's half of the Circled Serpent over to them for eventual destruction.

Zelia couldn't have been the one who betrayed Juz'la to Ssarm. Zelia had only heard the slaver's name for the first time a year before, when Arvin told it to her. Juz'la was faking her vengeful anger.

All of the threads came neatly together in a tight knot, however, if Juz'la was working for Sibyl.

Juz'la stared with unblinking eyes at Arvin as he considered his answer. Once again, Arvin was glad that Karrell's ring was on his finger.

"It sounds like we have a mutual enemy," Arvin said at last.

Juz'la smiled like a snake that had just swallowed a mouse. "Zelia's seed was wary of me, at first," she continued, "but she was also arrogant—and just as blinded by vanity as Zelia herself. The seed thought I was fooled by the body it wore. When I cast my domination spell, she never even noticed."

Arvin knew exactly what Juz'la was up to by claiming to have used a spell on the seed: trying to provide an explanation for the effects of the *hassaael*. He resisted the urge to touch the crystal at his neck. Tymora herself must have placed Thessania, the false storm-mistress, in his path. If she hadn't, he'd never have known what *hassaael* was. He pretended to scowl.

"Don't try that on me," he warned. "My psionics—"

"Are a match for my sorcery, I'm sure," Juz'la said. A flicker of forked tongue appeared between her teeth as she laughed. Then her smile was gone. "Here's what I propose. Go and get your half from wherever you've hidden it. Contact me with a sending, and I'll tell you where the door to Smaragd is. I'll steal Zelia's half and meet you there." She paused, measuring him with her eyes. "Agreed?"

Arvin stared back at her, pretending to consider the offer. According to the Dmetrio-seed's memories, it had been five nights since Juz'la had learned where "Dmetrio's" half of the Circled Serpent was— two full days before Arvin and Pakal had snuck into Sibyl's lair and stolen her half of the Circled Serpent. If Sibyl had known where the door was, she would have opened it during the time that both halves were in her possession, but she hadn't known where it was. *That* was what her dreaming minions had been searching for: the location of the door. They hoped their god would tell them.

It also explained why the Dmetrio-seed hadn't been killed already. Sibyl had probably hoped that Zelia would learn the door's location and relay it to her seed, allowing Juz'la to intercept the information.

There was the slim possibility, however, that Sibyl had learned the door's location in the two days since Arvin and Pakal had stolen her half of the Circled Serpent, and—an even slimmer possibility—that she had told Juz'la where it was. Before he killed Juz'la, Arvin needed to rule that out.

"Agreed," Arvin lied. "I'll go and get my half at once."

Juz'la gave a satisfied hiss and stroked the head of her viper. "Excellent. I'll summon Hrishniss. She can fly you back to wherever—"

Arvin didn't give her a chance to finish. Silver flashed from his forehead as he hurled a stream of ectoplasm at her. It struck exactly where he'd intended: the hand that was stroking the viper. Strands of shimmering ectoplasm wound themselves around both her hand and face, immobilizing and gagging her, and preventing her from casting any spells. As he cinched them tight, Arvin manifested a mental shield between them. If Juz'la used her magical fear on him, the shield would deflect at least part of it.

He drew his dagger and spoke over the droning of his secondary display. "If you want to live," he threatened, "you're going to answer some quest—"

Juz'la was no longer standing in front of him. She'd transformed into an orange-and-yellow snake and fallen to the floor. The entangling ectoplasm, loosened, lay in a heap, together with her dress. Juz'la stared out from its folds and hissed something at him in Draconic. Then she flicked her tail.

The ice-white ray that shot from it streaked through Arvin's shield, striking his dagger hand. Frost blossomed on the blade and his hand went numb. He tried to release the dagger but his fingers wouldn't unbend. At least she'd used a spell that wasn't fatal. She needed him alive as much as he did her.

Arvin drew more ectoplasm from the Astral Plane and shaped it into a construct. Still half-formed, it lunged forward, seizing Juz'la by the neck and tail. Her eyes bulged as it squeezed. Her serpent body writhed furiously, but she couldn't slither free.

"Release me," Juz'la hissed.

Deep inside his mind, Arvin heard a groan as his mental shield intercepted whatever spell she had cast at him; it nearly buckled under the strain. With a thought, he directed the construct to clamp its hand over Juz'la's mouth, gagging her.

"Where is the door?" Arvin asked.

He let the shield dissipate and transferred his energy to a different power point. Silver sparkled from his forehead as he slipped inside Juz'la's thoughts. She put up a good fight—getting inside felt like battering down a stone wall with his forehead—but the instant he was in, he had his answer. She didn't know where the door was, and she was, indeed, Sibyl's minion.

Arvin heard a hiss. The construct, neglected by Arvin for those few moments, must have allowed its grip to loosen. Juz'la spat out the words of a spell and touched it with her tail. Electricity flashed through the astral construct in jagged streaks. It exploded into a mist of ectoplasm.

Juz'la, freed, fell to the floor.

Arvin hurled his dagger, but the metal of the hilt guard stuck to his skin, tearing it and throwing his aim off. The dagger missed, burying itself in the heaped-up dress next to her.

Juz'la's tail flicked forward. A second lightning bolt crackled out of it, striking Arvin square in the chest. The smell of burning flesh filled his nostrils as every muscle in his body wrenched into a painful cramp. His heart faltered and his vision swam with jagged streaks of light. He sagged to his knees. Only by force of will was he able to prevent himself from blacking out.

"If you kill me," he croaked, "you'll never get the other half."

He heard a hiss of laughter. "Corpses can be made to talk."

She was bluffing. She had to be. Otherwise she'd have killed him when they first met. Full mobility had already returned to his fingers, though they felt as though they were on fire. Beside him, he could hear the crackling of incense in the burning oil. With an effort, he lifted his head, stared at Juz'la. She was still in serpent form.

"Tell me where it is," she hissed, "and I'll spare you."

Arvin felt a spell slither into his mind. He wanted to live. He *needed* to live; he was Karrell's only hope. He heard those thoughts aloud at the same time he thought them—but in a woman's voice. Karrell's?

"It's in a cave," he whispered. "In a bluff where the river bends. Where the flying snakes nest."

Equally strangely, he was calm when he said it. As if it didn't matter at all that he had just revealed the hiding place of the one thing that would allow him to save Karrell.

He heard a hiss of triumph. Then something stung his hand. Glancing down, he saw Juz'la's tiny black viper and twin specks of red on the back of his left hand. He'd been bitten.

The shock of it snapped him out of the spell Juz'la had snared him with. "No!" he roared.

Lunging to his feet, he slammed a shoulder into the brazier. It crashed to the floor, sending a wave of flaming oil racing toward Juz'la. She screamed as it engulfed her and shifted back into her yuan-ti form, but sticky smears of melted resin remained stuck to her, burning her skin. From head to foot, her body was a mass of seared red flesh. The burning oil, spread thinly across the floor and wicking into Juz'la's abandoned dress, illuminated her from below, throwing ghastly shadows across her face.

Arvin summoned his dagger and it flew out of the burning dress toward him. Catching it by the point, he hurled it at Juz'la. The blade buried itself in her throat. She fell to the floor, dead. The smell of burned flesh lingered in the air.

Arvin glanced down, found the viper, which was trying to slither away, and slammed a heel onto it. The tiny serpent died with a satisfying crunch.

It was cold comfort, however; Arvin could feel the viper's poison taking hold of his body. His left hand was already swelling; Karrell's ring was a tight, painful band around his little finger. He felt dizzy and weak; his heartbeat light and fast. He leaned over and vomited; it splattered onto his boots. He stared at it, shivering.

So this is how I die, he thought. Of a snake bite? After everything I've been through . . .

"I'm sorry, Karrell," he said aloud.

"Master?"

Arvin looked up. The half-lizard who had brought them the platter of fruit stood in one of the tunnels, staring at him, uncertain. He glanced at Juz'la, who lay face-down amid the burning oil. The scales on her head blackened and curled from the heat, peeling from her scalp like dry skin. Smoke thickened the air, making Arvin cough.

Arvin had stopped being ill, and his stomach started to uncramp. His hand still felt like all of the demons of the Abyss were tormenting it, but his heartbeat was slowing, becoming more steady. Amazed, he shook his head.

Maybe he would live.

"There's been . . ." he glanced at Juz'la, saw that the dagger that had taken her in the throat was hidden by the way her body had fallen.

"An accident," he concluded. He held up his grossly swollen hand. "Juz'la's viper bit me. I bumped into the brazier, and it toppled. The oil spilled out, and Juz'la was burned."

Realizing he should feign some concern, he moved to where Juz'la lay. The sudden motion, combined with his dizziness, made him reel. He turned the motion into a less-than-graceful squat, ignoring the tiny flames that licked at his boots, and pretended to be feeling for a pulse. As he did, he slipped the dagger up his sleeve. It was a clumsy palming, but if the half-lizard noticed anything, he made no comment.

"She's dead," Arvin concluded.

He started to stand, then noticed something that lay beside the body in the flaming oil: a tiny vial that must have been secreted somewhere inside Juz'la's dress. The dark liquid inside it bubbled from the heat, the cork that sealed the vial starting to char. Arvin picked up the vial before it burst and he blew on it, trying to cool it.

The half-lizard puffed out his throat, clearly agitated. He shifted uneasily on bowed legs, looking as though he'd like nothing better than to scurry away. "Master," he croaked. "What—"

Arvin stood, fought off another wave of dizziness. He stared down at the half-lizard. "Your name's Porvar, isn't it?" he asked.

The half-lizard nodded. There was fear in his eyes but also intelligence. He wasn't as far gone as the slave who had met Arvin upon his arrival.

Arvin smiled and manifested a charm. "I'd like to help you, Porvar."

The half-lizard blinked rapidly. His posture became a little less subservient.

"The Jennestaa forced you to drink a potion, didn't they?"

The half-lizard's throat puffed out in alarm.

"A good friend of mine was forced to drink a similar potion," Arvin said.

Porvar looked doubtful.

"It's all right," Arvin assured him. "You can trust me. I'm not yuan-ti. I'm human."

Porvar glanced down at Arvin's swollen hand. The flesh around the punctures was purple. "When vipers bite, humans die."

"Not this human," Arvin assured him, and it was true.

The dizziness ebbed, leaving him more certain on his feet. His left hand was in agony, though. He tried to flex his fingers and nearly cried out from the pain.

"There's a statue," Arvin said. "Dmetrio Extaminos brought it with him when he came to Ss'yin'tia'saminass. Take me to it, and I'll help you escape."

The half-lizard laughed. "Where to? The jungle extends to the horizon."

"Better free in the jungle than a slave here," Arvin countered.

The half-lizard blinked. Once. Twice. "Why do you want the statue?"

Arvin smiled. "I plan on smashing it."

The half-lizard considered this. "And the others?" he asked.

"There's more than one statue?" Arvin asked.

Porvar shook his head. "The ones in the pit. The halfings who are still ... whole. Will you help them, too?"

"I'll do what I can," Arvin promised.

Porvar's lips twitched. He turned. "Come. I will show you where Juz'la moved it to."

The corridor was only chest-high; Arvin had to walk bent over to follow. While the half-lizard's back was turned, he shook the dagger out of his sleeve and sheathed it and placed the vial in a pocket. Then he looped the wine-soaked cloth around his neck as an improvised sling for his swollen hand. He wished, belatedly, that he'd gotten Tanju to teach him one of the powers that stabilized and helped heal the body. Instead, he'd focused, those past six months, on powers he thought he might need in his battle with Sibyl. He hadn't expected to live long enough to require healing.

It soon became too dark to see, so Arvin followed Porvar with one hand on the half-lizard's shoulder.

The corridor they followed ran in sinuous curves for some distance, and Arvin was certain they were no longer under the pyramid. Every so often, they passed through another of the circular, multi-exited chambers. Most of them were filled with rubble, Arvin discovered after painfully stubbing his toe on a piece of broken stone.

Eventually, they drew near an illuminated chamber filled with yuan-ti. Arvin let go of Porvar and assumed a sliding, more fluid gait. He filled the minds of the yuan-ti with the illusion of scales on his body and slit-pupiled eyes. He wet his lips with his tongue, adding a serpent's forked flicker. Porvar glanced back at him, perhaps wondering why Arvin shuffled his feet, but the illusion wasn't directed at the half-lizard's mind. Arvin gave him an encouraging nod and gestured for him to lead on.

Soon Arvin smelled earth and mold and saw a dim light up ahead. Porvar halted a few moments later at the entrance to an enormous circular chamber. Easily fifty paces across, it was illuminated by moonlight that shone in through a portion of the ceiling that had collapsed. The moldy smell probably came from the rotted timbers that had tumbled into the room. Vines trailed in through the hole, brushing the spot where they'd fallen. Arvin noted the leaves, shaped vaguely like human hands, and the berries that were clustered in bunches like grapes. Assassin vine.

The chamber was crowded with pieces of weathered statuary that had, presumably, been scavenged from the ruins above. Stone snake heads with jagged, broken necks lay here and there on the floor. Some were no larger than Arvin's own head; others were chest-high. All had once been painted in bright colors, but the paint was flaked from them like shedding skin. Empty eye sockets had probably once held gems.

There were also a number of broken slabs of squared-off stone: stelae, covered with inscriptions in Draconic. The chamber also included a more-or-less intact statue that Arvin recognized from Zelia's childhood memories: the World Serpent, progenitor of all the reptile races. Lizard folk, yuan-ti, nagas, and a host of other scaly folk stared up at her from below, paying the goddess homage. They stood on the bent backs of humans and other two-legged races who crouched, like slaves, in perpetual submission.

Sounds drifted down the corridor behind them. Somewhere in the distance, a yuan-ti voice shouted. That couldn't be good.

"Where is the statue Prince Dmetrio brought with him from Hlondeth?" Arvin asked.

Porvar pointed at the far side of the room. "There."

Arvin sighted along the pointing finger. The statue stood against the far wall. It was small, no more than knee-high, with a gray-green body and wings that were covered in gilt. Pale yellow gems glittered in its eye sockets: yellow sapphires. Its hands were raised above its head, forming the circle that symbolized birth. Sseth reborn—the perfect hiding place for the Circled Serpent.

Arvin took a step forward but Porvan caught his arm, preventing him from entering the chamber. He nodded at the vines that trailed in through the ceiling.

"Stranglevine," he whispered, as if afraid his voice might awaken it.

Arvin smiled. "I know. I've worked with the stuff often enough."

Silver sparkled from his forehead, lengthening into a long, thin rope. Quick as thought, it wound itself around the assassin vines, binding them together. The plant, sensing it was under attack, began writhing like a snake. Arvin wrapped the far end of the shimmering rope around one of the larger serpent heads, stretching the assassin vine as tight as a lyre string.

"Wait here," he told Porvar.

He jogged over to the statue. A quick glance noted a slight discoloration; a sniff told Arvin that it was contact poison. He slipped off his improvised sling, wound it around his good hand, and lifted the statue with that. He didn't feel or hear anything shifting inside the statue when he picked it up. That worried him—Juz'la might already have removed its contents, and if she'd hidden Dmetrio's half of the Circled Serpent somewhere else, he might never find it.

Fortunately there was an easy way to find out if there was anything inside. Raising the statue above his head, Arvin slammed it down onto the floor.

Out of the shattered remains fell the lower half of the Circled Serpent. It glinted silver in the moonlight, the tiny scales carved onto its surface made a netlike pattern on the gleaming metal.

Arvin closed his eyes and heaved a huge sigh of relief. He'd done it! Both halves were his. Now all he had to do was find the door.

One thing worried him, however. Dmetrio hadn't kept the lead-lined box the Circled Serpent had been found in, which meant that something else had been hiding it from divination magic. The gray-green glaze on the ceramic statue must have had lead in it—but Arvin had smashed the statue, so that protection was no longer in place.

Arvin wished he still had his magical glove; vanished inside it, the Circled Serpent would probably escape detection. Without it, all Sibyl had to do was cast a location spell to find it.

A rustling noise behind him warned him that the ectoplasm that bound the assassin vine was starting to fade. He renewed it with a fresh manifestation, tying several loops into the rope he bound it with. Then he scooped up the Circled Serpent and tucked it inside his shirt, using his sling to tie it in place. He turned and motioned Porvar forward.

"Come on," he said, placing a foot in the lowermost loop of his improvised ladder. "Let's get out of here."

The half-lizard glanced nervously at the vine.

Arvin nodded toward the corridor. The shouting he'd heard grew louder. "We may have been found out," he said. "Do you *really* want to go back the way we came?"

Porvar shook his head.

"Then climb," Arvin instructed. "Follow me."

The climb wasn't an easy one for Arvin, despite his magical bracelet. He could use only one hand, and Porvar, below him, kept jostling the rope. Halfway up, Arvin's feet slipped and he nearly fell. Feet flailing, he clung to the vine with his good hand, trying to twist himself back around. As his feet found the vine again, something tickled the small of his back—a tendril of assassin vine, worming its way up inside his shirt. Cursing, he fumbled at it with his injured hand, but the vine curled around his waist and spiraled its way up his body. Within heartbeats, it tightened around his throat. Arvin hooked his arm around the vine and tried to pull the tendril off with his good hand but couldn't get his fingers under it. He traded arms, hooking the left one around the rope, and reached for his knife. The tendril tightened.

The vine jerked as Porvar shifted below. Arvin tried to shout at him to back off but the vine had already cut off his breath. He felt hands grasping his ankles, then his legs—what was the half-lizard trying to do, climb past him and escape? He tried to kick Porvar off, but the half-lizard gripped his legs too tightly.

"No!" Porvar hissed.

Arvin heard a chewing noise. Porvar grunted then wrenched his head to one side. The pressure on Arvin's throat eased. Glancing down, Arvin saw Porvar spit out a length of tendril. The half-lizard grinned up at him.

"You can stop kicking me now."

Unwinding the limp tendril from his throat, Arvin breathed his thanks.

The rest of the climb went smoothly. Getting out of the hole was tricky, but Porvar gave Arvin a boost from below. Arvin scrambled out and secured the Circled Serpent inside his shirt again. That done, he extended his good hand to Porvar, helping him clamber out. He backed Porvar away from the hole. When the ectoplasmic bonds evaporated, the entire assassin vine would come snaking up out of it.

They had emerged into dense jungle. The weathered remains of stone buildings loomed nearby, smothered in a thick layer of leafy vegetation. A few paces away, an enormous stone snake head stared with sightless eyes into the jungle. Trees stood like living pillars, their branches forming a dark canopy overhead.

Off in the distance to their right, something crashed through the jungle—several things, judging by the sound of it. From the opposite direction—the center of the ruined city—came yet more shouting. One of the creatures moving through the jungle was headed their way. The ground trembled as it drew closer. Arvin heard the crack of branches and saw trees moving. As it broke through the trees, he dragged Porvar into the shadow of the serpent head. An enormous reptile like the one he'd seen earlier lumbered past, a yuan-ti perched on a saddle on its back. The yuan-ti brandished a spear in each fist, and a feathered cape fluttered out behind him.

"The Se'sehen," Porvar breathed. "Ss'yin'tia'saminass is under attack."

"That's good," Arvin said. "In the confusion, you can escape."

Porvar gave him a level stare. "Not without my son."

"He's in the pit, isn't he?"

Porvar nodded.

Arvin struggled with his conscience. He'd retrieved the second half of the Circled Serpent—the only sane thing to do was shift into the form of a flying snake and get out. Now Karrell was counting on him. Arvin's *own* children would die if he failed to save them. Porvar was a stranger, trying to hold Arvin to a promise he couldn't afford to keep.

"Please," Porvar begged.

His whisper was all but lost in the crashing that surrounded them. Dozens of the giant lizards were thundering through the jungle toward the center of Ss'yin'tia'saminass.

Arvin sighed. "Which way is the pit?"

Porvar grinned, revealing a jagged set of teeth. "This way."

They hurried through the jungle, moving at right angles to the attack. More than once they had to stop and hide from other Se'sehen, also mounted on lizards. Eventually, the jungle opened up, and Arvin could see the cistern just ahead. He heard cries coming from inside it: the halflings. One of them was dead, impaled on the needle-like spikes. His face, level with the rim of the cistern, had turned a faint blue and was so swollen it was impossible to see his eyes.

Porvar stared, transfixed, at the corpse. "Poison," he croaked.

"Is your son good at climbing?" Arvin asked.

The half-lizard startled, then nodded.

"Tell the halflings to be ready to catch a rope."

Without wasting any more words, Arvin uncoiled the braided leather cord he'd fastened around his waist and began to climb a nearby tree. When he was high enough to look down into the pit, he tied one end of the cord to a tree branch and tossed the other down into the cistern, shouting its command word as he did so. The trollgut rope expanded, more than doubling in length. One of the halflings caught the other end.

"Is there something you can tie it to?" Arvin shouted.

The halflings looked around then shook their heads. The floor of the cistern was rough with broken stone, but none of the chunks was large enough to serve as an anchor for the rope. Arvin was just about to break the unpleasant news that one of them would have to hold it while the others climbed out when another of the enormous lizards hurtled toward them through the jungle. It smashed through the trees mere paces away from Arvin, sending the tree he was in whipping back and forth, and skirted the cistern, the yuan-ti on its back clinging grimly to its saddle. Arvin clung equally grimly to a branch with his one good hand.

As the giant lizard thundered away, Arvin heard a cheer go up from the halflings below. Glancing down, he saw that the lizard had knocked over a tree, which had fallen into the pit. Its trunk formed a ramp up to the rim. Already the halflings were scrambling up, Porvar's son in the lead. The half-lizard moved forward to embrace him, but the boy shrank back, frightened. Then, visibly screwing up his courage, he hugged his father. Porvar looked up at Arvin, waved his thanks, then hurried away with the others into the jungle.

"Nine lives," Arvin whispered.

He added a silent prayer that Tymora keep sending the halflings luck. To escape in the middle of a full-scale assault, they would need it.

Arvin, fortunately, would be out of there as soon as he could morph into a flying snake.

He cut the new growth from his trollgut rope and looped what remained over his shoulder. Then he started to draw energy up through his navel and into his chest. Only then did he think to touch his chest and make certain the lower half of the Circled Serpent was still there.

It wasn't. It must have fallen when the lizard brushed the tree.

A chill ran through him. His heart stopped racing a moment later, however, when he spotted it on the ground near the base of the tree. Aborting his manifestation, he scrambled down to grab it. He secured the Circled Serpent back inside his shirt and resumed his manifestation.

He tried to draw energy up through his navel, but all that came was a trickle. Only the tiniest amount of energy remained in his *muladhara*. He'd been spending it wantonly, neglecting to check how much remained. There wasn't enough to morph himself into a flying snake.

He'd have to walk out of Ss'yin'tia'saminass on foot.

He turned, trying to figure out which way the river was. It was somewhere to the east, but under the trees, in moonlight, it was impossible to figure out which way that might be. He decided to find a place to hole up, sleep, and replenish his *muladhara*.

He walked for some time through the ruins of Ss'yin, leaving the sounds of battle farther and farther behind. Enormous stone snake heads and low mounds that had once been buildings loomed out of the darkness on either side. He paused under a tree, looking for a sheltered place to perform his meditations. After a moment, he found a good spot: a circle of darkness in the side of a ruined building that was overgrown with vines—a doorway.

Dagger in hand, he pulled aside the vines and crawled into a corridor. He was taking a risk. Something else might have already claimed it as its lair. The corridor, however, ended in a pile of collapsed rubble only two or three paces into the building. It smelled of mold, and its floor was littered with dead leaves and other debris but it was otherwise empty.

Arvin collapsed, exhausted. He would sleep only a short time, he told himself, just long enough to refresh his mind so that he could perform his meditations.

He lay down, pillowing his head on his arms. No more than a quick nap, and . . .

A rustling noise snapped Arvin awake. He sat up, dagger already in hand. He'd slept for longer than he'd intended. Outside his hiding place, twilight was already filtering through the jungle. The air was steamy and hot.

The swelling in his left hand had gone down; he was able to move it again. The twin punctures on the back of it were still an angry red, but the agony had ebbed. The hand just felt stiff and sore.

He paused, listening carefully, and heard monkeys chatter to each other over the rasping *caw-caw-caw* of a jungle bird. The rustling noise had probably been the monkeys, swinging through the trees. Other than that, the jungle was quiet. Whatever the outcome of the Se'sehen attack on Ss'yin, the battle was over.

He considered performing his meditations inside his refuge but decided to take advantage of the animals outside. A quick dagger throw, and he'd have fresh meat. Then he'd restore his *muladhara*.

He crawled outside and stood, stretching out the kinks that came from sleeping on a stone floor.

A slight rustle of the leaves above his head was all the warning he got. A heartbeat later, a snake-tailed yuan-ti with green scales the exact color of the leaves around him swung down from the branch above him and yanked Arvin off his feet.

CHAPTER 9

Arvin gasped as he was yanked sideways by the yuan-ti. Its serpent tail coiled around the branch above, it swung like a pendulum, slamming Arvin against the trunk of the tree. An explosion of stars filled Arvin's vision; as he blinked them away he heard the yuan-ti land on the ground next to him. Something heavy coiled around his chest and squeezed: the yuan-ti's serpent tail. The lower half of the Circled Serpent dug into Arvin's ribs. The yuan-ti, a male with leaf-shaped scales whose raised tips feathered out from his face, squeezed tighter, driving the air from Arvin's lungs, then eased up just a little. He bared his fangs and hissed something in Draconic.

Arvin stared back into unblinking eyes. "I don't understand you," he gasped.

As he spoke, he reached deep inside himself and connected with the small amount of energy that remained in his *muladhara*. He manifested a charm and saw the yuan-ti blink. Sunlight slanted down through a gap in the forest canopy. The sun was rising, and the jungle was getting even hotter.

The yuan-ti hissed again in Draconic. Sweat blossomed on his body, stinging Arvin's skin. Unable to move his arms—the yuan-ti's tail held them fast—Arvin gestured with his chin instead.

"Se'sehen?" he asked.

The yuan-ti's head swayed from side to side. In a human, it would have been denial, but the gesture was accompanied by a gloating smile and bared his fangs. His tongue flickered against Arvin's face, savoring his fear.

Arvin decided to take a gamble. "Sibyl?" he asked. His good hand was pressed against his chest but still visible. Arvin tapped a finger against his chest. "Sibyl," he repeated. "I'm one of her followers, too."

The yuan-ti relaxed his coils. His face was triangular with slit-pupiled eyes, not the slightest bit human. He had human arms, however, though they too were covered in green scales. His forked tongue flickered against Arvin's chest. "Sybil?" he repeated.

Arvin nodded. "Yes. Yes. We're on the same side."

The yuan-ti smiled and released Arvin. "Sibyl," he hissed again.

A shadow flickered across the yuan-ti. Something big had momentarily blocked the sunlight. The yuan-ti looked up.

Arvin followed his glance and saw an enormous winged serpent silhouetted against the sky. He felt the blood drain from his face as he realized who it must be. With the arrival of dawn, the portal had once again activated. Sibyl had slipped through.

The yuan-ti said something to Arvin in a tense, urgent voice. He glanced up again at the winged serpent that circled above them. Then his tail uncoiled, releasing Arvin. He said something more, gesturing urgently at the jungle, then slithered rapidly away.

Arvin stared, surprised. It was almost as if the yuan-ti had been frightened off by Sibyl. Maybe he'd been Jennestaa, after all.

Time for Arvin to get out of here as well.

As he turned to go, he heard a sharp fluttering noise: air passing swiftly over massive wings. Glancing up, he saw the winged serpent hurtling down toward him. He ran, hoping to lose himself beneath the trees, and cursed. He had nothing to fight Sibyl with; he'd left the musk creeper net in the cave. He tripped over a vine, stumbled, then recovered and ran on. He—

Couldn't move.

Couldn't even blink as he crashed, still frozen in a running pose, to the ground. As he lay on the jungle floor, the only thing that was moving—swiftly enough to make him dizzy—was the blood rushing through his veins. Over the thudding of his heart, loud in his ears, he heard the rustle of wings and the prolonged thud of a serpent body settling on the ground.

A tic of despair tugged at the corner of Arvin's eye. He waited for Sibyl's fangs to strike.

"Arvin?" a familiar voice said. It sounded surprised.

Arvin could move again. He scrambled to his feet. When he turned around, he saw Pakal. The dwarf had an odd expression on his face. It looked as though he was trying to decide whether he was glad—or angry—to see Arvin again.

Coiled on the ground beside Pakal was the winged serpent Arvin had mistaken for Sibyl. Arvin saw that it was no abomination—or at least, unlike any abomination he'd ever seen before. From its wedge-shaped head to the tip of its tail, the serpent was covered in feathers that glowed at the touch of sunlight. Midnight blue shaded into indigo, then into red, orange, yellow, and green. It had wings white and lacy as fresh frost, each feather tipped with vivid turquoise. Its face, though that of a serpent, was set in a kindly expression. Its smile was neither sly nor gloating but serene.

A rosy glow emanated from Pakal's body, turning his skin a ruddy brown. He had one hand raised, two fingers extended in a forked position; claws were visible at their tips. He'd lost his blowgun, probably to the river, but his dart pouch was still attached to his belt. Pakal had obviously homed in on the Circled Serpent just as he had in Sibyl's lair. Smashing the statue had been a big mistake.

The winged serpent next to him stared at Arvin with eyes like twin moons. Without opening its mouth, it spoke to Arvin, mind to mind. Its voice was a soft female trill. *Which half of the Circled Serpent do you carry?*

Denial would have been pointless. The winged serpent radiated power. Even with a chance to perform his meditations, Arvin doubted he could counter it.

"The lower half," he said. "The one Dmetrio had."

Show me.

Compelled, Arvin's hand slipped inside his shirt. It pulled out the lower half of the Circled Serpent. The serpent nodded.

Arvin stared up at the feathered head. "What ... are you?"

A couatl, the voice trilled. *One of those Ubtao called home again. To the people of the jungles, I am known as Ts'ikil.*

Karrell's friend. Supposedly. "Are you an avatar?" Arvin asked.

Laugher rippled into his mind. *No. A servant of the god, nothing more.* The couatl nodded at the artifact in Arvin's hand. *Where is the other half?*

"It was lost in the river."

Was it? The voice sounded bemused. *Let us see.*

Arvin felt the couatl sifting through his thoughts, like a finger idly stirring sand. He clenched his hand around Karrell's ring. Without any energy to fuel his psionics, it was his only defence. The familiar rush of magical energy up his arm didn't come.

It does not block me because I made it, the couatl said.

The couatl rummaged a little longer in Arvin's mind then withdrew.

Arvin felt sick. He knew the couatl must have found what she was looking for: a memory of the cave where he'd hidden his backpack.

Pakal nodded in response to an unheard command and stepped forward. He held out a claw-tipped hand.

"Don't make her force you," he warned.

Reluctantly, Arvin handed the Circled Serpent to him. The dwarf tucked it into his belt pouch.

"Please," Arvin said, his eyes locked on Ts'ikil's. "I need to rescue Karrell. She's in Smaragd, pregnant, and about to give birth. I have to get her out of there. Just open the door that leads to Smaragd long enough for me to slip inside; I'll find my own way out."

For a moment, Pakal looked sorrowful. Then he snorted. "You really expect us to trust you?" The ruddy glow that surrounded his body intensified. The claws on the hand that held the lower half of the Circled Serpent lengthened.

Arvin tensed, ready to counter the attack he knew was coming.

The dwarf, however, turned toward Ts'ikil. "No," he said. "He might tell the Se'sehen where—"

The couatl must have given him a silent rebuke; Pakal backed down.

Ts'ikil turned to Arvin. *Karrell's plight fills me with great sorrow,* she said. *If I could shift to the layer of the Abyss she occupies, I would have attempted a rescue myself, but it's just not possible to reach her.*

Arvin's heart beat a little faster. His eyes were locked on Pakal's pouch. "It is possible. Now that we have both halves, we could—"

The risk is too great.

Pakal gave Arvin one last glare then climbed obediently onto the couatl's back. Ts'ikil coiled her body beneath her, unfurled her wings, and sprang into the air.

"Wait!" Arvin called. "Take me with you!"

Too late. Ts'ikil burst through the trees into the open sky and flew away.

Arvin didn't waste his breath cursing. Instead he threw himself into the *bhujang asana.* It took all the willpower he possessed to still his mind and enter a meditative state. Frantic thoughts of Karrell filled his head.

He had to hurry—

Stay calm! he growled at himself.

To fill his *muladhara* and morph into a flying snake—

Breathe in through the left nostril, out through the right.

To beat the couatl back to the cave where he'd hidden his backpack—

Breathe! Draw in energy. Force it down. Coil it into the *muladhara.*

Before Ts'ikil got there. Before she found the other half and destroyed—

Stop it! Still your mind! Control!

He completed his meditation then whirled through the five defence poses and five attack poses like a manic dancer. Sweat flew from his body as he thrust with his hands, twirled and kicked. At last he was done.

He yanked a mental fistful of energy into his navel—nearly making himself sick in the process—then up into his chest. The scent of saffron and ginger exploded into the air as he morphed. He did it clumsily, not caring that his serpent tail ended in two human feet or that his head, though tiny, was still human. What mattered were the wings. He thrust them out and muscled his way into the air, bursting out of the treetops like an arrow loosed from a bow. He wheeled, getting his bearings, then flew toward the rising sun. Ts'ikil was a black dot, silhouetted against its bright yellow glare.

Despite having learned how to extend his metamorphosis well beyond its normal duration, Arvin had to land several times and remanifest the power. Each time he rose from the treetops, Ts'ikil was farther away. An ache clutched at his throat as he saw Ts'ikil dive down toward the sinuous break in the jungle that was the river. The couatl would recover the other half of the Circled Serpent long before Arvin would reach the bluff himself.

Even though he knew it was hopeless, Arvin flew on. It seemed to take forever before he could see the river, let alone the bluff. Eventually, however, he saw the dark spots in it that were the caves and could pick out the one where he'd hidden the backpack. He spotted Ts'ikil coiled at the base of the bluff on a ledge beside the river. She was too big to enter the cave herself—she would have sent Pakal in to recover the other half of the Circled Serpent. There was no sign of the dwarf, however. Hope fluttered in Arvin's chest. Maybe he hadn't arrived too late, after all. Perhaps something had delayed Pakal and the Circled Serpent had not yet been destroyed.

Arvin was just about to descend toward the cave when something in his peripheral vision caused him to turn his head. Something big raced downriver. Another winged serpent, flying almost at treetop level, its dark coloration blending with the jungle below. There was no mistaking its black body and batlike wings.

Sibyl.

She was almost at the bluff.

Arvin activated his lapis lazuli. He didn't need to picture Ts'ikil in his mind, not when he could see her just ahead of him. *Ts'ikil!* he cried. *Sibyl is flying toward you from the north. She's almost at the bluffs.*

The couatl reacted at once. Her white wings unfurled like sails and she sprang into the air. As she rose, a turquoise glow began at her wingtips and spread swiftly to cover her entire body—some sort of protective spell, Arvin guessed.

As Ts'ikil rose above the bluff, Sibyl wheeled sharply. Her tail flicked forward, hurling a lightning bolt. It ripped through the air, striking the couatl in the chest. The turquoise glow surrounding her exploded into a haze of bright blue sparks as it absorbed the bolt's energy. A heartbeat later, the thunderclap reached Arvin, rattling his wing feathers. He dived toward the bluff, praying that neither of the combatants would notice him.

Ts'ikil retaliated with a flicker of her tongue that sent twin rays of golden fire crackling toward Sibyl. So intensely bright were they that they left streaks of white across Arvin's vision. When he blinked them away, Sibyl was surrounded by a roiling cloud of black that lingered at treetop level. Arvin at first thought it was the aftermath of the couatl's attack, then remembered the yuan-ti's ability to shroud herself in darkness. Sibyl's attempt to make herself a more difficult target, however, did nothing to forestall Ts'ikil's second attack. The couatl swooped down toward the patch of darkness with an eagle's cry. The trees around and below the darkness shuddered, as if caught in an earthquake. Arvin's ears rang from the sound of Ts'ikil's scream.

The darkness surrounding Sibyl started to dissipate, Sibyl's form slowly becoming visible. It looked as though she was struggling to stay aloft. Her wing beats were ragged and her head drooped. Ts'ikil swooped lower, closing in for the kill. Her wingtips brushed the uppermost branches of the trees.

One of them came to life. Whipping its branches upward, it hurled a tangle of vines into the air that wrapped around Ts'ikil's tail, snagging it and jerking the couatl to a halt. She tore free an instant later, leaving a scattering of brightly colored feathers behind, but the momentary reprieve gave Sibyl the time she needed to mount another attack. She sent a tide of darkness toward the couatl—a boiling cloud that had a greasy, greenish tinge. Some of it touched the jungle below, and leaves fell away from the tree-tops like scraps of rotted cloth. Then it engulfed Ts'ikil. For the space of several heartbeats, all Arvin could see of the couatl were a handful of dull feathers falling out of the cloud. Then Ts'ikil emerged. Ugly brown patches marred her rainbow body.

Sibyl had been using two of her hands to direct her spells; the other two held a glowing length of spiked chain, which burst into flame. She whirled it above her head and dived on Ts'ikil. One spiked end caught the couatl in the chest, knocking her sideways through the air, but not before the couatl twisted, lashing Sibyl's side with her tail.

Sibyl recovered swiftly and swung her chain in a second attack. It passed through empty space as the couatl vanished, her body disappearing from tail to nose. Sibyl hissed and flailed with her chain, but her effort was futile. Just as Pakal had in Sibyl's lair, Ts'ikil had turned her body to air.

She rematerialized a moment later behind Sibyl. Her tail lashed forward, knocking the chain from Sibyl's hands. It fell, still flaming, to the jungle below. Ts'ikil's tail flicked out again, coiling around Sibyl's waist. With a mighty backward thrust of her wings Ts'ikil jerked the abomination toward her and bit Sibyl's neck. Sibyl, however, twisted in her grip and bit back, her teeth ripping feathers from Ts'ikil's shoulder. Locked together, wings beating and tails thrashing, the pair of winged serpents crashed down into the jungle below.

By then, Arvin was approaching the cave where his pack was hidden. He felt a familiar tickle in his forehead. The iron cobra, it seemed, was still searching for him. It didn't matter; he could always outfly it. The battered minion was the least of his worries, at the moment.

As he entered the cave, his wings tingled. A moment later, his serpent body sprang apart into legs and his wings shrank in upon themselves, becoming arms once more. He landed awkwardly, his body expanding and resuming human form. He was glad the transformation hadn't occurred in mid air.

He spotted his backpack immediately at the side of the cave. It had been hauled out of its hiding place and opened, though the musk creeper net was still inside it. Arvin plunged his hand into the pack and felt around, searching each of its side pockets twice, then a third time. The box that held the upper half of the Circled Serpent was gone.

Kneeling, Arvin balled his fists. Pakal had found the second half of the Circled Serpent and made off with it. The dwarf could have been anywhere.

Outside, Arvin could hear the two winged serpents thrashing in the jungle. A moment later, he heard wing beats and the sharp whistles and dull explosions of spells being cast. A breeze wafted in through the cave mouth, carrying with it the moist smell of the jungle—and of burned feathers. Ts'ikil was in trouble.

Maybe Arvin could even the odds. He still had the musk creeper net. He rubbed the scar on his forehead that hid the lapis lazuli. He wouldn't be able to contact Ts'ikil a second time that day, but if he could lure Sibyl close to the cave mouth with a carefully worded sending, he might be able to hurl the net on her.

Two shapes streaked across the sky, just above the treetops on the opposite side of the canyon: Sibyl, with Ts'ikil in close pursuit. The abomination had a number of deep gouges down the length of her body, but Ts'ikil didn't look much better. She flew raggedly, favoring one of her wings. Arvin rushed to the mouth of the cave with his pack and leaned out, trying to see where they went, but the two winged serpents were already behind the bluff. He heard Ts'ikil's eagle cry and clapped his hands over his ears as her sonic attack struck the bluff, sending a shower of broken stone into the river below.

As he turned, his eye fell on something that must have fallen out of his pack: a thin strip of fabric that had been tied into a series of intricate knots. He recognized it at once as something he must have made, but when he tried to remember when, he felt a curious, hollow sensation.

He scooped it up and examined the knots. They were a code—one he'd invented himself, years ago—that was based on the silent speech used by rogues. Each knot, like a hand signal, represented a different letter of the alphabet. Quickly running them through his fingers, he deciphered the message:

R.E.A.R.C.A.V.E.T.U.N.N.E.L.H.I.D.D.E.N.I.N. M.O.U.T.H.S.H.A.D.O.W.A.S.P.S

"Hidden in mouth?" he whispered aloud. What did *that* mean?

The first part of the message was clear enough: there must be a tunnel, somewhere in the back of the cave. He had obviously hidden something inside it, then erased all memory of having done so. There was only one thing valuable enough to merit such a drastic step.

The Circled Serpent.

Arvin grinned. That explained why Pakal wasn't there. The dwarf had must have gone through the pack, reported to Ts'ikil that the other half of the Circled Serpent had been taken by someone, and been sent on a futile errand to track down the supposed thief.

Pocketing the cord, Arvin hurried to the back of the cave. He had to clamber up a slope to find the tunnel; it was hidden behind a column of rock and was bricked shut except for a small opening where two bricks had fallen out. Touching it dislodged still more bricks; the entire wall seemed loose. He'd expected to see the box containing the Circled Serpent just inside the tunnel's mouth, but it wasn't there. It was probably deeper inside the tunnel, but it was difficult to make anything out in the shadows. He'd have to wait for his eyes to adjust. A breeze passed over his shoulder; air flowing into the hole in the bricks. The tunnel must have a second exit.

The knotted cord had mentioned shadow asps. Heeding his own warning, Arvin sent his awareness down the tunnel in a sparkle of silver. If there were asps lurking in those shadows, he'd be able to detect their thoughts. The tunnel, however, seemed clear. He yanked at the bricks, clearing a large enough hole for him to enter. Then, dagger in hand, he crawled into the tunnel. His eyes slowly adjusted to the dim light.

A second cavern lay a short distance ahead. As he started to move toward it, his manifestation at last picked up the three serpent minds. Their thoughts were focused on moving forward, on the sensation of their insubstantial bodies slithering through stone. They were intent upon something that had entered the second cavern—that had just *appeared* there without warning a few moments before. They were dimly aware of a second intruder behind them—Arvin—but it was the one in the cavern they wanted.

Arvin had halted the instant he detected the asps, but he hurried forward. Belatedly, he realized the source of the breeze he'd felt when he first peered into the tunnel: Pakal's body in gaseous form. The dwarf must have been lingering in the cavern, watching Arvin the whole time. Protected by the armband that was the equivalent of Karrell's ring, his thoughts had gone undetected.

Arvin didn't bother moving quietly. Pakal would have heard the tumbling bricks and be expecting him to show up. He did, however, send his awareness on ahead of himself to observe what the dwarf was up to. A low droning filled the air as Arvin concentrated on the second cavern.

It was deeply shadowed, but Arvin was still able to make out a few details. At the center of the second cavern was an enormous serpent, its body coiled in a tight ball. Surprisingly, it had not stirred, despite the fact that Pakal stood with one foot on the serpent's jaw while forcing the mouth open with his hands. The mouth slowly creaked open, revealing a square object that rested against the serpent's tongue. Pakal kicked it, knocking it out of the serpent's mouth, then let the head drop. As he bent to pick up the box, three shadowy heads reared up out of the floor behind him.

Arvin couldn't bring himself to just stand by and watch Pakal die. Besides, if the dwarf was busy fighting snakes, Arvin could make a grab for the box.

"Pakal!" he shouted. "Behind you. Three snakes!"

Even as he spoke, he reached the end of the tunnel and could see what was happening with his own eyes. He manifested another power, and a thread of silver shot out from his forehead. One end of it wrapped around the box.

Pakal ignored Arvin's warning. He shouted in a deep, throaty voice that sounded like an animal's growl and gestured. Five glowing red claws detached themselves from the tips of his fingers and thumb and streaked through the air toward Arvin.

Arvin ducked, but the claws found his shoulder and raked through flesh. He gasped in pain and the power he'd been manifesting faltered. The thread of silver flickered and the box thudded to the floor.

The claws pulled back for another swipe—then disappeared.

Pakal was having problems of his own now. While his back was turned, the shadow asps had attacked. Pakal stood with one hand pressed against his leg, his teeth bared in a grimace. He ground out a prayer and swept his hand across the seemingly empty space in front of him. A heartbeat later the three asps were outlined in glittering gold dust. Pakal growled a second time and raked the air with one hand. Glowing red claws streaked toward the nearest of the asps. As they tore into it, black shadowstuff oozed out through the glitter that coated its body. With a flick of his hand, Pakal's claws tossed the body to the side.

Two more asps remained, however. They flanked him, slithered in close, and struck.

Pakal howled as their fangs sank into his bare legs. He managed to kill another with his glowing claws, but the third asp reared back and struck him again. The dwarf fell to his knees.

Arvin, meanwhile, steeled himself against the pain of his wounded shoulder. As blood dribbled down his right arm, he concentrated on the task at hand. He remanifested his power and used it to pluck the box from the floor. It sailed back into his hand. He caught it, then sent the thread of psionic energy back into the room and used it to yank open the pouch that hung from Pakal's belt. A crescent-shaped object fell out. It was wrapped in crumpled lead foil.

The other half of the Circled Serpent.

Pakal lunged for it, grabbed it with both hands, and fell heavily on top of it.

Arvin cursed. His psionic hand wasn't strong enough to lift a body.

The last of the shadow asps was still outlined in glittering dust, making it an easy target. Arvin leaned into the cavern just enough to give his arm some play, raised his dagger, then hurled it. He was almost surprised when the blade pierced the asp's head. Even though the dagger was magical, he'd half-expected it to pass right through the creature. The asp thrashed for a moment then stilled.

Arvin called his dagger back to his hand and waited. No more shadow asps appeared. He picked up the box that held the upper half of the Circled Serpent and stepped down into the cavern. Just to make sure there weren't any more guardians lurking within the stone, he sent his awareness sweeping in a circle around him. Nothing.

Still holding his dagger, Arvin hurried to where Pakal lay. He glanced warily at the enormous serpent that loomed over them. No wonder it hadn't moved; it looked as though it had been dead for many years. Its body was studded with gems, one of the largest of which—a stone that had been cut in a star shape—had fallen out. Arvin picked it up and smiled, realizing that the gem-studded body of the abomination was a fortune, ripe for the plucking with the shadow asps gone. That could wait, however. There were more important things to attend to.

He tucked the gem into a pocket, then bent and turned Pakal over. The dwarf's face was as gray as the stone floor on which he lay. His lips were an even darker shade and his eyes were closed.

"I'm sorry," Arvin told the corpse. "I tried to warn you, but ..."

Arvin pushed any thoughts of remorse firmly aside. Pakal could have helped him rescue Karrell. Instead he'd chosen to oppose Arvin. The bloody wounds in Arvin's shoulder were testimony to that. Even so, Arvin felt a twinge of guilt. He told himself that Karrell was what mattered, that the dwarf was the one who had started the fight, but it didn't help.

As he picked up the lower half of the Circled Serpent, tears of relief welled in his eyes. At last he had both halves of the key that would open the door to Smaragd. He could rescue Karrell.

If only he knew where the door was.

Or how to use the Circled Serpent, for that matter.

He'd worry about that later. For now, he had to focus on getting out of the cave and away from there, before whichever of the flying serpents won the fight—Ts'ikil or Sibyl—returned. He smoothed the foil back into place and picked up the box. It looked large enough to hold both halves. As he nested them together inside it, he heard a faint whisper.

Pakal's eyes were open. He was casting a spell. Arvin startled, nearly dropping the box.

" ... together," the dwarf whispered.

Arvin started to summon energy in preparation for a manifestation, but stopped when he realized

Pakal had merely cast the spell that allowed what he said to be understood.

"Put ... together," the dwarf repeated. Sweat blossomed on his forehead as he fought the effects of the shadow serpents' poison, straining to rise. His words were faint. "Push tail ... into head. That's how ... destroy ..."

His eyelids fluttered, then closed. His body went slack.

Arvin touched a finger to the dwarf's throat. A pulse still flickered there. Faintly.

Relief washed through Arvin. Despite the wound in his shoulder, he hadn't wanted the dwarf to die. "I will destroy it," he promised. Then, under his breath, he added, "Once I've rescued Karrell." That said, he stood. He looked down at Pakal, hesitated, then decided. If he left the dwarf there, Pakal would die.

He tucked the box inside his shirt, then bent and hooked his hands under Pakal's shoulders. Grunting, he hauled the dwarf into the tunnel. It was a struggle, crawling backward down the tunnel while hauling the limp body. His left hand was still sore where Juz'la's viper had bitten it. Eventually, however, he reached the first cavern. He paused for a moment before entering it, listening, but heard only the rush of the river below and the cries of monkeys in the jungle on the far side of the canyon. He realized his forehead had stopped tingling—a good thing, since it meant the iron cobra wouldn't be showing up. Maybe the dunking in the river had finally caused it to seize up.

He lifted Pakal out of the tunnel and took a moment to find his footing on the steep slope. He would set the dwarf down near the mouth of the cave, where Ts'ikil could spot him, then stuff the box into his pack, morph into a flying snake, and get out of there. He edged his way around the column that hid the entrance of the tunnel.

Standing on the other side of it was the dog-headed man. Arvin barely had time to blink in surprise before large golden eyes bored into his. Arvin turned his head to the side and tried to manifest a psionic shield, but he was too late. His eyes rolled back in his head, his body went slack, and his mouth opened wide in an involuntary yawn. He felt Pakal slip from his arms, then his own body crumpled into a heap on top of the dwarf's.

Arvin awoke with a jerk, his heart pounding. The dog-man—

Arvin leaped to his feet and drew his dagger. He shook his head violently, trying to throw off the cobwebs of sleep that clung to it. He looked around the cavern. The first thing he saw was Pakal, lying on the floor at his feet. The next was the dog-man, lying on his back. Bright red blood stained the golden fur of his face; it looked as though something had slammed into his forehead, hard enough to cave in his skull. More blood was splattered on the top of the stalagmite he lay next to.

Arvin slapped a hand against his chest. The box he'd tucked into his shirt was gone. His backpack still lay in a corner. Whoever had killed the dog-man had taken only the Circled Serpent. Arvin was close to weeping. He'd actually had the key to Smaragd in his hands, only to have it stolen from him again.

By whom? How had the dog-man known where to find him?

Arvin touched a finger to Pakal's throat and felt a faint pulse. The dwarf was still alive, though just barely. If it had been Sibyl who had returned, surely she would have finished both Arvin and Pakal off. What had happened?

There was one way for Arvin to find out. He drew energy up through his navel, into his chest, and exhaled slowly. The scents of saffron and ginger filled the air, and ectoplasm shimmered briefly on the walls of the cavern before evaporating in the jungle heat. The cavern blurred, shifted slightly ...

Arvin stared down at a ghostly reflection of himself. The dog-man stood over him, his mouth open in a grin, tongue lolling as he panted with silent laughter. He rolled Arvin over and tore open his shirt. The box fell out. Panting harder, the dog-man picked it up.

A second source of powerful emotion drew Arvin's eyes to the entrance of the cave. The dog-man's back was turned, so he didn't see the snakeskin carpet that drifted to a halt at the cavern's mouth, its fringe of tiny wings fluttering. A serpent that had been coiled on it slithered into the cavern.

The dog-man, at last alerted to danger, whirled. He visibly relaxed—then his body tensed up again. As if turned by an invisible hand, his head was wrenched to the side. He stared at the wall for a heartbeat or two, then exploded into a run toward it. As he reached the wall, he flung himself forward, smashing his forehead into the rounded top of a stalagmite in a spray of blood. Then his body crumpled into a heap beside the stalagmite.

The serpent regarded him for a moment with unblinking eyes. Then it shifted into yuan-ti form. It was, as Arvin had half suspected, the Dmetrio-seed. The seed strode forward, lifted the box the dog-man had dropped, examined it briefly, then opened it. Seeing both halves of the Circled Serpent, he hissed in delight. Triumph shone in his slitted eyes.

The seed gestured and the flying carpet floated into the cavern. He placed the box on it. Then he bent to examine Arvin and Pakal. He lifted the dwarf's leg and flicked his tongue over a patch of black that spread outward from the twin puncture marks left by one of the shadow snake's bites. Hissing softly, he dropped the leg. He turned to Arvin and lifted Arvin's hand. Unblinking eyes stared down at the bite marks on the back of it—punctures surrounded by a dark bruise. The Dmetrio-seed looked disappointed—he probably assumed Arvin was dead and was rueing not having killed Arvin himself—and let Arvin's hand fall. Then he stepped onto the carpet. He shifted into serpent form and coiled tightly around the box. With a flutter of wings, the carpet lifted from the ground and flew out of the cavern.

The last impression Arvin's manifestation gave him was the Dmetrio-seed's triumphant hiss. Then the vision ended.

Arvin stood for several moments, staring at the body of the dog-man. The Dmetrio-seed had acted with the decisive brutality Arvin had come to expect from Zelia; the seed had seemed fully aware, powerful and in control. The death of Juz'la must have broken the lethargy he had been languishing under. Arvin shuddered as he contemplated what the dog-man had been forced to do. He had seen Zelia dominate someone before—he'd experienced her psionic compulsions first-hand—but had never dreamed they could be so strong. His tutor, Tanju, had hinted that there were powers that could compel a person to take his own life, but this was the first time Arvin had seen them in action, and Dmetrio was merely one of Zelia's seeds. Arvin would be doubly wary from then on of any version of Zelia.

Especially the one that had both halves of the Circled Serpent.

Arvin rubbed his forehead, realizing that the tickling he'd felt in his forehead as he descended toward the cave must have been the Dmetrio-seed using his psionics to view Arvin at a distance. Arvin had shown the seed exactly where the cave was.

His left hand still throbbed where the viper had punctured it, his right shoulder was crusted with dried blood from Pakal's attack, and his chest felt bruised from the crushing the yuan-ti who had swept him into the tree had given him.

The deepest ache, however, was inside him. For a few brief moments, he had held the key to Karrell's prison in his hands, then it was gone again.

He took a deep breath and pushed the melancholy thought firmly aside. He reminded himself that it could have been worse. It could have been Sibyl who had claimed the Circled Serpent. At least Arvin knew how the Dmetrio-seed's mind worked. There was a chance that the seed would dutifully carry the Circled Serpent back to Zelia in Hlondeth—but only a slim chance. More than likely, the seed had decided to betray Zelia—all Arvin needed to do was find the door. If Arvin could find a way to locate the Dmetrio-seed before the seed learned where the door was, then perhaps . . .

The *whuff-whuff-whuff* of wings startled him out of his reverie. A shadow—large and serpent-shaped—passed across the mouth of the cave. A flying serpent, landing at the base of the bluff. Was it Ts'ikil returning? Or Sibyl?

Arvin scrambled across the cavern toward his pack. Plunging a hand inside, he seized the musk creeper net. He used his dagger to slash the rootlets that had grown into the pack, at the same time manifesting the power that would render him invisible. Then, cautious, he crept to the mouth of the cave.

CHAPTER 10

The marilith lowered its face to Karrell's and glared into her eyes.

"Naughty mortal," it scolded. "Don't you dare run away again."

Karrell, her legs held by a twist of the demon's tail, met the marilith's eye with a defiant look.

"Or what?" she countered. "You'll kill me? Go ahead."

The demon hissed. Its tail tightened. As it did, Karrell whispered Ubtao's name under her breath and brushed a hand against the marilith's mottled green scales. The wounding spell took effect, sending a jolt of pain through the marilith's body. The demon gasped and its coils loosened again.

Karrell felt the ground beneath her feet

grow soggy. The foul smell of rot drifted up from the ground—the jungle reacting to her spell. She distracted the demon by speaking again.

"By killing me, you'll only kill yourself," she reminded it.

The demon's eyes narrowed.

"Let go of me," Karrell demanded. She nodded down at her belly. "You know I can't run."

The demon tilted its head, considering. One of its six hands toyed with a strand of sulfur-yellow hair. A half-dozen dretches surrounded it. One of them scratched at its belly, setting the blubber there to jiggling.

"Mistress," it croaked. "Should *we* kill it?" Drool dribbled from its mouth as it gave a fang-toothed smile.

"Silence, idiot!"

A sword appeared in the marilith's hand. Without even looking at the dretch, it slashed backward, neatly slicing through its neck. The head landed in a tangle of ferns, surprised eyes staring blankly up at the sky as the body crumpled, its neck fountaining red. The other dretches sniffed the splatters, then dropped to all fours and began lapping up the flowing blood with their tongues.

The marilith ignored them. It gestured with the point of its sword at Karrell's distended belly. "Soon your young will emerge," it observed.

Karrell eyed the sword point and readied another prayer. If the sword pricked her, she'd need to inflict yet another jab of pain to convince the demon that the fate link still held.

"I'll need a healer to tend me," she told the marilith, "someone who can take away the pain and staunch my blood if too much of it flows, someone who can keep me alive if the birth doesn't go well." She gestured at the circle of slashed and trampled vegetation where the marilith's swords had whirled. "Open another gate; send me home. The odds of survival—for both of us—will be much greater then."

"No."

"If I die—"

"Then your soul will wind up on the Fugue Plain, even without a gate," the demon said, "where, instead of being claimed by Ubtao and taken to the Outlands, it will be consumed by Dendar." The marilith smiled, revealing yellowed teeth. "As I'm sure you noticed, the Night Serpent has developed a taste for the faithful."

Karrell blanched at that but managed to keep her voice steady. "All the more reason to keep me alive," she argued, "since your soul will also be consumed."

"All the more reason to keep you close," the marilith answered.

Karrell gestured at the dretches. They had peeled back the skin of the dead one's neck and fought over the right to suck the spinal cord.

"You sent them in to herd the faithful into Dendar's mouth," Karrell said. "Why?"

The demon gloated. "You haven't figured that out?" it *tsk-tsked*. "You're not as clever as I thought, half-blood. Perhaps there's too much human in you."

"Then pity me. Tell me why you want Dendar to grow so big. Is it so she'll be stuck inside her cave?"

The demon frowned. "What purpose would that serve?"

"It would prevent the Night Serpent from escaping when Sibyl opens the door to her lair."

"Why should we care if Dendar escapes?"

"Because . . ." Karrell was at a loss.

The marilith was right. Why indeed? For all the demons cared, the entire world beyond the Abyss—and all of the souls it contained—could disappear.

"Why should Sibyl want to open that door?" the marilith continued. "Hmm?"

"To reach Smaragd," she said. She waved her hand in a circle. "Through your gate."

The marilith gave a throaty laugh. "You truly are as stupid as you seem, mortal. Nothing living can enter the Fugue Plane."

Karrell knew that, of course, just as she knew that Sibyl was very much alive—and as mortal as she was. If she could keep the marilith talking, perhaps she could learn what was really going on.

"Sibyl could enter it by dying," she said.

The marilith sighed. "Who would claim her soul?"

Karrell deliberately blinked. "Why ... Sseth, of course."

The marilith started to say something, then bent until its lips brushed Karrell's ear. "You look tired. Rest. Sleep." It gave Karrell a wicked smile. "Dream."

Karrell flinched away from the demon's touch. The marilith's last comment had been an odd one. Since being dragged into Smaragd, Karrell had slept fitfully, one ear always open for the sounds of the marilith and its dretches. Her dreams had been troubled. With Dendar feeding on the souls of the faithful, any dreams Karrell had were certain to be full-blown nightmares, perhaps more than her mind could stand. Why would the demon want Karrell to do something that might harm her—and thus it?

With a suddenness that left her dizzy, Karrell realized what was happening. Sseth communicated with his worshipers through whispers and dreams, and Sseth was bound. The dreams he was sending had turned into a writhing nest of nightmares. *That* was why Karrell—why all of the yuan-ti—had been having such troubling dreams for the past several months, dreams that disturbed their sleep enough to cause them to wake up, hissing in alarm. Dreams of being bound, of feeling trapped, of being prey rather than predator, dreams that were terrifying in their imagery but not quite substantial enough or clear enough to convey whatever message Sseth was so urgently trying to send.

If Dendar gorged herself on the faithful—if she stopped eating nightmares—those dreams would come through, not in a trickle, as they had for the past several months, but in a terrible, mind-drowning rush.

Sibyl wasn't planning to enter Smaragd through Dendar's cave. Dendar was only the solution to her immediate problem. There had to be another entrance to Smaragd, one that Sseth knew—one that he was trying to send to his faithful through dreams that had become nightmares.

Whatever that route was, the Circled Serpent was the key. Of that Karrell was certain. She closed her eyes, praying that key didn't fall into the wrong hands.

Something stroked her hair—the marilith's claw-tipped fingers. "A copper for your thoughts," it hissed.

Karrell pressed her lips grimly shut. Inside her belly, her children kicked. They could feel her tension, her anxiety. Forcing herself to remain calm, she placed a hand on her stomach.

The demon stared thoughtfully at it. "Is it your time?" it asked. "Has it begun?"

One of the dretches rose from its feast and sniffed Karrell, its blood-smeared nostrils twitching. Karrell smacked its hand away.

"Not yet," she told the demon, meeting its eye.

It was a lie. Karrell's water had just broken; she could feel its warmth trickling down her legs. Her stomach cramped—a hint of the contractions that would follow.

She smiled up at the demon, hiding her fear behind a mask. "Don't worry," she told the marilith. "When my labor does begin, you'll feel it."

As she spoke, she sent out a silent plea. Arvin, she thought, if you're listening, come quickly. I'm running out of time.

❖ ❖ ❖ ❖ ❖

Arvin eased his head out of the cave and stared down. He'd had the net ready to throw, but lowered it again. It wasn't Sibyl who had returned to the cave, but Ts'ikil.

The couatl sat coiled on a ledge beside the river at the bottom of the bluff, her head drooping with exhaustion. Her body was badly burned in several places. Scorched feathers stood stiffly out from seared red flesh. Sibyl's black cloud had left oozing brown patches elsewhere along the couatl's length. Her remaining feathers had lost their rainbow luster and her wings were tattered. She held one wing at an awkward angle, as if it were broken.

Arvin opened his mouth to call out to her then hesitated. Maybe he should just sneak away while his invisibility lasted, strike out on his own and try to find the Dmetrio-seed. Unfortunately, even though Arvin had learned his psionics from Hlondeth's best tracker, he didn't have any powers that would allow him to hunt the seed down. He'd concentrated, instead, on learning powers that would help him infiltrate Sibyl's lair.

For what must have been the hundredth time, Arvin wished he hadn't broken the dorje Tanju had given him the winter before. It would have pointed, like a lodestone, directly at the Dmetrio-seed. What Arvin needed was a power that could do the same thing or—he glanced at Pakal's still form—a spell. Pakal had been able to track down the upper half of the Circled Serpent back in Sibyl's lair. Perhaps he could do the same with the seed.

The trouble was, he'd probably continue to insist on destroying the artifact.

Ts'ikil, on the other hand, had at least seemed sympathetic to Karrell's plight. Perhaps she might yet be persuaded.

Arvin negated his invisibility. "Ts'ikil!" he called. "Up here!"

It took several more shouts before the couatl raised her head. Either the cascade of the river below was drowning out Arvin's voice, or she was as far gone as Pakal was.

Arvin! Her voice was faint, weak. *What has happened?*

"Pakal is badly wounded," Arvin shouted. "Dmetrio has taken the Circled Serpent. He has both halves."

Arvin knew he was taking a huge gamble. If Ts'ikil had magic that could locate the Dmetrio-seed, she might go after him and leave Arvin behind, assuming she could still fly.

He felt Ts'ikil's mind slide deep into his awareness. Her mental intrusion was a mere tickle—far gentler than the pummeling Zelia had given him in her rooftop garden as she rifled through his thoughts. Memories flickered past in reverse order: the psychic impressions Arvin had picked up from the cavern, his encounter with the dog-man, Pakal's battle with the shadow asps.

"He looks bad," Arvin told her. He spoke in a normal voice, certain she was still listening in on his thoughts. "He's ... alive, but his skin's turning black. Can you help him?"

I will try. Can you lower him to me?

"Yes."

That said, he uncoiled his trollgut rope. He repositioned Pakal's belt across his chest, just under the arms, and made sure it was securely buckled. He attached his rope to it, passing a loop under each of the dwarf's legs to turn it into a sling. He carried Pakal to the mouth of the cave, eased him over the edge, and stood holding the end of the trollgut rope. "*Augesto*," he commanded. It lengthened, slowly lowering Pakal to the ledge below.

When the rope went slack, Arvin tossed the other end of it down. He stowed the magical net back inside his pack and slipped the pack on, then activated his bracelet. By the time he climbed down to the ledge, Ts'ikil was bending over Pakal, touching his wounds with a wingtip. She hissed softly as her feathers brushed across the puncture marks. In full daylight, Arvin got a better look at the blackness that surrounded each of the wounds. He'd assumed it to be bruising, but it was something much worse. The darkened areas on Pakal's legs seemed somehow insubstantial—shadows that clung to him, even in the full glare of direct sunlight. As Ts'ikil's wingtip touched them, it sank into nothingness.

"That's not good, is it?" Arvin said. Despite the wound in his shoulder, he bore the dwarf no ill will. Pakal had only been doing what he felt he must—just as Arvin had been.

For several moments, Ts'ikil said nothing. The river surged past them, a pace or two away, sounding like one long, constant sigh. From somewhere in the distant jungle came a faint scream: a monkey's cry. The stone of the ledge felt hot, even through the soles of Arvin's boots. He wondered if they shouldn't be moving Pakal into the shade.

No, Ts'ikil said. *Sunlight will hasten the cure.* She gave Pakal's wounds one last touch, trilled aloud—a melody as beautiful and haunting as that of a songbird—then sank back into a loose coil. *There. I have done all I can.*

"When will he regain consciousness?" Arvin asked.

A day. Perhaps two.

Arvin frowned. "That's too long. We need him to find Dmetrio now." He glanced up at Ts'ikil. "Can you—"

No. Pakal and Karrell were my eyes.

"Aren't there others you can call upon?"

None close by.

Arvin closed his eyes and let out a long sigh. "So that's it, then. The Dmetrio-seed has gotten away."

We will find him.

"How? You said—"

He will go to the door.

"Yes—but there's just one problem," Arvin said. "We don't know where the door is." He paused. "Do we?"

No mortal does.

Her choice of words gave him a surge of hope. "What about the gods?" he asked. "Can they tell us where it is?"

We have petitioned both Ubtao and Thard Harr. They do not know its location.

"What now?" Arvin asked.

We rest and gather strength. And wait.

"Here?" Arvin said. He glanced up at the sky. "What if Sibyl returns?"

She won't, not for some time. She was even more grievously wounded than I.

"She's not dead?" Arvin said. Part of him felt disappointed by the news, but another, larger part of him was glad. He wanted to be the one to kill Sibyl. To exact revenge for what she had done to Naulg, and for what her marilith had done to Karrell. He shrugged off his pack and set it on the ledge by his feet. "What, exactly, are we waiting for?" he asked.

You already know the answer to that question. We await a dream that Sseth will send to the yuan-ti. When it comes, we must act swiftly.

Arvin snapped his fingers. "The dream will provide the location of the door, won't it?" he said. "Then all we have to do is beat the Dmetrio-seed to it and lay an ambush."

Yes.

"A good plan, except for one thing," Arvin said. Feeling a little foolish—surely he was pointing out the obvious—he made a gesture that included Ts'ikil, Pakal and himself. "None of us is yuan-ti." He hesitated, looking at the couatl's serpent body. "Are we?"

Laughter trilled into his mind. *Not me*, Ts'ikil said. *You.*

Arvin blinked. "You think *I'm* yuan-ti?" he asked. He shook his head. "I'm human."

Yuan-ti blood flows in your veins.

Arvin snorted. "Why do you think that?"

That should be obvious.

"Well it isn't—and I'm not yuan-ti," Arvin said, "unless the potion the Pox forced me to drink left some lingering traces." He stared at Ts'ikil. "You know what I'm talking about, right? You saw that in my memories?"

The couatl nodded.

"That potion was purged from my body a year ago," Arvin continued. "Zelia neutralized it the night she found me in the sewers."

I was not referring to the potion.

Arvin thought a moment. "Ah. You mean the mind seed. It was purged, too, but a little of Zelia's knowledge still remains. Gemstones, for example. I know their value, both in coin and as raw material for constructing dorjes and power stones." He realized he was babbling, but couldn't stop himself. "Is that what you mean? Will my having been seeded a year ago enable me to receive Sseth's dream-message when it comes?"

Despite the couatl's frail condition, there was a twinkle in her eye. *I thought I spoke plainly, but I see that you haven't understood,* she said. *Once again: there is yuan-ti blood in your veins.*

She stared at his injured hand. "This?" Arvin asked, raising it. "Are you trying to say that the viper that bit me—Juz'la's pet—was a yuan-ti?"

The couatl sighed aloud. *Don't you wonder why its venom didn't kill you?*

"I got lucky," Arvin said, touching the crystal at his throat. "Tymora be thanked."

The viper was one of the most deadly in the Black Jungle. You have a strong resistance to snake venom.

"So?" Arvin was starting to get irritated by Ts'ikil's persistence.

Such a strong natural resistance is typically found only in those humans who are part yuan-ti.

"My mother was human!" Arvin said, his temper making his words louder than he'd intended.

And your father?

Arvin balled his fists. His father had been a bard named Salim. Arvin's mother had described him as a gifted singer whose voice could still a tavern full of boisterous drunks to rapt silence. That was where Arvin's mother had met Salim: in a tavern in Hlondeth, one she'd stopped at in the course of her wanderings. He wasn't a psion like her, or even an adventurer, but she fell deeply in love with him. They remained together only for a handful of tendays, but in that time they conceived a child. Then, one night, a vision had come to Arvin's mother in a dream: Salim, drowning, dragging Arvin's mother down with him.

Salim had been planning a voyage to Reth to sing at the gladiatorial games. It was an important commission—one not to be refused if he wanted other business to follow. He had already asked Arvin's mother to accompany him. He refused to believe that her dream was a premonition, but he had not known her long enough to know the extent of her powers. She had already made her dislike of gladiatorial games known, so Salim thought she was simply refusing to accompany him. He boarded a ship bound for Reth and drowned along with everyone else on board, just as she had foretold, when it sank in the stormy waters of the Vilhon Reach. Had Arvin's mother gone with him, she too would have drowned, and Arvin—still in her womb—would never have been born.

That was the extent of what Arvin's mother had told him about his father. She had described Salim as tall and agile, with dark brown hair and eyes, just like Arvin's. She'd never mentioned scales, slit pupils, or any other hint that there might have been yuan-ti in his blood.

Arvin didn't believe that his mother would have lied to him, but what if she herself hadn't known Salim wasn't fully human? What if Arvin really did have a trace of yuan-ti in his ancestry?

Impossible, he told himself. He had been inspected by Gonthril, leader of the rebels of Hlondeth, and pronounced wholly human. Humans with yuan-ti ancestry always had a hint of serpent about them, like the scales that freckled Karrell's breasts. If Arvin's father had been part yuan-ti, surely his mother would have noticed something.

Then again, perhaps she had. Maybe it hadn't mattered to her enough to mention it.

Why does the idea of having a yuan-ti heritage frighten you?

"It doesn't," Arvin snapped, "and get out of my head."

He felt the couatl's awareness slide away.

The intense heat of the jungle had made Arvin sticky with sweat. He stalked over to the lip of the ledge, kneeled, and pulled off what remained of his shirt. He splashed river water on his face and chest. It cooled him but didn't help him to feel any cleaner. He dunked the top of his head into the water, letting it soak his hair, then flipped his hair back. It still didn't help.

He didn't *want* to be part yuan-ti—he'd only recently gotten used to the idea that his children would be part serpent. He'd learned, by falling in love with Karrell, that not all yuan-ti were cruel and cold, but growing up in Hlondeth had taught him to be wary of the race. Yuan-ti were the masters, and humans were slaves and servants. Inferiors. Yet humans, despite being downtrodden, had a fierce pride. They *knew* they were better than yuan-ti. Less arrogant, less vicious, on the whole. Yuan-ti rarely laughed or cried and certainly never caroused or howled with grief. They were incapable of the depths of joy and sorrow that humans felt. They were emotionally detached.

Just as Arvin himself was.

The realization hit him like an ice-cold blast of wind. He sat, utterly motionless, water dripping onto his shoulders from his wet hair. Aside from the feelings Karrell stirred in him, when was the last time he'd been utterly *passionate* about something? He could count the number of true friends he'd had in his life on one hand. If he was brutally honest, they narrowed down to just one: Naulg, who had defended him at the orphanage when they were both just boys. After Arvin had escaped from the Pox, he'd set about trying to rescue Naulg and had eventually succeeded—but just a little too late to save his friend's life. If Arvin had been a little more zealous in his efforts, a little more passionate about his friend's welfare, might Naulg have survived? Was a lack of strong emotion the reason why Arvin had been so reluctant to take up the worship of Hoar, god of vengeance, as the cleric Nicco had urged?

Was Arvin, indeed, as cold-blooded and dispassionate as any full-blooded yuan-ti?

No, he told himself sternly. He wasn't. There was Karrell. He loved her. The need to rescue her burned in him, not just to rescue her, but to save the children he'd fathered. They *mattered* to him.

The fact remained that he *was* part yuan-ti. He couldn't deny it any longer, even to himself. It explained so much: why it felt so natural to morph into a flying snake, why his psionics were so powerful. Yuan-ti had a number of inborn magical abilities that mimicked psionic powers. Their ability to charm humans, for example. That was one of the first powers Arvin had learned. It had just come naturally to him.

Because he had yuan-ti blood.

He squared his shoulders. So what, he told himself. It doesn't change anything. I'm still the person I've always been. I just understand myself a little better now.

He turned, saw Ts'ikil watching him. "Were you listening to my thoughts?"

No.

"Thank you." He stood. "Tell me about the Circled Serpent. If I'm going after the Dmetrio-seed, I'll need to know as much about it as he does."

It is ancient—it was made at the height of the Mhairshaulk Empire. It was one of several keys, the rest of which have been lost in the intervening millennia. The sarrukh, creators of the yuan-ti and other reptilian races, erected a series of gates to other planes of existence. The keys could be used to open any of them.

"How?"

Ts'ikil ignored the question. *You think you can survive in Smaragd.*

"Karrell has for six months, pregnant and alone."

Not alone. Karrell is one of the k'aaxlaat. Ubtao watches over her.

"Even in Smaragd?"

Even there. Ts'ikil's eyes bored into Arvin's. *You, on the other hand, have yet to choose a god.*

Arvin touched the crystal at his throat. "I worship Tymora."

When it suits you.

"That's as much as most mortals can say."

That is true, but the fact remains: you are not a cleric. You will have no protection in Smaragd.

It took Arvin a moment to realize what Ts'ikil had just said. Hope surged through him. "You . . . you're going to let me do it, aren't you? Enter Smaragd." He tilted his head. "What changed your mind?"

I have not changed my mind. The Circled Serpent must be destroyed. A key that can release Dendar—that can bring about the destruction of this world—can not be permitted to remain in existence. She lifted her unbroken wing. Feathers hung from it in tatters. *I am injured; my part in this has diminished.*

She lowered her wing. *Fortunately, so has Sibyl's. She was equally weakened by our battle, and she does not know that Zelia's seed has the key.*

It has come down to a race between yourself and the Dmetrio-seed. If he reaches the door first and opens it, I fully expect that you will follow him inside. You must, if you are to save Karrell's life.

"That much is obvious," Arvin said.

Yes, but the course of action you must pursue is not. You will be tempted to rush to find Karrell first. Don't. Once the seed enters Smaragd, he will hurry to Sseth's side. You must concentrate on stopping him from reaching the god instead. If he succeeds in freeing Sseth, Karrell will be the first to die. She is the cleric of his enemy, and Sseth will know— immediately—where she is within his realm. With a thought, he will destroy her.

Despite the sticky heat, Arvin shivered. "What if

I manage to take the Circled Serpent from the seed and open the door with it?"

If you did, you would open a way for any who wished to follow.

"Couldn't I close the door behind me?" Arvin asked.

Not from inside Smaragd. The door can only be opened—or closed—from this plane.

Arvin thought for a moment. "I could leave the Circled Serpent outside with someone else, someone who could close the door behind me and open it again once I've gotten Karrell."

The couatl's laughter trilled softly through his mind. *With me, perhaps? Assuming I let you use the door and closed it after you, how would you let me know when it is time to open it?*

Arvin opened his mouth then closed it again. He already knew his lapis lazuli wasn't capable of penetrating Smaragd. It probably wouldn't allow him to do a sending from within that layer of the Abyss, either. Once inside, he'd be on his own.

"Can the key be carried into Smaragd then out again?"

To Arvin's surprise, the couatl answered. *It can, but if it is lost there, we would lose the opportunity to destroy it, and the gate would remain open.* Ts'ikil paused—long enough for Arvin to silently acknowledge what she meant by "lost." His death. *One of Sseth's faithful would eventually free him, and the key would fall into Sseth's coils. The god of serpents will be sorely tempted to release Dendar. The Night Serpent would readily agree to feed on the faithful of other gods until only Sseth's worshipers remain.*

Without worshipers to sustain them, the gods themselves would fade, Ts'ikil continued. *Only Sseth would remain.* She paused. *Is the life of one woman—however precious that life might be—worth such a risk?*

Arvin squeezed his eyes shut. It was—to him—but who was he to make that decision? He shook his head at the irony. He had hoped to persuade Ts'ikil into supporting a rescue attempt. Instead she was coming close to talking him into abandoning it and without, as far as he could tell, the use of so much as a simple charm spell.

"What if Sseth's faithful can't free him?" Arvin asked. "I'm no cleric, but I do know that only a god is powerful enough to bind another god. That binding is going to be hard to break."

That is true, but one of Sseth's mortal worshipers could accomplish it, if his faith was strong enough.

Arvin brightened at that. "Zelia's only a lay worshiper; she's no cleric," he told Ts'ikil. "If her seed's faith isn't strong enough to do the job, there's little danger in letting him open the door."

What if it is strong enough? Are you really willing to take so large a gamble, when it is souls that you are wagering with?

Arvin hesitated. The soul that mattered most to him was Karrell's.

Her future is assured, continued the couatl. *She is one of Ubtao's faithful, and her soul will be lifted to his domain from the Fugue Plain after she dies. Knowing that, you must ask yourself if rescuing the body that holds that soul is an act of love . . . or selfishness.*

"And our children?" Arvin said. "Would Ubtao accept their souls as well? Or would they be condemned to the torments of the Fugue Plain forever?"

The couatl said nothing for several moments. It was answer enough. She stared at Arvin's crystal.

Their fate is in Tymora's hands, she said at last, *because, in the end, it will all come down to a toss of her coin—to whether the Dmetrio-seed reaches the door before you. If it is open when you arrive, and you can stop him from freeing Sseth, you will get an opportunity to rescue Karrell.* She held up a cautioning wingtip. *Before you start praying to Tymora, you had better weigh the dangers and decide if one woman's life is worth the terrible consequences should you fail.*

Arvin closed his eyes. His heart tipped the balance heavily in one direction, his head another. Logic warred with emotion. He wasn't sure which would triumph—the human passion that surged in him whenever he thought about Karrell and the children he had fathered with her, or the cold, hard logic of the serpent that coiled around his family tree.

Only one thing was clear: he needed to find out where the door was. One way to do that would be to sleep, dream, and hope that one of his nightmares might contain a message from Sseth. He was so worked up by his conversation with Ts'ikil, however, he was pacing. Sleep would be almost impossible. He thought of the dog-man and his ability to render others unconscious and halted abruptly.

"Can you do that?" he asked Ts'ikil. "Put me to sleep with magic?"

The couatl gave him a sad smile. *I could, but your sleep would be deep and dreamless.*

Arvin paused. "I just realized something. If the Dmetrio-seed uses *osssra*—"

Ts'ikil looked grim. *He will enter a dream state more swiftly, and his dreams will be clearer than yours.*

"I don't suppose you're carrying any *osssra*, by any chance?" Arvin asked.

The couatl shook her head. *I came unprepared. Unlike you, I am not a psion.*

That made Arvin pause. Ts'ikil had used the right word—most people called him a "mind mage"—but had made the usual incorrect assumption. Not all psions could see the future. Arvin could catch glimpses, in a limited fashion. From Tanju, he had learned how to choose the better of two possible courses of action—to gain a psionic inkling of the immediate future, events no more than a heartbeat or two distant.

Ts'ikil had reminded him of one thing, however—his meditations. By using them, he could still his mind and force it into a state between waking and sleep. He could listen to his dreams, perhaps even seek out the ones Sseth was sending.

"You know," he said aloud. "That just might work."

Without explaining—the couatl could continue to read his mind, if she wanted to know what he was doing—Arvin lay down on his stomach on the ledge. Its stone was rough, so hot it felt as though it would burn right through the fabric of his trousers, but he paid it no heed. He was used to meditating in worse conditions, and had long since learned to block such trivial discomforts from his mind. He assumed the *bhujang asana*, arching his upper torso and head back like a rearing cobra. In a small corner of his mind, he smiled. No wonder he'd preferred that *asana* to the cross-legged position his mother used for meditation. He, unlike her, had serpent blood flowing in his veins.

And he was about to find out if it was enough to hear what Sseth had to say.

Arvin went deep. Deeper than his usual meditations, deeper even than he'd gone while under Tanju's instruction a year before in the abandoned quarry. He viewed his mind as he'd seen it then, as an intricately knotted net of memories and thoughts. But he viewed the strands as if through a magnifying lens. He could see not only the cords that were braided into each rope, but the individual thought fibers that made up each cord. A handful were a pale yellow-tan, mottled with irregular spots of black: hair-thin serpents with unblinking eyes and flickering tongues. Though he was reminded of the tendrils that Zelia's mind seed had insinuated, the sight of those serpents didn't stir up any unpleasant emotions. They were the legacy of his father's yuan-ti blood. Judging by the triangular shape of the head, Salim's ancestors had been pythons in their serpent form.

Bulges pulsed along the bodies of the hair-thin snakes like mice passing through a serpent's gullet: individual thoughts flowing through Arvin's mind. With deep, even breaths, he slowed them, putting his mind ever more at peace. He was distantly aware of his body sinking into a state much like sleep. His breathing and heartbeat slowed, and despite the fierce jungle heat, his body cooled slightly. His arms, however, remained rigid, supporting the *asana*.

Dreamlike images began to crowd into the darkness behind his closed eyelids. Fragments of memory floated by. Karrell's face and her voice, the word in her language for kiss: *tsu*. The warehouse and workshop Arvin had been forced to abandon a year ago, after the militia discovered the plague-riddled body of the cultist who had died there. And memories from farther back. Of the day he'd learned that Naulg had escaped from the orphanage, and the sorrow Arvin had felt at his friend not saying good-bye. Of his mother's face, the day she'd departed on what was to be her last job as a guide, and the tight hug she'd given him after placing around his neck the bead that enclosed the crystal he wore ever since.

He was distantly aware of his body, of a tear trickling down his cheek. It vanished quickly in the intense jungle heat.

He waited, watching the shifting images, drifting. Eventually, they began to blend in the way that dreams will. He was lying in a bed with Karrell, tenderly stroking her cheek, not in the room they'd shared in Ormpetarr but at the orphanage. The bed was small and narrow and hard, its straw-filled mattress scratchy. One of the clerics stood over them, frowning. The gray robe held out his hands, and Arvin saw that they were bound not with the traditional red cord, but with a serpent whose body was a tube of molten lava.

The smell of burned flesh and hair was thick in the room, coming from a lump of *osssra* that burned in a brazier in the corner. The brazier fell over, spilling a wave of lava across the floor. The *osssra* lay in the middle of it—a severed snake head. Its tongue flickered out of its mouth and wrapped around Arvin's wrist. He yanked it free but found himself trapped in the embrace of a six-armed creature—Sibyl, with Karrell's face.

Her stomach bulged like a dead body rotting in the sun. Tiny human hands erupted from it, the fingers seeding themselves like tendrils in his own stomach. He could feel them growing into him, burning their way up his veins toward his heart, which Karrell held in her hand. It pulsed, then lay quivering, then pulsed, then quivered again. She bit into it like an apple, blood-juice running down her chin and throat. Then she laughed with Sibyl's voice, a gurgling hiss like water bubbling through a sewer.

Stink surrounded Arvin, the stench of his own rotting flesh. The plague had found him. It had crept, disguised as his mother, into his bed, and rushed into his nostrils. Deep in his lungs, it festered. Inside his stomach, it grew, forming child-sized tumors that would burst and spread their seeds.

A scream echoed in his ears: his own. Dimly, he could sense Ts'ikil bending over him, touching his shoulder with a wingtip. That steadied him. The nightmare had left his arms trembling, his heart pounding faster than a rattler's shaking tail, his body drenched in sweat.

In the momentary reprieve granted by Ts'ikil, he was aware of the ache in his left hand, the crusted blood on his right shoulder.

Then he plunged back into nightmare.

It was as horrible as what had come before: twisted images of Karrell blended with Zelia, Naulg was swallowed whole by Sibyl, a silver snake coiled around Arvin's neck and tightened, slowly and remorselessly. In his dream, he saw his body convulse, his back wrenching backward in agony like a serpent's, until he was staring at his feet.

The image was unmistakable: the Circled Serpent, but was it a message from Sseth or just his own feverish imagination?

A heartbeat later, it was gone, replaced by scenes of infants impaled on fang-shaped stakes, a priest yanking Arvin's head back and forcing him to consume raw sewage while reciting his prayers at the same time, and Karrell—except that when Arvin tried to embrace her, she turned to shadow-stuff.

Nowhere, in any of the imagery, did he see a door.

It was getting increasingly difficult to continue. Had it been a normal dream, he would have woken up screaming long ago. Only the discipline imposed by a year's practice at meditation allowed him to continue for so long. That, and the lingering traces of Zelia's credo.

Control, he told himself savagely. If you want to see Karrell again, you've got to persevere.

The small portion of his mind that remained detached from his nightmares wondered what images Zelia's seed was experiencing. What would his nightmares be like? He doubted there was anyone Zelia cared for, save for herself. Certainly no one she loved. If Zelia herself was sleeping at that moment, she would probably be dreaming about her seeds turning on her.

The thought made Arvin smile. It gave him the strength to carry on.

The images swept relentlessly past. Arvin waded through a river of blood in which screaming human heads bobbed, suddenly found himself a winged snake stripped of his wings and plunging to his death, and saw a boil of pestilence rise on his stomach. He scratched it and a marilith erupted from the wounds his fingers clawed. He realized, suddenly and viscerally, how terrible a place sleep would be if Dendar did not feed on nightmares.

He had no idea how much time was passing. A tiny corner of his mind told him the sun still beat down on his prone body but with less intensity. There was a distant pang of hunger in his stomach and a full sensation that told him he would need to urinate soon. He fought a battle, however, and such things were trivial. The Dmetrio-seed had *osssra* on his side. Arvin had only his own will.

The nightmare images pummeled him, weakened him, wearing down his resolve. His body could endure the strain he was putting it under by holding the *bhujang asana* for so long, but his mind would soon snap. Already he could see the ropes that made up his mental net starting to fray. The sun's heat was making him lightheaded, and he would need to drink soon or he would faint.

A feather brushed his lips, bringing with it a trickle of water—Ts'ikil, lifting water to his mouth. Arvin sucked it greedily down—and saw, in his nightmare, himself suckling at Karrell's breast, only to find his head impaled by cold flat steel as the marilith shoved one of her swords through Karrell's back.

No! In his nightmare, he wrenched his head away. His eyes fluttered open, too-bright sunlight and the riotous colors of Ts'ikil's feathers swam before him, and his arms trembled. He collapsed, slamming his chest down onto hot, rough stone. For a moment, full wakefulness claimed him; he squeezed his eyes shut and straightened his arms, forcing himself back into the *asana*, forcing his mind back into the realm of nightmare.

Then he was aware of something that he hadn't noticed before. His forehead tingled. Either the iron cobra was closing in, or ...

Or someone else was scrying on him and trying to communicate with him.

Sseth.

With a croaked whisper, Arvin activated the lapis lazuli. He pictured Sseth as the god had been depicted in the Temple of Emerald Scales in Hlondeth—an enormous winged serpent with green and bronze scales looming over his worshipers. Distantly, he felt his mouth form silent words.

"Sseth. I am one of ..." he hesitated, fearful of telling an outright lie to a god, "one of your people. Tell me how to reach you."

The mental image Arvin had formed suddenly shifted. The statue he had pictured became flesh, and the face of a sleeping serpent filled his mind. Thick vegetation covered it: a tangle of leafy vines, bulging white rootlets, and interwoven tree branches and roots. Arvin's breathing faltered as he realized he was looking at the face of a god.

The eye opened. A slit pupil swiveled to stare at Arvin through the constricting lace of foliage. Arvin gasped as his awareness tumbled into it.

Into Sseth's own nightmares.

Sseth lay in his jungle domain, basking under a brooding purple sky, surrounded by his minions— the souls of his yuan-ti priests. His merest whim should have produced fervent, fawning service, but they had turned their backs on him. Without a word—ignoring even his commands—they slithered away. As they did, the jungle around Sseth came to life. Tree trunks glowed red then turned into tubes of lava. Vines became streamers of molten rock. These flowed over Sseth, burning him. The immense heat curled his scales like dead leaves. Then they crystallized, trapping him in solid stone. Trapped like an insect in amber—him! A god! He tried to open his mouth, but it would not move. The petrified vines had bound it shut.

He stared in mute fury as a dog-headed giant wearing a starched white kilt and golden sandals strode toward him, each of his steps crunching the petrified vegetation underfoot. Around the usurpur's head was the symbol of his power: a golden diadem of a rearing cobra.

The awareness that was Arvin had no idea who the dog-headed giant was, save that he was reminiscent of the dog-man who had followed Arvin all the way from Hlondeth. The awareness that was Sseth, however, understood that the head was not that of a dog, but of a jackal, a scavenger of the desert. It conveyed to Arvin the full extent of what that meant. It was no giant who strode toward him with an evil leer on his lips but a rival god, Set, Lord of Carrion, brother to jackals and serpents, King of Malice and Lord of Evil, slayer of his own kin.

Sseth raged. An angry hiss slipped between his clenched jaws.

Set grabbed his mouth in his massive hands and forced it open. He placed a golden sandal on Sseth's forked tongue, stilling it. Then he stepped inside.

Sseth tried to thrash away, but to no avail; the petrified vegetation held him fast. He felt Set force his way down his gullet. For a heartbeat, all was still. Then came a tearing sensation. To Arvin, it felt as though the skin were being flayed from his body. To

Sseth, who had a deeper understanding, it was recognized as skin sloughing free. Never before, however, had the shedding of his skin been so painful.

When it was done, Set stood before him, clad in Sseth's own green-and-bronze skin. A serpent head cloaked his own; through its gaping jaws Set's jackal grin could be seen. Then the rival god vanished.

Sseth tried to follow but could not move. His jaw, however, was still open. He snapped it shut, only to feel a tooth break against one of the petrified vines that bound him. Looking down, he saw that the tooth was embedded in the ground. It stood upright, like a miniature volcano, blood flowing from the broken tip like lava. Then the molten rock crystalized. Sseth stared at it, focusing his entire attention upon the tooth. Upon the crater at its tip. *Thisss* . . .

A sudden clarity came to Arvin's mind. He recognized that shape. The tooth had the exact contours of the volcano he'd viewed from the air while trying to get his bearings after coming through the portal. The broken top of the tooth had the same jagged edges as the crater at the volcano's peak. Sseth's message was clear: the door was inside that crater.

Yes, Sseth hissed. *Yesss.*

"How do I open it?" Arvin asked.

Too late. The sending was over. Blackness descended.

When consciousness returned, Arvin found himself lying face down on the ground. He must have collapsed a second time. Blood trickled from his upper lip where a tooth had torn it. The tooth felt loose in his mouth when he worried it with his tongue.

Ts'ikil bent over him, her expression anxious. *Did you learn where the door is?*

Arvin rose, shaking, to his feet. "You weren't listening to my thoughts?"

Sseth might not have spoken if I had.

The sun was low enough in the west that shadows from the cliff across the river had started to creep across the ledge on which they stood. Arvin turned and looked north. Peeking above the treetops was the distant mountain he had seen in Sseth's dreams. Inside its crater lay the door to Smaragd—the door that led to Karrell.

Ts'ikil turned in that direction. Her awareness slid into Arvin's mind. After a moment, she spoke. *Have you enough magic left to fly?*

Arvin had just been worrying about that. He'd taken the time to replenish his *muladhara* at the beginning of his meditation, but the numerous manifestations the metamorphosis power would require to carry him such a distance would certainly deplete it again. If he was going to do battle with the Dmetrioseed, he'd need to conserve his power.

Ts'ikil extended her good wing. Only one of her flight feathers remained intact and unbent; she nodded at it. *Take it.*

Arvin started. "You want me to pull your feather out?"

It will allow you to reach the volcano without wasting your power.

Arvin grasped it then hesitated. Was it some sort of trick? Would him having the feather somehow allow Ts'ikil to come along for the ride? To reach the door and prevent him from opening it?

No.

"Then why help me?"

Ts'ikil nodded at Pakal. The dwarf lay on the stone, the patches on his legs only slightly more insubstantial than the shadows that crept toward him. Then she stared at Arvin. *I help you because, even though I know what is in your heart, there is still a chance*—her lips quirked—*albeit only a coin's toss chance, that you will choose the correct path through the labyrinth that lies ahead.*

Arvin nodded. He grasped the feather and pulled. It slid cleanly from Ts'ikil's wing. He felt his feet drift away from the ground. He was flying.

Gripping the feather tightly, he took a deep breath. "I'll make the right choice," he promised Ts'ikil.

Though whether right for himself and Karrell—or for the world—remained to be seen.

CHAPTER 11

Arvin approached the volcanic crater warily. He had morphed his body into that of a flying snake as soon as he drew close enough to the volcano for a single manifestation to carry him the rest of the distance. The couatl feather was tucked inside his pack.

The lower slopes of the mountain were covered in thick jungle that gave way near its peak to bare black rock where nothing grew. Ancient lava flows had overlapped one another, leaving rounded puddles of frozen stone that looked like layered scales. The peak itself was a crater perhaps fifty paces across with a floor that looked like ropy, wrinkled black skin. Wisps of white vapor hissed from cracks in the rock, tingeing the air with a rotten-egg smell. The walls of the crater appeared thin and fragile. In several places, chunks of stone had broken away and fallen down the mountainside, giving the peak its jagged, broken appearance.

There was no sign of the Dmetrio-seed. Nor was there any indication of exactly where the door might be. Arvin had expected to see something like the portal he and Pakal had used or the circular dais in Sibyl's lair, but the crater appeared wholly natural.

He probed the area for any sign of psionic manifestations. There were none. Nor could he detect any thoughts.

He landed in a spot away from the venting gas, on hot black stone. Folding his wings against his body, he shifted the color of his scales from greenish brown to glossy black. He waited, one finger of his awareness touching his *muladhara*, ready at an instant's notice to manifest a power should the Dmetrio-seed arrive. As shadows crept across the crater's floor, he kept an eye on the sky.

After a time, he felt the tingling in his body that meant his metamorphosis was about to end. Still there was no sign of the Dmetrio-seed. He waited until his body had shifted back into human form before he scrambled to the lip of the crater. It would have been a difficult climb without his magical bracelet, for the rock was indeed as fragile as it appeared. He took a look around but saw nothing that might have been a flying carpet. No matter which direction he peered in, the sky was empty.

Perhaps the seed hadn't received Sseth's message.

Arvin laughed at the irony—that he, the last person who would ever embrace the serpent god, had been the only one to understand Sseth's plea.

He was growing impatient. Gods only knew what was happening to Karrell. She'd put on a brave front when Arvin had used Zelia's power stone to speak with her, but he had seen the toll that mere survival had taken on her. That had been days ago. Anything might have happened in the meantime. Karrell might be ...

He couldn't bring himself to contemplate it. Not there, not when he was so close. If only the Dmetrio-seed would show up, Arvin could get on with it. The waiting was the hardest part. When would the Dmetrio-seed figure out Sseth's message?

Another possiblity occurred to Arvin. Maybe the seed *had* figured it out. Maybe he'd decided not to betray Zelia but to convey the Circled Serpent to her as ordered. When Arvin had probed the seed's thoughts, a final decision had yet to be made. For all he knew, the Dmetrio-seed had decided to obey Zelia after all. The seed might be making his way back to Hlondeth even then ...

Arvin rubbed the scar on his forehead. There was one way to find out.

The scents of saffron and ginger mingled with the rotten-egg smell of the volcano as Arvin manifested a metamorphosis. Ectoplasm slimed his skin, adding to the discomfort of assuming a form even more distasteful than that of a flying snake. His body became slender, developing curves and breasts. His face took on a serpentine appearance. Even without a mirror to guide him, he could easily visualize his hair turning red as it lengthened, his tongue developing a bluish tinge as it forked. The scales that blossomed on his hands and face were the exact shade of green he remembered. He fought the urge to scratch his itching skin, venting his discomfort instead in a soft, feminine hiss.

Then he manifested his sending.

The Dmetrio-seed's face took several moments to coalesce in Arvin's mind. Eventually, it came into focus: dark hair that swept back from a high forehead, narrow nose and thin lips. His face was dappled in leaf-shaped shadow; he was somewhere outdoors. Eyelids drooped low over slit-pupiled eyes, and it looked as though the seed had just wakened. He lay on the ground, his body coiled around something that gave off smoke that caused his body to blur then become clear again, probably a brazier filled with burning *osssra*. That surprised Arvin. Perhaps the seed *had* decided to find the door and use it himself.

Arvin wasted no time on preliminaries; Zelia certainly wouldn't. He concentrated on the memory of her voice and shaped his own mental words with the inflections she would use.

The door is a volcanic crater at the head of the River Chun, he sent. *I am there. How quickly can you reach me?*

The Dmetrio-seed looked startled then wary. For a moment, Arvin wondered if something in his tone had given him away. *You want me to ...?* he started to ask, then caught himself. A sly smile crept across his face. *I will be there by sunset.*

The sending ended as he bent over and picked up the object he had been lying on—the flying carpet.

Arvin took a deep breath, glanced at the sun, then smiled. "I'll be ready for you," he promised. Then he began his preparations.

The Dmetrio-seed arrived exactly at sunset, when the sky to the west was a deep purplish red and the crater gloomy with shadow. He circled the peak on the flying carpet, staring down into the crater. Arvin, circling higher above in flying snake form, couldn't make out the expression on the seed's face but could imagine it. The seed, expecting a meeting with Zelia, would be puzzled at finding the crater empty. He would be probing for psionic energies or scanning the area for thoughts, perhaps even surveying the seemingly empty crater with a power that would banish illusions.

Arvin waited well out of range, not yet daring to make his move. He'd managed to lure the Dmetrio-seed there, but had the seed brought the Circled Serpent with him?

The flying carpet landed inside the crater. The seed stepped off it, hesitated, then pulled out a box that had been tucked inside his shirt. The seed looked around warily then shouted something, but Arvin was too high above to make out the words. Then the seed opened the box. Arvin saw a gleam of silver inside. He watched as the seed tossed the box aside and began to fit the two halves of the key together. While the seed was busy assembling the Circled Serpent, was the best moment to strike.

Arvin stiffened his wings and dived.

As he hurtled toward the crater, he clawed ectoplasm out of the air around him and shaped it into a flying snake that hurtled through the air next to him. A loud droning noise surrounded him as he gave his construct a single mental command—*seize it!*—and aimed it like an arrow at the Circled Serpent. Then he attacked.

Imagining his arms lashing forward, he sent strands of mental energy whipping through the air toward the Dmetrio-seed. The seed sent his mind slithering away into emptiness that left Arvin's attack with nothing to latch onto, then countered Arvin's attack with one of his own—a psychic crush that crashed through the mental shield Arvin had erected in front of himself and looped tightly around his mind. Arvin was barely able to remain conscious as it constricted, squeezing his thoughts together like the broken bones of a mouse in a serpent's coils. He tumbled through the air, his mind no longer in control of his body. Suddenly, he was human again. He slammed into the crater floor, knocking the air from his lungs. Dazed, he looked up.

The Dmetrio-seed was at the other side of the crater, struggling with Arvin's construct. It had seized the Circled Serpent in its mouth and was tugging on it while the seed clung grimly to it. Arvin forced himself to his knees, waving a hand. *That way*, he commanded. The construct obeyed, dragging the seed with it. At last, it wrenched the Circled Serpent from the seed's hands—but even as it did, a loud hissing filled the air. The seed glared at the construct and it exploded into a mist of ectoplasm. The Circled Serpent clattered to the floor of the crater, practically at the seed's feet.

Instead of picking it up, the seed whirled toward the real threat: Arvin. Surprise flickered across his face as he recognized his attacker. He visibly relaxed, then crooked a finger at Arvin—just as Zelia had done in the rooftop garden. Arvin felt a hollow open at the base of his spine; his *muladhara* opening, preparing to spill its psionic energies to the winds.

He smiled. The seed, just as he'd hoped, had chosen to toy with him instead of killing him outright. Arvin knew better than to use his psionics.

"Augesto!" he shouted.

The Dmetio-seed reacted immediately. A sharp hissing filled the air—his secondary display. His psionic attack struck Arvin even as it sounded, and Arvin felt the air rush from his lungs in an explosive breath. His lungs strained as he tried to inhale, but it was as if an invisible rope had cinched tight around his chest. Only by concentrating was he able to draw a thin, gasping breath.

The seed picked up the Circled Serpent, twisted it back into a circle, then bared his fangs in a delighted smile.

"This time, you won't have to play dead, Arvin," he hissed. "You'll *be*—"

A rumbling noise from the crater wall behind him interrupted his gloating. The seed whirled—just as a teetering slab of stone crashed down on him. Dmetrio vanished underneath the slab, which shattered explosively as it struck the crater floor.

Immediately, Arvin could breathe again. "Nine lives," he breathed, touching the crystal at his neck. Then he ran toward the fallen rock.

The seed lay in the middle of a scattering of broken stone—he either hadn't known any powers that would whisk him away or hadn't had time to manifest them. The falling slab must have struck him square on the head. His high forehead was caved in, and his jaw hung loose, attached only at one side. The arms and legs were likewise broken and bent, fragments of white bone protruding through bloody flesh. Even so, Arvin bent and touched a finger to the seed's twisted throat. As he expected, there was no sign of life.

Jumbled together with the stone were fragments of Arvin's trollgut rope. His trap had worked just as he'd hoped it would. He had tied off the slab of stone with his rope, then loosened it until the rope was all that held it in place. The astral construct had lured the Dmetrio-seed into position, and upon Arvin's command, the rope had lengthened, allowing the stone to fall.

Only one thing had not gone according to plan: the construct was supposed to have carried the Circled Serpent out of the way before the stone fell. Falling to his knees, Arvin scrabbled at the broken rock, clearing it away from the seed's body. The Circled Serpent was supposed to be indestructable, but a part of him worried, even so, that the rock might have dented it, preventing it from being used.

He heaved a sigh of relief when he saw where it had landed: inside a fold of stone that sheltered it from the crush of falling rock. They key was undented. Whole. Closing his eyes, he whispered a prayer to Tymora. He silently promised the goddess of fortune a hundred gold coins—no, a thousand—for her benevolence, then ended it with the plea that she extend the run of good fortune just a little bit longer.

"Just long enough for me to rescue Karrell," he said.

Then he stood. Slowly, he twisted the Circled Serpent back into a circle again. He was careful not to press the head toward the tail; that, he had learned from Pakal, would cause it to consume itself.

When it was a circle again, he walked to the center of the crater, a confident smile on his lips. Last summer, one of Gonthril's rebels had used a magical device to open a secret passage in the Extaminos gardens. The Circled Serpent, Arvin reasoned, had to work in the same manner. Just as Chorl had done with his hollow metal tube that night, Arvin bent and lightly tapped the Circled Serpent against the ground. Instead of emitting a musical tone as the tube had done, the Circled Serpent struck the stone with a dull clank.

He waited, but no door opened.

Arvin tried again.

Nothing happened.

Arvin stood, thinking. He tried holding the Circled Serpent parallel with the crater floor, then turned it a right angle to it, then held it parallel again. He tried walking in a circle around the crater, first in one direction, then the other. He tried drawing a circle on the stone with the Circled Serpent.

Still nothing happened.

The sun had disappeared below the horizon, and stars started to appear in the sky above. Inside the crater, all was in shadow. Arvin was worried but refused to admit defeat. He would solve the puzzle. Perhaps the Circled Serpent worked more like Naneth's teleportation ring. He tried gently tugging it, then laid it on the ground and stood inside it, on tiptoe, with both feet, but wasn't transported anywhere.

He tried to recall everything he had ever gleaned from the guild about opening magical doors. He tossed the Circled Serpent into the air, spinning, but nothing happened. He rolled it around the circumference of the crater—a task made difficult by the pile of broken stone covering the Dmetrio-seed's body—but neither action triggered its magic.

Though the night air was cooling, he could feel anxious sweat beading on his forehead. There *had* to be a way in—but how? Perhaps, like the portal he and Pakal had used, the door to Smaragd would only open at certain times of day, or maybe it could only be opened by a follower of Sseth. Was that why Ts'ikil had seemed so unconcerned about the key winding up in Arvin's hands?

If that was the case, why all the dire warnings about what would happen if Arvin were to enter Smaragd? Those only made sense if there was a way Arvin could use the key.

He pondered. How would one of Sseth's faithful use the key to open the door?

He felt a familiar tickle in his forehead: the lapis lazuli, warning him that someone was scrying on him. Ts'ikil? If so, her timing was impeccable. Arvin had just located, in one of Zelia's memories, a possible solution to his problem.

"If you're watching, Ts'ikil, it's too late," he announced. "I've made my decision."

Bracing his feet, he held the Circled Serpent out at arm's length in his right hand. Then—imitating the motion he'd seen in Zelia's dream-memory of her visit to the temple in Hlondeth—Arvin moved it in an undulating motion.

The sign of Sseth.

A ring of glowing red appeared around the edge of the crater. A wave of heat pressed in upon Arvin from all sides. He saw he was surrounded by a thin line of lava. It formed a perfect circle around the edge of the crater. The line of red expanded. As Arvin watched, it grew to the width of a palm, charring the Dmetrio seed's body with its intense heat. One of the fragments of the rock that had fallen from the lip of the crater above began to melt.

Arvin grinned. He'd done it! He'd opened the door. But—he shot a glance at the lava that bubbled inside the circle that surrounded him—did the entrance to Smaragd indeed lie through the molten interior of a volcano? If so, only an immortal would survive the passage through it.

The floor of the crater tilted suddenly, sending him staggering to the side. He clung to the Circled Serpent, and after an unsteady step or two, found his balance again. It felt as though the floor of the crater had become detached—was it floating on a bed of lava? The crack widened farther still, its edge creeping inward toward the spot where Arvin stood. Already the moat of lava was nearly a pace wide.

The tickling in his forehead continued to intensify until it felt like a hot ember burned within his scar. Something made him look up: a flicker of darkness against the starry sky near the lip of the crater. With a start, he saw a hooded serpent peering down at him. As it humped its body up over the edge of the crater, he heard a scraping sound—the rasp of metal against stone.

The iron cobra.

It slithered into the crater, its battered metal body scraping against the stone. Arvin backed away from it but was forced to halt as the unsteady floor tipped still further. The cobra, too, halted, just on the other side of the circle of lava. It stared at Arvin across the molten rock, its dented face illuminated from below by the red glow. Then it drew back into a coil, preparing to spring across the gap.

Swiftly, Arvin drew energy into his third eye. He hurled a line of sparkling silver at the iron cobra, looping it around the serpent's neck. As the iron cobra began to move, he yanked.

Unbalanced, the cobra toppled into the lava. It thrashed, trying to escape, but began to melt. Soon nothing remained except a bubbling layer of melted metal. For a heartbeat or two, gleaming red eyes glared out of the glowing puddle. Then, with an angry hiss, they vanished.

So did the sensation in Arvin's forehead.

The iron cobra had been following Arvin. Had it given Sibyl his location?

If so, there was little Arvin could do about it now. He teetered on the circular slab of stone. The heat grew steadily more intense. The ever-present damp had long since evaporated from his clothes. His skin felt hot and dry. He could use the couatl feather to fly above the crater, but if he did—if his feet weren't touching it when it at last opened—would he lose his chance to enter Smaragd?

If indeed that door did lead to Smaragd. What if it opened onto another plane—the Elemental Plane of Fire, for example?

Or even just the interior of a volcano, which would just as certainly kill him.

The circle of stone tilted, throwing Arvin to his knees. He started to slide toward the lava, then found a toehold and handhold and scrambled back up the tilting surface, balancing it once more, but not for long. The crack of lava was several paces wide, steadily closing in on the spot where he huddled.

A flapping sound, high overhead, made Arvin look up. He saw a winged serpent silhouetted against the sky. Ts'ikil—or Sibyl? It flew awkwardly, with sudden lurches, perhaps due to a broken wing.

As it wheeled above the crater, Arvin recognized it as Sibyl. The abomination's black wings were tattered and her body was crisscrossed with deep lash marks and burns from her battle with the couatl, but her face was alight with a wicked grin as she suddenly dived toward the spot where Arvin lay.

Arvin tried to wrestle his backpack off, hoping to get at the net it contained. At the very least, he could ensure Sibyl's death before he himself died. It was impossible to hold the Circled Serpent, cling to the rock and reach his pack all at the same time. Something had to go. The Circled Serpent, he decided, hurling it beyond the line of lava, but even as he wrenched his backpack in front of him and tore the flap open, Sibyl struck the edge of the circle of stone. It flipped upside down like a pot lid, spilling Arvin not into lava but into a black nothingness. He fell, still clinging to his pack, and saw Sibyl dive past him. Above them both was a circle of bright, flaming red in an otherwise purple and brooding sky. Below was thick jungle.

A *long* way below. Far enough for the fall to kill him.

Arvin fumbled desperately inside his pack, searching for the couatl feather, as he fell toward the trees below.

Karrell awoke with a scream. For several moments, she struggled to escape from the dream that clung to her like a heavy shroud, blocking all sensation of the waking world. She had been swimming in a bowl of venom, trying desperately to keep her head above water to prevent the deadly poison from slipping past her lips. The pool, at the same time, was an acid that ate into her flesh. It was gnawing a hole through her stomach, which pulsed as her children struggled to free themselves. If they did break free, however, they would die. Their first breath would be a lungful of liquid poison.

Arvin was in her dream as well. He stood at the side of the pool, holding a silver rope in his hands. He twisted it, tying it into a loop, then threw it. Karrell caught it and looped it around her wrist, but it coiled around her tooth instead. Arvin yanked the silver rope he held, forcing her mouth open. The venom rushed in, gagging and drowning her, and . . .

With a whispered prayer to Ubtao, Karrell shoved the dream memories aside. She sat up, expecting to find the marilith hovering over her. Instead the demon's attention was fixed upon the sky. It was difficult to see details through the thick screen of jungle, but something was happening up there, almost directly above them. The dark purple clouds swirled in a spiral around a circle that glowed a dull red.

"What's—" Karrell gasped as a contraction twisted her gut, "happening?" she managed to finish at last.

The demon gave no answer. Fortunately, it hadn't noticed her flinch. It watched, transfixed, as a bulge appeared below the circle of red in the sky. The bulge lengthened like dripping sap, then fell toward the jungle below in a bright red, bubbling streak. An explosive hiss of steam rose from the jungle as it struck.

Whatever was happening, Karrell was thankful for the distraction. After their earlier discussion, she'd pretended to take the demon's advice. She'd closed her eyes, feigning sleep, hoping that the demon would attribute any grimaces she made to nightmares and not to a pain that it didn't feel. Exhausted, Karrell had actually fallen into a restless slumber, but when she was awake she was unable to hide the agony that cramped her stomach every few moments. Her face, she was certain, was as pale as parchment. Sweat trickled onto her lips, leaving the faint taste of acid on them.

When the demon turned to her, Karrell glanced up at the sky, redirecting its attention there. "Are we in danger?" she asked, hoping the demon would interpret her look of discomfort as fear.

"Stay here," was the demon's only answer. It gestured, and half a dozen dretches appeared. "Watch her," it instructed them. "See that she doesn't leave this spot. Use your magical fear to herd her back here, but do not harm her."

The dretches nodded their bulbous heads and grunted. One or two of them fixed beady eyes on Karrell and smiled, revealing teeth like broken needles.

The marilith disappeared.

Karrell tried to stand, but a wave of agony forced her back to her knees. She could feel an intense pressure deep in her pelvis; her children, straining to be born.

"Ubtao," she panted. "Not in this place. Not now. Not *here*."

The layers of rotted vegetation beneath her hands and knees quivered as she spoke her god's name, turning to slime. Acid ate into her palms. Staggering upright, she wiped them on a nearby tree. The bark sprouted needles that tore her skin. The ground underfoot continued to liquefy, and Karrell sank into putrid water past her knees before her feet finally settled on something solid.

The dretches giggled—a loathsome, gurgling sound as vile as the bubbles rising through the putrid water in which they stood. The slimy stuff lapped at their bulging bellies, but they didn't seem to mind it. One of them bent over and slurped some into its mouth.

When her contraction ended, Karrell stared, panting, at the dretches. They stood in a circle around her, scratching their bellies, sniffing. They were stupid creatures—her success in avoiding them after her escape had already proved that—but they had powerful magic at their command. She'd seen how they'd driven the souls of the faithful.

She could hear more explosions in the jungle as yet more streaks of red fell from the sky. The circle of red in the clouds was brightening, bathing the clouds around it in an eerie glow. It was, she was certain, a gate—though why it was opening was anyone's guess. If it connected with the Prime Material Plane, however, she might at last be able to summon a creature that could help her.

"Ubtao, hear me," she said. "Send me allies in my time of need." She trailed a hand in the murky water and pictured the animals she hoped to summon. Small and swift, with silver scales.

She felt her awareness shift. It flew up through the jungle canopy into the sky. Toward the circle in the clouds and through it. Somewhere in the world beyond, it plunged into a river that flowed through the jungle, and . . .

Tiny motes of silver burst from Karrell's fingertips, rapidly expanding into full-sized fish. A school of fish, blunt-faced and silver, with gaping mouths filled with teeth jagged as broken glass soon swarmed toward the dretches and bit before the demons even had time to blink. By the time Karrell lifted her dripping hand from the water, the pool in which they stood had turned from murky green to bright red.

The dretches wailed, gurgled, swatted at the water that boiled around their legs and bellies, but to little effect. One of them went down immediately, yanked sideways by its own entrails. Another thrust a finger into the water, loosing a cloud of noxious vapors into it, but though one or two of the piranha floated to the surface, belly up, the rest continued their savage attack. Another dretch went down screaming, then a third.

Karrell staggered out of the pool, gagging on the fumes from the dretch's spell. A lash of fear struck her as one of the remaining dretches cast a spell at her, but it only hastened her onward. She had to stop a moment later, when another contraction struck, but when she continued, walking unsteadily, there were no sounds of pursuit. The allies she had summoned from her homeland had done their work.

She staggered on and a few moments later came to the spot where the first drip from the sky had landed. It had punched a hole through the trees, smashing them aside and scorching its way down through leaves and vines as it fell. It lay in a crackling red heap, lumpy and soft as bread dough, its edges a crusty black. Steam hissed from the jungle all around it, and even from a distance of several paces, Karrell could feel its intense heat.

Lava? What was lava doing dripping from a gate in the sky?

She glanced up at the circle of red; it was bright enough that it hurt to look at it. She had a better idea of who might have opened it—someone important enough for the marilith to have abandoned Karrell to the dubious guardianship of its dretches.

The circle in the sky suddenly flipped open, revealing a clear patch of starry sky. Two shapes tumbled through: a black, winged serpent with four arms, and a human, arms and legs flailing as he fell.

"Arvin!" Karrell cried, certain it was he.

He crashed into the jungle, not far from the spot where she stood. Karrell winced and felt a pang deep inside. She whispered Ubtao's name, praying that Arvin had survived. If she could reach him, use her healing magic . . .

Another contraction gripped her, forcing her to her knees.

When it was done, she glanced up. The winged serpent flew in an uneven spiral. It lurched sideways every few wingbeats like a drunken man. It was close enough that Karrell could see who it was.

Sibyl. Wounded or unwell, but there. In Smaragd.

Karrell felt a cold fear wash through her. Her head spun and she thought she was going to be sick. Sibyl had achieved her goal. She had found a way into Smaragd. Unless something was done—immediately—she would free Sseth and become his avatar. Karrell's mother's people—the humans of the Chultan Peninsula—would be crushed like mice in a serpent's coils. For unlike the Time of Troubles, Ubtao would not also walk the world in avatar form. There would be no one to battle Sibyl, save the *K'aaxlaat* and any other mortals brave and foolish enough to stand with them. Even these an avatar would sweep aside.

Another contraction gripped her, bringing tears to her eyes. She clung to the tree next to her, but its bark suddenly became spongy and gave way. She tried to climb to her feet but could not. She simply didn't have the strength to rise.

"Ubtao," she whispered. "Help me, not for my sake, or even for . . ." she clutched her stomach as another contraction wrenched at it. Something tore between her legs; she felt warm blood running down them.

"For my children," she gasped, "but for all my people.
Lend me ... your power. Send me the weapons ... I
need ... to stop ..."

The marilith's voice boomed out over the jungle.
"Sibyl!" it cried. "This way! Sseth lies here!"

Another wave of pain forced Karrell's eyes shut. As
they closed, one of the trees adjacent to the crackling
lump of lava burst into flame. From behind closed
eyelids, she could see the flicker of the flames, but
by then the pain inside her was too great for her
to care. She groaned, panted, then groaned again,
waiting for her children to be born.

❧ ❧ ❧ ❧ ❧

Arvin, barely conscious, lay in a tangle of vines
and broken branches. He had found the couatl
feather at the last moment, slowing his fall just
enough to avoid being killed—but not enough to
avoid being injured. He was dimly aware that one
leg was twisted uncomfortably beneath him, that
his face and arms were scratched and bleeding, that
there was more blood in his mouth and a ringing in
his ears, but he couldn't summon up enough energy
to care about it.

Something sticky dripped onto his face from
a broken branch above his head, something that
gummed his nostrils and lips and tasted faintly of
acid. The air he breathed had a sickly sweet odor, like
rotting fruit. The stench was worse than the sewers
of Hlondeth.

He didn't care.

A swarm of tiny flies buzzed around him, landing
and walking with sticky feet through the smears of
blood and sap that covered his face, then rising again,
buzzing around his ears and into his nostrils.

He didn't care.

Somewhere nearby, someone shouted Sibyl's name, a booming, demonic voice that brought back terrible memories.

His eyes flickered open.

He sat up, noticed that the couatl feather was still in his hand. As he stood, a streak of fire raced through the jungle toward him. He gasped, tried to activate the feather's magic, but before he could rise into the air the fire reached him. At the last moment it zigzagged around him, setting a tree a few paces away on fire, then continued on its way. He watched it go, his mouth hanging open in surprise. It was no ordinary fire, but one that scribed a neat line through the jungle, igniting only those trees and bushes in its path—magical flame that burned the vegetation it fed on to ash then continued to burn in empty air.

Arvin touched a hand to the flame. It was like touching an illusion: he felt no heat, no pain.

He shook his head, and blinked. Was he dreaming? Was it another of the nightmares Dendar had failed to consume?

"Sibyl!" the voice cried again—more strident. "*This* way!"

Glancing up, Arvin saw the gate the Circled Serpent had opened—a circle of bubbling lava, framing a patch of clean, starry sky.

It was no dream. He'd done it. He'd entered Smaragd.

A shape swept by overhead. Dark wings against a purple sky.

So had Sibyl.

A second line of fire rushed through the forest, crisscrossing the first. A heartbeat later, Sibyl swept past. She seemed to be following it. Craning his neck, Arvin watched as she flew away with ragged wingbeats, wheeling and twisting in the sky, pursuing what must have been a twisting, convoluted path.

"Sibyl!" the voice cried again from somewhere to his right. "Over here! Under the swords!"

The cry was followed by a whirring, crashing sound. It sounded as though the jungle was being hacked to pieces, as well as set on fire.

There was no time to wonder what was happening, or why. Arvin struggled to his feet and discovered he'd been lying on his backpack. He picked it up. The net was still inside, and he thanked Tymora for that. And for breaking his fall without breaking his bones. "Nine—"

Halfway to his crystal, his hand paused as the realization finally sank home. He was in *Smaragd*.

Mentally reaching for his lapis lazuli instead, he pictured Karrell's face. It came to him immediately. Her eyes were screwed shut, her mouth open and gasping. A grimace of pain etched deep lines into her cheeks and forehead. Her hair hung around her face in a disheveled mess. As he watched, she gagged and was nearly sick.

It didn't matter. Joy surged through him, fierce as the fire that bathed him in its glowing light. Karrell was alive!

Karrrel, he sent. *It's Arvin. I'm in Smaragd. Tell me where you are.*

Karrell's eyes opened briefly. Then she screamed. And panted. Grimaced. Then spoke in a ragged voice. *Ubtao's fire*, she gasped. *Follow…*

Of course! The fire. Slinging his pack over one shoulder, Arvin held out the feather. He rose into the air, then flew along the path the fire had burned through the forest. Wary of Sibyl spotting him, he flew within the flame. It blurred his vision and filled his ears with a roaring crackle. More than once, he came to places where the path doubled back across itself. He chose a direction at random the first three times, then realized he was lost in a maze. He paused, hovering in the air, uncertain which way to go. He didn't have much time. If he was to rescue Karrell and stop Sibyl from freeing Sseth, he had to move quickly, to decide quickly.

Saffron and ginger wafted through the flame and a droning noise rose above the crackle of flame as Arvin manifested his power. Which way? he asked himself. Straight ahead, left, or right?

He turned to the right, and an eyeblink-quick flash of a possible future flashed through his mind: him flying on and on through the jungle, until the fire finally died, then a scream, Karrell's.

Straight ahead and he got a flash of the marilith demon, swords whirling above its head, a pair of hands cupped to its lips as it shouted. Behind it was an enormous serpent head under a netlike tangle of vines. The ground beneath Arvin's feet trembled as the serpent's mouth craned open. Its eye fixed on Arvin, somehow seeing him through the slit Arvin's power had sliced through time.

My child, it hissed. *Free me. Join me.*

Arvin hung, transfixed, on the words. The god had spoken directly to him, mind to mind. Sseth's voice entered a place, deep inside Arvin, that he had not known existed, found it empty, and filled it with an overwhelming, almost sexual desire. Arvin was yuan-ti. He was *worthy*, worthy of power beyond his wildest dreams, power that would grant him anything—*anything*—his heart desired.

Karrell? he pleaded. *Karrell can live?*

Yes! the voice hissed. *Yes, yes! She will be yours, for eternity. Yours!*

"You lie," Arvin gritted.

The vision ended. Taking a deep, shuddering breath, he shook it off. Then he turned left and flew on.

He spotted Karrell a moment later. The line of fire ended where she hunkered down on all fours and in rags, trembling against the pain of giving birth. Already Arvin could see the head of one of the children crowning. A few moments more, and he—or she—would be born.

"Karrell!" he shouted, landing and enfolding her in his arms. "I'm here."

She sagged against him, and for a moment they simply held each other.

"Our children?" Arvin asked. "Are they—"

"Soon," Karrell gasped.

Arvin glanced up. The gate was still open but was far overhead, out of reach. He could fly up to it with the couatl feather—might even be able to do so while holding Karrell—but not while she was giving birth.

She clutched his hand. "Arvin," she gasped. "Be . . . you . . ."

"Hush," he told her. "We're together." He forced a smile. "I'll figure out a way to get us both out of here."

Karrell shook her head. "Behind . . ."

Belatedly realizing Karrell had been trying to warn him, Arvin turned . . .

Just in time to see Sibyl reach the end of the line of fire and skid to a landing behind him.

CHAPTER 12

Sibyl landed awkwardly in a loose coil. Arvin could see now why she had been flying so unevenly. There was a trickle of dried blood under each of her ears. Ts'ikil's cry must have burst both of Sibyl's eardrums. As she folded her wings against her back and steadied herself against a tree with two of her four hands, Arvin scrambled for his pack. Ripping it open, he found that tendrils of musk creeper had once again grown into the leather. Cursing, he slashed these with his dagger.

Sibyl's magical fear struck him.

Arvin fought back, even as the fear drove him to his knees. Forcing his will against it was like trying to shoulder his way through an icy wall of water. It slammed against him, trying to shove his mind back into a tiny corner of itself where it screamed, cringed, and wept.

He fought it down. Like a man staggering under a massive weight, he rose to his feet. Hands shaking, he hauled the net from the pack and lifted it to shoulder height, preparing to throw ...

Sibyl's glare intensified. So did the magical fear. Arvin felt tears pour down his face. The net sagged in his arms then slid from his hands.

Sibyl bared her fangs in triumph. Then she turned her attention to Karrell.

"Well, well," she hissed. "A cleric of Ubtao, in Smaragd? How stupid of you to reveal your position with that spell. I would tell you to prepare to meet your god, but there's only a hungry serpent where you're going." She laughed, then cocked her head, savoring the pain of Karrell's labor. "Go on," she taunted. "Try to run."

Arvin stared at the net that lay at his feet, his entire body quaking. Control, he urged himself. Fight back! Reaching deep inside his *muladhara*, he grasped a thread of energy and yanked it up into his chest. He breathed out, heard a droning noise fill the air, and imagined a protective shield in front of him.

Sibyl's magical fear broke upon it and was deflected to either side.

Arvin scooped up the net and hurled it. The throw was perfect. The net opened in mid-flight and landed on Sibyl's head and shoulders.

"*Absu—*"

Sibyl was swifter. She shifted into a tiny flying snake.

"*—mo!*" Arvin shouted, completing his command.

Too late. Sibyl escaped through the large weave of the net. She hovered above where it lay on the ground. She darted sideways then reappeared in her humanoid form next to Arvin. She towered over him, easily three times his height.

"You may have escaped my temple," she hissed, "but you won't escape Smaragd."

She flicked her tail. A lightning bolt shot from it, striking Arvin square in the chest. He was hurled backward into a vine-draped tree. At a spoken word from Sibyl the vines came to life, whipping themselves around him. He managed to wrench one arm free, tearing his skin as the suckers of the vine were ripped from it, but the vine wrapped around it once more. He tried morphing into flying snake form, but the tendrils tightened instantly, holding him fast. Abandoning that manifestation, he resumed his human form. Sibyl watched with unblinking eyes, smirking at his struggles.

The net lay on the ground a palm's breadth from Karrell, yellow flowers blossoming from its knotwork. Its fibers began to unweave, sending pale green tendrils questing up into the air, searching for a mind to drain.

Karrell continued with her labor, her head down and hair trailing, grunting as another contraction gripped her.

Struggling against the vines was futile, but Arvin's mind was still free. He clawed ectoplasm out of the air and shaped it into a construct with great hooked claws and a mouth that gaped wider than a serpent's and sent it hurtling toward Sibyl in a sparkle of silver that clouded his vision.

Sibyl met it with a shouted word in Draconic. The construct exploded into a cloud of tiny, shimmering flies that circled harmlessly around her head. With a shrug of one wing, she brushed them aside.

Sibyl was even more powerful than Arvin had feared. Had she already become an avatar? No, there hadn't been time, but the thought gave him an idea.

A droning filled the air around him as he tried to force his way into her mind. If he could convince her, even for an instant, that she had heard an unconditional summons from her god, she might leave. A simple splicing of her memories would be all it took. He pushed against her will, looking for the tiniest chink in her mental armor through which his own mind could slip.

Sibyl forced him back. Then she hissed. Her tail began to glow with an unbearably bright light then whipped forward. As the tip of it slapped against Arvin's face the brightness exploded, filling his entire vision. He blinked but could see nothing but white. He was blind.

He could no longer see Karrell, but he could hear her deep, shuddering groans. He could also hear, over Sibyl's hissing laughter, the soft pops of the flowers on his net releasing their compelling dust. Sibyl, he had seen in the instant before he was blinded, was still too far away from the net to be affected by the dust, but Karrell was close. Too close.

"Karrell," he shouted again. "Get away from the—"

His teeth slammed together as what must have been a second lightning bolt struck him. Muscles rigid, he fought against the blackness that threatened to swallow him. He had been foolish, he realized, to attempt to rescue Karrell alone. He should have tried harder to convince Ts'ikil to come with him. He pictured the couatl as he'd left her on the ledge, realized he should have at least told her he was entering Smaragd. Even wounded, the couatl was the one creature who might actually be a match for—

No. There was one other who might be able to beat Sibyl in a head-to-head fight.

The marilith demon. Arvin knew just which card to play to get it on his side: the fate link.

Allowing his body to go limp—playing dead—Arvin pictured the demon in his mind. The face was easy to visualize. It had seared itself into Arvin's memory on that terrible day that Karrell had been drawn into the Abyss. Sulfur-yellow hair framing an angular face with wide lips and a V-shaped frown, the hair whipping about in an invisible current. The body, female from the waist up, but with six arms. Below the waist, a writhing serpent's tail covered in green scales that shimmered as though they had been dipped in oil.

As Arvin made contact, he saw the marilith whirl, a hiss on its lips. Its mouth silently framed a word: "You!"

Sibyl is about to kill Karrell, Arvin sent. *Teleport to Karrell. Now!*

The demon didn't bother making a reply; its image simply vanished from Arvin's mind. A heartbeat later, he heard a *whoosh* of displaced air that announced its arrival. He was already busy manifesting a power. His face felt cool where ectoplasm coated it. Blurry images filtered in through the skin of his forehead and cheeks as they became sensitive to light. Two towering shapes, confronting one another.

Suddenly he could see again.

The marilith cuffed Sibyl away from Karrell and screeched something at it in Draconic. Sibyl hissed angrily and snaked her tail toward Karrell. The marilith flung out all six hands, and swords appeared in them.

Arvin smiled. Drawing air deep into his lungs, he charged his breath with psionic energy, then he blew the scents of saffron and ginger, first at the marilith, then at Sibyl, linking their fates.

The shouting was dying down and the marilith was lowering her swords. Time to stir the pot a little. Arvin manifested a second power, insinuating himself inside the demon's mind. It was an ugly mind, volatile and irrational, filled with violent fantasies that centered on what it would do to the worthless dretches—the creatures that were its minions—who had clearly shirked their duties. It bubbled with loathing over the fact that Sibyl—an insignificant *half*-demon—possessed the one necessary quality that would allow her to become Sseth's avatar: a mortal soul. But the anger that had boiled like lava through the marilith just an instant before was already cooling. Sibyl had agreed to deal with Ubtao's worm later, *after* she became Sseth's avatar. Once the chains that bound the human's fate with the marilith's had been severed, the impudent cleric and her squirming, loathsome spawn could be safely crushed. The marilith, Sibyl had just promised, had nothing to fear.

Fear, Arvin thought. He seized the emotion and braided it together with the marilith's frustration and her ideas of how minions should be treated to form a new memory: Sibyl telling the demon that it had better learn to obey her, and that the demon—worthless dretch!—had better learn that its needs were insignificant, that Sibyl was Sseth's chosen one, that she would deal with Ubtao's cleric when it suited her, and if that time had already come, and if that meant the marilith's miserable life would end, well then—

A scream of utter fury ripped through the demon's mind. *Ungrateful spawn! I should never have agreed to—*

A sword slashed down. Connected. Blood sprayed as one of Sibyl's forearms was sliced open from elbow to wrist. Marilith and abomination screamed as one. The demon stared at the identical wound on its own arm. Arvin felt a shadow of the demon's pain and gasped. He clung grimly to its mind. Swift as thought, he added a new memory: Sibyl, grabbing the demon's arm as the sword descended and deliberately twisting it so the blade struck Karrell, instead—causing a wound to spring up magically on the marilith's arm—then Sibyl somehow being wounded in the arm herself by the sword as the demon yanked it away from her again.

It was a crude image, one the demon would have recognized for false in an instant just by glancing down at Karrell, but its blood was up, anger frothing through its mind. Screaming, it launched itself at Sibyl, all six blades flashing.

The demon was lightning-fast, but Sibyl moved even more swiftly. Serpent body writhing, she avoided the slashes. Twin streaks of red shot from Sibyl's eyes. They plunged into the demon's chest, punching hot red holes. Identical wounds appeared on Sibyl's chest. She reeled back, glanced down at them—then at Arvin. Her tail twitched toward him, but before she could blast him with another lightning bolt, the marilith lopped off the tip of Sibyl's tail. Sibyl screamed at it in Draconic, but the demon was in full fury and did not notice that its own tail had been severed as well.

Sibyl, however, had learned something from the exchange. Instead of fighting back, a dark shimmer pulsed from her body: magical fear. It slowed but didn't stop the marilith's attacks. Jungle vines whipped around the demon's body. It sliced them apart and kept coming. In the distance, Arvin could hear wings flapping—another demon, summoned by the marilith to join in the fray?

The vines holding Arvin had loosened somewhat, and he strained against them, trying to get free. Sibyl and the demon were in the way, and he couldn't see Karrell. Had she breathed in the dust and fallen victim to the musk creeper's compulsion?

He caught a glimpse of Karrell crawling toward the net. She reached out, grasped it with both hands, drew it closer to her.

"No!" Arvin shouted.

Karrell staggered to her feet, drawing the net still closer to her. Tendrils reached eagerly for her head.

Arvin tore at the vines. If those tendrils rooted in her scalp. . . .

Sibyl flicked her tail, smearing blood across the marilith as it slapped home, and shouted something in Draconic. The demon was transformed. One moment, it was a massive creature with six arms and a serpent's tail; the next, an ordinary human with six swords lying at her feet—a human who gaped down at the smoking holes in her chest, the blood draining from her lacerated arm, and the abbreviated stump of her left foot . . . then collapsed.

Arvin ripped free of the vines at last and raced for Karrell. "The net!" he screamed at her. "Throw it at Sibyl!"

She did. The net sailed out of her arms—and missed its target. It landed on the now-human demon, enveloping it.

Karrell's face went white. Then another contraction staggered her. Grunting, she sank back into a crouch.

Sibyl whipped around, hissing, her red eyes furious. Her tail lashed forward, catching Arvin around the chest, trapping his arms against his sides. It squeezed . . .

"Karrell," Arvin cried. "I—"

The squeezing forced the air out of his lungs, preventing him from saying more. Then, abruptly, it stopped.

Arvin tore his eyes away from Karrell and looked up at Sibyl. The abomination stared over his head, a vacant look on her face. Like a suddenly loosened cloak, her coils fell away from Arvin. He stepped out of them and saw, behind Sibyl, the marilith demon. Still in the human form Sibyl had transformed it into, it lay, draped by the net, its eyes empty. Strands of yellow musk creeper had rooted in its scalp and wormed their way in through its ears, nose, and mouth. They pulsed as they drained the last vestiges of its mind. Already it had been rendered an empty husk.

Sibyl, linked to it by Arvin's psionics, had suffered the same fate. The abomination's chest still rose and fell, but her mind was a gaping ruin. She was as good as dead.

Arvin ran past both abomination and demon and lifted Karrell in his arms. He felt tears streaming down his cheeks. "The net," he said. "I thought . . ."

"Ubtao," Karrell whispered—though whether it was an explanation or a plea, Arvin couldn't tell. She groaned—deep and long—and her body shuddered.

Arvin glanced up at the sky. The circle of red was still open, and the wingbeats he'd heard a moment before had grown closer.

"We've got to get out of here," he said, knowing even as he spoke that there was no hope of escape.

A shadow fell across them. Arvin reached for the dregs of energy that remained in his almost depleted *muladhara*, then glanced up.

"Ts'ikil!"

The couatl landed gracefully, despite its injured wing. Her condition had improved. New feathers had sprouted in several of the bare patches and her wings were less tattered. Ts'ikil trilled softly as she stared at Karrell, then touched her with a wingtip.

Arvin stared up at the couatl. "How . . . ?"

Your sending.

"But I didn't . . ."

Ts'ikil smiled. *Yes, you did. You called out to me, asking me for aid—then very unflatteringly compared me to a demon.*

"I did?"

Karrell groaned, reminding Arvin of more urgent concerns. "Can you fly Karrell out of here?" he asked. "Quickly, before she—"

I can do better than that, now that the door is open, the couatl said, pointing up at the hole in the sky. She extended her other wingtip to Arvin. *I can take her home. Take her hand, and touch me. We will step between the planes.*

Arvin scrambled across hot, black stone to the spot where he'd thrown the Circled Serpent. The trip to Karrell's village had taken less time than a heartbeat. They'd spent only enough time there to explain what was going on to Karrell's startled clan and see her safely into a hut. Then Ts'ikil and Arvin raced back to the crater again. The gate to Smaragd had already started to close; a thin crust of wrinkled, almost-hard stone covered the opening. It crackled and steamed, releasing hot gases that stung Arvin's eyes.

He blinked, clearing them, and spotted the Circled Serpent lying near the edge of the cooling lava.

"There it is," he told Ts'ikil.

He started to pick it up, then yanked his hand back. The silver didn't look hot, but it had burned his fingers. He blew on them, then manifested a power that lifted the Circled Serpent into the air.

Ts'ikil hovered above, her wings fanning away the worst of the heat. Arvin moved the Circled Serpent toward her, but the couatl shook her head.

You should be the one to destroy it, she said. *You have earned the right.*

Arvin nodded. He enlarged the invisible psionic hand he had created, then squeezed, forcing the tail of the Circled Serpent into its mouth. He felt a sudden tug, and the artifact yanked itself free. A hissing filled the air—louder than the crackling of the cooling lava—as the Circled Serpent spun in mid-air. Arvin backed away, one hand raised to shield his face. Faster and faster the Circled Serpent spun, the head following the tail, until it was a blur of silver in the air. Then it disappeared.

The volcano gave a shuddering rumble. Then all was quiet. Arvin lowered his arm and looked down, and saw that what had been crusted lava a moment ago was cold, solid stone. A breeze blew across the peak of the volcano, cooling the sweat on Arvin's face.

He glanced at Ts'ikil. "That's it?" he asked. He had expected something more.

The couatl smiled, then nodded. *It is done.*

"Then let's go. I want to see my children."

Arvin leaned back against the wall of the hut, his infant son cradled in his arms. The boy was quiet, but earlier he had been competing with his sister in a crying contest. The twins were small— the combined effects of sharing the same womb and the lean nourishment Karrell had found in Smaragd—but they seemed strong enough, and they had powerful lungs.

The boy had brown eyes, like Arvin, a fuzz of brown hair, and a pattern on his smooth skin that might one day become scales. The girl had Karrell's high cheekbones, darker hair, and a slightly forked tongue. Both had human arms and legs, but what was most important was that both had survived.

So had Karrell, though the labor had been hard on her. She lay in a hammock, nursing their daughter.

Arvin watched as two women of the Chex'en clan fussed over the new mother, fanning her and offering sips of cool water. They looked like Karrell—close enough in appearance to have been her mother and sister, though Karrell had said they were only the clan midwife and her apprentice, both distant cousins. Each of them had Karrell's long black hair and dusky skin.

It had been some time since Arvin had slept, even though three days had passed since Ts'ikil had spirited them out of Smaragd. The birthing had taken the remainder of that first night, and the days and nights since then had slipped past in a blur. Arvin hovered somewhere between dozing and wakefulness. The heat of the jungle didn't help, nor did the fact that he kept slipping, in his drowsy state, into the minds of his son and daughter. The link with them came so easily it was like breathing. One moment his thoughts were his own—the next, his mind was overflowing with simple sensation: the sweet slide of milk down his throat, the gentle touch of a warm body against his, the blur of his mother's or father's face as they stared down at him with adoration.

It was easy to let his mind drift. The worst was over. Sibyl and the marilith were as good as dead, their minds empty shells. Sseth was securely contained within his domain, bound and brooding. Pakal had recovered from his shadow wounds and gone back to his people, and Ts'ikil had also fully healed.

Yet . . .

The younger woman came to Arvin and said something to him in her own language, then gently lifted his son from his arms. It was time for Karrell to feed him. Arvin reluctantly relinquished his son. He had been enjoying the feel of the infant's soft breathing against his bare chest. He stood and straightened the loincloth one of the Tabaxi men had given him, then crossed the hut to Karrell's hammock. As he brushed his lips against her forehead, she gave him an exhausted smile.

"We did it," she whispered. "We stopped Sibyl. It's over now."

"Yes," he said.

Yet . . .

He needed to think, to shake the lethargy from his mind. He stroked his daughter's head, and his son's, then squeezed Karrell's hand.

"I'll be outside," he told her.

The hut was circular, made of saplings that had been bound together. The roof was a rough dome covered with broad leaves, laid in a pattern like shingles. It was one of perhaps a dozen huts occupying an oval clearing that had been hacked from the jungle. At one end of the clearing stood a pitted chunk of black volcanic stone, studded with "thunder lizard" claws—an altar sacred to both Ubtao and Thard Harr. One of the wild dwarves who also made their home in that part of the jungle was prostrated in front of it, his hands extended toward the stone, fingers curled like claws. The clan's meeting house was at the opposite end of the clearing. In the distance behind it, smoke rose from the trees. That was where the rest of the clan was, clearing new land for crops. Arvin could just hear the faint thudding of their axes. Lulled by the sound, Arvin stood, staring at the jungle.

A woman's shrill cry from inside the hut jerked him out of his half-doze. He raced inside, nearly colliding with the midwife. She shouted something at him in her own language, pointed at her assistant, who knelt on the ground next to Karrell. The assistant lifted one of the twins—their son—and blew air into his open mouth in short, rapid puffs. Arvin's entire body went cold at the sight.

"What's wrong?" he cried.

Karrell didn't answer. Her lips were moving rapidly as she bent over their daughter. She gave Arvin a quick, terrified glance as she whispered a prayer. Arvin clenched his fists. Something had gone wrong. Both twins had stopped breathing, but Karrell's magic would save their children. It *had* to.

Then Karrell exhaled, as sharply and violently as if she had vomited the air from her lungs. She clutched at her chest and struggled to inhale.

"What's *wrong?*" Arvin shouted.

Karrell shook her head. She tried to speak, but couldn't. She made a frantic gesture at their daughter. The girl's lips were starting to turn blue. Arvin scooped the girl up, only to have her wrenched from his hands by the midwife. The elderly woman began blowing air into the infant's lungs.

Karrell swayed, still trying to gasp air into her lungs. Her eyelids fluttered.

Magic. It had to be, but why?

No, not magic. A memory hovered dimly at the back of Arvin's mind. Of himself gloating as he manifested that very same power.

No, not himself.

Zelia.

A droning hum filled the air as Arvin manifested a power. Silver sparkled from his eyes; a thread of it led out the door. He raced after it across the clearing. It led where he'd half expected it to: to the dwarf who stood, a smirk on his face, next to the holy stone.

One of Zelia's seeds.

Arvin hurled a manifestation at the dwarf-seed as he ran. Droning filled the air around him as he tried to batter his way through the seed's defenses, to crush his opponent's mind to dust, but the seed was ready. His mind slithered away from Arvin, leaving him grasping emptiness. Then the seed attacked. A fist of mental energy punched its way through Arvin's defenses then coiled around his mind. Too late, Arvin tried to throw up a shield against it. He could feel strands of energy moving this way and that inside his mind, weaving a net that held him fast. There was a quick, sharp tug—and the net closed, trapping his consciousness inside. Arvin could feel himself standing, was aware of his chest rapidly rising and falling, of his heart pounding in his ears—but the will that normally controlled his actions was tightly confined. He could imagine himself manifesting a power, but his *muladhara* seemed far away. His mind couldn't reach out to it from behind the net that had trapped it. Made stupid by a lack of sleep and the urgency of stopping the attack on Karrell and the children, he'd done just what the seed wanted—rushed blindly into psionic combat.

The dwarf-seed smiled, as if reading his thoughts. For all Arvin knew, it was.

"Arvin," the seed said in a husky voice that was unsettlingly similar to Pakal's, except for its smirking tone. "How obliging of you to run right into my coils."

Arvin tried to talk. All he could manage was a low moan. He felt drool trickle from the edge of his mouth.

The seed smiled. "Where is Dmetrio? Where is the Circled Serpent?" Silver flashed from his eyes as he spoke.

Arvin tried to resist the awareness that slid deep into his mind but couldn't. In another moment, the seed would learn that Dmetrio was dead and the Circled Serpent destroyed. The worst of it was that Arvin knew exactly how the seed would react—with rage at the fact that Zelia's plans had been thwarted—and with gleeful satisfaction at having caused Arvin the greatest anguish possible by killing the children and Karrell.

Then it would kill him.

If Arvin could have closed his eyes, he would have. He didn't want to see the dwarf-seed gloating.

What he did see surprised him. The seed suddenly jerked and his eyes widened. He whirled, and as his back came into Arvin's view, Arvin saw the dart that had lodged in the seed's neck.

"No!" the seed gasped. "Not—"

Then he fell.

As the rigid body struck the ground, Arvin felt the net that held his mind fray then suddenly loosen. He saw Pakal step from the jungle, blowpipe in hand. Astonished, he gaped at the dwarf—but only for a heartbeat.

Karrell, he thought. The *children* . . .

He turned and raced back toward the hut.

As he neared it, he heard a baby's cry. Then another. Then Karrell's voice, thanking Ubtao. He plunged inside and saw Karrell holding both children in her arms, tears streaming down her cheeks. The midwife and her assistant stood nearby, relieved looks on their faces.

Arvin fell to his knees beside Karrell. "By the gods," he said. "I thought I'd lost all three of you."

Karrell closed her eyes and took a shuddering breath. The children in her arms continued to cry, strong, healthy wails. Arvin gently stroked his son's hair then his daughter's. They were *alive*. He touched a hand to the stone that hung at his neck.

"Nine lives," he whispered to himself.

Karrell's eyes opened. They bored into Arvin's "It was her, wasn't it?"

Arvin nodded grimly. "One of her seeds."

"Is it—"

"Dead?" Arvin asked. "Yes, Tymora be praised. By a stroke of her luck, Pakal happened to be—"

Hearing something behind him, Arvin turned. Pakal stood in the doorway, arms folded.

Arvin crossed the hut and squatted in front of the dwarf. "You saved my life," he said, "and Karrell's, and our children's." He let out a long sigh. "I thought you'd gone back to your people. How did you manage to show up in just the right place and at just the right time?"

Pakal grunted. He said something in his own language—a brief prayer—then spoke in the common tongue. His eyes were smiling. "Having me watch the village was your idea. You anticipated that a seed might come."

"My idea?" Arvin echoed.

Pakal nodded. He touched a thick finger to Arvin's temple. "The memory. You erased it."

"Ah." Arvin said. Suddenly understanding his lingering unease.

Karrell passed the twins to the other women and rose to her feet. "You *knew* that a seed would attack us?" she said, rounding on Arvin. "You might have told me."

"He could not, Karrell," Pakal said. "The seed might have probed your thoughts and learned that I was lying in wait for it."

Karrell continued to rage. "You risked our children's lives, just to eliminate one seed?" she shouted. "You might have killed this one, but what now? Will you erase all of our memories of what just happened and send Pakal back into the jungle to wait until the next seed comes? And the next? And the one after that?"

Arvin balled his fists. Karrell was right. More seeds would come. Arvin and Karrell might flee, but there would be no guarantee that wherever they chose to hide wouldn't be home to another of Zelia's seeds, and once Zelia learned the Circled Serpent had been destroyed, she'd stop at nothing to have her revenge. As she'd demonstrated, killing Arvin alone wouldn't be enough.

Pakal interrupted that grim thought. "There *is* a way to end this," he said. He turned to Arvin. "Before you erased your memory, you told me to remind you of this: one year ago, you stripped away Zelia's power to create seeds at will. Since then, she has been able to seed only two people: Naneth and Dmetrio. Both are dead. All of her other seeds—those created before Zelia met you—do not share her animosity toward you. They simply do as Zelia orders. To them, you are just another target for them to kill. Eliminate Zelia, and no more such orders will be given."

"That much is obvious," Arvin said, "but it raises one big question. Did I happen to tell you why I didn't set out for Hlondeth at once?" He glanced at the twins. "Aside from the obvious reason?"

Pakal smiled. "Before confronting Zelia in her tower, you needed to learn more about its defences," Pakal answered. "I have a spell that allows me to question the dead—and the dead cannot lie."

Arvin smiled. "Not a bad plan," he said. "I wish I'd thought of it."

Pakal grinned. "You did."

Arvin glanced at Karrell. The anger had fled from her eyes; determination had replaced it. "I'll come too," she said. "My magic—"

"Is needed to protect the children," Arvin said. "If another seed should find them while I'm gone. . . ."

Karrell's mouth tightened. She held his eyes a moment longer, then nodded. "Do it," she said. "Kill her. End this."

❧ ❧ ❧ ❧ ❧

Arvin and Pakal strode across the flagstone plaza toward the pyramid that dominated the center of the city. Ss'inthee'ssaree was as ancient as Ss'yin, but unlike the Jenestaa, the Se'sehen had worked hard to reclaim it from the jungle. The buildings that ringed the plaza had been repaired and restored to their former glory, their stonework cleaned and remortared. The serpents that twined on their carved facades had been repainted in bright colors. The flagstones underfoot were smooth and even, without so much as a tendril of vine growing between their cracks.

They were also stained with dried blood. House Extaminos had not only triumphed over the Se'sehen in Hlondeth but had carried the fight to the Black Jungle. Sibyl had inadvertently shown them the way, when she used the portal on Mount Ugruth to follow Arvin and Pakal. House Extaminos controlled what had once been the Se'sehen stronghold.

Flies rose lazily into the air as Arvin skirted the largest of the dark brown stains that marked the plaza. The corpses of those who had fallen in battle had been carried away, but the smell of death still rose from the sun-hot stones.

A score of Hlondeth's militia stood guard in front of Arvin's destination: the pyramid that housed the Pit of Vipers, a temple identical to the one that had been Sibyl's lair, a temple that contained the one-way portal the Se'sehen had used to reach Hlondeth.

Though they were sweltering in bronze chain mail and flared helmets, the Hlondeth militia was alert. They lowered their crossbows and snapped to attention as Arvin approached. Their officer—a halfblood with a narrow, black-scaled face that echoed those of the twined serpents embossed on his breastplate—touched his sword hilt to his chest, then bowed low.

"Lord Extaminos," he said. "We thought—"

"You are paid to obey, not think, Captain Vreshni," Arvin said, neatly plucking the officer's name from the man's mind. He raised his chin haughtily, as

Dmetrio would have done. His forked tongue gave his words an imperious hiss. "Accompany me to the portal. I have urgent business in Hlondeth."

"Yes, Lord Extaminos," the officer said, bowing a second time. He sheathed his sword and gestured at the pyramid. "This way."

Arvin turned to Pakal, who had also disguised himself as a yuan-ti. The dwarf's illusion was perfect; his body appeared twice as tall as it really was and slender as a serpent's. The tattoos on his body had become a pattern of snake scales, his matted braids were gone, and the necklace of claws and teeth around his neck had become a ring of tiny, sparkling jewels set into the scales of his chest, shoulders, and back. The only detail untouched by his illusion was the armband of gold, set with a turquoise stone, on his upper right arm.

"You may go," Arvin told Pakal in a cold voice. Using his lapis lazuli, however, he bade the dwarf a more pleasant farewell. *Thank you. For everything.*

Pakal returned his grim smile. *Thard Harr watch over you,* he sent back. *And ... good luck.* He bowed then strode away.

Arvin followed the officer, moving his feet with a sliding motion as Dmetrio had done. The metamorphosis had been an easy one; Dmetrio's appearance was still fresh in his mind. The club-toed feet, however, were tricky to walk on.

The pyramid was tall and narrow. It resembled a series of ever-smaller blocks set one upon the other. Each of the four sides was dominated by a stone serpent that seemed to be slithering down the stonework, its head resting upon the ground, and their four tails twined together at the top of the pyramid. The serpent that decorated the front of the pyramid had its mouth open wide, and its fangs looked as though they were solid silver.

Arvin suppressed his shudder as he followed the officer into the mouth. It reminded him a little too closely of Sseth. The mouth was open wide enough that Arvin could walk upright, but an edge of the officer's flared helmet scraped against one of the silver fangs, causing him to duck.

A smooth ramp led down to a chamber filled with soft green light. The walls were carved to resemble scales. A forest of serpent-shaped columns held the weight of the pyramid above at bay. A sweet scent lingered in the air under the heavy musk of snake—*osssra*, Arvin realized a moment later. Though the braziers that dotted the floor were cold and dark, the stone walls were impregnated with the stuff.

More militia—six halfblood officers, two of them armed with wands—stood guard in front of a gilded statue: one of the stations of Sseth. The god was depicted in his twin-tailed form, his tails encircling a black obsidian globe that represented the world. Wings flared out from his shoulders, and under each wing was an arched entry. These led to corridors that curved away to the right and left.

The officers bowed as Arvin approached. One of them touched a hand to his helm. "Shall I inform Lady Dediana of your imminent arrival, Lord Extaminos?"

"No," Arvin ordered. "Tell no one."

Confusion flitted across the officer's face but was quickly hidden by his bow. "As you command, Lord Extaminos."

Arvin waited for Captain Vreshni to indicate which of the corridors led to the portal. The captain did a moment later by turning slightly toward the left entrance. Arvin strode into it as if he'd known all along which route to take. The captain scurried after him.

The corridor spiraled down past slit windows that opened onto a central room. Just like the room in the temple under Hlondeth, it was dominated by a dais of black obsidian. The snakes that had once slithered around it were dead. They'd been reduced to ash; a burned stench lingered in the air. Judging by the scorches on the walls, someone must have let loose a blast of magical fire—one of House Extaminos's wizards, perhaps.

Just as in Sibyl's lair in Hlondeth, the portal room's only other exit was framed by the beastlord's snarling face—it probably led to a similar temple. More militia stood guard in front of the exit, looking alert and watchful. Captain Vreshni indicated a path had been cleared through the ash, allowing passage to the dais.

"If you please, Lord Extaminos."

Arvin started to thank him, then remembered whom he was impersonating. "Go," he said curtly, dismissing him.

The captain bowed his way out of the room.

Arvin took a deep breath then stepped onto the dais. For several heartbeats, nothing happened. Then the portal activated. He felt a dizzying lurch—and found himself standing in the same room as before.

No, not the same. The corridor beyond the beastlord's face was choked with rubble and the lantern light was stronger here. Arvin could hear soft breathing and the creak of a crossbow being drawn. Whoever was guarding this room was invisible.

Refusing to flinch, Arvin drew himself up and glanced imperiously around the seemingly empty chamber. As he did, he manifested the power that would allow him to listen in on their thoughts.

There—one of them was casting a spell. It was divination magic: a spell that would confirm whether the visitor who had arrived so abruptly was, indeed,

Hlondeth's missing prince. As the spell quickened, Arvin slid deeper into her mind and neatly snipped out the memory of what her magic had revealed: a human who bore no resemblance whatsoever to Lord Dmetrio. He spliced an image of his metamorphosed form into the hole he'd just created then withdrew.

"Show yourself," he commanded.

A yuan-ti appeared before him. She was a dark-haired woman with yellow scales, wearing the high-collared robe of Sseth's clergy. One hand held a snake-headed staff that rested on the floor. She frowned for a moment, like someone who'd just walked into a room and forgotten what they'd been looking for, then bowed.

"Lord Extaminos," she said. "Welcome back. Your mother will be pleased to hear that you have returned."

"Do not inform her ... quite yet," Arvin said.

The cleric, straightening, arched an eyebrow.

"There is someone else I must speak with first."

Her thoughts bubbled with curiosity. She held her tongue—but not her magic. Arvin felt energy surge from Karrell's ring, up through his arm and into his mind, shielding it. For just an instant, he slipped the ring from his finger and concentrated on a familiar face—Zelia's—filling his mind with it until the image crowded every other thought out. Then the ring was back on his finger again.

The cleric's lips parted in a smile, baring the tips of her fangs. She hid it behind a bow. "I will escort you, Lord Extaminos. During the attack by the Se'sehen, a number of humans took the opportunity to ... cause some problems. The streets are still not entirely secure."

She was thinking about Gonthril. The rebel leader and his followers had been stirring up trouble, it seemed. More than that, several sections of the city, including a stretch of its waterfront, had fallen into human hands, but once the militia returned from down south, she was thinking, all that would end. The uprising would be crushed and the slaves who had dared to claim their freedom would be put back in their place.

"You will show me to the surface, then resume your duties here," Arvin commanded.

"As you wish," the cleric demurred.

Her thoughts told him much more. Lady Dediana had grown suspicious of Zelia of late, suspicious of the hold the mind mage seemed to have over the royal son. The queen suspected a plot—and "Dmetrio's" insistence on not telling his mother about his return had confirmed it. He would be watched. Carefully.

Arvin smiled to himself. Years of working for the Guild had taught him how to slip away from even the most persistent watchers, and his psionics would take care of any who was armed with magic. Meanwhile, the cleric would confirm Lady Dediana's fears. If Arvin was unsuccessful in his bid to take Zelia down, House Extaminos would surely finish the job.

For the moment, however, there was someone he needed to make contact with, someone he needed to persuade to help if his plan was to come to fruition.

"Your concern for my well being is ... appreciated," he told the cleric, "but also unfounded. I can take care of myself."

❧ ❧ ❧ ❧ ❧

Arvin stared across the table at Gonthril. The rebel leader hadn't bothered to disguise himself, save for the cloak hood he'd just allowed to fall back against his shoulders. His rebels—for the moment—had control of the waterfront, including one particular tavern.

The Mortal Coil.

Arvin smiled when Gonthril had suggested it as a meeting place. When Arvin had used a sending to contact Gonthril, he'd wondered if the rebel leader would bother to reply. It had been a year since they'd last seen one another. That they were meeting in the place where Arvin's troubles had begun was ironic. The head of the serpent was closing in on the tail.

Though the harbor outside was nearly empty of ships—most had fled when the Se'sehen attack began—the tavern was just as Arvin remembered it. Pipe smoke had stained the coiled-rope ceiling that had given the place its name, and the air still smelled of unwashed sailors and ale. The circular walls were still damp and the benches were as hard as ever. The only "patrons," however, were Gonthril's people, who stood alert and ready, crossbows in hand. Nobody was behind the bar—and nobody was drinking.

Gonthril looked the same but somehow older, aged by a year of hiding and fighting. Arvin, too, had aged. The two men still looked as close as brothers. Gonthril's eyes, however, were blue, and the little finger of his left hand was whole.

"You said you had something to offer me?" he asked. "Something I would find valuable?"

Arvin nodded and leaned forward in his chair. "Information."

"About what?"

"House Extaminos. Its secrets ... and its weaknesses. Everything your uprising needs to succeed."

Gonthril's eyes glittered. "Tell me more."

"There's a yuan-ti," Arvin began, "a mind mage named Zelia."

"I've never heard the name."

Arvin smiled. "That doesn't surprise me. Zelia makes a point of keeping out of the public eye. She controls a network of spies who have infiltrated not just House Extaminos but every major yuan-ti House in Hlondeth."

"How?"

"By passing themselves off as members of those Houses. The family members are eliminated, and the spies take their place."

Gonthril frowned, and thought a moment. "These spies—are they dopplegangers?"

Arvin's eyesbrows raised. The rebel leader had a quicker mind than he'd expected. "In a manner of speaking, yes."

"The information they have gathered—is it written down?"

"No," Arvin said. "It's all inside Zelia's head, but there's a way to get it out."

"How?" Gonthril asked, skepticism plain in his voice.

"By killing her. Once that's done, I can put you in touch with a cleric who can speak with the dead."

Gonthril's eyes bored into Arvin's. "Why do *you* want this woman dead?"

"For several reasons," Arvin answered. "The simple answer is that if I don't kill her, she'll kill me." He spread his hands. "That's not what really concerns me. Zelia won't stop there. She'll also make sure my wife and children die."

Gonthril's eyebrows rose. "You've been busy, this past year."

Arvin had to smile.

Gonthril's expression turned serious again. "What if the information in Zelia's head turns out to be of no use to the Secession?" Gonthril said, "I'll have wasted my resources. There's an entire city of yuan-ti that need killing and precious few humans bold enough to do the job."

Arvin fought to keep his smile from wavering. Gonthril's hatred of the serpent folk ran deep. If he realized that Arvin was part yuan-ti—and that the wife and children Arvin was trying to protect were as well—the only "help" forthcoming would be a crossbow bolt in the back. He was glad, yet again, that Karrell's ring was still on his finger.

"Zelia is worth killing for other reasons," he said.

"Convince me."

"You've heard that Sibyl is dead?" Arvin asked.

Gonthril nodded. "So House Extaminos says."

"It's true," Arvin assured him. "Now Zelia is trying to pick up where Sibyl left off. Sibyl was only pretending to be Sseth's avatar, but Zelia actually stands a chance at becoming just that."

"How?"

"It's complicated, but the short answer is this: Sseth is bound inside his domain. He needs someone to free him. Whoever does this will be rewarded with anything they ask for. Zelia knows of an artifact called the Circled Serpent—a key that opens a door to Sseth's domain. Using it, she can free him—and become his avatar."

Gonthril whistled under his breath. He sat in silence a moment, then reached inside his shirt and pulled out a chain that was looped through a ring—a wide band of silver, set with deep blue sapphires. He took it off the chain and slid it across the table to Arvin. "Put it on."

Arvin did, reluctantly. He remembered the last time he'd worn it. With the ring on, he'd be unable to tell a lie. If Gonthril asked directly about the Circled Serpent, Arvin would have to tell him it had already been destroyed. Gonthril would assume everything Arvin had just told him was a lie, and Arvin would have to fight his way out of the Mortal Coil.

He resisted the urge to glance at the half-dozen crossbows pointed at him. Instead he took a deep breath. Control, he urged himself. He didn't need to tell the whole truth about the Circled Serpent—he just had to concentrate on answering Gonthril's questions as succinctly as possible.

Gonthril looked him square in the eye. "Do you work for House Extaminos?" he asked.

Relief washed through Arvin as he saw the tack Gonthril's questions would take. He smiled. "No," he answered, his voice firm and level. "As I told you when you asked me that question a year ago, I work for myself."

This time, it was the truth.

"Is the story about wanting to kill Zelia a ruse to trap me?"

"No."

"Is your name really Arvin?"

Arvin frowned. "Of course."

"Are you a doppleganger?"

Arvin laughed. "No. What you see is what you get. I'm—" He was about to say "human" but checked himself just in time. He shrugged. "I'm Arvin."

Gonthril nodded then gestured for Arvin to take off the ring.

Arvin did and passed it back to Gonthril. The rebel leader slipped it back on the chain and hung it around his neck.

"What's the Seccession's part in your plan?" the rebel leader asked. "What do you need us to do?"

"Not the Seccession," Arvin said. "You. I need someone who can pass as me without having to resort to magical disguises. I'll be playing the part of one of Zelia's spies—a spy that has 'captured' Arvin. It will be dangerous and unpleasant, but if Zelia reacts as I expect her to—and believe me, I know her well—it will give me the chance to take her completely by surprise."

"I see," Gonthril said. For several moments, there was silence. Gonthril glanced at one of his rebels. The man gave a slight shrug then nodded.

Arvin waited for the rebel leader's reply.

"I'll need to know more details, of course," Gonthril said, "but so far, you've got my interest."

Arvin heaved a mental sigh of relief. He hesitated then decided to broach the question that had been nagging at him for some time. "Before we get into the details, there's one thing I neglected to ask the last time we met," he said, his voice low enough that Gonthril's people wouldn't hear it.

"Go on," Gonthril said.

Arvin waved a hand between them. "We look enough alike to be brothers," he whispered. "Is there any chance that we might be?"

Gonthril gave a tight smile. "My mother had a very strong spirit. When I was growing up, I often heard her tell my father she wouldn't be bound to any one man. We may—you and I—very well have been fathered by the same man."

"Did your mother ever mention a bard named Salim?"

"No."

"Then your father—"

"The only man who earned the right to be called 'father' was the man who raised me," Gonthril said in a stern voice. His expression was grim. For a moment, Arvin was worried he'd offended Gonthril.

"That man is dead," Gonthril continued, "as is my mother. They died in the so-called 'Plaza of Justice' the year I turned thirteen, executed for a crime they did not commit, but that didn't matter. They were human, and 'insolent to their betters.' Even as they were led to their deaths, they refused to go quietly and shouted insults at the yuan-ti who had condemned them." His eyes grew fierce. "I decided to carry on that tradition of defiance. That same year, I joined the Secession."

Arvin listened quietly, surprised by how much he and Gonthril had in common. Each of them had been forced to make his way in the world alone. Their lives, however, had taken very different paths.

Gonthril shrugged. "You don't need to convince me that we're related," he said. "I'm helping you for the good of Hlondeth—for the benefit of humans everywhere—not because of some blood tie we may or may not share."

Arvin nodded, his face neutral, but his heart was beating quickly. Was the man across the table from him really his brother? Arvin's mother had believed that Arvin was the only child Salim had ever fathered—but what if the bard had been lying to her—or simply hadn't realized that a previous liaison had produced a child?

It would be ironic indeed if the leader of a group dedicated to returning Hlondeth to human hands turned out to be part yuan-ti.

Gonthril had already moved on; he leaned across the table in a conspiratorial hunch. "Now tell me your plan. In detail."

CHAPTER 13

Arvin walked toward Zelia's tower, herding his captive ahead of him. Gonthril had a blindfold over his eyes and his hands were bound behind his back. His feet were hobbled, so he staggered when Arvin shoved him forward. The bonds looked and felt tight but were special knots that could be loosened in an instant by tugging the right strand. The rebel leader played his part to perfection, never once complaining about Arvin's rough handling.

When they reached the door, Arvin waited. Tension knotted his stomach. The seed Pakal had killed in Karrell's village had told him of the tower's defences—about the strip of copper hidden within the doorframe that would manifest a catapsi on any psionicist who entered and the invisible mage mark designed to take care of non-psionic intruders. The seed had also told him how to get past them. A pressure plate high above had to be pushed with a far hand manifestation as one stepped through the door. It had alerted Arvin to the dangers that lay within. Even so, Arvin had to steel himself as he knocked then waited for the door to open. The bottle he held in his left hand was slippery with sweat.

Control, he told himself. Then he smiled. He was thinking like Zelia—which was just what he wanted.

Arvin's crystal hung around Gonthril's neck and Karrell's ring was on one of the fingers of Gonthril's right hand. A glove on his left hand hid the fact that his little finger was whole. The disguise wouldn't stand up to scrutiny, but if all went well, Zelia wouldn't get a chance to make a close inspection.

As the door swung open, Arvin grabbed Gonthril by the hair and forced him to his knees.

He had been expecting some minion to answer his knock, and was surprised to find Zelia herself staring out at him. Then he realized that it was probably one of her duplicates.

It looked like Zelia, though, down to the last pore. Long red hair glowed in the light of the setting sun, and her green eyes matched the color of the scales that freckled her cheeks and hands. She wore a yellow dress of watered silk that plunged low between her breasts and left her arms bare. The scales that covered her body were a deep sea green. She glanced briefly at Arvin, then at the captive. Her eyes flashed silver as she manifested a power. Then she frowned.

"It's the ring," Arvin told her, "but let him think what he likes—he's powerless. I drained him with a catapsi."

His voice sounded strange in his ears. It matched the form he'd metamorphosed into: Dmetrio. He'd spent extra care in shaping his body, down to the last detail. The hair that framed his high forehead was thinner and darker than his own, and his scales were the exact shade Dmetrio's were. His body was leaner, his groin a smooth surface with his genitals tucked inside a flap of skin. His posture and movements were fully those of a yuan-ti. He swayed, rather than standing square on his two stub feet, and kept his lips parted, tasting the air with his tongue.

A hissing filled the air, though Zelia's lips remained closed. "You're right," she said a moment later. "His aura is empty."

"If it wasn't, the door frame would have drained him," Arvin chuckled.

Abruptly, she looked up at Arvin. He was ready for her. As her eyes flashed silver a second time, he pulled energy into his throat and imagined his hands sweeping through the air in front of his face, washing his thoughts clean. At the same time he concentrated, simultaneously manifesting the power that allowed him to shape sound. The droning of his secondary display became a sharp hissing noise—the sound the Dmetrio-seed would have made, had it been the one manifesting the empty-mind defense.

Zelia *tsk-tsked*, shaking her head.

Arvin shrugged, adding a feminine sway to the gesture. "What did you expect?" he said. "None of us like to reveal all of our playing pieces at once, do we?" He glanced past Zelia into the tower. "Where is she?"

The duplicate didn't bother to pretend she didn't know who he was talking about. "In the study."

She opened the door wider, an invitation for Arvin to step inside. He did, taking care to deactivate the traps in the door as he passed through it. Zelia hung back, waiting for him to prove that he knew where he was going, which he didn't. Her body language, however, spoke volumes to someone trained by the guild. The slight turn of her hips plus her deliberately averted eyes pointed him in the right direction. Shoving Gonthril ahead of him, Arvin crossed the entryway and made for a door on the right. The handle was trapped with a venomed needle, so Arvin pushed the secret button as he turned it, preventing the needle from springing.

The study had a basking pit and walls hung with slitherglows that filled the room with soft, shifting rainbows. The scent of oil lingered in the air. The only piece of furniture was a small cabinet opposite the door. The room was unoccupied; the basking pit was empty. Arvin turned as Zelia closed the door behind her. One hand still knotted in Gonthril's hair, he forced his "captive" back to his knees.

"Where's Zelia?" Arvin asked.

Zelia cocked her head. "Right here," she said, touching her chest with a slender finger.

Arvin didn't believe it for a moment.

Gonthril shifted suddenly, twisting in Arvin's grip. "You bitch!" he shouted, rearing to his feet. "You killed Karrell! I'll—"

Arvin manifested a simple power, shaping the sounds in the room. As a loud hissing filled the air, he shifted one of the fingers of the hand that held Gonthril's head, giving a two-tap code. Gonthril reacted according to plan, writhing and moaning as if his brain were burning. Arvin wrenched Gonthril's head back, exposing his throat, and bared his fangs.

Zelia caught his arm. "Don't be so hasty," she hissed. "Let him suffer a little more. Let's savor this."

Arvin twisted his lips into a sadistic smile. "I know," he said. "Let's fuse him."

"No!" Gonthril cried. "Not that!" He tried to force his way to his feet but Arvin shoved him down.

As Arvin pretended to be busy subduing Gonthril, he heard a chuckle from the seemingly empty air next to the cabinet. A second Zelia appeared in the room, standing next to it. She was dressed identically to the first—aside from their positions in the room, it was impossible to tell them apart. Arvin was almost certain it was the original, or maybe the first Zelia was the original and the second was the duplicate. It would be just the sort of mind game she would enjoy.

This second Zelia stepped swiftly forward and flicked her fingers against Gonthril's face. Silver flashed in her eyes a third time. Gonthril's shouts of protest became muffled howls as his lips fused together. The flesh of his legs joined, and his arms melded with his torso. He crumpled downward into a ball, his body smoothing and folding in upon itself until it resembled a wrinkled lump of clay through which the ropes that had bound him passed. Hair and fingernails were still visible, as were the two holes in what had once been his nose. Gonthril breathed through these rapidly.

Arvin felt a dull horror as he glanced down at the lump that had, a moment before, been a man, but so far, his plan was holding together. Zelia had swallowed the bait he'd tossed her and had repeated her previous error, fusing Gonthril's fingers together, ensuring that Karrell's ring could not be removed. It was up to Arvin to keep her occupied, so she would not slice it free.

The first Zelia gestured toward the far wall. "Roll him over there," she ordered.

Arvin obliged. As he tumbled Gonthril against the wall, he kept one wary eye on the Zelias. At the first hint of suspicion on their part, he would begin his attack.

The second Zelia regarded him with unblinking eyes. "So, 'Dmetrio,'" she said. Why haven't I been able to reach you? Where have you been?"

Arvin turned. "I had a run-in with an old friend of ours," he answered. "Juz'la."

The second Zelia gave him a sharp glance. "What of her?"

"She, too, quit the Hall of Mental Spendor," Arvin said. "She's working for Sibyl now."

Zelia's eyes widened.

"Or perhaps I should say, Juz'la *was* working for Sibyl," Arvin said. He ended with one of Zelia's gloating smiles.

The first Zelia cocked her head. Her tongue flickered from her lips. "You'll have to tell me all about that," she said. "Later."

As if at some unspoken signal, both Zelias swayed toward him. The first one ran a hand down his bare chest, toying with his scales; her tongue flickered out again, touching his chest.

"Interesting perfume," she said. "It tastes like ginger."

Arvin forced himself not to recoil though his skin crawled. He nodded. "I thought you might like it."

The second Zelia lifted the hand that held the bottle. "What's this?" she asked.

"The best wine in House Extaminos' cellars: a truly exotic vintage," Arvin answered. He nodded at the lump that was Gonthril. "I thought it would be appropriate to celebrate before we swat the gnat."

Out of the corner of his eye, Arvin caught a flash of silver from the Zelia who had moved slightly behind him. She was manifesting a power!

Despite knowing that he was already a heartbeat too late, he plunged into his *muladhara* and started to draw energy into—

The cork popped from the bottle, startling him. As it drifted over the shoulder of the Zelia whose eyes had flashed, Arvin realized what power she'd just manifested—a simple far hand to pull the cork. She would have been suspecting treachery from her seed—contact poison on the neck of the bottle, perhaps.

"Drink," she said.

The first Zelia stared up at him, the tips of the fangs showing as she smiled. One hand continued to stroke his chest. Behind her, Gonthril rocked back and forth in a futile effort to free himself, moaning softly.

Arvin lifted the bottle in a toast first to one Zelia, then the other. "To the sweet taste of victory," he said. He drank deeply. The wine was indeed a fine vintage, better than any he'd drunk before, but all he tasted was the *hassaael*'s perfumey flavor, which prickled his nose. That, and a faintly bitter undertone that was his own blood.

He licked his lips with a forked tongue. He glanced between the two Zelias, as if uncertain which to pass the bottle to first. He still couldn't be certain which was the real Zelia and which was merely a duplicate. The one giving the orders might be the original—or she might just be playing a clever game. For all he knew, both women were duplicates.

He hoped not. Two Zelias were enough to deal with.

The one stroking his chest took the bottle. A cabinet opened, and three delicate crystal glasses floated through the air toward her. She poured the wine into them, set the bottle down, and passed one glass to Arvin, the other two to the second Zelia—then took Arvin's face in both hands and kissed him. It took all of Arvin's self control not to flinch away from her and still more effort to return the kiss. Their forked tongues entwined briefly, then she pulled away. She glanced at the first Zelia, nodded, then took one glass and raised it in a toast. The other Zelia returned it but didn't drink the wine herself until the first had swallowed hers.

That decided it. The Zelia standing slightly behind Arvin had to be the original. The one that had met him at the door was taking the chances, tasting his mouth to see if he'd really consumed the wine, then drinking it herself.

The second Zelia clinked her glass against Arvin's then drank. Arvin resisted the urge to smile as he sipped from his own glass. His guess had been right: the Dmetrio-seed hadn't known what *hassaael* was, and neither did Zelia.

Lowering her glass, the second Zelia stared with a smile on her lips for several moments at Arvin—then coiled an arm around his neck and drew him close.

"You said you have both halves?" she breathed, her breath heavy with the scent of the potion.

Arvin smiled. "Yes." He nodded down at Gonthril. "Your plan worked beautifully."

"Where are they?"

"In a safe place." He raised his glass to his lips and started to drink—

The arm around his neck tightened, preventing him from swallowing. Zelia's green eyes blazed. "You weren't thinking about trying to keep it for yourself," she hissed. "Were you?"

The grip eased enough for Arvin to swallow the wine that was in his mouth. "The thought never even entered my mind," he answered.

"Liar," she spat. She gave him a steely look. "You know what happens to seeds who defy me. You'll deliver them, as promised, and we'll reap our reward." Then she smiled "Before we deal with that, let's have a little fun."

That surprised Arvin. He'd expected her to demand that he hand over the Circled Serpent immediately.

That was, in part, why he'd tricked her into drinking the *hassaael*—so that he could persuade her to wait. His deception was going even better than he'd hoped, and that worried him. There was something he was missing—but what?

The second Zelia had dropped to her knees. Feeling her fingers on the laces of his breeches, Arvin stiffened, then forced his body to relax. He looked down and faked a lustful smile as he choked down his revulsion. There was a time he might have found Zelia alluring—but that was long passed.

Time to plant the suggestion and let the potion do its work. He pulled the first Zelia close, pretending to kiss her. "I don't want to share you," he whispered, deliberately making his words just loud enough for the second Zelia to hear. "Get rid of her."

As he spoke, he manifested a fate link between the two. The scent of saffron and ginger rose in the air, and he scratched his chest. He'd never manifested a power in her presence that caused that particular secondary display, and he counted on them to mistake the smell for his "perfume."

If either woman recognized it as a secondary display, they made no comment. They were too busy matching each other, glare for glare.

"What are you waiting for?" Arvin cried at the standing Zelia. "Strike!"

Each of the Zelias hesitated for a heartbeat. Then the air filled with a loud hissing. Under the influence of *hassaael*—and goaded by their own suspicious natures—they attacked each other. Each reeled back as the other's power struck. The kneeling Zelia's eyes rolled back in her head, and the standing Zelia blinked, then shook her head. Eyes flashed silver, hissing lashed through the air and ectoplasm sheened first one then the other woman as powers were hurled back and forth.

Arvin tossed in an attack of his own. He lashed the mind of one Zelia with a whip of psionic energy, then sent tendrils of thought into the mind of the other, constricting and crushing her mind. His concentration held for the first attack, but in the middle of the second, the sound he'd been shaping into a hiss reverted back to a low drone.

One of the Zelias whirled. "Arvin!" she shouted, pointing at the lump that was Gonthril. "He's using his psionics. He's used a suggestion to turn us against each other!"

In the heartbeat of silence that followed, Arvin heard a faint crunch. He knew at once what it was: Gonthril biting down on the thin-walled ceramic vial he'd been holding in his mouth—the potion Arvin had purchased from Drin earlier that evening. Arvin silently cursed.

Not now! Arvin sent. *They're both looking right at you!*

Too late.

The magic-dispelling potion inside the vial did its work. Gonthril's arms and legs sprang apart. A quick twist of his hands—just as Arvin had taught him—freed the bonds around his wrists, and a sharp kick freed his ankles. He tore off the blindfold and spat out the remains of the vial, then leaped to his feet.

Arvin lunged for Gonthril, dragging him to the side. "I'll deal with him!" he shouted at one of the Zelias. "*She's* the one who manifested a suggestion on you."

Instead of resuming their attack as he'd hoped, the Zelias turned toward him.

"Do you want to become an avatar or not?" Arvin screamed at the duplicate. "Kill her!"

The Zelias exchanged a knowing look, and Arvin suddenly worried that he'd mistaken the original for the duplicate. Before he could correct the error, both women's eyes flashed silver. Their mouths parted slightly in surprise, one a heartbeat after the other, as they glanced between Arvin and Gonthril.

"He's split himself," they hissed as one.

Arvin felt the blood drain from his face. They'd just seen through his metamorphosis. Releasing Gonthril and shouting, "Attack them!" he threw up a mental shield. Next to him, Gonthril leaped forward, shouting the word that would turn the rope that had bound him to stone. He whipped this improvised weapon around like a staff, aiming at the closest Zelia's head.

She ducked, but the other Zelia had time to manifest a power. A wall of psionic energy slammed into Arvin, knocking him to the ground. Out of the corner of his eye he saw Gonthril crumple too, his nose and mouth leaking blood like he'd just been smashed in the face with a brick. Despite the roaring in his ears, Arvin heard what sounded like the tinkle of tiny bells—a hallucinatory noise that was another of Zelia's secondary displays. Dazed, he tried to mount a psionic defense—only to feel his *muladhara* open and spill all of its stored energy in a swirling rush.

The Zelias must have seen the distress in his eyes. They smiled.

"You ... haven't won," Arvin gasped. "I destroyed ... the Circled Serpent. You'll never become ..."

The eyes of the Zelia on the left flashed. Arvin felt her awareness enter his mind. Powerless to stop her, he felt her rifle through his thoughts. The memories she was looking for floated to the surface of Arvin's mind—memories of the Circled Serpent being destroyed. She probed further, and earlier memories floated to the surface of Arvin's mind: the dog-headed man confronting him in the cavern, then a skip ahead to Arvin learning that the Dmetrio-seed had killed him and fled with the Circled Serpent.

"So he did betray me," hissed the Zelia whose eyes had flashed. "The fool. He could have ruled Hlondeth."

The other Zelia cocked her head, still staring mockingly at Arvin. "What made you think I *wanted* to become an avatar?" she asked.

Frowning took too much effort. Arvin's entire body felt like one big bruise. Something felt loose inside his chest. Intense agony shot through him with each breath. He couldn't muster the strength to lever himself off the floor; he could barely raise his head. Beside him, Gonthril lay still. Dead or unconscious, Arvin couldn't tell.

"Why . . . wouldn't you?" Arvin asked.

He was surprised that the Zelias hadn't killed him yet. They wanted to gloat over their victory, it seemed. If he could keep them talking, maybe he could still make the *hassaael* work for him.

The Zelia on the left—Arvin had lost track of which one was the original but suspected that she was the one—answered. "Because Set's followers will reward me so well for destroying the key."

"Set's . . . followers?" Arvin repeated dazedly. Then he understood. The dog-man who had followed him up Mount Ugruth—Zelia was working with him. Working *for* him. Arvin had been wrong. She hadn't wanted to become an avatar at all.

"Exactly," she hissed, obviously still listening in on his thoughts. "The Dmetrio-seed was merely supposed to rule Hlondeth, once Dediana was out of the way." She *tsk-tsked*. "A pity that he grew greedy." She sighed melodramatically. "They all do in the end."

The Zelia to the right had been silent for some time; Arvin noticed her frown, as if concentrating on something intensely. Then her eyes slid sideways in a furtive glance that was directed at the first Zelia.

Odd that he couldn't feel both Zelias inside his head. It was almost as if . . .

He spoke quickly, even as the thought formed in his mind. "She's drained you," he gasped. "She's going to kill you. She said 'me,' not 'us.' If you kill her first, she—"

Zelia, too, must have known how to control sound. Arvin heard a hissing and no more words emerged, even though he was still talking.

He smiled. Zelia had just played right into his hand.

Swifter than a cobra, the duplicate twisted and bit the other in the throat. The original Zelia recoiled, one hand pressed to her wound. She removed it, then blinked in surprise at the twin beads of blood on her fingers.

Both women began breathing with tight, shallow gasps; their faces a bright red. Blood trickled from the nose of the original Zelia.

"You fool!" she hissed at the duplicate. "Can't you see what he's done? He fate linked us! You're going to die now, too." She shook her head. "Why did you . . . I would never . . ."

"Yes, you would," the duplicate panted back. A blue forked tongue flicked away the blood that flowed from her own nose. Her lips twisted in a wry grimace. "In fact . . . you just . . . did."

The first turned to Arvin, her eyes wild. "Set . . . curse you," the original panted, "and drag . . . your soul . . . to the . . . Abyss!" Then she collapsed.

A heartbeat later, the duplicate fell on top of her. For a moment, both bodies were still. Then, like dough melting in the rain, they flowed into one another until only one Zelia remained.

Dead.

A brittle laugh erupted from Arvin's lips. He no longer cared about the agony in his chest. Victory sang in his ears. He'd done it! Defeated Zelia! Karrell and his children were safe.

"I've already been to the Abyss," he whispered, "and back again. Now it's your turn."

Still lying on his back, he reached out with one hand. He was able—barely—to reach Gonthril's neck. Under his fingers he felt a faint lifebeat. Gonthril was alive.

Arvin let his fingers linger on the crystal at the rebel leader's throat. "Nine lives," he said.

He chuckled weakly. It had taken him at least that many to claim his revenge, but he was alive and Zelia, dead.

Arvin used the stone in his forehead to manifest a sending. When it was done, he closed his eyes. In a moment or two, once he'd rallied his strength again, he would manifest another sending, calling upon the Secession to rescue him and Gonthril. But for the time being, he would rest. His part was, at last, over.

Out over the Vilhon Reach, thunder grumbled once then stilled.

In a hut deep in the Black Jungles, an infant finished suckling at his mother's breast then fell asleep beside his sister.

Their mother smiled.

NEW YORK TIMES BESTSELLING SERIES

R.A. SALVATORE'S
WAR OF THE SPIDER QUEEN

The epic saga of the dark elves concludes!

EXTINCTION
Book IV
LISA SMEDMAN

For even a small group of drow, trust is the rarest commodity of all.
When the expedition prepares for a return to the Abyss, what little
trust there is crumbles under a rival goddess's hand.

ANNIHILATION
Book V
PHILIP ATHANS

Old alliances have been broken, and new bonds have been formed.
While some finally embark for the Abyss itself, other stay behind to
serve a new mistress—a goddess with plans of her own.

RESURRECTION
Book VI
PAUL S. KEMP

The Spider Queen has been asleep for a long time, leaving the
Underdark to suffer war and ruin. But if she finally returns, will
things get better...or worse?

www.wizards.com

FORGOTTEN REALMS®

STARLIGHT AND SHADOWS IS FINALLY GATHERED INTO A CLASSIC GIFT SET!

BY ELAINE CUNNINGHAM

"I have been a fan of Elaine Cunningham's since I read *Elfshadow*, because of her lyrical writing style."
– R.A. Salvatore

DAUGHTER OF THE DROW
Book I

Beautiful and deadly, Liriel Baenre flits through the darkness of Menzoberranzan where treachery and murder are the daily fare. Seeking something beyond the Underdark, she is pursued by enemies as she ventures towards the lands of light.

TANGLED WEBS
Book II

Exiled from Menzoberranzan, the beautiful dark elf Liriel Baenre wanders the surface world with her companion Fyodor. But even as they sail the dangerous seas of the Sword Coast, a drow priestess plots a terrible fate for them.

WINDWALKER
Book III

Liriel and Fyodor travel across the wide realms of Faerun in search of adventure and reach the homeland of Rashemen. But they cannot wander far enough to escape the vengeance of the drow, and from the deep tunnels of the Underdark, glittering eyes are watching their every move.

ED GREENWOOD

THE CREATOR OF THE FORGOTTEN REALMS WORLD

BRINGS YOU THE STORY OF
SHANDRIL OF HIGHMOON

SHANDRIL'S SAGA

SPELLFIRE
Book I

Powerful enough to lay low a dragon or heal a wounded warrior, spellfire
is the most sought after power in all of Faerûn. And it is in the reluctant
hand of Shandril of Highmoon, a young, orphaned kitchen-lass.

CROWN OF FIRE
Book II

Shandril has grown to become one of the most powerful magic-users in
the land. The powerful Cult of the Dragon and the evil Zhentarim want
her spellfire, and they will kill whoever they must to possess it.

HAND OF FIRE
Book III

Shandril has spellfire, a weapon capable of destroying the world, and
now she's fleeing for her life across Faerûn, searching for somewhere to
hide. Her last desperate hope is to take refuge in the sheltered city of
Silverymoon. If she can make it.

www.wizards.com

DRAGONS ARE DESCENDING ON THE FORGOTTEN REALMS!

THE RAGE
The Year of Rogue Dragons, Book I

RICHARD LEE BYERS

Renegade dragon hunter Dorn hates dragons with a passion few can believe, let alone match. He has devoted his entire life to killing every dragon he can find, but as a feral madness begins to overtake the dragons of Faerûn, civilization's only hope may lie in the last alliance Dorn would ever accept.

THE RITE
The Year of Rogue Dragons, Book II

RICHARD LEE BYERS

Dragons war with dragons in the cold steppes of the Bloodstone Lands, and the secret of the ancient curse gives a small band of determined heroes hope that the madness might be brought to an end.

REALMS OF THE DRAGONS
Book I

EDITED BY PHILIP ATHANS

This anthology features all-new stories by R.A. Salvatore, Ed Greenwood, Elaine Cunningham, and the authors of the R.A. Salvatore's War of the Spider Queen series. It fleshes out many of the details from the current Year of Rogue Dragons trilogy by Richard Lee Byers and includes a short story by Byers.

REALMS OF THE DRAGONS
Book II

EDITED BY PHILIP ATHANS

A new breed of Forgotten Realms authors bring a fresh approach to new stories of mighty dragons and the unfortunate humans who cross their paths.